To my mentor Ron Hilton,
best regards,

Honor Must Prevail

Siege of the Red Clans, Book One of Honor Trilogy

IAN D. SPIER

Disclaimer: All characters herein and all organizations herein are works of fiction. Any resemblance to persons or groups living or dead are wholly coincidental.

Paperback ISBN: 978-1-5356-0321-8
Hardcover ISBN: 978-1-5356-0695-0

WHITE PEAKS
SERPENTS TONGUE
FROST GAP
VOSTIOK PLATEAU
NORDRANAYA SHELF
NORTH BREAK
ICEFANG
BITTER FORK
GRIZZLY RIVER
VOSTIOK RIVER
HORN RIVER
WOLF RIVER
VIZNOR HILLS
NORTH PINES
FROST LAKE
LAKE THALU
TURTLE LAKE [SYNDICATE]
MERCI RIVER
GAP OF MOGAI
STRAIT OF VIZNOR
HAUNTED RIDGE
MIST RIVER
WINDWALL
DRAGON RIVER
RIVER MOGAI
MOGAI VALE
DAGGER LAKE
GREEN VALE
TALOS FOREST
AMA
XANTIR STRAIT
DRAGON RIDGE MOUNTAINS
STONE VALE
PINE RIVER
XANTIR HILLS
STONE RIVER
GOBLIN PASS
FALCON PASS
BORDER LAKE
RIVER VANIKI
FOREST OF VALANTIR
IRON RIDGE
DABANI PEAKS
MAZA PLAINS
WEST WOOD
WEST BOLT
EAST BOLT
MODAR RIVER
AGAMA DELTA
DABANI PLAINS
BAZU PINES
YE HO
CROC RIVER
LAKE MAHA
MOJARA DESERT
BLUE FORK
WEST RIDGE
IZIMAL
PALMS
IZIMAL SANDS
STRAIT
RIVER LUNA
VAJA PLAINS
VAJA STRAIT
TIGER PEAKS

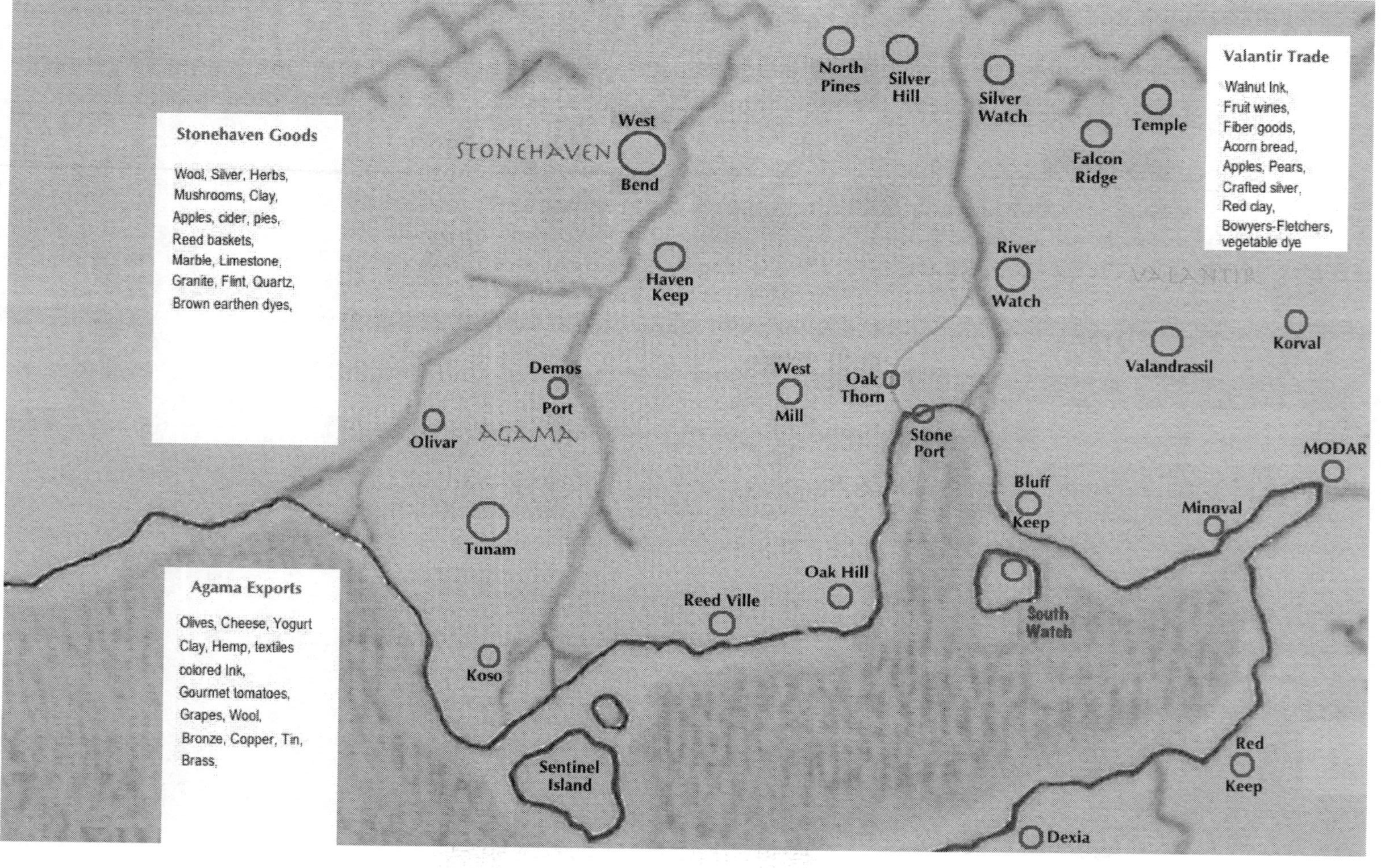
Stonehaven Goods
Wool, Silver, Herbs,
Mushrooms, Clay,
Apples, cider, pies,
Reed baskets,
Marble, Limestone,
Granite, Flint, Quartz,
Brown earthen dyes,
Agama Exports
Olives, Cheese, Yogurt
Clay, Hemp, textiles
colored Ink,
Gourmet tomatoes,
Grapes, Wool,
Bronze, Copper, Tin,
Brass,
Valantir Trade
Walnut Ink,
Fruit wines,
Fiber goods,
Acorn bread,
Apples, Pears,
Crafted silver,
Red clay,
Bowyers-Fletchers,
vegetable dye
STONEHAVEN
AGAMA
VALANTIR
West Bend
North Pines
Silver Hill
Silver Watch
Temple
Falcon Ridge
Haven Keep
River Watch
Korval
Valandrassil
Demos Port
West Mill
Oak Thorn
Stone Port
Olivar
MODAR
Bluff Keep
Minoval
Tunam
Oak Hill
Reed Ville
South Watch
Koso
Sentinel Island
Red Keep
Dexia

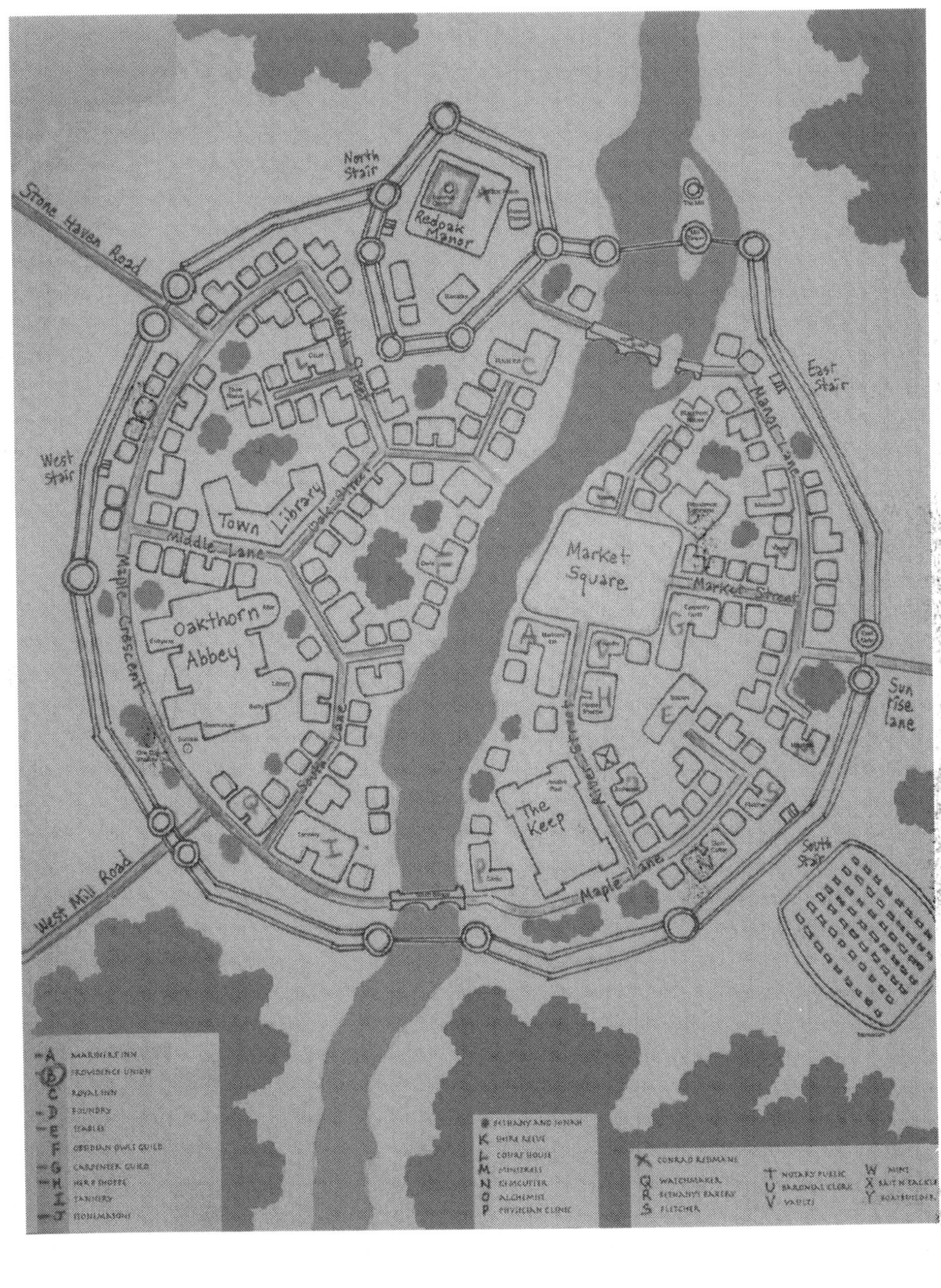

North Stair
Stone Haven Road
Redoak Manor
North Street
Town Library
Middle Lane
Maple Crescent
Oakthorn Abbey
West Stair
East Stair
Manor Lane
Market Square
Market Street
Sunrise Lane
The Keep
Maple Lane
South Stair
West Mill Road
A MARINERS INN
B PROVIDENCE UNION
C ROYAL INN
D FOUNDRY
E STABLES
G CARPENTER GUILD
I TANNERY
J STONEMASONS
K SHIRE REEVE
L COURT HOUSE
M MINSTRELS
O ALCHEMIST
P PHYSICIAN CLINIC
Q WATCHMAKER
S FLETCHER
T NOTARY PUBLIC
V VAULTS
W MINT
Y BOATBUILDER

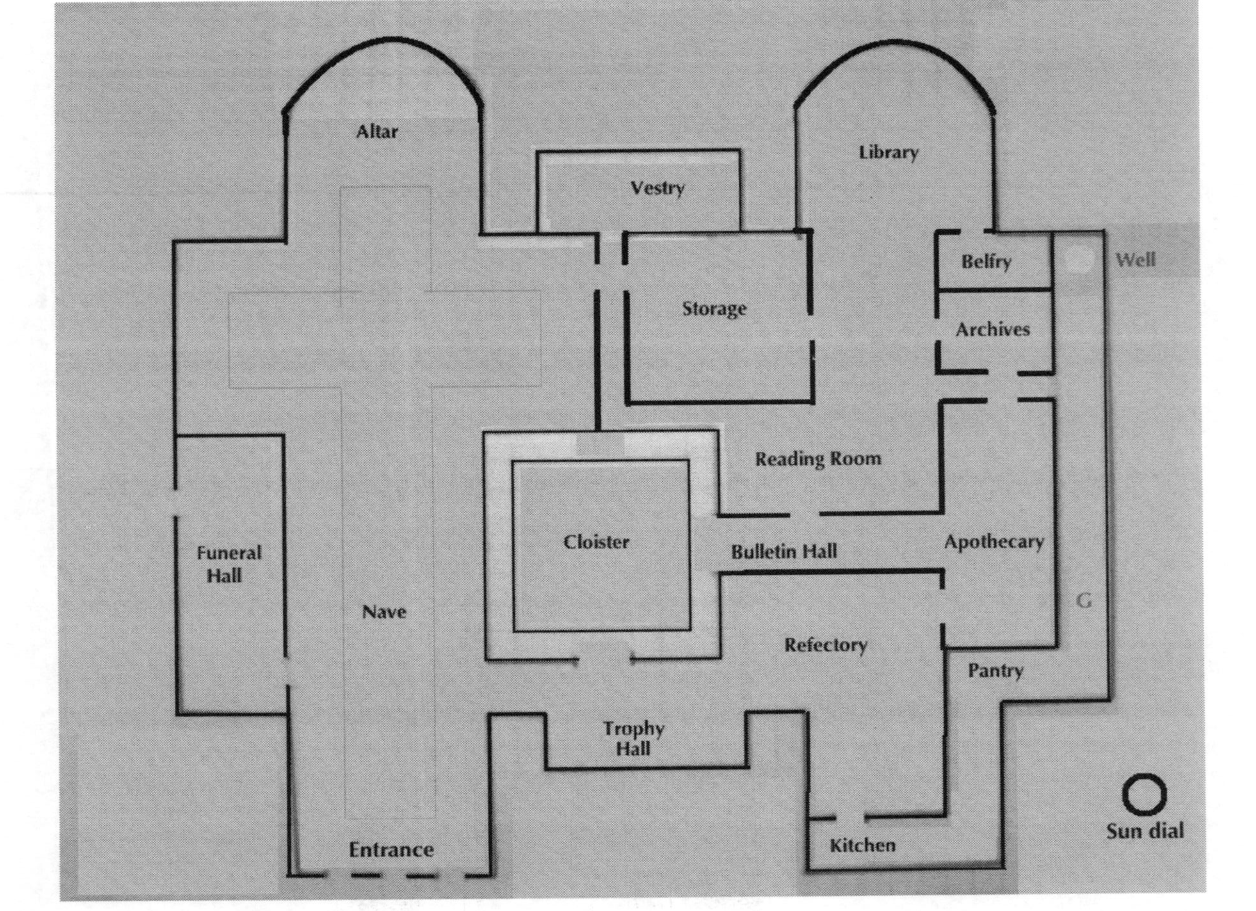

Altar
Vestry
Library
Belfry
Well
Storage
Archives
Reading Room
Cloister
Bulletin Hall
Apothecary
Funeral Hall
Nave
G
Refectory
Pantry
Trophy Hall
Sun dial
Entrance
Kitchen

Table of Contents

Acknowledgements

While this work might have been possible alone, the quality would have suffered without the help and advice of many friends, colleagues, fellow writers, mentors, family and hired help. In somewhat random order, I would like to thank the following: my friend and sounding board, Michael, mentors Ron and Fran, my friend Lisa B., my stepmother Donna, my professors Anthony, Nancy and Judy, my friend Kimberly, Karyn Dolan, Monica, Lori and Windy, my stepsister Justine, my peers on Main Street [both living and ascended], also Susan from Kansas, the late RJ from Buffalo, and many others whose knowledge has added to my own. Thank you.

Additional Credits

Some of the material regarding centaurs has been adapted from or inspired in part by online excerpts of *The Herd Lord* by Beth Hudson Wheeler, and Eleanor Ray. Used with permission. *The Herd Lord* is Beth's first published book. The names used for the centaurs in *Honor Must Prevail* were borrowed or adapted from Greek references. Other sources of inspiration include Greek mythology, philosophy, politics, the web, and life.

Introduction

"Let it be said: the many roads to power or especially to wisdom are paved with much suffering, including, first and foremost, our own. I was an impetuous child, like my mother was. Early on, I had the curse of piercing the veils of time, but never the hearts of men, even today. Men claim to value truth, but they abuse, vilify, and ridicule those who dare speak it. For the truth brings pain, and men always blame the messenger. They would just as well blame the falling of the snow on the southern migration of the birds in autumn. I did not ask to be a messenger. I was born this way. Forever different from others, often outcast, scorned, hated. The truth is a burden. Of all creatures, only man prefers the lie. I have often wished I were an otter or a dolphin instead. They seem happy with their lot. Indeed, they love the water more than I, and usually live in peace. I was not so lucky."

— *The Oracle Tyrianna*

Chapter One
Dire Warnings

At high noon in the Korathian capitol city of Kozos, the markets, inns, and taverns had wall-to-wall patrons, most were in rags, celebrating a big harvest of beets, carrots, kale, pumpkins and raspberries. Scattered white and gray clouds blew westward in the autumn breeze. Tonight would be the full moon of September, in the year of the Raven, Stonehaven Reckoning 1564, the sixth century of the second age.

In the northern quarter of the city, near Dagger Lake and the forest dominating the shores at the outskirts of the surrounding countryside, the inn known as the Falcon's Perch, with its walnut post and beam structure was now host to a curious young lady of five foot nine with medium-length, wavy, dark amber hair framing her high cheekbones. She had a slender jaw and arched slim, dark amber eyebrows and was wearing a white cotton tunic with yellow braided silk trim, under a jade green wool cloak matching her entrancing, round, deep emerald eyes. She had a dazzling silver ring on her left hand, inlaid with hematite and abalone, set with a single crystal of double terminated quartz. Such a ring was well beyond the purse of most commoners in their tattered gray, green, and brown wool with patches of hempcloth. She strode proudly to a large oaken wine barrel and promptly ascended on top of it, proclaiming: "People of Korath! Listen well to the vision of ..."

The crowd mumbled their interruptions, with many whispers of "Elf-witch" and "crazy teenager" circulating, none of which amused a tall man in the corner, who crossed his bare arms over his light brown deerskin vest and gave an intimidating frown with the chiseled jaw he bore. He stood six foot four, and his taut frame had the menacing muscle tone of large jungle cats. He raised one jet-black eyebrow under his short, cropped and slick jet black mane with a prominent widow's peak. His deep set, dark icy blue, almond-shaped eyes fixed straight at the lady. She gave a slight surreptitious nod to him before speaking again. "Listen! Dark days descend on all. The darkest in three generations!"

Several men interrupted her, yelling: "'Course it's gonna be dark! Winter's comin', missy!" "No drinks for her. She's had enough already!" "Hey, lady! Shove off! Take your business elsewhere ..." This was followed by many more insults. At this, her long hair flared out as a gust of wind tore through the room from out of nowhere. She struck the floor with her hickory staff, and her eyes brightened akin to silvery moonlight.

"Enough!" she thundered. "The great sundering draws nigh, and the great war will soon drop at your doorstep! His army marches as I speak, against three champions who cannot stand alone against a sleepless malice ! You must join them! The moonchild has spoken!" Her eyes faded back to normal, and she now stood, as if half-asleep, unaware of what she had just said. One drunk stepped forward, mead dripping from his dark curly beard, and muttered, "Moonchile, eh? When I geh ter see yer fanny (hic)?"

As the drunk reached forward to grope her budding curves, his buckles and buttons suddenly came undone, and he fell painfully face first at the foot of the barrel. Half the crowd dropped their mugs and doubled over in fits of laughter. An ugly old woman with long, curly salt and pepper hair on a body shaped like a butter roll, wagged her finger in fury. "Bewitched my nephew Kurt, she did! That vile tramp! Was lookin' straight at him when he come undone! Father Malsain was right! Cain't trust no Elves no more! TAKE her!"

A couple dozen patrons moved forward to do so, but were knocked flat by a blue wave of force that came from all directions, leaving only the young lady and the tall man in the corner standing upright. The man pointed to the doorway, "Go! Quickly!"

The lady ran for it, and the patrons got to their feet to pursue, but the tall stranger barred their path. They attempted to wrestle him out of the way, but he was stronger than ten of them combined. Then they shoved, also to no avail. When they broke bottles, he drew forth his trident and struck it sideways against the door frame; the sound of it shattered the glass in their hands and assailed their ears, making them unable to stand, let alone sit upright or even kneel. When the ringing stopped, he was gone. One man staggered to the door and could not tell which way they had fled.

A fruit vendor pointed north. "They went that a-ways, through the park." The patron nodded his thanks. "What they do anyway?" asked the vendor.

"Never you mind," said the patron. "Nobody would believe me anyhow."

Moments later, a mob was moving north in pursuit of the "riff raff." They caught sight of their quarry at the forest's edge several hundred yards away and realized those two were superior runners; the city folk would be out of breath long before they caught up on foot. Most doubled back; a couple stayed to watch, and six returned on horseback.

"Through those trees over there." One of the patrons pointed.

None of the six riders had any tracking ability, and even with two parties flanking east and west of where they last spotted the strangers, the search was hopeless. It was a big forest. The lake was forty miles away, an hour on horseback, and that lake was forty miles wide in the middle, nearly 200 miles long. Without a trail to follow, they'd be starving and sleep-deprived before catching them. "Father Malsain won't be happy about this at all ... he's going to rip us a new hole over losing the rabble-rousing Elf-witch and that other foreigner."

* * *

Later that night, far westwards in the barony of Oakthorn, the full moon rose in the east behind the trees bending under the howling winds of a raging thunderstorm. A slender and wrinkled old diplomat named Obsek, with his long, bent nose, sunken eyes and wiry, unkempt white eyebrows, was attempting to negotiate a treaty with his host, Baron Bravane Redoak the Third, often called Bravane the Younger, a barrel-chested, red bearded, square jawed, blue-eyed, and broad shouldered giant of a man at six foot seven; a generous host where food was concerned, but quick to interrupt any and all attempts by the diplomat to explain the "benefits" of the treaty with the Kingdom of Razadur. Obsek nearly toppled over in fright, his heart skipping a beat as the Baron's chain-mailed fist struck the great dining table in outrage, toppling the empty goblets like so many chess pieces. Bravane protested in a booming voice of discontent, "Power? Am I to believe a warmongering Kingdom such as Razadur is going to offer power worthy of what your king demands as his price? Kazius Auguron and all his men are FOOLS to think I will accept these terms! A blind man could see through this thinly veiled stalling tactic and land grab designed to bleed my city of everything my people have worked for! You babble nonsense while he hatches some plan to cheat me. How stupid does he think I am? Power, indeed ..." Bravane then fell silent, pacing the baronial dining hall as if Obsek did not exist. Despite the obvious insult and Obsek's proximity to the fireplace, he felt a chill and a tremor in his fingers. Obsek reached for more wine to settle his nerves, just before the Baron returned to the table, his large framed body looming over the remains of the salted pork and glazed carrots.

Bravane eclipsed all the wall torches from this position, such that Obsek was completely in his shadow. Obsek's eyes shrank back into their sockets with fear, and a sheen of cold sweat appeared on his neck. Obsek downed a gulp of wine and squirmed as the baron displayed a menacing and satisfied grin. The room was getting blurry, and Obsek's forehead grew unbearably warm. His ears started ringing, and his thirst grew no matter how much wine he consumed. He struggled to stay upright, as though the room was wobbling, and try as he might, Obsek found no evidence of poison in his drink. His eyes grew heavy, his tongue dry, his throat itchy, and it took every ounce of will to speak. "My king is not without mershee ... [hic] ... but do not think you know more of power than he or hish captainsh ..."

No sooner had Obsek spoken the last syllable than a great clap of thunder outside the manor startled him out of his chair. He tumbled to the floor. His teeth were chattering now, his bones felt cold, and his ears hot. The room spun without stopping, and his head throbbed with constricting pain, as if he were under a cider press.

Obsek could barely register the baron's words, let alone think anymore. He clawed at the leg of the dining table, attempting to pull himself upright. His grip was weak, and it sounded as if the very rain pelting the stained glass windows and their iron grillwork with lead soldering and veins was mocking him. Bravane just stared at him, unaware of Obsek's true condition, dismissing the symptoms as nothing but fear and liquor.

The baron spoke as Obsek struggled into his chair like some two-foot toddler, "Your king and all who serve him are delusional and arrogant not to realize the price of a so-called power that destroys the land we live on. The water in Razadur is tainted black, the air is fouled, the herbs withered, mottled, blighted, and dying. The animals likewise. What sort of mad idiot neglects and abuses the land they live on? The gods are surely punishing him as we speak! Only fools practice such stupidity, and such fools will not find welcome in my presence, or in my home! Go to your king and tell him this ..." Bravane then scribbled some words on the treaty as Obsek mumbled curses under his breath and weakly emptied the last half of his wine goblet on the carpet. Bravane pretended not to notice. As Obsek grabbed for the treaty, his arms stretched out to their limit, the baron sunk four inches of steel into Obsek's ribs with such force that the diplomat dangled a foot above the floor, his eyes wide in shock, despair, and terror. His jaw hung limp, his breath a gravelly rasp; in seconds, his eyes froze, never to move again.

Bravane then threw Obsek's body onto the checkered gray alternating slate and granite tiles near the fireplace, and tossed the treaty into the flames, followed by the half-empty bottle of wine that Obsek had chosen. Bravane exclaimed, "Your toast, your treaty, your king are all refused, and this meeting is adjourned!"

A knock at the door intruded on his wandering thoughts, and the voice of his most trusted honor guard asked him, "Sir? We heard a commotion ..."

Bravane responded, "I am quite well, but I require a discretionary hand in here!"

The honor guard captain thus entered and shut the door, and immediately sensed something foul on the breeze, an odor of contagion and stagnation. Captain Conrad Redmane the Bold then noticed the body of Obsek and asked: "Shall I send for the physician, sire?"

Bravane almost jumped. "The treaty! Curse the family temper! I need to salvage the treaty! I need it as evidence!"

Redmane closed his eyes and sighed with his head down. It was one of those days again, which happened almost every year. Bravane the Younger was a good man, considering the bad family history of the previous two generations of Redoaks. Conrad helped Bravane stamp out the burning treaty and managed to save about three quarters of it. The corners were browned, and three burn holes in the parchment made deciphering the terms difficult, but the basic message was clearly an offer of stale bread crumbs compared to what Kazius the Cruel demanded in return. He insisted on taking half of Oakthorn's output of lumber, fish, silver ore, crops, and livestock in times of peace, and greater shares during war.

"Like we would ever spit on the alliance we already have with the Elven Kingdom of Valantir, which his father Arius tried to destroy! How stupid does he think we are?" Bravane the Younger muttered aloud.

Conrad did not answer, as he knew his baron was not asking for an opinion. But after a minute of his baron pacing madly, fidgeting and chewing his knuckles, Conrad could see he was temporarily incapacitated. "Sir? This man is not a fitting decoration for the floor ..."

Baron Bravane the Younger retorted, "I know! He cannot stay here ... the king of Razadur will pounce on any excuse to make war, just as his father did. Kazius has already sent troops out of Black Falls. The scout report arrived just yesterday! We are between a tornado and quicksand!

Conrad interjected, "I have an idea, Lord, but must act quickly by your leave, sir."

The baron bowed his head and nodded. "Do what you must."

The Captain, thus, went to summon the baron's physician James, and gave careful instructions for where to take the body. They needed to be quick and attentive to cloud cover with the full moon out, though the rain was still heavy. Once their task was done, Conrad turned southward to pay an evening visit to his old friend Savadi

Aksara the Humble. But along the way, a shadow was on the prowl, and called to him from the concealment of the trees near the abbey.

"So it is true? Auguron has played his hand after all these years? Hmm?" Conrad warily approached the tree to size up the rogue.

This strange man, in his black woolen cloak and gray leather armor, with a nose for dangerous information, silvered hairs on his eyebrows, practiced tone of voice, calm posture, who balanced a dirk on his gloved fingertip, was certainly no mere apprentice, but a seasoned veteran in the shadow business.

The eyes, most of all, showed the stranger's savvy and poker face behind the rogue's mask.

Conrad the Bold called back, "I know who you work for, so I should ask *you* what transpires in Razadur!"

The man in gray leather answered, "I have nothing whatsoever to do with Razadur, nor does Umbral, who sends his regards, Captain."

Conrad frowned, responding: "Tell Umbral that he can gain my good favor by bending ears and noses in Kazius Auguron's direction, and be warned that his troops have already left Black Falls. And shadows will be collecting hazard pay if I get something especially useful!"

To which the stalker replied: "So, the diplomat is dead, yes?"

Conrad shot a warning glance back. "You had best keep a tight rein on that information. Kazius will stoop to anything to achieve his ends, or did you not know how his father Arius and the Bloodhammers nearly destroyed Oakthorn?"

The shadow nodded. "Oh, we know the local history quite well, especially that particular chapter, Captain. Very well, indeed. But we are not much concerned with the noisy Bloodhammers, who could not surprise a sleeping ox to save their lives. It is the Blackwolf Den you should worry about, should they be summoned into service by the Crown of Razadur." And with a sarcastic undertone, he added, "Pleasure doing business, Captain."

Conrad's burgundy red woolen cloak was soaked by now, even though the rain was starting to lighten up. He took an instant dislike to the rogue who just vanished, and Conrad was eager for this evening to be over and done with. He walked up to the main door of the abbey, and scanned north and west for anyone watching before he went across the front lawn and through the secret door to the cellars under the Trophy Hall. He found his friend Savadi Aksara, the physician general, down there doing inventory on the medicinal roots and mushrooms.

Savadi continued his work as he spoke, "Good to see you, Brother Conrad. What is this weight I sense on your mind? As to why I am here so late, we are low on remedies for the fever going around. Lore Keeper Henry and two arbiters, Dhasa and Darana, plus their students are unable to perform their duties."

Conrad raised an eyebrow. "Illness? How long ago?"

Savadi the Benevolent responded, "Not more than three days ago."

Conrad was very displeased at this, mumbling, "The diplomat arrived that day to arrange tonight's meeting, now he is dead. One of Umbral's men already knows. This is not good, Savadi. The baron is still haunted by family demons, he is not ready for the prophecy."

Conrad's friend just smiled. "Your worry has merit, such is your job here, but I tell you he will find his way. Farseer Andar keeps me informed. How is your father?"

Conrad began, "My father has been unwell ever since the diplomat arrived. My sister has three maids looking after him. He is already frail, and keeps losing weight by the day. We do not know how long he has."

Savadi shook his sad face. "Terribly sorry. I pray the Creator has mercy."

Conrad confided his fears, "Savadi, my faith is failing me. Razadur is ready for war, the baron got a report just yesterday. I was not there to read it. The baron is crumbling. Our harvest is not in yet, and you know my mother is gone."

Savadi smiled again, adding, "She still watches over you, you know, and Summer is very proud of what a fine man you have become. Delightful woman, I still have one of her landscape paintings in the attic. Exquisite talent ..."

Conrad sighed, a single tear forming in his eyes. "You ... are able ... to speak ... with her?"

Savadi replied, "Oh, yes, her spirit wanders here often, in the upper levels. Summer and Wardkeeper Sasha were very close, and they both tell me we are not alone in this abbey."

Conrad asked, "What does *that* mean? Who else is here?"

Savadi paused, weighing his words. "Well, Arius never truly died. Sasha says he does not require sleep, and sets his will against the wards on this sanctuary. He has gained dark powers since his defeat many years ago."

Conrad stood there, incredulous. "And *how* are we supposed to fight *both* of them?"

Savadi smiled again. "We have many allies."

Conrad stood silent, brooding with fingers clenched, wondering how his friend could be so optimistic in the face of doom. They were all going to die this time; Conrad was certain. Many allies indeed, he thought. Where were they, if this prophecy is to be taken so seriously? Why wait? Why not be done with the Auguron menace once and for all? And Savadi, beloved and dear friend and wise mentor, physician-general of the Emerald Order that he is, just smiles while war is brewing three-hundred miles away. Conrad took a couple fast paces to the opposite wall and withdrew a bottle of mead, which he silently raised to Savadi's health as he took the stairs back out, and uncorked it in the rain on his way back to the manor.

Thus began another conflict between Razadur and the breakaway kingdoms of the Itana Empire, a war long in the hatching, long in suffering, and long expected by historians who visited the library, and the lorekeepers who maintained it. There were three libraries: The City Library, the Baronial Manor Library, and the Monks' Library. The City Library was by far the largest, and also in greatest need of maintenance. Some old man had fallen asleep there with his pipe still lit some years ago, and other mishaps had happened since, including the great fire/ Bloodhammer raid of 1533. Years later, Baron Bravane the Younger himself had once spilled wine on several old books, which got him forever banned from that section of the library, and a new policy made that he had to trade a book of equal value or buy the book outright in any other section. The Reeve and the Magistrate both sided with the library on this. They all hoped the baron would one day triumph over his demons, due to the sins of his fathers. Conrad knew better than anyone; he was there when the worst of it happened.

Conrad trod the muddy streets, turning east and then northeast, passing the Royal Inn on his way home, which was now closing up for the night, and two barmaids had just locked the door when they caught sight of him, by the light of a street lantern. They knew, of course, who he was; his red and gold enameled breastplate was unmistakable, even on this rainy night with clouds obscuring the moon. The blonde one just smiled and nodded her head in greeting, and the brunette looked at him head to toe, giggling in a giddy way. Conrad noticed and smiled back, waving hello. The barmaids hurried home, and Conrad was still wearing a half-smile by the time he entered the manor gate. Sergeant Mill greeted him there and reported that the baron had drunk himself to sleep again, and had to be carried up to his own room.

"Very well, as you were, Sergeant," Conrad the Bold said with the customary salute. He then proceeded upstairs to verify that the baron was safe and sound, before searching for the scout report. After much rummaging in vain, he found it in the baron's library on a reading table.

FIELD REPORT

Miles Longbranch,

Forward scout in service to Bravane Redoak the Third, Seventh Day of September, Year of the Raven.

Forces sighted marching through the Southwest of Korath, 200 miles north of Black Falls, several banners identify main army of Bloodhammers, supported by the Dragonwhip Trolls, and other Infantry. Total estimate:

Three-thousand men, no sign yet of Kazius among them. Status updates to follow.

This was written four days ago, just before the arrival of the diplomat Obsek to arrange the meeting. No wonder the Baron had been in such a bad temper. Kazius had not bothered waiting for the results of the negotiations. An army that size was unlikely to travel over the Iron Ridge mountains, nor to take the long route through the northern territories. The shortest approach was through Valantir, which had already paid in blood at the battle of Shadval, on the border of Razadur, west of the Iron Ridge. But something did not fit. Conrad knew that Valantir could easily repel an army of three thousand, and Kazius, arrogant though he was, must also have known this, which would mean he was meeting another force along the way. Was it eastern mercenaries and pirates? A force of goblins, more trolls, or something more horrible? Perhaps Arius himself? Conrad paced the room for hours, racking his brains before exhaustion took him early next morning. He slept upright in the library chair and did not wake until well past dawn. Sergeant Mill woke him up to report that Conrad's stable boy was now ill with fever, and nobody fed Conrad's horse yet.

Conrad snarled, "You woke me up for *this*? And why in a settlement of over a thousand people, could nobody feed the horse? Remind me someday how *you* got to be a sergeant!"

The other honor guards averted their eyes, looking at the floor and hiding their faces, leaving Mill to face Conrad's sleep-deprived, irritable wrath alone. "For s-s-s-services r-rendered, s-s-sir ..." he muttered weakly.

Conrad yelled, "EXACTLY! You couldn't do *one* more, like feeding a horse? Was that beyond your ability? I ... never mind. Leave! Get out of my way!"

Alex Mill, otherwise known as Alex the Meek, backpedaled in near panic, almost toppling a bookcase in his haste.

Conrad stormed out of the manor, ready to strangle someone and cause an uproar. His mood was reflected overhead in a dreary overcast sky of dull gray, diffusing the daylight.

"Another foul day begins," Conrad grumbled to himself as he went to feed and groom his horse, bred from the same stock as the baron's. "Sorry, Bill, I know this is not your fault. Jake is ill, and Alex the Meek is being stupid today, and I did not sleep well because I'm in charge when Bravane can't pull it together, and Kazius ... well, he was born on the wrong side of the bed ..." Bill just blinked and bumped noses.

"Love you, too, Bill. I see Jake let the food run low again ..." Conrad grumbled again, seemed everything was up to him now. He just hoped the next load of oats was in today and he returned to the manor for scrambled eggs and smoked herring before leaving on another errand to the abbey.

This time, he walked along the riverbank, right past the headquarters of the Obsidian Owls Guild, where a familiar voice greeted him from a rooftop: "Back so soon, and no effort at all to cover your tracks? An amusing charade, Captain, you are making this child's play."

Conrad ignored the taunt. His patience was exceptionally thin today. There was no time for games. "Think what you will, thief. Your opportunities for hazard pay just multiplied. The enemy is already moving through Korath as we speak. Three-thousand men who are expected to be joining a larger force on the way here, we don't know who. I need as many eyes as can be spared, and bonuses will be added for disrupting their operations. Missing food, missing cog pins, maps, plans, orders ... I want them handicapped and hobbled in every possible way. Am I plain enough for your amusement now, Rogue?"

The man in gray leather laughed aloud, and replied, "For hazard pay, Captain, I can forgive your little jab. We shall speak again. Yes, I look forward to it." He even bowed this time, his eyes alert but friendly.

Conrad Redmane continued on his way, thinking, just maybe the guy was not so bad after all. MAYBE. Conrad entered the main door of the abbey, and right away, he knew something was wrong. There was no sign of morning mass, the halls were much too quiet, and the hair on his neck was standing up. He went into the refectory. There were plates left half-empty on the tables, but there was no sign of struggle. There was some menace emanating from the very walls, something Savadi had mentioned the other day ... Conrad drew his sword from his scabbard, and unslung his shield from his shoulder, and searched further. The kitchen, empty. Pantry and greenhouse, both empty. He searched the apothecary. Everything was intact, no broken glass, no spills, also no people, not even a sentinel. The library was empty of lore keepers, scribes, and the menace felt especially strong in this corner. He kept scanning, no blood on the floor, no broken furniture, no windows ajar, no torn draperies, no muddy footprints, and in the north wing of the library, a solitary book had been dropped on the floor, pages facing up. It was a history of Valantir: from antiquity to the tragedy of Shadval. It had fallen open to the 1490 Treaty of Westwood, an alliance between the Elves of the Westlands, the Elves of Valantir, two Kingdoms of Men, and the Faraway Elves of Talos to the East. A single bookmark had fallen on the floor, a purple silk ribbon. Conrad could feel his pulse pounding in his neck, with beads of sweat still forming every passing minute. His senses were on high alert, seeking answers to why nobody was where they belonged.

Conrad found nothing amiss in the storage room or in the bulletin area by the stairwells, and a layer of dust at the bottom of the stairs suggested nobody had gone into the cellars this way. He heard a clatter in the refectory around the corner, and ran to confront the source of it, and a poor rat scurried between his feet. Conrad blurted, "Lucky you are still alive, you little rascal! Don't _do_ that!"

Conrad the Bold paused to catch his breath, returned to the bulletin area and went upstairs. The dorms were all quiet, but he could hear whispers from the third level above. As he ran to investigate, his sleep-deprived brain was robbed of subtlety.

Suddenly, a loud voice called his name, "Watcher Red Bear, also known as Conrad Redmane, stand and be judged for suspicion of treachery in the death of Keymaster Ramus! What have you to offer in your defense, criminal?" It was the voice of Arbiter Eledar the Unforgiving, the only member who had voted against Conrad's acceptance into the Emerald Order. Conrad stood there in shock; he could not believe his ears. Always, Conrad had honored his duties to his baron, his town, his people, and the Order, and this arrogant arbiter had the audacity to call him a *criminal* without a fair trial?

Eledar spoke again, "He was found dead in West Mill last night while you were unaccounted for!"

Conrad thundered back, "ARBITER ELEDAR, you have abandoned wisdom to accuse me thus, with naught but coincidence to support your rash conclusions and to indulge your bitter nature and personal vendetta! I hereby claim the right to face my accuser and see firsthand the evidence you would employ against my good name, unless you have NONE to offer, you vile snake!"

Eledar scowled in naked contempt of Conrad, and spoke in a prideful and sneering tone of ridicule, "You had motive and opportunity, and I will prove it beyond all shadow of doubt!"

Conrad countered, "Where is the evidence, Eledar? You can claim all you like, but I do not see full council present. You are the ONLY arbiter facing me, and have only one sage supporting you, who is a well-known yes man for your agendas! This is far short of a fair tribunal. How bold you have grown, to so nakedly force your will and twist the truth for some evil at my own expense, which you have longed for all these years! No, Eledar, you will cease this deception at once, or I shall run you through and remove your misbegotten head from your rotting carcass! Give me an excuse, you madman!"

Arbiter Eledar, in his pride and arrogance, would not listen, and motioned for the two sentinels present to arrest Conrad on the spot, the very man who had trained every last sentinel and watcher. Conrad was already on them before Eledar could finish the gesture, clipping the watcher on his left under the chin with his shield, knocking him to the floor, and ducking under the one on his right, striking the pommel of his sword against the back of his opponent's right knee, toppling the second man. Next, Eledar was dead in two strokes, exactly as Conrad had warned him. The sage fainted away, and as the two sentinels attempted to rise, he kicked one and slammed the other, rendering both unconscious. Conrad ran quickly to the stairs, jumping a flight, and colliding with the walls on his way down. He exited the funeral hall on the north side, and headed straight for the Owls' Guild, arriving in just over a minute, completely out of breath after a dead run. The agents on duty recognized his armor and allowed him to pass.

He staggered into the headquarters, with a fierce look in his eyes, that promised peril and suffering to anyone who barred his path or provoked him. "UMBRAL! I ... want ... answers ... yesterday! I have been ... falsely accused ... of murder ... the keymaster ... I want ... the parties who did it ... my honor ... tarnished ... <u>very</u> ugly mood ... no more games ... <u>who</u> did this?"

Tyton Umbral the Mysterious simply sat forward in his throne, an elegant but unadorned chair of mahogany with brass caps on the feet, and regarded this angry, desperate, and exhausted man in his guild quarters as a tiger regards another jungle cat hunting on his turf.

Tyton's dark brown eyes were cool but sharp, reading Conrad's confidence, his stance, the heat and alertness of Conrad's eyes, the fresh blood on his armor and his sword, the strength and angle of his grip, and weighed Conrad's reputation. Quite calmly, Tyton decided to play along and humor the Captain. "It is not my wish to see you unhappy, Captain. That would be bad for business. Where shall we begin looking?" Tyton asked matter-of-factly in his exotic accent.

Conrad tried to read Umbral's eyes, and found them nearly impenetrable.

There had been no sound of malice, no fear, and only the barest whisper of annoyance in his carefully worded response. This man was even more than his reputation as grandmaster of the Owls had suggested. Tyton was also the only member of the Providence Co-operative to meet his obligations entirely by correspondence. He knew because Conrad's sister, Bethany, and her friend Rachel chartered and run that Co-operative. It was apparent that Umbral was playing it cool, and it was up to Conrad whether to trust Umbral's word or not. Refusing seemed like a bad idea, and there was not much time to waste. Conrad replied wearily, "My accuser says Ramus was killed in West Mill last night. This is the best clue I have."

Tyton appeared satisfied with Conrad's answer, and the only sign of his mild amusement was his eyebrow lifting a quarter inch. "Very well, Captain. West Mill it is. I suggest you divest your armor in favor of leather, as what you have on is too well recognized, if you get my meaning." Tyton snapped his fingers, and two of his veterans led Conrad to another room. Tyton called after him, "I promise you will get your old armor back once we clear your name."

Conrad did not argue. The man was correct. The gold enamel and the signature crest of a red bear was a certain giveaway that he could ill-afford while he was a fugitive from adverse conditions beyond his control or understanding. The agents going on this mission were all prepped in twelve minutes. The team split into four pairs. Tyton would lead Conrad over the wall, while other teams exited by the Southwest and northwest roads, with the 4th pair somehow bypassing the river grate. Conrad looked puzzled, but then, he only had a couple hours of sleep.

Once they had all met up a couple miles outside town, Tyton explained it was a good way to avoid undue attention. Conrad just shrugged. Tyton informed everyone that they would forage for food along the way, and stop only twice for rest, as West Mill was a full day's journey on foot.

Conrad groaned, "No horses?"

Tyton shook his head. "Horses leave a trail, attract attention, and require more maintenance. We can avoid detection better on foot."

Conrad groaned. He would be grateful if Kazius and all the other scheming bastards would just die. His faith in humanity and justice was already failing before Eledar finished it off. And by the time the team stopped for a rest, Conrad had collapsed.

Chapter Two
Chaos

Under a bright sky, a young lady emerged from the river two nights after Tyrus and Tyrianna were chased by a frenzied mob out of the Falcon's Perch Inn and the capitol city of Kozos, thirty miles away from the village of Pine Slopes, a tiny settlement at the foot of the Barrier Mountains that shielded Korath from the goblins and exiled Dwarves of Zara-Mogai to their northwest.

"Very noble of you to look after me, but I've managed pretty well on my own for the last several years, Tyrus," Tyrianna said.

He gave her a skeptical look. "But not against a mob that big, Tyri. Neither of us would have lasted very long in there."

Tyrianna scowled. "Fine! Be that way! Just wait until I find those daggers that Kazius is after! Then I won't need a guardian!"

Tyrus shook his head in disbelief. "You are too young to know about his father, Tyri. His body was never found. He survived both the battle of Shadval and the raid on

Oakthorn. Arius is far deadlier and more diabolical than Kazius."

Tyrianna retorted, "Well, how come I've never seen him? Arius must be chicken!"

Tyrus said nothing after this; it was clear nothing would change her mind.

Tyrianna growled in frustration at his silence, "I hate when you do that!" She then stormed off into the mountains, with Tyrus following a minute behind. She had a knack for getting into trouble.

* * *

Within thirty minutes, they saw smoke up ahead, a mile away over the next rise through the canopy of scattered pine forest. It was billowing much wider than a normal chimney would. Somebody was in danger, and they quickened their pace to investigate. As they closed within a hundred yards, the source became obvious. It was a house on fire, the only house visible on this side of the mountain. Tyrianna stopped in her tracks, spreading her arms slightly, clenching her fists and bowing her head.

Tyrus called, "No, Tyri! Wait! Don't —"

But he was too late. She teleported the final distance to the house and looked around for signs of anybody inside the log cabin, but the smoke was too thick, and she did not know how to put fires out without water. Tyri was on her knees, coughing, by the time Tyrus caught up. He pulled her away from the smoke and set her down on a big boulder.

"Wait here," he said sternly. Tyri was too busy coughing to do anything more than nod. Tyrus went to look for a log and called to the house, "Stand back!"

Next he rammed the door and tossed the log away from the flames.

There was nobody inside. He turned away from the house just as a salt and pepper-haired middle-aged woman in white cotton robes with gold trim arrived and pointed a hand at him, shouting, "Get off my land!"

Tyrus was then hit with a lightning bolt, and Tyrianna screamed, "No-o-o-o-o-o!" But Tyrus was still standing, trying to explain, "This is not what you think! We didn't do this!"

Next, the woman in white waved her arm in a sweeping crescent motion, and clouds formed overhead, and the air suddenly dropped twenty degrees in a matter of seconds. She called down freezing rain over the house, and then hailstones.

Tyrus drew his trident once more, and slammed it pommel side down into the ground, causing a shock wave that snuffed the dying flames. The woman looked surprised. When Tyrus made no more sudden moves, she relented. "Well, okay, maybe you were here to help after all. You can call me Ravenna. Sorry about that. Although you look none the worse for wear, that would have fried a normal person. What are you?"

Tyrus answered, "My people are known by many names, including Myrmidons. We have long had immunity to the eels under the sea. This is a friend, the only one of her kind." He extended an arm toward Tyri, who gave a forced, toothy grin and waved nervously.

"Uh, hi! Nice weather today ..."

Ravenna made a half-smile and went to inspect her house, saying, "Yep, that looks like powder burns ... this has to be the handiwork of those Lawgiver cultists ..."

Tyrianna asked, "Are they known to hate Elves and chase them out of town?"

Ravenna looked closer at Tyri. "Yeah, you do resemble an Elf, except for the round chin and wider jawbone. Father Malsain is behind those mobs, I promise you that. Been stirring up hate for years now, and the royal family of Korath turns a blind eye to it. They try not to offend anybody, but they just make it worse."

Tyrianna just shrugged. "If you say so ..."

Ravenna told her, "I just did. And there's not much left of my things or the house, rotten scoundrels. They were biding their time until I had to take the wash to the hot springs ..."

Tyrianna said, "I'm sorry. We tried to put it out sooner ..."

Ravenna waved her hand, responding, "Not your fault, child, this is on Malsain's blind followers. And it's them that will get a right cross when they see me next. Best we be rid of Korath for awhile, where were you off to anyway?"

Tyrianna answered, "Back to the safety of Valantir. They adopted me after I ran from home."

Ravenna observed, "I suspected you could not have been from Korath. They don't like odd folk much ..."

Tyrianna just shook her head. There was a melancholy in the girl's tone and posture, Ravenna noticed. Something about home and history was dreadfully painful to her, and Ravenna was wise enough not to press the issue. So they headed southwest toward Falcon Pass, and Valantir.

* * *

Meanwhile, in Oakthorn, the baron was now waking from yet another nightmare. Each time was the same, Bravane the Younger, waking in a cold sweat, his hands trembling so bad they bruised on the nightstand, while his heart hammered against his chest like iron shod hooves on the road at full gallop. Bravane quickly drank down a shot of rum to settle his nerves, waiting for the terror to subside. Soon after, his first cousin Amanda, the daughter of his uncle Alex Redoak the wise, arrived to check on him. She found him curled in a blanket on the floor by his fireplace, mumbling incoherently as he did during his worst episodes. Without speaking, the dark-haired Amanda sat behind him, leaned his head into her lap, stroking his forehead as he shivered and cried like a small infant. Amanda, her parents and the Redmane/ Blackthorn clan were the only family Bravane had nearby, other than Helen. His father lived in exile after a terrible tragedy, and the grandfather died a few years ago. It was common knowledge that the Baron would have crumbled long ago without his cousins and uncle, and even with their help, he was barely keeping it together. Amanda waited for the Baron to nod off to sleep before leaving, and informed Sergeant Mill that the Baron was not well today. Alex Mill just shrugged when Amanda asked where Conrad was.

Amanda searched Conrad's room, then the stables, then crossed the river to the house of Conrad's sister Bethany. By luck, Bethany Blackthorn was home. She was nursing little Jacob, her second child, in the kitchen. "What brings you today, Amanda?" she said. "I had been preparing the feast for our neighbor's tenth anniversary, such a wonderful couple, you met them, yes?"

Amanda stood puzzled for a moment. "Oh, yes! John and Amber, of course!"

Bethany noticed a strange expression on Amanda, and the next moment, Jacob was howling and crying. "Oh, sweetheart! Mommy's right here, honey. It's okay. Everything is fine, baby," Bethany cooed as she rocked him gently in her arms. After several minutes, he calmed down and went to sleep. And Bethany tucked him into his little crib.

On returning to the kitchen, Bethany asked Amanda what was wrong. "It's Conrad. He's missing. I can't find him, and the baron is a mess," Amanda said.

Bethany went to close the front door, and then explained, "One of the sages and two watchers have accused Conrad of a double murder. Everyone says he killed the keymaster and a senior monk, but this makes no sense. I know my brother. Wherever he is, he is seeking to restore his honor. He will not rest until he does. This is all I know until my husband Jonah returns. He will know his facts better than the idle gossiping rumormongers at the square, who have nothing better to occupy their minds with than to be pointing fingers."

Amanda looked pale, and her eyes had enlarged, clearly overwhelmed by the drastic chain of events, including the dead diplomat, whose body was found outside the barony walls on the North Road to the capitol of West Bend minus his modest coins.

A maid passed by with a bucket, informing Bethany, "Fetching another pail of water for Connor, milady."

Bethany called back, "Thank you. Nell."

Amanda got up to leave. As she did, she fixed her sad eyes on Bethany as she said, "So sorry about your father being ill, such a good man."

Bethany gave a weak smile. "Thanks. I hope your family is well."

Amanda replied, "Same as ever, Mum in the tower, Dad looking after her. You know ..."

Bethany nodded and then gave Amanda a hug before opening the door. "I'll let you know when my brother returns."

Amanda shuffled back to the Redoak Manor, and noticed clouds keeping the town in shadow. The vitality of the barony seemed to be drained away by it. She did not know how Bethany could be cheerful while

Conrad was a fugitive. The baron was losing his mind, Connor was sicker than he ever was, and Alex the Meek was no help at times like these. Sure, the fellow was loyal, but he had no command ability, and simply did not belong in a high-ranking position. And why was Bravane in charge, instead of her father? The rules of succession were so confusing. Her father was older and wiser, and had only ruled in Bravane the Younger's stead until Bravane the Third came of age. Alex Redoak was clearly loved by many, and Bravane, simply pitied and tolerated. Amanda felt powerless to do anything, simply having a name only granted wealth, not always credibility and respect. Always the problem of freewill, people only did what they could understand and what they were ready for. And the rumormongering lot in the square couldn't care less about Conrad's loyalty, honor, and bravery when he was such easy pickings for their forked and fickle tongues. Amanda never knew her maternal grandfather Morgan, who died in a house fire long before she was born. But she had heard stories about the land he first lived in, tales that her mother heard while Morgan was alive. The Union of Xantir, it was called. A land far to the west of Stonehaven, known for powerful wizards and a more sensible government than the one in West Bend, wherein the council spent days debating such trivia as which way the council members ought to lace their boots. Nothing ever got done, and they wasted away resources. Men were such doddering fools, except for her father Alex the Wise and cousin Conrad. And sure enough, there was Sergeant Mill at the gate of the manor.

"Is this gentleman with you, Lady Redoak?"

Amanda looked around, and there was a drunken man following her, ale dripping from his beard and a leering face with a smile of broken teeth.

"Certainly <u>not</u>, " Amanda hissed, as she snapped her fingers and pointed at the drunk.

Two honor guards immediately grabbed the drunk by the shoulders and steered him away from the gate, toward the courthouse. More men jumped out from behind a tree, and a tall, bald one put a burlap sack over Amanda's head while another clubbed Sergeant Mill on his head. A fourth one attacked the men escorting the drunk. The tall man punched Amanda in the stomach and hoisted her over his shoulders. A fifth man threw a rope down from the wall, and in almost no time at all, they were all gone over the northeast wall outside the manor grounds.

* * *

Within the town, other ruffians had opened the stables and let all the horses loose, while yet one more group let loose the prisoners from the Reeves building. The Obsidian Owl headquarters had two vantage points to the street between them and the Reeve, and it did not take long to see what had happened. Veteran Gray Owl was in charge while Grandmaster Tyton was away on a field mission.

"Owls! To arms! Blackwolves in the city! Open sanction to kill enemy rogues on sight!"

The honor guards were all busy rounding up horses, with not enough left over for anything else. Only when Sergeant Mill regained consciousness was anyone aware that Amanda was missing. Alex Mill tried in vain to find someone with command ability, besides the incapacitated baron. Without Conrad around and with Jonah Blackthorn, Bethany's husband, quite busy rounding up horses or prisoners, that left only Alex Redoak the Wise, who was in the tower keeping Myra company. Mill tried to avoid the manor tower, simply because Myra, Amanda's mother, was disfigured as a child in the great fire of Stonehaven Reckoning 1533 that killed Myra's parents. The boy who saved her life as a child was now her husband. And everyone called Alex Redoak "Uncle" or Alex the Wise to distinguish him from the meeker Alex Mill.

The Sergeant also dreaded going to the other Alex, in fear of what Alex Redoak might do to the man who failed to protect his daughter Amanda. But if Mill neglected to report, it would look so much worse, and his own wife Moira would never forgive him. Mill closed his eyes in resignation, clenched his teeth, and went to the manor tower. He stood by the door, trying to breathe normally, staring at the floor, hoping he would not get yelled at. All his life, he got yelled at. His adoptive siblings got away with larceny by framing Alex. When Alex tried to hide, he got lectured that he should be making friends; when he was seeking friends, he got mocked for being shy, and rumor was that his wife had married out of pity. Then the door opened. Amanda's father stopped short on his way to check on the baron. "Alex! What brought you here?"

Alex Mill tried to find his voice, but his tongue was not working. Alex Redoak prompted, "Is something wrong? There is, isn't there? Speak, man!"

Alex the Meek stammered, "I tried, sir, I tried to stop them ..."

Uncle Alex the Wise interjected, "Stopped who? What happened?"

Mill the Meek answered, "Bandits, sir. They ..."

Alex the Wise blanched; horror crept over his face. "Where is Amanda?"

Mill began to cry. "They clubbed me over the head. They took her ... I'm very sorry, sir ..."

Amanda's father raged, "GET IT TOGETHER, man! Go find her! NOW! That is a direct order. Do you understand me?"

Alex Mill nodded vigorously and staggered back down the stairs. The elder Redoak turned to his wife. "Myra, love, I will do everything possible to get her back. I love you, darling. Be safe." He quickly donned his chain mail and leather vest, before kissing his wife and grabbing his sword on the way out. Myra sobbed inconsolably as her eyes and throat burned with tears. Amanda and Alex Redoak were everything to her. Myra was alone in the tower again, fearing her world was ending. Myra wailed, "NO-O-O-O-o-o-o-o-o-o-o-o-o! My baby ... not my baby! Don't take my baby!" Her quaking voice echoed in the tower stairwell, haunting any and all who could hear her cries of despair.

Chapter Three
Trails Uncovered

Near West Mill, under a vast canopy of dull clouds, Conrad stirred from a long sleep to see that there were two people watching him at the campsite. One of whom turned to check him over. "We hear you had a bad week, Captain. Tyton thought it best to have you stay behind. Fatigue would have made you a liability if we ran into enemies."

Conrad thought, Oh! Is that all? A bad week was putting it mildly. He yawned and stretched, wondering if the others had found any trail yet. While it was nice to have a day off from his normal duties and responsibilities, he wasn't sure how much of this he could stand. He knew other people counted on him, and he had a noble ancestry to live up to. His great grandfather James Redmane had fought alongside Bravane the First, against the invasion of the Southwest alliance by the nation of Izimal in Stonehaven Reckoning 1490, fifth century of the second age. Conrad could not begin to say how old the Elven calendar was.

The lorekeepers of Oakthorn Abbey had told Conrad that Elves lived five hundred years, and their medical lore was astounding, even Savadi often said so. Perhaps the Elves knew a cure for the fever. Any prophecies about that? Conrad wondered. And how did the Elves not predict the battle of Shadval in 1540, the year after Conrad was born? The Elves paid dearly with many lives to reduce the presence of chaos fanatics, the most fearsome of which was Lorenna Saint Noir. Legend said she single-handedly obliterated hundreds of Elven priests and mages, before she was finally slain in "the knight's gambit." Stonehaven would have fallen twice as fast as the Elves did. Magical bloodlines were few and far between among humans. Most of those wizard families were from Xantir.

One of Conrad's great grandmothers, Amber Silverwing, was a Druid from Xantir. Amber died soon after Bethany was born in 1541. For Amber's generation, 62 years was a remarkably long human life. Conrad began to notice a growing headache, punctuated by sharp pangs of hunger. He suddenly realized that he had only had one meal yesterday, and poor Bill! Conrad had only fed him once, and the oats were almost empty! He stood up quickly, too quickly, and his vision went from colored to gray to black, as he lost his balance and fell flat on his back. The owls rushed to help him sit upright.

Conrad sat dizzy for several minutes. What could have made him be in such a hurry? Then he remembered — his horse! He needed to go feed his horse! The owls restrained him, saying, "Whoa there! Where in the blazes are you going?"

Conrad muttered, "Bill, my horse ..."

The owls answered, "Somebody would have fed him by now ..."

Conrad panicked. "You don't understand! Sergeant Mill is a spineless half-wit! The stable boy is with the fever! I have to feed my horse!"

The taller owl set him straight, saying, "We are forty miles from Oakthorn, and you'd collapse without food before you got there. Someone else will take care of it."

Conrad weakly protested, "but ... but ... the baron is ..."

Again, the taller owl corrected, "We know about the baron and his nightmares. His uncle will step in."

Conrad slumped. "I suppose you're right ..."

As Conrad was rubbing his temples, the owls suggested a foraging trip. Conrad thought, Oh, this will be interesting, as I know almost nothing about foraging, let alone mushrooms. There was never enough time to learn such things while the elder family members who have these skills were alive. I may wind up three shades of green before the day is out. That, or starve, lovely choice. This was the third rotten day in a row, and Conrad wished it would stop.

One of the men had a canvas bag, which, as the minutes crept by, they managed to fill with wild garlic, elderberries, wild carrots, cattail roots, dandelion greens, and walnuts. Conrad was amazed at how easy it was, compared to how impossible or arduous he believed it would be. The two men next to him shrugged their shoulders as they watched with amusement the sour face Conrad made when tasting white carrot and dandelion greens, the noises and funny faces he made while eating wild garlic, his grunts and curses as he tried to crack the walnuts. Conrad was greatly relieved the elderberries gave him no problems. He dearly missed the gourmet delights that his sister made back home, and thought to himself that he would never take her cooking for granted ever again.

* * *

Later that day, the main party returned from their field mission west of where Conrad collapsed. Grandmaster Tyton announced, "We eavesdropped on the locals at the inn, questioned a couple farmers, and ascertained the time and location of the murder. It is due north of here. Let's go."

Conrad asked what time Ramus was killed.

Tyton the Mysterious answered, "The very same night the diplomat died."

Conrad asked again, "When the diplomat's body was found, or before that?"

Tyton smiled. This guy did not miss a trick.

Tyton added, "Circumstances also suggest that the diplomat carried the fever into Oakthorn. We are awaiting further evidence, but Obsek's body has vanished, one of my men was savagely tortured and killed near the scene. To a casual observer, he fought a losing battle against a dozen opponents. To a skilled tracker … it was a single assassin, the most sadistic of his kind, who serves Arius alone. It was his mark. And no, he is not a Blackwolf.

He is single-mindedly ruthless. Blackwolves lack the patience to ever become anything close."

Conrad asked, "So you know this enemy?"

Tyton nodded and said no more, which in itself was creepy, as Tyton Umbral was the essence of deadliness; for someone, anyone, to give *him* pause, was unimaginable. Conrad tried not to think about it.

As they approached the vicinity of the murder scene, Tyton silently pointed at clues to see if Conrad was paying attention. The hoofprints were clear enough; a visitor had been here, and the track led back to Oakthorn. Other clues were tougher to spot. Conrad began to think the Obsidian Owls were all mentoring him in their own fashion. There were some bent blades of grass, scratches in the dirt, indentations in the soil, and over there, they sighted bloodstains in the dirt. Tyton gestured Conrad over and directed him, adjacent to the scene. Tyton made many hand gestures, showing the outline of where the body had fallen, where he had crawled, and where he had finally died. When Conrad had a look of resignation and confusion, Tyton finally spoke: "These marks were his elbows, these, his knees, and here, the Blackwolves hastily grabbed up some coins, but missed one over there under the tree root, which must have rolled on its edge."

Conrad responded, "How are you so certain who they were?"

Tyton led Conrad to the campfire. Red wine stains littered the grass, and some animal bones sat in the ashes. "The signs fit the information overheard at the inn. Three strangers paid for a room in the coin of Falcon Ridge from Valantir, never ordered food, smelled of venison and red wine. Look, these are deer bones. These men arrived long before the diplomat," Tyton explained. "Ramus cannot just skip work without arousing suspicion. He had to give excuses to his wife and to the baron before meeting here. These prints here ... Ramus was standing. He got stabbed from the front, while arguing with the rogues. He falls clutching a pouch in his right hand. Here is an imprint of the coins under his elbows and knees, and..."

Tyton walked to the tree to retrieve a coin. "Match this to the impressions and read it."

Conrad squinted as he read, "Twin kingdoms five, twenty suns survived ... what does *that* mean?"

Tyton explained again, "The motto refers to the twentieth anniversary of Shadval and the two races who stood against the forces of chaos. Elves and men from five lands. This gold coin was minted 1560, four years ago. The battle of Shadval further cemented the Treaty of Westwood between those five lands. One of your ancestors died there avenging the horrors of '33."

Conrad searched his head. His father never set foot there, and Conrad's grandfather Seamus died in the great fire. "I give up. Who was it?"

Tyton answered, "Susan Redmane, your great Aunt ... and the mother of Bravane the Elder, making her the baron's paternal grandmother."

Conrad slapped himself on the forehead. "Of course! I forgot."

Tyton continued, "This suggests several things.
One, Ramus was bribed before his death, and two, the Blackwolves passed through Falcon Ridge at the northern edge of Valantir. We need more evidence to confirm this. It is likely the body was carried on the back of that horse. If we encounter any Blackwolves, kill on sight."

Chapter Four
Bounties

Ravenna held up a hand in the stark shadow of a pine tree to halt the two traveling companions. There was a gathering of six men near the mountain pass, with one clearly in command. "So the girl is the same one?"

A second man nodded. "The description fits at least two other posters. Wanted for murder in Black Falls, and vandalism in Mojara. Kazius offers 400 Gold Eagles alive, 200 dead. Mojara offers one hundred gold for identifiable remains. Kozo-Makan offers 250. High price for such a young kid."

The leader shot a withering look over his spectacles. "I am not concerned with her youth or what you choose to do with her as long as I get my … justice. The lawgiver frowns on trespass and sorcery. You say they lost you in the forest?"

The second man nodded again. "They did, never saw anything on two legs run like those two …"

The Father held up a hand to stop him. "That's all I needed to know, Cooper. Off with you! Summon the assembly to the North Hall, and I want that young prince Adam in attendance. Now go!"

The man bowed. "Yes, Father !"

And as the men dispersed, Ravenna told her new friends not to wait up, but to get to safety. "But," Tyrianna protested in a harsh whisper, "I have to know —"

Ravenna cut her off. "With bounties like that, not wise to get so close to the chopping block, girl. You get to safety, hear?"

Before Tyrianna could answer, Tyrus said, "A sage caution." And nudged Tyrianna towards the open pass.

Tyrianna protested in a sinister hiss, "You have no right! Leave me alone!" Tyrus ignored her. She continued, "Who do you think you are, ordering me around, you big —"

Tyrus halted her, seized her shoulders, and said, "I promised your mother I'd keep you safe. The sea is my home, too, Tyrianna. I know who and what your mother is. And I'm sorry about Kaedrus."

Tyrianna now had angry tears burning her cheeks. "Sorry won't bring my father back! Stuff your sorry!"

Tyrus' stern look was his answer. A promise was a bond, and that was the end of the matter where he was concerned. It pained him to see one so young harbor such hatred, regardless how Kazius Auguron might deserve it, for the suffering inflicted by his men during the Tax Raid of 1551, the year Tyrianna's father died in Mojara. Tyrianna was half-mortal, and had been hurt before. She got into enough trouble as is. Tyrianna screamed some more, "I don't need you overbearing grown ups treating me like some child!"

Tyrus halted again, crossing his arms. "Oh? You have some plan for outrunning the mob a second time, getting back into Razadur and Black Falls undetected, and finding Kazius all by himself with no weapons or allies? You survived the last time by sheer luck, and let's not forget, you *missed* your intended target! You killed his younger cousin Jason! A child !"

Tyrianna let out a guttural yell of fury at him as she slammed her staff into the ground, and the blue shock wave knocked Tyrus off his feet this time. She then crumpled to her knees, sobbing. Tyrus got back up and noticed a mob in the distance. "Tyri, we need to go ... quickly!"

But Tyrianna would not move. She just kept saying, "Not fair ... it's not fair that he still lives ..."

Tyrus had to pick her up over his shoulder and haul ass away from the mob a quarter mile east of them. As strong as he was, Tyri's weight caught him off-balance. And the safety of Valantir was many miles away. Tyrus gambled that the foothills to the south of the pass were closer and would afford him cover. But as he crested a hill thirty minutes later, he saw the army of Razadur advancing in his direction. He estimated three thousand of them. "Neptune's beard! What foul luck!" he exclaimed.

He turned southwest, perpendicular to the advancing troops, and kept running. Two hours later, Tyrus was out of breath, and scanning for places to hide. As he crept uphill into the timberline, He caught glimpses of fire on the north side of the pass. But he was too far away to see who or what was responsible. A blackbird circled overhead once before ducking below the trees.

Minutes later, an exhausted Tyrus was startled by a woman; it was Ravenna.

"Zounds! How did you manage to get here so quickly?" Tyrus asked.

Ravenna smiled. "A secret of mine. Anyway, Malsain hoodwinked the young prince into cutting a big swath of forest between Kozos and the Jagged Lake by predicting a dire winter ahead. That man is as devious as they get."

Tyrus countered, "Arius would certainly give him a contest."

Ravenna shrugged. "If the rumors have any truth to them ..."

Ravenna looked at Tyrianna, sitting on a rock, forlorn and helpless. Then she looked at Tyrus, raising one eyebrow and motioning with her eyes at Tyrianna, to ask what happened. Tyrus just shook his head in the negative. Ravenna shrugged. "Well, we can't stay up here long. If they beat us to Valantir, bad things will happen."

Tyrus answered. "You try running with extra weight for two and a half hours. We are low on food and water and in no shape to run for two more hours."

Ravenna frowned. "Hmm ... that is a problem ..."

Tyrus added, "I saw fires on the North side of the pass, but could not tell the source; it was too far away. I doubt it was Elves."

Ravenna pondered for a minute. "Most likely, goblins or trolls. But I cannot fathom trolls ever bowing to Kazius, and he knows better if they won't. So it has to be goblins or … it could also be exiled Dwarf clans or the chaos cults. Either way, it's bad news. Well then, stand over here and join hands."

Tyrus raised an eyebrow. "now what?"

Ravenna insisted.

Tyrus grudgingly walked over to the rock where Tyrianna sat, and they all joined hands.

"Close your eyes and … open."

With a wave of dizziness, Tyrus looked, and saw they had reappeared a mile west of where they had been. Tyrus looked nonplussed. "That buys us, maybe, twelve minutes."

Ravenna retorted, "Well, I had to think of *something* … didn't I?"

Tyrus said, "Okay, fine, but can you slow them down?"

Ravenna answered, "Now that you mention it, yes, I could."

Tyrus finished, "Please do."

Ravenna strode a hundred paces out to the pass, held her staff high, and closed her eyes. She spoke in a language Tyrus did not understand, and after a full minute, as a gust of wind blew by, she brought the staff down hard, causing a split on the end, and the ground shifted and groaned, opening a fissure perpendicular to the pass, hundreds of feet long and twice as deep, fifty feet wide. Ravenna crumpled, exhausted. And two things happened, first, the army on the other side of the chasm had to fan out to get around the obstacle, and two, the fires got closer, and a smoky cloud seemed to rise up, which turned out not to be a cloud at all, but a volley of arrows!

Tyrus yelled, "INCOMING! Tyrianna, take cover!"

Tyrus leaped over the prone form of Ravenna, drew his trident, and twirled it in spherical arcs to deflect the arrows around him, one got through, piercing his left shoulder. He looked for Tyrianna, and she was gone. He called for her, and got no answer. Cursing at the top of his lungs, he slammed the pommel of the trident to the ground, sending a shock wave at the advancing hostiles. They all toppled and scrambled to their feet, back into kneeling positions. They fired again, Tyrus deflected with greater difficulty this time, and one more got through, piercing his leg.

"TYRI! Do something!" he yelled.

She faded into view in front of him, weaving a spell of some kind, chanting in yet another language Tyrus did not know. Her eyes blazed white, and a wind howled past, sweeping away the next volley, tumbling the hostiles and scattering their quivers. She continued chanting, and one by one, the shadows cast by the enemy, lifted off the ground, and attacked its counterpart. Tyrianna, then, fainted in exhaustion. It was up to Tyrus now and whatever strength he had left. He snapped off the feathered ends of the arrows and pulled them through. He grabbed one of Tyrianna's daggers and ripped a couple scraps of cloak to bandage his wounds while the enemy fought their own shadows. Some of the enemy fell, but overall, they were winning and would soon attack again. He tried to rouse Ravenna, to not much avail. Tyrus had no more time to lose. He hoisted Tyrianna over his right shoulder, screaming in agony as he did so. And he limped as fast as he could back into the foothills and the timberline, heading west by southwest to Valantir. Cracks of lightning in the distance told him Ravenna was awake and angry.

"Give them hell for us," he groaned and continued limping.

Chapter Five
Proof

Amanda awoke, gagged and bound, in a bed of pine needles and maple leaves on the ground. Trees surrounded the camp, and the remnants of a misty rain clung to her cloak. Her captors were gathered around a campfire, drinking red wine and doing impressions of armored guards chasing horses, while roaring with laughter. She attempted wriggling away from the camp, but her feet were tethered by a rope to a low branch. She had no clue where she was, or even the day of the week. But she was hungry and helpless, that much she knew. She struggled against her bindings, and achieved nothing. Seething hatred welled up as she studied the men, etching their faces in her memory. And something else caught her notice. Each one had a tattoo on their right shoulder, the outline of a wolf head, in solid black. They were a gang of some kind. And they were roasting some poor animal on a spit. Her stomach growled. Her hatred fanned even hotter. She silently vowed to make them pay for this indignity in blood. Drunken maggots, all of them. Vile thugs. She'd rip their eyes out when she got a chance, without question. Every last miserable one of them would pay.

* * *

"Any sign yet?" Alex Redoak asked the man in charcoal gray leather.

"Yes," answered the veteran. "This track turns north from here. Their stride is unsteady, both from extra weight and their drunken stupor. And … look there … (pointing) … do you see?"

Alex squinted. "No … wait … yes, I do see it … a wisp of smoke."

The owl replied, "They are as arrogant as ever. Will have them by day's end."

Alex cracked his knuckles. "Yes, by God, they shall rue the hour they laid a hand on my daughter!"

The lead rogue motioned for the others to flank the river on both sides, and off they went. Farther north, other pairs of eyes also noticed the telltale fire and smoke, and had already encircled the camp. None of the Blackwolves had noticed until one got up to go relieve his bladder by a tree. He met a pair of eyes on the feathered end of an arrow pointing right at his heart, and immediately wet himself, and whimpered. A voice behind him asked, "What the hell, Danny? Step on a snake, didja?"

In answer, a dozen archers stepped out of concealment from the trees, every last one an Elf decked in green wool cloaks, green silk robes, and the painted white emblem of Valandrassil on their tabards, the great tree of Valantir.

One bore the icon in a circle of gold, and it was he who spoke: "You are not recognized in the Treaty of Westwood, and having evidence of hostile intentions (pointing to the young woman tied up in ropes and rags), you are now prisoners of the Elven crowns." He produced a wand from his sleeve and flicked at each of the rogues, one by one. They were suddenly numb, limp, and unable to stand upright. "Take them away," he commanded. The Elf in charge then kneeled next to the lady and undid her gag.

Amanda said, "Thank you. Much obliged."

He asked, "Your name, miss?"

She answered, "Amanda Redoak of Oakthorn."

The Elf bowed his head. "We have not forgotten the family of Bravane the First. We are honored to be of service." As he continued to undo her bindings, he asked, "Have they harmed you at all?"

Amanda replied in hot indignation at the rogues, "They have dragged me from my home, assaulted our guards, starved me, and gloated about letting the horses loose. They are, perhaps, guilty of murdering the keymaster Ramus and allowing my second cousin to take the blame, making him a fugitive."

The Elf nodded. "I see. And your cousin is?"

Amanda told him, "Conrad Redmane, Captain of the Guard ..."

The Elf looked shocked. "The signs! The unsleeping menace is advancing his pawns. You must return home at once and warn them!"

Amanda challenged, "*What* signs? Who are you?"

The Elf answered, "I am Andrath of Valantir. Your captors crossed our border."

Amanda was not satisfied. "*What signs?* What did you see?"

Andrath paused, and began, "The great war which begins with the sundering of the brotherhood. Conrad is also known as Red Bear and is foretold in our legends. My mother recorded this in 1492, by your Stonehaven reckoning. After the invasion by Izimal and the Vostiok rebellion. To Elvenkind, this was not so long ago. You must hurry!"

Amanda still did not understand, but got to her feet and dusted herself off. Andrath motioned for two Elves to escort her back home. Amanda asked one more question, "Is there anything to prove Conrad's innocence?"

Andrath raised an eyebrow, then replied, "We will search their belongings right now." He snapped his fingers. "Aerdwen, see to it."

The other Elf bowed. "Yes, sire."

They were still searching the bags when Alex Redoak arrived.

"Amanda! Thank heavens you're safe!"

He ran to embrace her, and she hugged back while fixing a cold, wrathful eye on Sergeant Mill, who shrank from her gaze. While the Elves were picking through material evidence, finding coins from Razadur, coins from Falcon Ridge, plus an unknown currency, dried berries, smoked venison, red wine, maps of Oakthorn, West Mill, Falcon Ridge, rope, snares, bait, daggers, fishing hook, and of all things, a hand-sewn cloth doll, Andrath asked Amanda why a rogue would carry a doll. Amanda went to look at it, and blanched white. "That's Opal's doll!" Amanda exclaimed. "Ramus's daughter. They threatened his daughter! This was her favorite, made by her late grandmother! Those blasted rogues! I'm going to rip their eyes and tongues out!"

Andrath stopped her. "They will be surrendered to your Magistrate after we are done with them, Lady Redoak."

Amanda scowled and turned away from him, her ears hot with rage, as she cursed under her breath. Mill stumbled away from her; he had never seen her this angry and hoped to never see that look again. Amanda stopped in midstride, turned one more time, and grabbed the dried berries along with the red wine. "They won't be needing these ..."

Andrath nodded. "As you wish."

Amanda took the doll as well, before departing. Alex Redoak whistled for the horses, who appeared a couple minutes later, to bear their riders home.

Chapter Six
Out of the Shadows

Tyton and Conrad and the others snuck back into the city, and the logical place for the body of Ramus was the abbey's funeral hall, which Conrad had been in too much hurry to exit last time. Tyton gave commands for three men to create a diversion in the south wing and obtain some medicinal herbs if they could, while Conrad, himself and one veteran searched the hall in the north wing. Once his men snuck past the watchers at the front door, the rest was easy. They ascended the support columns in the main hall of the nave and waited for the patrol to reach the north end. They dropped down, sped through the cloister, past the bulletin room, and rounded the corner to the apothecary to "borrow" some herbs and potions, before hiding in the greenhouse, waiting for the sound of the patrol.

When the watchers passed by, they ran south through the pantry, leading the patrol back to the main door. As the patrol ran outside, other watchers joined the chase,

Tyton and Conrad snuck into the funeral hall, where the bodies of Eledar and Ramus lay. Both had been prepared in cedar oil, frankincense and myrrh for burial. Ramus was blanched from dehydration, and next to his coffin a small chest contained items found on his person; a pouch with just one gold eagle coin left in it, plus his wedding ring, a pocket watch, a letter to his family, and the dagger that killed him.

Conrad fell back, stunned by the recognition of this exact dagger. He had lost this one two years ago on a hunting trip. It had a walnut handle and a chrome butt cap with an inlaid topaz crystal. But as the murder happened the same night as the diplomat's demise, and West Mill was sixty miles from Oakthorn, why would anyone there take a stranger's dead body this far, or was this all planned? Did Eledar himself take the body? Conrad had to know; he needed more evidence. Why were the Blackwolves after the keys? How did all this fit into the agenda of Razadur? Conrad continued searching in vain, his rage and his anxiety eclipsing the ability to reason, making his thoughts run wild without focus or moderation. Conrad knew only that he would be a hunted man until he had solid proof of who killed Ramus. He failed to notice when Tyton gave the signal to leave.

The Obsidian Owls obeyed instantly, and Tyton hung back for a few more seconds, hoping Conrad would follow. Finally, he could wait no more and vanished into the night. So Conrad was still present when the watchers returned, and saw him next to the bodies, looking as if he was tampering with evidence.

"Watcher Red Bear, your rank is suspended, and you must stand trial in the town court!" one of the men yelled.

Conrad spun and snarled like a jungle cat, poised like he would charge at them and rip them in half with his bare hands. They backed away in fear of the scorching rage in his eyes and bared teeth. Conrad leaped forward, extending his arms as he neared the doorway, slamming them both against the doorframe, knocking the wind from them. Conrad sailed past as they fell, running with all the speed his adrenaline could muster away from the abbey. He ascended the western stair to the town wall, and vaulted over the edge, dropping 15 feet to the ground and rolling back onto his feet without missing a single stride. Conrad fled south into the forest, and was soon gone from sight before his former comrades could follow. Much as Conrad wished otherwise, his life, which was once the envy of many, was now the envy of none, and would remain thus to the edge of death itself.

Alex the Wise and Lady Amanda Redoak returned too late to be any help to Conrad. A very drunken Baron Bravane the Younger himself opened the manor gate to let them in and hugged Amanda close after she dismounted. "I'm so sorry for letting everyone down," he sobbed.

Amanda stopped him. "No need, cousin. Nobody blames you for your hard life. This is not your doing.

Look!" Amanda handed him the doll. "Ramus was threatened and bribed before his death. This is Opal's doll! He would have done anything to protect her!"

Bravane muttered uncomprehendingly, "But who? Who is behind this? And why?"

Alex Redoak spoke up, "The men who kidnapped my daughter work for Auguron. They had coins from Razadur, which are spurned in all the five kingdoms that honor the Treaty of Westwood. And one of the Elves spoke of a prophecy which predicts 'the sundering of the brotherhood' whatever that means. Along with some unsleeping menace moving pawns in a great war. Kazius is such a pawn. He is mortal, he is arrogant, he is no match for the trickery Arius was capable of. Arius likely blames all of the Redoak clan for the death of his wife Lorenna during the Battle of Shadval in 1540, not long after you were born."

Bravane stared blankly at Alex, trying to comprehend what he had just heard. "Sundering? What brotherhood? What are you talking about?" the baron mumbled.

Uncle Alex put a hand on Bravane's shoulder and said, "Let's talk inside."

Bravane nodded.

Alex tried to explain again, "The men, a bunch of rogues from Razadur, work for Kazius. We think they killed Ramus. This doll was in their possession, which rightfully belongs to the daughter of Ramus, and we have the Elves across the river to thank for my daughter Amanda 's safe return."

Bravane still did not understand, with so much drink clouding his mind, so Alex gave up.

He went upstairs to give Myra the news that Amanda was safely home. Amanda tried to get through to her cousin. "My captors work for Kazius ..."

Somehow that registered; Bravane looked up. "What? He sent men to kidnap you? What is he after?"

Amanda continued, "Perhaps to force an agreement to the burnt treaty we found. Or to force a surrender ... is there something else we don't know?"

Bravane nodded, but said nothing. Amanda pressed him, "Well? Are there <u>other</u> motives for framing our noble Conrad in a murder and kidnapping <u>*me*</u>? I deserve to know, cousin, and I <u>*will*</u> find out!" She had a tone in her voice that even a drunken baron recognized. When Amanda bent her stubborn will to something, she had a way of making it happen. And she knew many of Bravane's secrets, which she would use to her advantage if she absolutely had to. Plus, he owed her a debt. Without the support, advice, and assistance of Uncle Alex and cousin Amanda, he would have been run out of town years ago, if not locked up in a clinic. He handed her the Longbranch report. Amanda's jaw dropped. "Oh, my God ... this is the great war the Elf was talking about, but how can three thousand get through Valantir?" Bravane gave a blank look and shrugged. Amanda got up. "Since Conrad is not here, there is only one man who can help ..."

Bravane slumped forward onto the table in resignation, knowing he had no say when he was deprived of his wits.

Amanda would do what she had in her mind to do, and there was no changing it.

Amanda marched right out the manor gate, turning south, passing the Royal Inn on the way to the owls' guild quarters.

Tyton was amused to see her. "Well, what an interesting turn of events to see you here, are you acting in the baron's stead now? Or do you have other business?"

Amanda showed him the Longbranch report, and began to recite the Elven prophecy.

Tyton spoke, "We know about the Elves; my men helped find you, after all. And we know who captured you. They are called the Blackwolves and were present in West Mill the night Ramus died. There is evidence tying them to the murder scene. And they tell me you identified the doll. Thank you. We just need a few more pieces of the puzzle to clear Conrad's name. We also know Kazius is not stupid enough to attack Valantir with only three thousand men. He has something else up his sleeve. Goblins, perhaps. Or exiled Dwarves. Both harbor a deep hatred of Elves. The other unknown is whether or not the Syndicate or the nation of Korath will get involved. You are obviously seeking my help, as Conrad was. How can we help you?"

Amanda found she somewhat liked him already. No nonsense, right to the point, calm, cool, collected. Not hard to admire.

She began, "Is there a way to help Valantir and find Conrad?"

Tyton smiled. "Finding Conrad would be easier than helping Valantir. And my men would want hazard pay for such a thing as getting involved in front line combat. Are you authorized to make that promise?"

Amanda paused. "Well, my father ... he would be."

Tyton smiled again. "Yes, he would be. But thank you for the report." He hands back the paper. "This was useful. We look forward to business with Alex. A wise man. You have his eyes."

This was the most curious silk-tongued dismissal Amanda ever heard. The logic of his argument was rock solid. She could not muster any anger at him. Tyton really was a master of his craft. She wanted to stay, but there was nothing more to gain by it. Amanda had met her match. She left pondering the meaning of everything. Tyton could probably charm a raging bull if he wanted to; maybe he already had. Conrad had to be in a truly ugly mood when his honor was tarnished. What else did Tyton know? He had a look as if nothing ever slipped past him. Was this only legend, illusion, tradecraft, and charisma? Or was he truly omniscient? No, it couldn't be; only the gods knew everything.

But he had to know something about the deaths that she did not. That was his profession after all. The shadow of shadows, a force of the night, rogue, assassin, spy, saboteur, perhaps more. Amanda would probably never know. Tyton measured every word as if it was gunpowder. Getting into the vault of his mind was near unthinkable.

She entered the manor again and retired upstairs for the night, after assuring her mother she was fine. "Yes, Mom, I'm just exhausted. I'll be fine in the morning. I love you."

Myra would not let Amanda go right away, holding her hands and touching her good cheek to them, to banish all doubt that this was her daughter. Amanda kissed her mother's forehead. "I'm fine, mom. Good night."

And peace returned to the Redoak Manor for a single night, at least.

Chapter Seven
Courting Disaster

Tyrus awoke in a strange bed and sat up with a start. He saw his trident leaning against a far wall, and his clothing folded at the foot of the bed. His wounds had healed, and the room was sheltered from rain above, but not wind. It was open air, showing bright daylight, and it was now evident, he was in a treetop. Tyrus had never been inside the Elven dwellings before. But where was Tyrianna? Was she safe? He dressed quickly to go look for her. And which city was this?

Outside his door, an Elven sentry bowed in greeting. "Welcome, Tyrus, to the border city of Korval. We trust you are well?"

Tyrus nodded, asking, "Where is Tyrianna?"

The sentry replied, "She is resting. She was quite hungry last night. We thank you for saving our friend."

Tyrus noticed the crest on the sentry's green silk tunic. It was a circle of twelve white trees. Perhaps a symbol of the border cities?

Tyrus suddenly realized, "The armies were right behind us! With torches and archers!"

The sentry nodded. "Indeed, they were. Our friend and ally Ravenna got here first. They had to turn back on account of weather."

Tyrus laughed in spite of himself; dry humor from an Elf was the last thing he expected to hear. The sentry waited for Tyrus to catch his breath before asking, "I can lead you to the dining hall, if you so wish." Then, he bowed again.

Tyrus answered, "Yes, very much. Thank you."

They descended halfway down the spiral stairs that circled the trunk of the tree, and crossed a rope bridge with planks to a bigger tree with a large loft adorned with carved leaf and interlaced-knotted patterns of grapevines, images of sweet potato vines, and stylized icons of trees. These were painted in one of three ways — dyed with black walnut pigment, or dyed with green algae, some finished in linseed oil only, with modest accents here and there of silver and gold. Tyrus was impressed.

At the great oak table, which was an elongated oval with four rounded corners, a morning feast was laid out. Silver vessels of spring water, bottles of berry wine, honey mead, pans of acorn bread, wheat bread, jars of almond paste, raspberry jam, and pickles, plates of broiled salmon, dried fruit (including dates, figs, raisins and sun-dried pears), wild garlic, boiled potatoes, and raw leafy greens with dill weed. Tyrus dug in heartily. And his hosts regaled him with what they knew of Father Malsain, who was obviously turning Korath against the Elves. "He leads the

Lawgiver cult. We suspect him of far more. His rise to prominence coincides with bandit and mercenary activity in the area. He has no known connections to Razadur, but this cannot be ruled out. The citizens of Korath are led to believe Malsain can banish monsters. We think this to be a falsehood, but we have little evidence or testimony to substantiate either way. And contacting humans native to Korath for reliable intel has been nearly impossible. Ravenna is the only one who is able and willing. We are in her debt."

In between sips of berry wine and spring water, Tyrus asked, "I know why Kazius and Mojara have placed bounties on Tyrianna, but why is Kozo-Makan involved?"

The Elf known as Andiri answered, "We do not know, but we suspect they have business dealings with Kazius. Kozo-Makan is home to many bands of mercenaries. Beyond that, we are unable to say."

Tyrus paused before speaking again. "Tyrianna speaks often about visions of a great war and three champions. We were chased out of Korath for this. What do you know about the visions?"

Andiri replied, "The scrying waters tell us of an unsleeping menace in the north, who will break the order and bring chaos anew, which we fought at Shadval in 1540 by Stonehaven record-keeping. His bloodline is scattered over the many lands, and his pawns are many. The champions you speak of are represented by a bear, an owl, and a lion. We are convinced we know who the bear is. Further, it is said that a lame Redoak will pledge itself to a goddess and bring peace to the many lands. This prophecy led certain wicked families of humans to make war on tribal peoples wherein lametree families existed. The Bazadanis far to the south still hate the Augurons for this injustice. The Dabani and Bazu peoples are under a truce, in exchange for trade relations with Razadur. But they will not raise arms against Valantir. More than this is unclear."

Tyrus thanked Andiri. With nothing more to say, he simply continued eating.

* * *

"Bring forth the accused parties," said one of three Elves seated behind a seven-foot in diameter stump of petrified wood.

The sentries brought five men tied in ropes.

Mediator Elgar spoke: "You are all hereby charged with hostile trespass in the Five Kingdoms, as well as conspiracy to kidnapping and assault upon peaceful guardians of a noble family. The latter two charges will be tried in Oakthorn. Do you hear and comprehend the nature of these charges?"

One of the bandits opened his mouth and hesitated to speak.

"Furthermore, under Elven law, if you refuse to testify, you forfeit the right to protest our decision. Is this clear?" The men nodded. "Scribe will record a nod of yes to the question. Tribunal has now commenced. Trial of five does versus the Kingdom of Valantir, court of Valandrassil in session."

Elgar placed an hourglass in the center of the stump. "Now, if you will raise your right hands. Do you swear, by the stars and moon, to present your facts truthfully with honor, fairness, and full responsibility?" Hushed whispers are exchanged.

"Be advised. Refusal to take the oath shall be admission of ill will and count against you in our decision. Does the accused five deem themselves competent to understand?" They nod. "Scribe will record affirmative nods." Elgar paused and began anew. "The rights of the accused are as follows: by the Treaty of Westwood, all foreign parties will have a swift but fair trial, with the following limits on protests: you may contest on procedure, evidence,, or witness, only by placing hand or head, if a hand is lacking, on the metal disc in front of you. Failure to act in a civil manner shall be construed as a violation of the oath you have just taken. Is this clear?" They nod again. "Accused have nodded yes. You may now sit."

They were then seated at a smaller and shorter stump of petrified wood.

Elgar spoke again, "Will the royal counsel now step forward to present the case?"

A reddish-blond Elf with brown eyes stood and approached the stump. Turning his right shoulder to the three presiding mediators and facing the assembly, he spoke with his palm upturned toward the bandits. "These five accused were seen with a human captive inside the borders of Valantir. Said captive is also an ally of Valantir. It was the Lady Amanda of Oakthorn, which clearly establishes hostile designs in their trespass."

One of the five stood to speak, and Elgar stopped him. "Accused will follow the protocol of protest, or stand in violation of oath. Please place your hand on the disc and state the category of your protest."

The man stuttered, "Wh-what were those again?"

Elgar rolled his eyes and shook his head momentarily, and repeated the categories, "You may protest on procedure, evidence, or witness."

The bandit chewed his lip, straining to remember, which was difficult for a Blackwolf, as they are rarely sober. "Uhh, procedure."

Elgar answered, "Scribe shall register contest by first doe on procedure. As well as tribunal's first warning on protocol. Counsel for the accused, please stand." He does.

"Please state foundation for contest."

The defense counsel (a half-Elf) replied, "Request conference with accused parties."

Elgar frowned. "Session has only just begun. You have two minutes before penalties accrue for abusing procedure." And he struck a maple rod on a suspended hollow log section of cherry wood.

The counsel for the accused spoke to his appointed adoptees in a whispered hiss, "What do you idiots think you're doing? You were late getting up, after getting drunk all night and could not be bothered to participate in crafting your own defense? The barony of Oakthorn will not be as lenient when you face charges there, of much greater penalty than mere trespass! You five get it together or forget any hopes of finding mercy! You hear?"

Elgar announced, "One minute left."

One of the bandits whispered, "We were tracking some girl named Bitter Rose, and got her mixed up with the Amanda chick."

The defense counsel answered, "You moron, the Elves know who Bitter Rose is, and she does not look remotely like Amanda. You better pray I think of a better idea, or you five are done for."

The bandits sank their heads in defeat, looking like scolded children.

The counsel rose to approach the stump again. "The accused pleads mistaken identity concerning the lady Amanda. They were seeking the bounty on a fugitive from Razadur."

Elgar asked in return, "Then the accused is familiar with the bounty poster and the description of said fugitive?"

The defense counsel immediately saw the trap and no way out of this one, answered in a tone of defeat, "Umm, yes, the accused claims familiarity with said poster."

Elgar : "Can the accused produce the original poster or a copy thereof?"

Now even the drunken Blackwolves saw the trap. They were done for. All five tried to run for it. One Elven sentinel clothes-lined a runaway with a long staff. The other four ducked under him. A second runaway was tripped and captured. Three made it to the edge of the platform. The surest way out was to jump. One overshot the sloping roof of a lower level and shattered his left leg on the ground. Another missed his footing and hit the ridge of the roof right on his groin. He slumped to his right, slid sideways off the roof, and broke his neck. The last man, Danny, slid upright on the roof and tumbled to the ground. He ran westward until he reached the river an hour later, escaping pursuit by miraculous luck.

Elgar dryly observed to the remaining assembly. "The actions of the accused five, specifically flight from administration of justice, is now construed as admission of guilt and as violation of oath. Sentence will be decided in 24 hours. Court adjourned." And in a whisper to the counsel for the accused as Elgar patted him once on the back, "They just saved you two days of work."

The counsel showed a wry half-smile and replied with a sarcastic "Ha ha."

The two Blackwolves above were escorted back to a cage, while the third one with the broken leg below was taken to the infirmary.

* * *

Tyrus awoke in the strange bed again, bolting upright when he smelled the trace of smoke in the wind. He ran to the doorway to see, and miles away, he could see the glow of fire in the early dawn far to the east of Korval. Tyrus called out, "FIRE! Away in the east! FIRE!"

Elves everywhere sprang into action, and a sleepy Ravenna also appeared in her nightgown from around the corner on the catwalks. Tyrus witnessed her transformation into a bird and her flight straight to the source of the trouble. Tyrus grabbed his trident and went to find Tyrianna. Most of the Elves were evacuating westward, and a handful (a couple dozen) were gathering their staves, wands, pouches, and other items on their way to attempt quelling the fires. Tyrus could tell they knew it was a trap, and many would not return alive. He found Tyrianna and said, "This is your choice, child. Stay here to help or flee westward. Whatever you choose, it must be NOW."

Tyrianna looked at him oddly. This was the first time ever, in years, that he had given her a choice. And there was something in his eyes, an expression she had sometimes seen in her father's eyes. Eyes that trusted in her, when Daddy was showing her how something worked. Her father, Kaedrus Moondreams, was of another land across the winding sea to the south, in Mojara, who died in the tax raid of 1551 at the hands of the Crimson Hoods (tax collectors from Razadur). Tyrianna was only six then, and her hatred of Kazius Auguron had burned ever since. The townsfolk of Dexia called Tyrianna's father "Crazy Kaedrus" because of his visions. The fleets of Razadur and Mojara knew Tyrianna as "Bitter Rose" or the Sea Witch. She was stronger than most humans her age and could outrace a dolphin in its own element. Thus she sent scores of ships to a watery grave with scores of dagger-sized holes in the bottom of the hull. Tyrus still stood there, waiting for the water sprite's decision.

"We should help," Tyrianna finally answered. "I owe them for sheltering me all these years."

Tyrus nodded and bowed. "So be it. We will help."

Away in the East, they could see storm clouds gathering, and smoke still billowing over a raging forest fire. Even Ravenna might be overwhelmed by the size of it.

Chapter Eight
Reckoning

Conrad was still adjusting to the sink or swim school of foraging, learning to make do with wild carrots and everything else he sampled from a brief exploration with the Obsidian Owl guild. And he slept in trees or on beds of pine needles and straw made crude shelters and started making tools out of flint, plant fibers, twigs, and branches, with plenty of scratches on his hands from learning the hard way. In a couple days, he had a fishing spear and a net and had lost several pounds in the midsection. Conrad spoke to nobody, kept no journal or physical record, and wrote no letters; his companions were now the moon and the stars. His life was food, sleep, and fashioning tools. He studied the animals, learning the squeaks of rabbits, the prancing of deer, the habits of bears, and the unexpected cunning of fish. His instincts, driven by hunger, became sharper, his reflexes quicker, observations sharper, such that he knew the smell of rain on the wind, the acoustics of cold air, of fog and rain, the smells of people, or, at least, the few who wandered this far into the forest; in short, he was becoming as dangerous as the Obsidian Owls themselves. He was becoming a force of nature and felt a presence he had known as a child — his great grandmother, Amber, who died when he was only two. He just knew without knowing how. But even now, bad luck could find him.

One autumn night, as he settled into his tree, he overheard sounds of children stealing his supplies. One boy in particular was very bossy, his height and posture suggested he was the oldest of the three. Conrad also heard whispers between them about "the crazy man of the forest." From these unflattering remarks, he concluded his chosen refuge was no longer safe and sympathy from any elders was unlikely, regardless how he got his supplies back. This left him only trickery and element of surprise as his best strategies. He leaped from his perch into their midst and bellowed his best imitation of a bear growl, which had the desired effect of stark terror. The oldest boy turned white and ran at top speed in total panic, screaming with his eyes wide as grapes fit to burst. The other two followed right after, dropping tools as they fled. Conrad gave chase, pretending to limp, but he grew bored after a minute of pursuit. He picked up his tools on the way back. He ventured farther south to get away from the outlying farms.

He stopped at the edge of the swamp that borders the great bay thirty miles south of Oakthorn, and just west of Stone Port. Instinct stopped him; he didn't know why. He searched the area, nobody was watching, the animals were quiet. Still, he had a feeling something was out of place. A light breeze blew past and overturned a few leaves on the ground. When he looked at his feet, there was a steel wire pulled taut underneath some of the leaves. He carefully followed the wire to a tree with a bow trap rigged in its shadow.

The number one suspect was the Blackwolves. This was Conrad's chance to get even. A sinister grin crept over his face, as he scouted the area to verify his hunch. A quarter mile west, he found them. Three men seated around a campfire. Conrad caught the scent of the venison and their telltale brand of red wine. The trees they sat under hid the smoke, but not the reflected light of their fire. These were sloppy amateurs, but Conrad knew even amateurs could be dangerous. It was time to even the odds through deception and craft.

Near the bowtrap he had spotted earlier, he dug hollows under the tree roots and covered them over with twigs, bark, straw, and dirt. Closer to the creek, he slopped some wet algae over some pebbles in the shade of a tree that had big roots sticking up, and in the river itself, he rigged a tripline to some underwater weeds with brachiated taproots. Then he crossed to the other side of the creek, gathered some wild foods, and waited.

The day after, a solitary black wolf bandit arrived to see if any animals were caught. Conrad heard the man hit something wooden, yelling in panic as he fell, followed by a scream of sharp pain, then curses, groans, and moans thereafter. Conrad could also hear the crinkle of leaves as the man crawled away from where he fell. The others would show up soon or abandon their injured comrade.

A minute later, the rogue had only moved forty feet on one good leg and one functional arm. Conrad still waited.

"Come on damn you! If I have to hunt every last one of you vermin, I will by God ..."

Two more agonizing minutes later, the others showed up to help their fellow rogue.

"What took you so long? Damn it! I'm bleeding here!" the downed man hissed.

The second man retorted, "Locals up north say the woods are haunted by some wild bear man ..."

Conrad had to clamp both hands over his mouth to stifle his laughter. The man on the ground threw leaves at the able bodied comrade. "What rubbish! There's no such thing as a bear man! Now get me out of here!"

Conrad watched patiently until their backs were turned. At first opportunity (and clear shot), he flung a pebble at the shorter one and bounced it off his skull over the right ear.

"Ow! Something hit me!"

The other one said, "Just falling walnuts, you wimp!"

The short one shot back, "That was no walnut!"

The next pebble hit him right in the face, dazing him, and dropping him flat on his back.

The bleeding one on the ground winced.

A third pebble hit the last one standing in the chest. He flew into a rage and ran right across the creek towards

Conrad, his ankle caught the trip line, and down he went before he could take another breath. He coughed and sputtered, struggling to get above the water. He lasted only two minutes. The dazed one was too scared to get up again, while the bleeding one shoved at him to no avail, knowing he was a dead man if the other two failed. Conrad stood up and threw more pebbles to taunt the coward on the ground. Finally the injured one bit him on the ankle.

"Ow! You bloody idiot!" the other yelled.

The injured man yelled back, "Get him!"

The short one just hid behind a tree. Conrad laughed, taunting, "Ooo, the bear man is gonna get you. Better go beg Kazius for mercy!"

THAT did it, the short one came charging like a stung bull. Conrad laughed as he ran. He led the rogue up a hill past brambles and underbrush, and as Conrad cleared the crest of the hill, he ducked out of sight and snuck behind a tree. His pursuer stopped at the crest, knowing something was wrong. The blackwolf saw Conrad a second too late. He was already locked around his throat with both hands. The rogue tried to wrestle out of the chokehold, but Conrad was too strong. A desperate kick to Conrad's shins bought the rogue a moment's breath before Conrad slammed him into the tree and then threw him right into the brambles.

The pain of the bruises and scratches made the rogue unable to run, and his eyes went wide in fear, knowing he had just been outmatched. The rogue hobbled and limped away as fast as he could, while Conrad sauntered casually after him, with the wicked grin of closing for the kill. Conrad spotted a two-pound rock on the ground, with the shape of a skipping rock. He spun it hard right at the rogue, hitting him square in the back. The rogue howled in agony. The injured comrade at the other side of the creek closed his eyes, knowing the end was coming.

The short man could not stay upright; the pain was too great. He crawled in desperation, whimpering with eyes wide as saucers. Conrad strode with clenched fingers, slowly approaching the disabled man, and the rogue screamed before the end, quickly silenced by a snap of his neck. The last man, with a twisted leg and a crossbow bolt through his arm, sobbed, "God! No ..."

Conrad grinned again. "He has heard and judged. And you pigs owe me!"

With that, Conrad kicked him hard enough to crack ribs. The rogue spat blood and had not enough wind to speak anymore. Conrad picked him up by the collar and head-butted him. The man fell, cross-eyed, writhing in pain, dazed, helpless, and resigned to his inescapable fate. Conrad grabbed him one last time to deliver a right cross that ended it. Conrad went looking for his tools, and they were, once again, missing. There must have been one more bandit, scared witless. So he checked the rogues' camp. He saw signs of scattered food and someone who packed in a hurry. Some venison was left on a skewer. Conrad sniffed at it to see if it was poisoned, then took a single nibble. It tasted funny, so he spat it out and tossed the rest. Conrad estimated he had been out here a week. Maybe the owls found something by now. Home would be better than losing equipment all the time.

Chapter Nine
In Absentia

Bravane the Younger woke up from a long sleep, after days of absorbing duties that Conrad used to do, and most other men were too sick with the fever to take over. Between assessing the winter provisions, getting the locks changed, more obstacles in the ongoing investigation to clear Conrad's name, to training new recruits for the town's defense, the baron was oft deprived of both food and sleep, to the visible effect of his great exhaustion. Sergeant Mill was still incompetent as ever, Bravane turned more and more to his uncle Alex the Wise for advice. While Savadi the Benevolent asked more and more for signs from the abbey's farseer, the oracle named Andar.

"The way is dark for Red Bear, his future, hidden beyond my sight, but he carries a great weight, almost unbearable. He will witness ruin, the sundering follows him, he cannot escape. Death will strike again, haunting his steps. More enemies approach, their numbers grow, even my kindred from Valantir are pushed back. The dark hour has come."

Andar had been correct about many things and now his words invited despair. He was young as Elves go, a mere 49 years and 11 months. Savadi spent double the usual time in prayer and meditation, hoping for inspiration to guide them all. If any was to be had, it was dreadfully slow in arriving. Savadi prayed for Conrad's safe return, for truth to be known and peace to return to the abbey, which had split into factions — those who sided with Conrad Redmane against the cold, cruel Eledar the Unforgiving (whose barbed tongue was legend) and those who favor strict authority and order. Savadi did his best to be neutral, but it was a hopeless task. Savadi's duties to the injured brought him in direct contact with hot-tempered watchers who thought Eledar was the strong (and unforgiving) leader that people needed, as opposed to Conrad, who appealed to empathy and reason, instead of draconian rules and regulations.

When Savadi needed to adjust his teaching schedule at the Co-op, which Bethany helped run, Rachel Kemp (the manager-in-residence) informed him that Bethany was ill with fever. Savadi felt the air leave his body. Of all things to happen now, the family closest and dearest to him was being hit especially hard. Rachel was at a loss what to tell him. The physician-general of Oakthorn was such a kind man, always giving his time to people in need. There was just not enough of him to go everywhere. Rachel tried to sound confident in her words: "She will be happy to see you."

Savadi smiled weakly as he left. He had the slow, joyless stride of an old man going to his children's funeral, and Savadi was only thirty. Illness and death was exactly what sent baron Bravane the Third's mother Helen Aristodemos into the abbey under a vow of silence last year, losing her sister (and Conrad's mother) to heart failure. Helen had stayed in Oakthorn with her son when her husband went into exile. She was now rarely seen anywhere but the cloister and altars. Helen, who was in her autumn years at 50, took no guff from anyone, and not even the impossible-to-please Eledar the Unforgiving dared to correct her when he was alive. He insulted the cooks whenever he fancied to do so, even one as talented as Bethany, who catered weddings and anniversaries, and one day Eledar went too far by insulting Bethany's children. She had reacted impulsively as many a mother would have done, burning him with a face full of hot soup. Even Eledar's yes man dared not say a word about it, and a small handful of monks cheered for a scant few seconds before falling silent.

Bethany was but one street around the corner from the Co-op, five doors away on River Street. The three maids were now working double-time between Bethany and her ailing father. Savadi met Nell at the door who was fetching another bucket of water. He entered to check on Beth, and when she was awake enough, gently inquired if any word on Conrad came back yet. Bethany shook her head no. Savadi left in worse spirits than ever. Townsfolk whispered to each other as he passed them joylessly on the way back to the abbey. They took it as a bad omen to see Savadi looking haggard and melancholy. Savadi shuffled his tired bones like a dying man in great sorrow, finally arriving at the abbey and going straight to the cloister, where Helen did her daily walking meditations. He broke into sobs when she was five paces away and fell to his knees. Helen had a knowing look of compassion and offered one hand to help Savadi up. Savadi took it after a minute of weeping, and slowly rose to follow her to a tree in the south corner. They sat facing each other. Helen held her palms out vertically, Savadi slowly willed his hands to do the same, and their palms touched. Helen closed her eyes and bowed her head ever so slightly. Savadi's head slumped low. Moment by moment, the heat of her hands entered Savadi's fingers, chasing away the doubts that plagued him in secret and stirring memories of Andar's visions and of the one and only copy available anywhere in the Oakthorn Barony of the Elven prophecies, locked away underneath the abbey, that good things will follow the ending of the great war. Savadi wept again. His eyes showed relief and gratitude. He began to apologize for his faith faltering, but Helen held a finger to his lips and shook her head no. She then pressed her palms together and bowed. Savadi mirrored the bow in slow motion. Savadi rose to his feet, still sad, but no longer bent with the weight of the entire barony.

* * *

In Redoak Manor, Bravane the Younger was losing weight in a bad way, grouchier than usual, and at his wit's end with so little reliable intel about the troops from Razadur. Where are they now? Who joined forces with them? Why does the Kingdom of Korath put up with Kazius? Why is Kazius Auguron risking a showdown on land with Valantir? Is there something in the winding sea that jeopardizes the fishing fleet of Stonehaven? And why is Alex Mill still such a spineless wimp? Bravane kept feeling a gnawing emptiness every time he passed the baronial stable and Conrad's horse, Bill. Bravane had begun feeding him a couple days ago. Bill was the only thing Bravane could not be angry with. The baron hated almost everything else. His own bed was too lumpy; it gave him cramps in his tired, aching back, the cooks had become clumsy, things were missing from the manor, thanks to crafty people who pretended to be on the baron's business when Alex Mill was on duty. Goblets with the Redoak crest on it were gone, many bags of grain, some silverware, a chess set, one of the baron's good cloaks; even some of his books and maps were gone. Bravane was exhausted, overwhelmed, and ready to scream at the drop of a quill. Sergeant Mill tried to avoid him at all costs, which proved nearly impossible. The baron yelled at him each and every day now.

Today, Bravane the Younger rode his own horse into the market square, on his way to visit Bethany. Savadi met Bravane the Third on his way back to the abbey, and said there was still no word on Conrad. At this news, Bravane rode to the Royal Inn for a tankard of mead. After his third fill, some honor guards arrived to lead him back home.

Bravane shoved at them to keep their hands off, and after a long standoff, they backed away to the far wall waiting for the baron to collapse. After three more fills of mead, he slumped onto the table. The crowd shook their heads as the baron was dragged outside and slung over the saddle of his own horse by five men. The owner of the inn, Rebecca, had a sad look as they rode away.

The chatter was pretty gloomy after the baron was out of sight. The silver mines up north had almost been emptied by the fever. The pumpkin crop was at a low yield. The one and only surplus this year was the fish. Rumors about the death of Obsek were also going around. Why was he outside alone on the north road? And what would happen when Razadur found out he was missing? Kazius would probably burn Oakthorn to the ground like his father tried to do. Oakthorn only survived that time because of a freak hailstorm that rained down stones the size of walnuts that sent everyone ducking for cover, followed by freezing rain. The events that year of 1533, turned Brent Redoak into a broken, miserable man and a stain on a proud family. He nearly bankrupted the treasury and ruined the barony. Brent Redoak died three years later in 1536.

The damage to his sons, Alex the Wise and Bravane the Elder, was already done. Now his grandson, Bravane Redoak the Third, was a drunk almost like him. While his mother, Helen, was a silenced recluse inside the abbey. Further talk among the people supported the opinion that the baron's "noble" cousin Conrad Redmane, who was nowhere to be seen, sought to save his own skin, instead of facing trial. If he was so innocent, what was there to hide? The speculations coiled and twisted into complete fabrications and falsehoods. Some began to think he was an agent of Kazius Auguron and some beautiful exotic bride was waiting for him in Razadur. After this rumor started, the next round of drinks tasted horrendous, and the patrons all forgot about Conrad while complaining that the inn had gone to the dogs and the drinks tasted like goat piss. They all left in disgust after twenty minutes of raised voices and whining.

The blonde barmaid whispered to the brunette, "You really like him, don't you?"

Rebecca nodded yes.

"What did you do to make them all leave?" the blonde asked.

Rebecca gave a sly wink and answered, "Oh, just a little salt and vinegar. That's all."

The blonde doubled over in laughter and kept giggling the rest of the afternoon. Cleaning up only took an hour, and the inn closed early.

Rebecca told her friend, "You can do whatever you like. I'm visiting someone. I won't be at peace if I don't."

The blonde nodded, hugged Rebecca farewell, and walked home. Rebecca walked across the north bridge that crossed the river dividing Oakthorn and proceeded to Bethany's house. They had worked together a few times at weddings. The door was open, and Nell was sitting, exhausted, on the grass, desperately catching her breath.

A big bucket of water was next to her. The other two maids were busy inside, and Bethany had a visitor seldom seen anywhere. The mother of the baron, better known as Helen Aristodemos, Bethany and Conrad's maternal Aunt. Helen was laying on hands over Bethany, with little Jacob crying in his crib next to his mother. Rebecca waited quietly. Helen motioned her over. Rebecca hesitated a few moments, before she finally humored Helen. As Rebecca sat, Helen extended a hand, palm facing up. Rebecca hesitated again. Helen's eyes glanced at Bethany and met Rebecca's again, while tilting her head. So Rebecca took the hand offered. The hand was hot, and had an aura. Rebecca was almost afraid. Why does such a powerful woman want Rebecca's help? Helen's other hand lightly brushed Bethany's hair near her left temple. Rebecca felt uneasy; she wanted to say something, but her words were not for Helen. She wanted to ask something, but no longer dared to. Helen nodded her head slightly toward the other room as she let go of Rebecca's hand. Rebecca obeyed, glad to be released from an awkward scene.

The other room was the one Connor lay in. Rebecca did not understand her purpose here until she began to notice the features that Conrad inherited from this old man before her. The deep blue eyes were growing clouded and weak. Rebecca could not help thinking of Conrad himself. How she had fancied him the other night in the rain and how angry she felt when the patrons invented a story about Kazius arranging a bride for Conrad. Those patrons were not there to see Conrad helping his sister with her catering, or how many times Conrad stepped in while his cousin Bravane was incapacitated as baron. Or how glad Conrad was when Bravane assumed command again.

Conrad was clearly loyal to his family. Conrad deserved better than what happened four years ago in 1560. His fiancée Mandy left town with a merchant named Adrian. They had settled west in the capitol and, within a year, were exiled from there, too. Adrian was bad news wherever he went, and nobody ever forgave the woman who had abandoned Conrad and broken his heart. Mandy was known as a self-indulgent woman who craved expensive gifts and who threw tantrums when she did not get her exact expectations met. It was obvious Mandy liked the gleam of Conrad's armor more than she liked the man who wore it. Poor Conrad did not see it, he was easy prey. And here was Conrad's father, suffering. Connor lost his wife (and Helen's sister) last year, and looked as though he would soon join her. Rebecca reached out a hand to feel his hair as she spoke the words, "You have a fine, honorable son, sir. I hope I may get the chance to know him better. I wanted to tell you while you could still hear me. I hope the fates will soon take pity on us."

Connor stirred from his delirium for a moment, and though his eyes could not focus on her, he faced Rebecca with a weak smile on his lips, and a single tear ran down his cheek as he whispered the words, "Good ... son ... " and faded out again.

Chapter Ten
Bitter Fruits

"My fellow Korathians, I regret to inform you that a young boy accidentally set fire to the Elven Forest of Valantir, and that the Elven scum will soon attack in force to retaliate, my brothers," announced Father Samuel Malsain under a dark sky of gloomy clouds, in his black robe and skullcap, with a white tunic underneath, and his unruly beard hanging a foot off his chin. "We must ready our defenses and save our children from these vile heathen savages. And this," Malsain held up a bounty poster, " is a fugitive you may find among the godless savages. She is wanted for evil witchcraft, willing defiant sabotage, reckless murder, and wanton theft. Do not face her alone. She is highly dangerous."

A farmer spoke up, "Those troops I saw the other day, what were they for?"

Malsain gave a hollow-sounding, contrived laugh, answering "Why? They were sent to contain the plague now raging inside Stonehaven. We don't want our people to catch a nasty fever, do we?"

The farmer bowed, "N-no, o-of course, not. I didn't mean to doubt you, Father."

Malsain smiled, but his eyes were icy cold, hard, and full of malice as he made a shuffling motion with both hands, dismissing the crowd and sending them home. Three men stayed nearby in the shadow of a pillar, wearing red and black armor, the colors of Razadur, not Korath. The man in the middle wore a regal-looking cape and a steel crown. His guards both carried pole axes. The man in the cape spoke curtly as he strode into plain sight, "The girl was sighted at the inn, you say?"

Father Malsain answered, "I do not answer to you, Kazius. I just want the bounty. I take orders from a man in the north. His identity is no concern of yours."

Kazius retorted, "If I so desired, I have at hand plenty of information to share about your dirty side business. Even the royals would rise up in outrage."

Malsain bluffed, "Rumors, Kazius? You know how ignorant these peasants are. They are conjuring rubbish. And the rogues who work for you are even dumber."

Kazius clenched his fists, and his eyes narrowed into half-moons. "Say whatever you like, Malsain. One of your orphans has found asylum. A very reliable witness. Your little cult would never trust you again if word got out about the children. You think about that next time you feel so high and mighty."

Father said nothing, as a look of indignation crept over his face. Kazius flashed a cruel and toothy grin. Malsain finally spoke, "You enjoy blackmail too much, Kazius."

Kazius gave a cold smile. "Glad we understand one another, Father. Carry on. Good luck capturing the girl. A feisty one, she is. Your favorite kind, I hear ..."

Malsain turned purple. "Get OUT!"

Kazius bowed mockingly. "So sorry to inconvenience a man of the cloth ..."

Malsain's knuckles turned white, as he pointed to the door. Kazius gave the cruel grin again and left.

* * *

"Where is the nearest source of water? Lake, river, anything?" Tyrus asked the most senior-looking Elf.

Andiri answered, "Korval is fed by a spring, there is not enough to use against this fire, the closest river is ten miles away. If Ravenna cannot contain this, the forest is lost. We have already lost a dozen people to goblin archers. We are outnumbered hundreds to one, the best we can hope for is a stalemate or holding action. We are hard-pressed every which way."

Tyrus clenched his fists in frustration and rage, "There MUST be a way. I <u>*will*</u> find it!"

Into the fray he went, twirling the trident at full speed to deflect more volleys of goblin arrows as he advanced on the enemy in between burning trees. Elves all around were conjuring wind and water to hold back the flames, while Ravenna was farther ahead, underneath the clouds of hail and freezing rain, casting lightning bolts at the goblins, and hundreds of charred remains bore testimony to her anger. Tyrus advanced in front of her, and said "Zap me!"

Ravenna raised an eyebrow, doubting if she heard correctly, and Tyrus said emphatically, "DO IT!"

She called down bolts from the clouds, which he took full force with his trident held high. His body crackling with the charge, he yelled his rage and slammed the pommel double fisted with all his weight behind it into the ground, sending a surface tremor into the heart of the enemy, stunning every last one. All the goblins, the exiled shadow Dwarves, the Bloodhammers, the Dragonwhip Trolls, the mercenaries, many thousands of them. He had also snuffed half of the flames at the eastern edge of the forest, allowing the Elves to seize the advantage. The few enemies to regain their feet were hit with paralysis spells, and Tyrus ran into their midst, raking their throats with the forked end of his trident. Tyrianna could only watch in horror, seeing, for the first time, what the reality of war truly was, with the smells of fear and combat and rage so thick in the air she was nearly choking on it; her visions were not nearly this vivid or personal and up close. It was hatred and bloodlust and savagery to Dwarf anything she had seen during the Tax Raid of 1551. This was not a bunch of tax collectors kicking a feeble man and mocking him; it was raw, bestial, and bloody rage and savage, unfettered violence — kill or be killed. Tyrianna began to crumble to her knees in tears, her hands over her mouth. "Oh, Mother, I had no idea. I'm so sorry …"

Tyrus held his own, until some Dragonwhip Trolls in the rear brought up a ballista, and launched a massive bolt at him. Tyrus deftly brought the trident up to deflect, but even as the massive bolt diverted up and away from his torso, the force of impact tore the trident out of his grasp as he tumbled backward. The trolls scurried to crank the arms back into firing position and reload, praying they were faster than Tyrus. Tyrianna saw Tyrus fall and ran to help him from hundreds of yards away, and Ravenna gave chase, to protect her. Tyrianna felt the world moving in slow motion, her every bounding leap and heartbeat abnormally long and loud, her own voice dragging out forever in protest: "No-ooooooo-oooooooooooooo!"

Goblins began to regain their footing in sufficient numbers; the Elves could not stop them all. They rose into kneeling positions and took aim at Tyrus, Tyrianna, and Ravenna. A flash of light blinded them all as a gust of wind swept away the few arrows that launched, and a tall, angry, powerful woman with long flowing red hair in a gown of green serpent scales, wearing a chrome tiara of inlaid abalone, a pair of pearl and sterling silver bracers with blue lapis stone inlays, appeared with glowing white eyes, brighter than the moon, who spoke in absolute conviction, with a voice no mortal woman could muster, a high-end baritone with a chilling reverb, "GET AWAY FROM MY DAUGHTER!"

A second gale force gust of wind scattered their quivers, tore the bows from their hands, the helmets from their heads, and made them unable to stand upright, tumbling them like children before a tropical storm. The minor goddess known as Syrene strode with absolute authority, her left hand outstretched, palm wide open, and 5 bolts of forked lightning leapt from her hand, striking long chains of enemy targets, frying them where they stood, leaving smoking, charred black mockeries of life. Hundreds fell in seconds, thousands ran in terror, leaving their weapons scattered behind like broken furniture after a disaster. Even Kazius Auguron himself, two miles away, dropped his spyglass in utter shock. "Oh … SHIT …"

It all made sense now, why finding the daggers was so difficult. Kaedrus Moondreams never had one; the mother must have had one all along. Nobody had ever seen the mother anywhere, except her family. Her bearing went beyond royalty. She was a goddess, and Kazius had pissed her off. "General Axegrind, I think we should retreat …" Kazius said with barely contained fear in his voice.

His general bowed. "Yes, sire."

Kazius added, "Find us a suitable hideaway in the mountains and tell the men the bounty on the girl is cancelled."

In secret, Kazius began to hunger anew for the platinum dagger of old legends, a relic of power said to endow control over wind and water. The old hermit who sold the information many years ago said it was in or near the sea. And there had been this crazy man on the coast of Mojara whose daughter survived impossibly long submersions underwater, and was thus known as the sea witch. But Kazius had to rethink his entire strategy in light of the girl's mother. And the Blackwolves seemed to be taking a very long time returning with the hostage he'd sent them after. "Why am I surrounded by buffoons who can't do their jobs?" Kazius muttered to himself.

General Axegrind scowled and turned an icy stare at Kazius while he was not looking. The general thought, The main army will arrive in less than fifteen minutes at current speed and heading, and the fires are almost completely gone now. Today was a complete disaster for morale, personnel, and position. Another defeat like this would turn into mutiny or desertion. If it was mutiny, Axegrind could turn that to his own advantage.

* * *

In the capitol city of Valandrassil, Syrene presented a carved staff to Andrath as thanks for sheltering her daughter all these years and then gave Tyrus a silver ring with inset lapis, amethyst, and hematite for his several moons of service in protecting and mentoring Tyrianna. In parting, Syrene finally hugged her daughter close, much to Tyrianna's embarrassment. There were no words for what Syrene wanted to say, and it was too soon anyway. How could one impart thousands of years of knowledge to a teenager? With nothing more to say, Syrene simply kissed her daughter's forehead and vanished in a gleam of light.

There was a long silence afterward. Finally, Tyrus spoke, "No more visits to Korath anytime soon."

Tyrianna gave a weak half smile and replied, "Nope."

Andrath led them to the dining platform, where many of the Elven leadership sat, already eating. Each one nodded their heads at Tyrianna in recognition of their special guest, the water sprite whom they had adopted as one of their own. A previous conversation started back up, the main topic of which was some humans. Elgar spoke, "One rogue remains at large; the other three are now halfway to Oakthorn. There is also the matter of finding a suitable quarry for fortifying the mountain passages against another invasion by Razadur, by Zara-Mogai, and perhaps even Korath. We hear that Malsain now has the young prince Adam Silverlane in his pocket. We are, thus, cut off from Talos to the east. Unless they risk revealing technology that Kazius would stop at nothing to obtain. Or Arius, for that matter."

Tyrianna whispered to Andrath, "If the Great War was foreseen so long ago, why have the leaders only now acted?"

Andrath smiled. "Because a long life is not satisfactory if we neglect our pursuits of happiness altogether, nor is it ethical to take agressively bold actions against a crime that has yet to happen. We would have made an enemy of Korath long ago and done Malsain's work for him."

Tyrianna just sat, looking puzzled.

Andrath added, "Someday you will understand."

Tyrus smiled and tried to hide it.

For the remainder of the meal, the conversation drifted to matters too dull for Tyrianna to take any interest in, and it certainly had nothing to do with Tyrus and his fields of knowledge either. Thus, they quickly grew bored and went to explore the area.

Tyrus advised his young friend, "Appreciate the scenery while you can, it would be very lucky for all this to be the same ten years from now."

Tyrianna had a puzzled look again and asked with genuine curiosity, "What did you see when you were young, Tyrus?"

Her oath-bound guardian raised an eyebrow, this was a new turn of conversation, quite unexpected from a rebellious adolescent. "Myrmidons rarely have any contact with surface dwellers, you know that, right?" Tyrianna nods.

"And I agreed to watch over you after your father died, simply because it was well-known your half-siblings could hardly care less what happens to you. They are self-absorbed gods with petty jealousies and easily injured pride. My people isolated themselves long ago when humans first invented the cannon and mounted them on ships. We, too, have a history of warfare, but humans were possessed of far greater bloodlust than any other race except the Dwarven exiles, the dragonwhip trolls, several of the goblin tribes and other carnivores. I have heard much, but seen little until I accepted a duty to keep you safe. There is not much to tell that you have not seen yourself."

Tyrianna responded, "Yes, but you are near my father's age. I've never known war, except in visions. It's not the same as being IN one, up close."

Tyrus nodded, then spoke, "True enough. In your father's lifetime, my people fought against hydras, dragons, tritons, nagas, sharks, giant turtles, rogue whales; certainly you must have seen some of these."

Tyrianna nodded. She had seen the sharks and turtles and whales often enough. They continued conversing for hours, taking in the sights of the forest.

Chapter Eleven
Dust

"Look, mister, this foreign coin is mighty unpopular over here. I can't accept it," the farmer told the man in a burlap cloak and leather armor as he handed it back.

The man smiled and produced a bottle of wine. "I'll trade you this then. The previous owners won't be needing it where they went to."

The farmer gulped. "O-okay ... no need to get violent ... can't be too careful these days. Hop on then ..."

Conrad boarded the back of the wagon cart and tossed a coin to the farmer anyway. "I'm also buying a bag of your oats."

The farmer frowned and said nothing, thinking it best to get rid of this fellow as soon as possible. Thirty minutes later, the wagon stopped outside the southwest gate of Oakthorn to wait in line with the other out-of-town merchants. The crowd consisted of about a dozen people, plus their carts and beasts of burden. When the farmer met the gatekeepers, he turned to speak to someone who was not there anymore. The gatekeepers just shook their heads, thinking this was another old farmer whose memory was failing.

The farmer sputtered, "He was just here. Some strange fella that gave me the creeps ..."

The shorter gatekeeper replied, "We'll keep our eyes open," as a hunched-over man followed a merchant inside, carrying a sack of grain over his shoulders.

As he turned right to approach the south bridge and passed a tree obscuring the view from the gate, he rose to his full height and followed the riverfront north on the western bank. There he kept to the riverside until he neared the owls' guild quarters. Two apprentices barred his path. "Who goes there?"

Conrad flashed a sly smile. "I believe Tyton has some information I paid him for. And it's above your pay scale."

The apprentices looked at each other nervously. Then they looked back to where Conrad had been a moment before. Around the corner, they saw a corner of fabric. They approached warily, weapons drawn, and attacked ... a bag of oats, while Conrad snuck in the front door.

The veterans inside recognized him, and let him pass. The apprentices ran in after him until Tyton waved them off. "No need. We know this man. Welcome back, Mister Redmane." Tyton then sized up the evidence on his men, from the stray threads caught in the cross piece of a dagger, and the oats clinging to their boots, and observed with a dry and sardonic tone, "Well, that bag of oats won't menace us again, will it?"

The apprentices turned beet red and scurried out of sight.

Tyton turned to Conrad again. "We heard about some 'bear man' in the woods, who obviously fights better than the drunks who bungled a kidnapping. Admirable handiwork, Captain. I underestimated you."

Conrad was taken aback. "Kidnapping? Who? You're not part of that, are you?"

Tyton gave a weakly amused half-smile, "No, Captain, and were it not for Lady Amanda, we might have little hope of clearing your name. When the Elves rescued her from the rogues, they found an item in the men's bags that strongly suggests the wolves had used the keymaster's daughter as a bargaining chip. They got close enough to steal her favorite doll. And these rogues are soon to be delivered for trial here. My men will ensure they do not escape."

Conrad thought a moment. "But how does a doll clear me? And what do you mean 'you underestimated me'?"

Tyton smiled again, a bit brightly. "You took out three of them, in minutes, with only your bare hands and salvage materials. I would have bet 50 percent odds they'd have given you more trouble. But you fought like a tiger. My best student told me this last night." Conrad relaxed a little. "So, about that doll …"

Tyton brought his fingers together in contemplation, "Yes, the doll, plus other evidence, will be presented at their trial. We shall see. I predict the bumbling oafs will seal their own doom. I'm quite amazed that Kazius still gives them a job at all. Then again, Kazius does not inspire loyalty in men of greater intelligence and ability. Quite the opposite. Your armor is still safe here; perhaps you'd like to have it back?"

Conrad weighed his options. "Too soon to say. I doubt I would be a welcome sight here. But I do stand a better chance of staying dry at night in the town. Plus, my fishing supplies have vanished."

Tyton gave an understanding nod. "If your old life should become undesirable, you would be welcome here as an honorary member."

Conrad bowed his head. "Thank you."

Before Conrad could finish another thought, a new visitor entered the front door, and they were both shocked and pleased to see a familiar face. "Cousin! Amanda was very worried about you! Welcome back!"

Alex the Wise swept Conrad into a bear hug and then clapped both his shoulders.

Conrad answered in a voice of worry, "What's my status these days?"

Alex Redoak replied, "In a moment. I came here on business." Then he turned to Tyton and said, "The treasury is in bad shape. Our meager harvest, the fever, and other conditions have hit hard. I can only promise one week of hazard pay. Further negotiations will depend on updates from Valantir."

Tyton nodded his head and, with a slightly restrained chill in his voice, said, "Understood. We will consider the offer. Thank you."

Alex and Conrad promptly exited, and Conrad retrieved the bag of oats with a few holes in it.

* * *

Bravane had been stone drunk again the day Conrad returned and was so disgusted with Sergeant Mill by now that he would not allow anyone but Amanda and her father to disturb his many naps. He wanted to fire Mill as soon as possible, but none of the recruits were ready to replace him. Thus, the news of Bravane's cousin returning home was late to reach him.

Bravane bolted upright when Amanda told him. "Oh, Lord! I look a terrible mess, don't I? Where is he now?"

Amanda informed him, "He is keeping vigil over his father at the Blackthorn house. The fever is destroying his body. We don't know how he's lived this long."

Bravane struggled to marshal his thoughts. "Has Helen … my mother … seen him?" Amanda shrugged; she did not know.

Bravane answered his own question, "She must have. She has a gift. The healer's hands.

And she is the last surviving Aristodemos of her generation. A proud family from Agama. I never dared showed my face among them, being too much like my grandfather … "

Amanda interrupted, "Cousin, they all know what happened. The shame is not yours ..."

Bravane countered, "Oh, yes, it is. Look at me. Too drunk to welcome my loyal friend and cousin home ..."

Amanda had had enough. Her fury seized her. Her eyes widened, her face reddened. "STOP IT! Is this what you want, to let life pass you by while you breastfeed your self-pity? You are a fucking BARON! Are you going to just sulk up here while Kazius lays waste to our allies in Valantir? And where is Miles Longbranch? Probably dead. People are dying around us. Your brother is long dead, and you insult his memory by wasting the breath you have left in your body! How many of your relatives have fought and died to protect the land we live on? HOW MANY?"

Bravane sat there in shock, unable to speak. Amanda may as well have thrown ice water in his face. "You think about that, cousin, while you still HAVE relatives, people who love you as is, but would gladly see you start living up to your potential that you keep drowning in that bottle!"

With that, Amanda spun on her heels and left to pay her respects to Conrad's ailing father, while Bravane stared at the last couple ounces of rum in his bottle on the nightstand. There, was the stuff that numbed his nightmares, made the pest of a Sergeant Mill go away, only to have them all return hours later ... Bravane feared he would never be free. And suddenly, he saw Obsek in the bottle, the look on his face as he died, and then, no pain. Nobody misses Obsek anyway. But Bravane? Who the hell cares about him? And what does Amanda gain by all the help she gave him over the years? Bravane wrestled for control of his thoughts; nothing made sense anymore. His whole life was a blur, empty, meaningless, an utter waste. His father, Bravane the Second, tried to kill him after Donald died, for which Helen never forgave her husband. Alex the Wise or Conrad the Bold would make a better Baron than what the town had now, what was the use of his life? The tendrils of despair closed around him as Bravane reached for the last of the rum, and in his trembling stupor, he tipped the bottle crashing to the floor. Bravane fell to his knees, sobbing. "Noo-o-o-o-oooooo! It's not fair! Damn it!"

That should please Amanda, he thought bitterly, to see me weeping over a few ounces of spilled rum ...

"No, that's not true ... she would just stare in disbelief ... or laugh."

Then he saw a vision of Amanda picking up the broken glass. That was more like the real Amanda. A vision of Uncle Alex just crossed his arms and frowned while a phantom of Conrad shook his head and turned his back. In stark panic, the baron pleaded, "No, wait! Come back! I need you! Don't leave me!" Bravane suddenly realized he was talking to thin air. "Gods, help me ... I don't know what to do anymore ... " Bravane crumpled into a lonely ball on the floor, sobbing until he fell asleep.

* * *

"I'm here, Father. I've returned," Conrad said in a somber tone of mixed reverence and sadness. Connor struggled to see his son at the bedside, but all the colors were gone, and shapes were all blurry. Connor could hardly breathe; his muscles were so wasted away. His mouth attempted to form words, but could not. Nor could he lift his own hand for more than a quarter second. Devi tugged at her uncle Conrad's cloak, "Is grandpa dying, uncle?"

Conrad said nothing as he knelt down to caress her head and gave a quick hug, with resignation on his face. "Nell, please summon Savadi. Father's eyes are almost empty. I do not think he will last the night."

Nell left for the abbey just as Amanda arrived. Conrad was trembling, trying to stay strong, but the tears would not stop. Bethany lay in the other room, dried up from her own fever, and attempting to feed Jacob spoonfuls of goat milk. Jonah was rather glum from weeks of watching his father-in-law suffer, now his wife and son, too. Devi instinctively hugged her uncle again, from the side, and Conrad slowly slumped to one knee and now openly sobbed as he hugged his niece close.

In the other room, Bethany could hear her brother, and she knew their father was passing tonight. She, too, began weeping and gave Jacob to her husband Jonah as he kissed her forehead.

Two of the maids were now resting, exhausted. Thirty minutes later, Savadi appeared with Nell and Helen. Not long after, Connor Redmane breathed his last. Conrad was sitting against the wall, his head bowed over his bent knees, as Savadi recited a short prayer. And one by one, visitors arrived and left, offering flowers and bread, and Rebecca the barmaid stopped by for a visit, saying very little, not daring to put Conrad on the spot at this hour. Helen gave a knowing smile and nodded to Rebecca as she passed by, bowing slightly and blinking once. Rebecca returned the nod.

* * *

News traveled quickly, and Alex Redoak informed the baron, his nephew, of Connor's death. The baron, though tired and weary and irritable from having his sleep interrupted, within minutes he understood, much as he needed Conrad's strength, courage and hope, at this hour, there was none to give because Conrad needed the same. Bravane's memories paraded before him, of times spent with Conrad. The day Conrad saved his life up northwest at the waterfalls, to Conrad's short-lived engagement to Mandy, up to the birth of Devi and the passing of Conrad's mother. Bravane was ashamed to realize that he only thanked Conrad for saving his life and only gave heartfelt support when Summer Aristodemos suddenly died. Other times, Bravane only offered half-hearted advice, a few jokes, and some drinks. He looked up at Alex, and the elder Redoak recognized a change in Bravane's eyes. The somber look of remorse on a long, weary face. It was Conrad's turn to have Bravane's loyalty and strength, and Bravane owed him that. Just as he owed gratitude to his cousin Amanda, his uncle Alex, and his own mother Helen. Bravane held his head in his palms, rubbing his forehead, wondering where he would find the strength to repay Conrad and everyone else. Bravane began, "Alex, I have a favor to ask … "

Alex Redoak turned and waited to hear more.

"Could you … bring some cheese and mead to the stables, and I'll take them to … "

Alex finished, "Yes, of course."

Chapter Twelve
Revelations

"What news, herald? Speak quickly. I am a busy man!" snarled Kazius Auguron at his messenger.

The herald sank to his knees. "Advance party encountered problems in Falcon Ridge and are long overdue for updates."

Kazius snarled again, "That's obvious, you idiot. What of Obsek? What happened to him?"

The herald answered, "No word from him either, sire. He may have fled or turned traitor."

Kazius bellowed, "HAHAHA! Obsek is incapable of such defiance. You may leave now, imbecile."

Minutes later, a lone rogue entered the main camp, looking quite hungry, exhausted, dirty, and full of insect bites, scratches, bruises, and nobody dared to show pity on him. Pity for anything was taken for weakness by Auguron's chain of command.

Kazius taunted, "Well, look what the cat dragged in ..." Looking at the Blackwolf with naked contempt and revulsion, he continued, "Well? OUT with it! What took you idiots so long? Have you done what I sent you to do?"

The rogue swallowed hard, trying to avoid eye contact. "I don't know how to tell you — "

Kazius cut him off. "That you are total morons and I should throw you in the blood arena for sport? What are you saying, rogue?"

The lone Blackwolf responded, "We have been decimated by a rival guild and a man named Conrad. The Elves captured us before we could bring Amanda here. B-but, the Elves know who Bitter Rose is and ..."

Kazius heard enough, lunged screaming at the rogue, kicking his teeth in.

"Of COURSE, the Elves know who she is, you buffoon! They hid her for all of five years! You don't deserve payment, or food, or even the dirt and labor of burial! GET OUT, you worthless dung beetle!"

Danny rolled over, scampering on all fours to dodge another kick, and whimpered like a puppy full of porcupine quills as he clambered upright to run. The trolls jeered at him, the goblins cackled, and the Bloodhammers guffawed, making the rogue more afraid and desperate to get away. His eyes watered as he realized he *never* had friends among them; it was all a lie. Further proof came in the form of pebbles and rocks pelting him as they all chased him out of camp.

* * *

He ran all night until he could not take another step, fell completely spent on the battlefield with the burned corpses left by Ravenna and Syrene, where the vultures were picking scraps. Why an Elf would save him from the birds, nobody knew. But he did.

Days later, the rogue awakened in Korval, on a bed of straw in a cage.

"Wha this for?" he mumbled.

An Elven sentry replied, "You were identified yesterday by your tattoo and your eyes as one of the five bandits. You are to be delivered to Oakthorn for trial."

Danny slumped on his back. At least this was better than Kazius. But what a choice ... this is not the life he had hoped for. He thought he would have easy money to party for weeks on end, and then ... well, he never planned that far ahead. Maybe that was the problem. And in one corner of his cage, he spotted a silver plate, with a mug of water, half a loaf of bread, and some cheese. He dove for it, and tore into the cheese and bread like the starving man he was, punctuated by loud gulps of water.

The ordeal of the last several days had somehow purged his need for alcohol; he did not know how or why, and did not even care. The rumbling pangs of hunger, relieved by his meal, the best he had eaten in what seemed like weeks, had driven all such thoughts of parties and wine into irrelevance. Once done with all that was on the plate, he asked the sentry, "Is there more I might have? I'm really hungry." His wounds had only begun to heal, and he did look a bit pale, so the sentry inquired on his behalf. Twenty minutes later, another meal arrived, exactly like the one before. But Danny ate it without complaint, and then fell asleep again.

* * *

"The beasts have returned! The farmer is dead! Look here! He's got claw and fang marks all over him," one citizen said to his neighbors.

"But Father Malsain was supposed to banish them all. How can the beasts be back?" said another.

A third man, a hunter, examined the body. "This is not the handiwork of an ordinary beast. This was as tall as a man, with claws like a bear. The farmer's throat is slashed from ear to ear. I've never seen a beast able to do that so cleanly. This beast is evil and cunning."

A clamor arose among the dozen onlookers, "What do we do, if Malsain can't keep this thing at bay?"

The hunter interrupted, "I'm not so sure anymore. We only had Malsain's word for it, and this is the same farmer who asked about those troops marching through. Something don't add up. This is way too convenient for the Father."

The crowd looked shocked. "*How dare you question* Malsain! He warned us how high and mighty those Elves are, and that girl proved it!"

The hunter rebutted, "What makes any of us an expert on Elves? She was provoked by a drunk, as I recall!"

A fat guy predicted loudly that Malsain would banish the hunter for this heresy, to which the hunter replied, "Banishment don't scare me."

The fat guy asked, "Oh yeah? What could be worse than that?"

The hunter smiled and pointed at the dead farmer. The crowd fell quiet.

* * *

Elsewhere in Korath: "What do you mean he canceled the bounty? That two-faced, cheating bastard, making me look like a fool! Kazius will regret this insult! Where is he?"

His assistant replied, "Somewhere in the mountains, Father, and he has a bigger purse —" Malsain backhanded the assistant hard enough to draw blood. "None contradict me with impunity, NO ONE!"

The assistant saw a maniacal look in Malsain's eyes he had never seen before. Along with an inhuman red glow. As the assistant crawled backwards to get away, Malsain shredded his own robes to reveal a werewolf, the stuff of nightmares. The assistant sprang into a dead run towards the main door, but Malsain leapt from pillar to pillar like a giant orangutan and landed on the assistant thirty feet from the door. The evening shadows and torch lights distorted and magnified Malsain's lupine features, while a lone blackbird in the rafters witnessed the agonized death screams of the assistant.

Chapter Thirteen
Epiphanies

Andrath summoned Tyrus and Tyrianna to an early breakfast, and they were the only ones present on the dining platform. Tyrianna looked uncomfortable and asked nervously, "Why are we sitting here alone?"

Andrath replied, "The royal counsel has requested special escorts to Oakthorn. I agreed to ask for your help."

Tyrianna looked outraged. "Escorts? The answer is no! I am not for sale!"

Andrath corrected himself, "Not of that nature. My apologies. We are responsible for safe delivery of a prisoner to trial in Stonehaven. Perhaps you would like to speak to him first. And then make up your mind. I humbly ask you to reconsider."

Tyrianna folded her arms and scowled, the rebel in her back at the fore.

Tyrus volunteered, "I'll speak to him and give Tyri my opinion … "

Tyrianna retorted, "Ohhh, no, you won't! I'm going to see with my own eyes. You are not making my decisions for me!"

Tyrus shrugged. "As you wish."

A flustered Tyrianna shot back, "Don't patronize me! I mean it!"

Andrath glanced sidelong at Tyrianna with a cocked eyebrow and pretended not to hear, turning his attention to his food. Tyrus rolled his eyes and shook his head before finishing his meal and walking off to locate the prisoner. Tyrianna bounded after him with only half her plate finished.

"I was starting to like you before you got all high and mighty again!" she snarled, with uncharacteristic venom.

"Tyri," he began, "in spite of your gifts, your passions cloud your perceptions. Thats exactly why Kazius is still alive. You are blinded by rage and saw his younger cousin too late. You cannot unfire a crossbow bolt once loosed. Nor did you think before dashing into a smoke filled burning house. Blindness has consequences, Tyri. Thats why you have a guardian. You don't know what some humans will stoop to. You don't control your anger ..."

Tyrianna cut him off. "I know full well what that troll dung tyrant of Razadur is capable of. His men killed my father!"

Tyrus corrected, "Kazius is not the only enemy; his father is out there somewhere, blaming the five kingdoms for his wife Lorenna's death, and then there is this Father Malsain ..."

Tyri yelled back louder, "Malsain? He's a coward who hides behind his followers ..."

Tyrus gave up. There was no reasoning with the girl when she was this furious. They walked in sullen silence to the cage where Danny was kept. Unfortunately, Danny was still sleeping, and the sentry would not allow them near.

Tyrianna clenched her fists and strode away in a tantrum. Tyrus whispered to the sentry, "As impatient and impulsive as ever ..."

Tyrianna forgot her troubles when Ravenna returned with garments in tatters, complete with scratches, bloody gashes, scabs and bruises all over, otherwise looking pale and sweaty on the verge of collapse. Tyrianna ran to lend support before Ravenna fell over the railing, and asked, "What happened?"

Ravenna's voice was a dry, agonized whisper, "Malsain ... werewill ... demented ..."

And Ravenna slumped onto Tyrianna's shoulder, spent.

Tyrianna called out, "HELP! Ravenna's injured! help!"

Tyrus ran to them immediately and scooped Ravenna with both arms, following the nearest Elf to the healer's sanctuary. Tyrianna was beside herself, not knowing the first thing about medicine and pleading with the Elves to show her what to do. The senior physician put one finger to his lips, then gave her a small towel soaked with herbal tonics, and instructed her, saying, "Hold this ... here." He guided her hand to a large bruise and said, "Hold it gently but firm."

Tyrianna complied. The other healers continued washing the gashes and scratches and performing the laying on of hands. Tyrus paid attention to the jars, bottles, and bowls of powdered roots, bark, leaves, extracts and the labels on their containers, comprehending only a tiny fraction of their medicinal uses.

* * *

Hours later the same day: "I'm sorry I snapped at you," Tyrianna murmured softly, her head cast shamefully down at the floor next to Tyrus. He merely nodded his head politely and bowed, saying nothing. They went to see Andrath at lunch, and other council members were also seated.

One voice reported, "We have located a suitable quarry for the construction of the barriers. How many troops can we spare for protecting the workers?"

Andrath answered, "One thousand men for certain, maybe two." Andrath nodded to acknowledge the arrival of Tyrianna and Tyrus. He continued, "Ravenna is resting. But Danny's security detail has to leave by morning. The Oakthorn trial is mere days from now, and he should arrive with ability to speak on his own behalf."

Tyrianna whispered an apology to Andrath, and he smiled at her kindly, whispering back, "No harm done." To the council, he added, "We now know the truth of Malsain's claims to banish beasts and monsters, a trick easily done because he IS one, a werewill to be precise ...

and a clever liar, which we already knew. Korath is under his influence, making him as much a threat as Kazius if not greater. We may need assist from Talos. Is there a scout best suited to make such a perilous journey through the hostile territory of Korath?"

Another voice chimed, "I have such a one in mind, two, actually. I will ask them within the hour."

Tyrianna ate her small portions quickly, not having much appetite since Ravenna was injured, and soon went to go visit. The attendant on duty made Tyrianna promise to be quiet and not wake Ravenna. She complied, after making certain Ravenna was still breathing. She sat watching, for long minutes, and gave a weak smile and a wave when Tyrus stopped by after he finished eating. Tyrianna looked again at Ravenna, such a tired face, yet peaceful. An older woman who knew suffering, but not fear, so it seemed. She knew things, had lived already, and had mastered powers that many mortals had not. Her wavy salt and pepper hair fanned out over the bedsheet, catching the light from wind-chimes thirty feet away in the midday sun. Time did not pause this way in the visions. Tyrianna was never immersed in the visions, only observed them like a bird in flight overhead or as someone watching a stage production from 60 yards away. This was real. Tyrianna did not know Ravenna's age, but by appearances, she must be at least 40. Ravenna slowly stirred and winced as she tried to sit upright. Tyrianna gasped, and Ravenna slumped flat on the bed again. "Not to worry, child. I've endured worse."

The young watersprite had a look of disbelief; she had not known such pain, not even when sinking ships in deep waters.

Ravenna whispered, "I know that look. You doubt my word. I can also tell you don't have any children. But what do I know?" Ravenna patted Tyrianna's hand and blinked. "I had a son in 1549, born in Xantir rather than at home because my family refuses to let me marry the man I loved. I am a daughter of Kings, my father died in Shadval, and my brother now rules Stonehaven in the capitol of West Bend. The man I love is a commoner. And for this, we are shunned. So believe me when I say I've endured worse."

Tyrianna exclaimed, "That's horrible! Why?"

Ravenna responded wearily, "That's how royalty is. The paternal line inherits the property and titles, the women marry into a different noble family. The man I love did not have desirable property, and should something happen to my brother and his son, they don't want a commoner claiming royal inheritance. So my son and his father are shut out of sight, essentially given bribes to keep quiet. The servants watched me like a hawk, until I had to leave both my families behind or go mad. This was before I picked up new abilities. I was going to go back after Malsain was exposed or eliminated. That plan did not work so well."

Tyrianna got a sad look, leaned over the bed, and gave Ravenna a hug. Ravenna just lay there in bewilderment for a few moments, and then her hands drifted up to return the hug.

Chapter Fourteen
Duty Calls

"You WILL allow the funeral here, or I will bring the Reeve, the Magistrate, and as many honor guards as necessary; your personal squabbles with my cousin will wait, Arbiter. Do I make myself clear?" Bravane the Younger hissed at Arbiter Dhasa the dour, who had recovered enough strength to resume his duties. Dhasa gave the baron a dirty look of revulsion and hatred as he answered, "Yes ... very clear."

Bravane added in restrained anger, "You will get the standard fee, not one copper-pence more. And if I hear any more grief about this, you will be the new focus of my temper. Do not cross me, old man."

With that said and done, Bravane turned to leave, receiving dirty looks from the watchers who remained loyal to the memory of departed Arbiter Eledar the unforgiving. Bravane gave a menacing look right back. Savadi made no eye contact with either faction. He bowed politely and followed Bravane outside.

"So sorry for this. The council has been locked in bitter debate, whether to readmit Conrad into the Order, and I've never seen them so … punitive and hateful. Farseer Andar says this is just the beginning of the great sundering. A sleepless malice has taken root inside the walls. The wards we put up are crumbling."

Bravane stopped midstride. "Wards? What wards?"

Savadi answered, "Somewhere between the Quake of 1513 in Zara-Mogai, and the Bloodhammer raid of 1533, Arius had discovered ancient chaos relics after torturing a member of the original Order in Thalu to the northwest. The wards on the abbey are designed to keep Arius out."

Bravane gave a look of disbelief.

Savadi explained, "As physician to the lorekeepers, I hear many of their stories. Henry most of all."

"And how is my mother?" Bravane asked.

Savadi responded, "Glowing and sharp-witted as ever, but few ever notice because of her vows."

The Baron nodded his head. "I know she was fond of her sister. Wonderful woman … both of them."

They continued in silence to the baronial manor. Amanda greeted them in the main hall, and Savadi suddenly remembered, "Andar also says to expect the arrival of allies from sea and land soon. Including a 'goddess-born sprite.' He was unable to elaborate further."

Then he bowed to Amanda, "Greetings, Lady Redoak."

Amanda bowed back. "Conrad is in his room, and Mill has vanished without a word …"

Bravane blurted out, "No great loss …"

Savadi pretended he did not hear, but Amanda saw the hurt in his eyes. She knew Savadi to be a kind man. Behind Amanda, her father Alex the Wise appeared, "Bad news, nephew. The fever has all but shut down the silver mine. The treasury continues to dwindle. If this continues, we may not be able to afford hazard pay at all."

Bravane groaned in exasperation. "Raise the price on our fish and everything else. Use your own judgment. I don't want trade relations to suffer much."

Alex mused aloud, "What about requesting help from Agama and Valantir? Or from West Bend for that matter?"

Bravane made a sour face, "No, King Goldlion is still sore about his last visit here. That was messy ..."

Alex cut in, "Was an innocent mistake, Baron. You did apologize, yes?"

Bravane shook his head no. "I was too embarrassed to speak. I just wanted to crawl under a rock and die."

Alex spoke again, "You are still a third cousin once removed, whatever else he may think of you. Or do you wish to make our people easy pickings for Kazius Auguron when he gets here?"

Bravane slumped. "My wishes are but wasted pennies these days, like always."

* * *

That same week in Oakthorn, all was ready for the funeral of Connor Redmane, father of Conrad and Bethany and grandson of James Redmane, the hero of 1490.

Conrad's eyes darted around as he entered the abbey, half-expecting an asp, cobra, or viper to strike at any minute. The majority of the watchers and both arbiters gave him dirty looks as he passed the main hall and entered the funeral area. One watcher with an ugly scar on his left cheek even declared outright, in a sneering tone worthy of Eledar himself, "You will never be admitted to our order again, betrayer. The arbiters have decided yesterday to ban you from the premises, effective tomorrow. Your baron has no say in this, pig …"

Conrad locked cold, murderous eyes with the watcher for a full ten seconds that stopped the flow of funeral visitors, lips curled up to show his teeth, and fingers clenched as if to strangle a bull, after which Conrad finally spoke in icy menace, "I am GLAD to be rid of your miserable company, PAWN, you and ALL of your smug, self-righteous kind, ESPECIALLY Eledar, who whispers weak praises from the lips when the sun shines, but carries scorpion venom to the sickbed after dark, you scavengers!"

The entire assembly froze in stunned silence. The stare-down continued until Bravane nudged Conrad to take a seat, and Savadi was most hurt of all, leaving the crowd to weep in solitude. Nobody saw Rebecca leaving, unprepared for tensions this thick at the abbey. Before anyone could start another scene, Bravane cleared his throat, approaching the lectern, with Jonah and another guard at his sides.

Bravane began, "Citizens, friends, witnesses, it is my sad duty to preside over this occasion, the passing of a humble and good man, the latest statistic in a year of hardships. May his spirit go to his reward in peace, reunited with his dear wife, my aunt, and Conrad's mother, Summer Aristodemos from the land of our neighbors in Agama. I speak now in defense of my cousin, a man that I owe my life to, as many of you know. We have reason to expect his name will be cleared soon. And it would be unwise to speculate the details we may discover when agents of Razadur are brought to trial at last. Security around this trial has been doubled, to ensure the safety of all concerned. Thank you in advance for your co-operation. We have also heard that Kazius Auguron has already made war on Valantir, and our help may soon be required to fend off the hostile armies of Razadur. I also plan to find out what has become of Miles Longbranch. I realize my family line has not always led with wisdom or kindness ..." At these words, the assembly nodded, amazed at his candor, the mood of the room shifting from open contempt to half-hearted acceptance. "Now, in deference to the family of Connor Redmane, I bid you good day." Bravane stepped away from the lectern, and pointed his upturned palm toward it as he faced Conrad, bowing slightly and nodding. The room shifted again to naked hostility.

The new patriarch of the Redmane clan studied the assembly for a minute before making a move to stand up. The expressions ranged from fear to hate, indifference and worry. Finally, Conrad had enough of the nonsense and summoned up his defiant courage again, rising to his full height, flexing his shoulders and striding authoritatively to the lectern to deliver his father's eulogy. "My father was a good man, maybe not the most courageous or wise, but he was honest and kind. He went the full mile when able, helped a neighbor dig a well (makes eye contact with Amber and John), helped others fix a fence or wagon wheel. He also had a kind word for people down on their luck. I shall miss that rare quality ..." His eyes met the watchers on his low note, "He brought people together. His kindness will not be forgotten. Nor the gentle spirit of my mother. I can only hope those who knew my parents will carry their example forward. Thank you for attending, and special thanks to Redoak Manor for helping my family in this hour."

With those words, Conrad returned to the table. Jonah was next to speak, followed in turn by other townsfolk whose lives were touched by the Redmane family. When the speeches were over, Helen took the lectern, to the amazement of everyone. But true to her vow, she did not speak. She simply placed a dried flower reverently on the stand, brought her palms together, and stood in silent prayer. A minute later, she passed by Bravane's table, giving a hug to her nephew Conrad, then Jonah, then her son Bravane, then Bethany, then Amanda and Alex the wise. Then Helen made her exit from the funeral hall. No other monk present had any words of kindness. This lack of courtesy was not lost on Connor's relatives. The ill wind of malice went both ways. Thus it was no wonder when the Red clans took their leave from the abbey to eat at the baronial manor instead of joining everyone else in the refectory at the meal hosted by the monks.

* * *

"But I must go. You know why, darling," Jonah said mournfully to his wife Bethany. "Oakthorn can only promise a few hundred men to help Valantir. If not for the Elves, there would be no Oakthorn. I have to go seek audience with the King, and Conrad has yet to be vindicated at trial. I will be as quick as I can."

Bethany protested, "Why you? And why now of all times," sobbing, "with Father dead … I need you … "

Jonah hugged his wife and whispered, "Because Mill has gone missing, and Amanda has to be at trial as well, along with her father."

Bethany dug her nails into the folds of his cloak, clinging for dear sanity. "It's not fair. You know that." She spoke with streaks of tears on her face.

Jonah answered softly, "I know, honey," and hugged her one more time, kissing her forehead as he parted. "I love you. I will return. I promise."

Bethany sulked. "You better …" before turning her face away.

Jonah shut his eyes as he turned, and then left.

Bethany rested her fingers over her belly, a worried look on her face. A third was on the way.

* * *

In the manor, Bravane was tossing and turning, half-asleep and knocking over yet another bottle of rum, which he had half-emptied during dinner after the rift with the abbey. He muttered aloud, incoherently, as visions gathered in his dreams. He was riding his horse in a faraway land, covered in fog, with occasional leaves falling around him, from black and gray trees. Even the leaves were the color of lead and charcoal. Up ahead, spires pierced the fog, gradually revealing a castle as Bravane approached. It was slate roof over grayish-white stones, the main gateway unattended and ajar. The iron grillwork was bent and battered, and vines had begun creeping over the outer walls. A single leaf spiraled in front of him, a soft breeze nudging it through the entrance. Bravane followed. Once inside the castle, his horse vanished. He saw a tower looming ahead, in the middle of everything. An oak door with a brass ring handle, sat slightly ajar. Another gust of wind opened the door further.

Bravane stepped out of the gray haze, into the world of colors. Still no people. The room looked feminine, adorned with mirrors, paintings and tapestries. A grand hallway led away from the main tower, and faint echoes of giggling women led him in that direction. Something else drew him to a particular mirror in the hall. It stood framed by translucent white silk curtains. As Bravane walked up to it, he saw the surface had wrinkles in it. And his reflection in this mirror had a hole in it, and as he turned to and fro, the hole remained in place over his heart. It was as if a break in the mirror had mimicked the shape of a dagger, and inside that hole was solid lead. Bravane began to clutch his chest, feeling both heavy and hollow.

His other hand reached out, and as he touched the mirror, it broke into a shower of pearls that scattered at his feet on the stone floor. The voices down the hall laugh at him. An emptiness tugs at him, but to where? He wanders aimlessly in search of … something. A perfume of mint and strawberries drew him down a hall to the right, which opened into a bedchamber. He hears a baby's cry around a corner. The sound hit him in the chest with a stabbing pain, he falls backward over the bed and tumbles on the floor. He rises onto his knees, gasping for breath, one shoulder still touching the floor. He hears the baby being taken farther away, somewhere to his left, out of sight. The absence of the child hurts even more, turning his insides to jelly. He crawls to the window for fresh air, clutching at the sill in great agony. A trail of coins, all tarnished and scratched, spilled on the floor like blood. Bravane struggled to stand up, to follow the trail. Before he finished his first stride, he saw a swarming of rats from where the coins led. They rush past the baron and out the window to a hay-wagon just beneath. Bravane bolts awake in bed with his heart hammering in his ears and caught a blinding ray of the rising sun right in his face. He fell back in bed, clutching his eyes and chest. As his eyes recover, he inspects his ribs. Nothing broken, just a sore spot over his heart. No ordinary dream, if such a thing ever existed. Bravane groaned as he dragged himself out of bed.

Chapter Fifteen
Bitter Rose

Tyrianna fell to her knees, eyes shut, teeth clenched in great pain as she clutched her head, feeling as though her eyes were being twisted and pulled out of their sockets. "AAaaaaaaaaaaaaaa … the sundering … it begins … the champions all in danger … the darkness spreads from the North … must hurry … please stop … the paaaaiiiii-n …" and Tyrianna collapsed on the ground.

The Elven guards waited for Tyrus to lift her up before continuing their march. Danny kept staring; he heard tales of oracles and seers, never saw one in person. Further, his earlier revelation that Kazius abused "friend" and foe alike, Danny now wondered what this girl could have possibly done to deserve so many bounty posters. Just a teenager for mercy's sake. He could see plainly now that she did resemble the Elves who had adopted her, and both he and the girl shared a debt to Valantir. Danny would have been a meal for the vultures and crows had an Elf not found him. Kazius was hated and feared by his subjects; Danny had seen the dungeons, and the arena of blood, and the way the Crimson Hoods destroy property and limb while collecting taxes, and he heard whispers in the dark between commoners, referring to Kazius as the "cruel bastard." It did not matter as long as Danny was paid and left alone. It was dumb luck that Danny had not offended him sooner; now the dice finally jinxed. Bitter truth changes everything.

Danny had lived under a curtain of deception and paid for it. If this girl could truly see into other places and futures, perhaps she could make sense of his life. And thus, for the first time in his devil may care existence, Danny prayed for the well-being of someone he barely knew. Tyrus raised an eyebrow, saying nothing. Ravenna was still resting in Valandrassil and would join them later in Oakthorn. When the party set camp at nightfall, Danny was bound exactly as Amanda was during her kidnapping, as if Danny needed more reminders of his squandered life. He grumbled for many minutes before going to sleep. When dreams came, the land was covered in ash, the skies an unforgiving charcoal gray, completely blanketed in storm clouds. Tyrianna and the Elves were in chains, underfed and pale, with tattered rags barely hiding their welts and bruises, goblins jeered at them, cackling like imps. Kazius strode by, in red armor dotted with wicked barbs dripping a foul, sticky, evil-looking purple resin, fire in his eyes, laughing his most cruel, heartless laugh ever. Danny pleaded for the prisoners to be released. Kazius just kicked him in the teeth like last time.

"Filthy maggot, you dare ask ME for mercy? You craven weakling!"

With the word "weakling" echoing in his head, Danny jerked awake, vowing to make Kazius pay for his cruelty.

Danny struggled against his bonds when he woke up for the third time. Those Elves really knew how to tie knots. If it had been by an amateur, he would be free already. Or about as free as any man in his position could be. Without money, friends or allies. If he ran away, all chances of befriending his companions would vanish. He had not forgotten the generosity of the Elves when he was exhausted and starving. He knew for certain Amanda would never forgive him. Thus he clung to the hope that the young oracle Tyrianna could make sense of his life. He had to know. So he waited for the others to get up. It felt like hours, with his thoughts churning about. Kazius obviously had had something go wrong with his agenda. He had always ordered his men to do the bloody work; everyone knew Kazius could fight. It was not fear that held him back. But when he kicked Danny in the teeth, there was an edge in his voice, of rage, insanity and fear. Not afraid of Danny, but someone else. Kazius was an overgrown child throwing a tantrum. Something dear had been denied. Danny was never privy to whatever that could be. Kazius was not the trusting type. The sullen, brash, arrogant Monarch of Razadur was so obsessive about security and his past that he never even mentioned in the bounty poster who had been murdered.

The bounty was 400 Gold Eagles if Bitter Rose was taken alive, 200 dead. Kazius put up the bounty four years ago, and nobody collected yet. Danny began to suspect the reasons why. Tyrianna and Bitter Rose were one and the same, the Elves honored her as one of their own.

The Elves who took first watch were now waking up. And third watch was now free to undo Danny's bonds. Danny rubbed his wrists to get some feeling back into them, and flexed his fingers for ten seconds. Breakfast was more bread, cheese, and water. Tyrianna and Tyrus were up in time to join the small meal. There was one day's march ahead to reach Oakthorn.

They avoided the road, in the event of more bandits. Tyrianna noticed Danny watching her and asked, "Why do you stare at me, bandit?"

Danny averted his eyes, "So much to ask, and so little time. Sorry."

Tyrianna got defensive. "Why would my life be any business of yours?"

Danny was cornered, just like the tribunal he ran from. He sighed and shut his eyes while searching for the words he wanted. "You can see things in other places and times. Maybe even make sense of why I am here."

Tyrianna gave a sarcastic chuckle. "Oh, right! Just like that, huh? Tell you the meaning of life, the names of your children, the cat, the dog, and how on earth you live happily ever after. Good luck with that one."

Tyrus interjected, "Grumpy, are we?"

Tyrianna snapped, "Don't start with me! I didn't ask for my skull to be full of hornets yesterday. That hurt even more than the shadowbending at the mountain pass.

Maybe you should try it someday ..."

Danny mumbled in a soft voice, "Beats having teeth kicked in by Kazius's metal boots, or landing chestnuts first, on a ridge beam and breaking one's neck like someone I knew ..."

Tyrianna puzzled at him for a second. "Chestnuts? OH! Hah ha ha ha ha ha ha ha haaaaaa ... oh, that's good! A squirrel somewhere must have peed itself watching ..."

* * *

Danny was silent and sullen until lunchtime, though the dead one was not really a friend at all. Danny just could not see any humor in it. Tyrus had no interest in the trial or Danny, so he also said nothing. So the Elves began talking about prophecies.

"The unsleeping menace in the north has already sent his plague, and his pawns are preparing for the sundering ..." one of them began.

Danny asked, "What is the sundering?"

An Elf explained, "It will turn brother against brother, turn the sacred to profane, and sorely test the faith of all. Even Kazius himself is a pawn, therefore, so are you."

Danny protested, "Now wait a minute! I don't work for that bastard anymore!"

Tyrianna challenged, "Oh, yeah? Since when?"

Danny hung his head, answering in a defeated tone, "Since he did this ..." He showed his missing teeth. Then, he added, "And he said I was not worth the labor to bury."

Tyrianna quipped, "Oh, gee! Kazius in a bad mood? What a surprise ..."

Danny had enough, so raising his voice, he said, "Why do you treat me like this? You never saw the nightmare where Kazius chained all of you and I was begging him to let you go! You didn't see me at the edge of starvation and death! You know nothing about my life!"

Tyrianna retorted, "I'm not the one facing trial, thief."

Danny stared at her in icy indignation and corrected, "You would be overjoyed to get fair trial if Kazius ever caught you. You'd go straight to the dungeon, or the bloodsport arena or be sold into slavery. Maybe even become a concubine. You think about that, Oracle."

Tyrianna realized he was right and spoke no further.

* * *

An Elf gave the hand sign to stop and duck, and the party halted, crouched low to the ground. The foremost Elf examined some tracks in front of him. "We have been spotted hours ago. A human has made haste to report our whereabouts. We will change course north of the road. Be alert."

Danny did not like the sound of this. The other Blackwolves could be plotting to kill him if they knew Danny was defecting. It was time to make peace with the girl, since his days could be numbered. "Look, I'm sorry I was hard on you. I know better than most how cruel and merciless Kazius is. His men may kill me soon. I don't want any hard feelings."

Tyrianna quipped, "Really? Better than most? Did you know that Kazius gave the order to kill my father? A man who never hurt anyone! He stole my innocence, my faith, my happiness, my childhood! Don't give me that!"

Danny stood in shock. "That explains everything. Why he wants you so bad. You tried to kill him and missed, didn't you? Someone close to him died. Yes, makes perfect sense. I'm sorry about your father."

Tyrianna raged, "Nobody gets it! A thousand apologies can't bring him back! I don't want your sorry!"

Tyrus spoke finally, "So you are going to punish everyone who shows you compassion, Tyri? Are you going to push them all away, even your own mother?"

Tyrianna turned on Tyrus, but he was ready for it. "YOU! Always you treat me like a child! My mother knows nothing about death! She's fucking immortal!"

Tyrus calmly answered, "So you think she does not miss your father? Nothing could be further from the truth, Tyri. She loved him; she loves you. And you push everyone away, even the Elves who have adopted you as their own. All but one human."

Tyrianna was still furious. "And who would THAT be, Tyrus? Tell me, if you are so freaking smart!"

Tyrus smiled. "I have seen it. Do not even try to deny it. You've become fond of Ravenna."

Tyrianna blurted, "THAT old woman? HAH! You really … " then she grumbled, "Damn you, I hate it when you're right. STOP smiling!"

Tyrus bowed, forcing his face to relax into a blank expression. "As you wish."

Danny paused for a minute before speaking again. "We have more in common than you think." Tyrianna looked angrily in disbelief. "I owe my life to the Elves. I would have died in the mountain pass if not for them. I am no longer any friend of Kazius. He abuses friend and foe alike. His arrogance is legend, but I had always been too drunk to care. I was sober when he kicked my teeth in. Strange how things work … "

Tyrianna scowled and turned her back to him, whispering to herself, "Damn grownups …"

Chapter Sixteen
Only Human

Baron Bravane Redoak the third gathered his best men together in the manor for a private ceremony, except for Jonah, who was already riding toward West Bend to seek audience with the King. "Uncle" Alex had a hand on Conrad's shoulder, saying, "told you. Nothing to worry about."

Bravane the younger summoned Conrad forward, announcing, "Conrad, old friend, cousin, it would please me if you accepted your old job back. I don't care what the gossipy peasants think. You have as much honor as the lot of them together, and twice as much courage."

Conrad bowed reverently on one knee. "Thank you, sire."

Amanda was the only woman present, standing behind the baron on his left, with a smile at Conrad who was dear family to her as well.

Bravane recited the words, "Do you, Conrad Redmane, hereby accept the rank of captain with the duties and responsibilities thereof?"

Conrad spoke, "I accept, sire, with honor."

Bravane continued with one hand on Conrad's head, "I therefore reinstate your rank with all powers and privileges vested therein. Welcome back."

With that, Bravane clasped hands and pulled his cousin up, clapped him on the shoulder, and then they strode into the feast hall, to celebrate over mead and garlic roasted chicken with salted potatoes and dill weed.

* * *

Elsewhere, a scout arrived, out of breath, slumping to his knees in the guild hall. Tyton ordered his men to get the scout some water. "Just nod yes or no. Did you see them and avoid detection?"

The scout nodded yes. Tyton smiled. "And they are on schedule?"

Again the scout nodded yes.

"Good. I want a detail of four men to prevent their escape. They will not get away this time. If you see them run, kill them. Justice has been long overdue."

One of his men returned with water for the scout, poured some over the scout's head, and offered the rest to drink.

"I shall be overseeing this operation myself. Assemble in one hour."

* * *

"You can all stay here if you wish, I prefer to be as far from Malsain's known haunts as possible. There will be more victims exactly like the farmer, mark my word. You'll be lucky to go thirty days without seeing one. I'm leaving, and don't bother asking where to," the hunter declared. With that, he mounted his horse and left.

Soon after, a short balding man with a deformed leg and large ears slipped away from the small crowd into the shadows of the trees. He ambled northwestward into the foothills, and by day's end he found the cave.

"I brought fresh robes, master."

Father Samuel Malsain barely acknowledged his presence.

"The hunter knows; he does. He left town before I did. What will Father do?" his servant asked.

Malsain growled, "We return to Zara-Mogai. Someone else will have to finish the job here. Those Elves are up to something. Kazius ruined everything."

His servant bowed to hide his face, not daring to show disagreement. "Yes, Father, as you say."

Malsain donned the robes and continued stuffing a sack with candleholders, goblets, and coins. He left the church in a hurry and bits of straw still clung to some of his loot. "Go on ahead to notify the Alpha leader. And do be careful not to anger him. Bad things happen around him."

The servant bowed again as he backed away, out of the cave. He peeked in to add, "Rumors say Kazius suffered setback in mountains. His army, demoralized. Heavy losses to violent storm."

Malsain challenged, "WHAT Storm? Why has no one seen it? This reeks of magic, the lawgiver is not pleased. Now GO!"

The servant did as commanded. Malsain mumbled to himself after the servant was gone, "The hunter will rue the day he interfered with my work."

* * *

Kazius finally gave the order to return to Razadur until he could solve the morale problem. To the last man, all of his soldiers and minions were more terrified of Tyrianna's mother than they were of Kazius. His scowl and his foul mood hardly improved one iota since he banished the bungling rogue from camp, who was certain to be vulture food by now. Kazius had been after the five daggers for 13 years. One under the sea; another in some temple in Valantir, and every bandit that attempted to steal it was dead. He watched with annoyance as his men packed up tents, and continued pacing so much there was a circular rut in the ground. Within the hour, the long march home began. General Axegrind was in a foul mood as well. Petty fistfights broke out all day; the chain of command was crumbling. The only thing they did not have to worry about was food — they still had plenty of that.

* * *

"Thank you, kind sir, for transporting us," the woman said as she carried her young child off the ferry.

"Not so fast, missy. I don't do this for free. The other half, please."

Her husband obliged, handing over the other 40 gold eagles. They were now in a strange land, far from home. The coast had enough trees for shade and nourishment, but further inland was mostly sand and rock.

"Tell you what, since yer new here, ye foller dat dere street on the right, and talk to a guy in the map shoppe, tell him that Johnny sent ya. He'll find a nice living arrangement for ya. But keep yer eyes open for pirates."

On the way, they narrowly dodged a bar brawl that spilled out into the street. And inside the store he was directed to, Alex Mill saw all sorts of strange men. Including a man with a red hood and cloak, red leather bracers on both wrists, red leather boots, and a red tabard covering black leather armor. The effect was unnerving.

Alex wanted to hide, but he had to protect his wife and child. The man in the red hood turned as they approached the counter on his right. His cloak opened enough to show his battle axe swinging off his belt. Alex gulped hard, and the man in red grinned with malice. He obviously relished the effect he had on ordinary citizens. The merchant behind the counter whispered, "Hey, not in my store! Bad for business. I'll give you an extra bottle for the trouble."

The man in red smiled and patted the shopkeeper on the shoulder. Then he left, but not without fixing his evil eyes and a cruel grin on Alex on his way out.

"What can I do for you strangers?" the merchant asked.

Alex's wife spoke, "A man named Johnny said you could arrange a place to live."

The merchant beamed. "Yes! Of course! I just renovated a nice home that you can have for, well, let's see now, 200 gold should do it ..."

Alex stammered, "B-but that's more than a cow!"

The shopkeeper nodded. "Right you are. Best I can offer right now."

Alex asked, "What if I trade you my armor?"

The merchant approached closer to inspect under the burlap cloak. "I know that pattern anywhere. Yer from Oakthorn across the sea!"

Alex gulped again. Something was not right.

"Ok fine! I'll knock off a hundred for the armor, including shield and helmet. Hurry before I change my mind."

Alex had little choice, and the merchant knew it. The armor came off. The wife attempted small talk, "And what is your name, kind sir?"

The merchant grinned, "Call me Adrian. Everyone does. And here comes my lovely wife, Mandy. Hello, Dear. Was just selling the renovated house to these newcomers." Adrian made certain to hide the armor from his wife's gaze, as Alex counted out the hundred coins.

Adrian's wife stopped to chat. "Have I not seen you somewhere? I know I have. What was that place called? Up in the north, near those Elves, talented race; they make wonderful wine, but alas they care not for metals and gems as we do. Their loss, poor dears ..."

Adrian interrupted, "Mandy darling, these people must be hungry after a long journey. Let them settle in first. My wife loves to talk. We can have lunch sometime when we all have a few hours."

With that, he shooed them out the door and gave them directions to the house. "Oh, yes! You will need this as well." Adrian handed them a key.

Alex's wife added, "What about the deed?"

Adrian chuckled. "Oh, yes, the deed. How silly of me, of course." He hurried behind the counter then back. "Here you go."

Mrs. Mill folded the deed and tucked it away in her bags, to keep it away from the bar crowd that was just now calming down outside. Alex bowed nervously, feeling naked without his armor. His wife waved at Adrian and turned to make haste to their new home.

Around a corner, the man in red watched and grinned. He strode directly into the bar, and minutes later, he left again, with two more Crimson Hoods behind him.

Alex was inspecting the house, which was quite empty and still had a couple holes in the thatch roof. A knock at the door scared the daylights out of him. He ignored it at first, the next knock was much louder. Alex looked at his wife and child, reminding himself he had to protect them. The third knock was louder yet, just before the men kicked the door in.

"You there! Who do ye think ye are, not paying the tribute and the travel tax?"

Alex stammered, "What tribute? A thousand pardons, sir. We did not know ..."

The Crimson Hoods all laughed, and their leader announced, "Pardons don't buy anything, and the locals have neglected to tell you that everyone in Mojara pays tributes to Kazius, except for an uppity sea witch with a price on her pretty head. The bounty for her is 100 gold, put up by the dock-master, lost a lot of ships to that little brat. We might forgive your ignorance, if you see her and send word. But right now you owe us ten eagles for travel tax, and twenty for the tribute. You have one week to cough it up. Have a nice day."

And as they left, Alex Mill realized he had no tools to fix the door.

* * *

The outer walls of Oakthorn were now visible, and Danny stopped in apprehension. The Elves assured him he was well-protected, but Danny took no comfort in their words.

"I'd like to make peace before I go in. I'm not your enemy anymore, miss. After my testimony, I might soon be a dead man, especially if the others are still loyal to Kazius. I know I can't bring your father back. Giving my testimony might be the bravest thing I ever do in my life. I was a coward for many years, and I'm still afraid of Kazius. Most people in their right minds would be. Please don't be mad at me."

Tyrianna finally turned to look him in the eyes. Her eyes softened and lost their cold indifference. She was not sure how far to trust him, but now at last, she did not hate him. She extended her hand. "Okay. Truce."

Danny clasped her hand gracefully and bowed his head. Up ahead, a trumpet sounded. Two columns of armored men formed a corridor to protect Danny from the crowds. As the Elven party got closer to the eastern gate, Danny could see men in charcoal gray leather behind the armored columns. He recognized them right away as a rival guild of thieves; he did not know the name. Danny wanted to run, but the Elves surrounded him on all sides, and Tyrus brought up the rear. One look at the muscle tone on Tyrus, standing six foot four and had to weigh over 250 #, banishing feeble hopes of getting past him. The fear in Danny's eyes was obvious to the Obsidian Owls.

Danny could tell, by their eyes alone, how deadly they were. Another benefit of sobriety, which Danny would have been glad to do without for a while. He cringed at every motion of the rival thieves' heads as he filed past the armored honor guards, his own eyes were on the verge of hysterics and sobbing. The columns folded in to follow the Elves, and the formation turned left to the southern bridge over the river. Several of the peasants were throwing tomatoes and pudding in Danny's direction, half of it hitting the guards. Danny was as terrified now as he had been running away from the goblins and trolls. Tears rolled down his face in spite of his attempts to hold them in. Tyrianna was jolted by visions of her father flashing in her mind, of that fateful day when he was mocked by frightened peasants while the Crimson Hoods beat Kaedrus to death with clubs and knuckledusters.

Tyrianna screamed in panic, "STOP IT! ALL OF YOU! No more!" As she cried tears of rage and despair, her hands raised and a blue wave tumbled all the peasants, leaving alone all the non-aggressors.

Tyrus knew right away what happened and moved to shield Tyrianna. The peasants sat wide-eyed for a moment on the ground, and dispersed in fear northward toward the market square. The Elven party and their escorts crossed the bridge without further incident.

Danny was led to his own cell in the Reeves' building, adjacent to the other remaining three surviving Blackwolves, who immediately spat at him and tried to grab him through the bars.

"Turncoat! Betrayer! Never once tried to free the rest of us, you worthless dog!"

Danny cowered in the corner farthest from his former comrades.

Two deputies opened the cell door to show the Blackwolves who was in charge around here, wielding dark walnut clubs with leather straps and knocking the legs out from under the three wolves and shoving them toward the other wall.

"You three behave, or we'll give you something else to complain about!"

The oldest wolf challenged "Oh, yeah? You and whose army?"

The taller, athletic deputy answered, "Oh, you think yer funny, do ya? We'll see how funny you are in a couple hours. Just watch!"

The deputies backed out and locked the door again.

The oldest wolf yelled back, "And what's this with no decent food, you horse dropping? Last time we had wine and cheese, instead of your dried up bread, bath-water and piss!"

The deputy just grinned and walked away. Danny did not like the sound of this and missed the Elves already, who all left the building after the cell was locked. The stone floor was very cold, and the bench that recessed into the wall was not much better. Danny's former comrades kept giving him dirty looks and making silent threats with their hands. The minutes dragged out too long in here, there was nothing to do, nowhere to go.

* * *

Tyrus, Tyrianna, and the Elves arrived at the baronial manor and were greeted near the gate by Alex Redoak and his daughter Amanda, who thanked the Elves again for her rescue. A light dinner of spiced yams and turkey was served in the dining hall by baron Bravane's kitchen maids, while the Elves traded stories of current events.

"The foundations for the outposts at the Falcon Pass are underway at long last, wehile scouts have reported the armies of Razadur have retreated south and are regrouping. Malsain, however, eludes us. We expect to have more information soon."

Conrad asked, "Why is Kazius in retreat? He has never done so in his career ..."

Tyrus explained with a devilish gleam in his eye and sly grin on his face, "Tyrianna's mother can be very persuasive."

Tyrianna was shocked at his choice of words, hastily adding, "She fried entire scores of them where they stood, saving me from a bad end ... saved all of us, really."

To which one of the Elves responded, "Saved the entire forest. There were not enough Elves to contain the fire and fight off the goblins. Were it not for Syrene, all of Valantir could have burned to the ground. We owe our gratitude to Tyrianna, who courageously sought to rescue Tyrus."

Tyrianna looked away in embarrassment.

The Elf continued, "The forest is our home, and that of countless birds, mice, and creatures. But for a small action to help your friend, we might not be sitting here. One should never assume our decisions have no influence over the course of events."

Tyrianna mulled it over a minute while Amanda raised a goblet to acknowledge the merit of the Elf's words. Ravenna arrived to join them just before sunset.

Tyrianna asked, "What is Kazius after, besides the daggers?"

Bravane stammered, "What daggers?"

The senior Elf answered, "Land, wealth, power, dominion. The entire Auguron family line that we know of has sought after these things. All save one born in Vaja many years ago. Later in 1529 Stonehaven Reckoning, he vanished from all public records. Erik Auguron is rumored dead, much like Arius Auguron. We do not know their exact relation. Erik was a rebellious child, and hot-tempered, but had none of the other Augurons' greed and cruelty. We think he was murdered."

Conrad had a suspicion mulling in his head about Vaja and Erik. Ravenna took the lull in conversation as an opportunity to ask what was left of the food. Bravane looked fidgety as he passed her the entrees.

Ravenna put him at ease, "My brother has forgotten the whole thing, Baron. Not to worry."

Tyrianna looked to her right at Ravenna, somberly whispering, "Glad you're okay."

Ravenna smiled and rested one hand on her shoulder affectionately. The bruises had almost vanished, and the gashes were fading to pale pink welts. Ravenna said, "I have the Elves to thank for that."

* * *

"Tell me again why we left? You acted as if your life was in danger, dear ... " the wife said.

Alex Mill tried to avoid eye contact.

"We don't have enough money to do this again. We are stuck here, but we deserve to know why, darling. We seemed safer in the five kingdoms."

Alex answered, "I had to leave. Bravane was always yelling at me, and the trial was about to begin and ... "

His wife gasped. "Alex, are you a fugitive?"

He blurted, "Yes! I mean ... no. I'm not. But everyone will look down on me as the guard who let Amanda be kidnapped. They all hate me now. Everyone is going to know ..."

His wife yelled in fury, "You *what*?"

Alex winced and braced himself with hands raised in fear to ward off attack.

His wife Moira snapped, "You abandoned your baron when they might need your testimony as to who kidnapped Amanda?"

Alex pleaded meekly, "They don't need me, they caught three of the bandits. Nothing I say is going to matter ..."

Now his wife DID slap him. "You coward! You stranded us here with these tax collectors and pirates and made my adoptive mother sick with worry because you were afraid of mere gossiping peasants? You *sicken* me, Alex Mill! You've really done it now!" With that, she walked out the door, slamming it. The door fell off its hinges again. Mrs. Mill screamed in rage through the doorway, "OOOOOO, I hate you!"

Alex began sobbing on his knees. Mandy walked by and stared through the open doorway, watching Mrs. Mill storm off toward the town well.

* * *

Mandy continued past, to her husband Adrian's shop, interrupting a round of haggling with his customers.

"Adrian darling, you really should fix that door. It's an eyesore, you know. Makes our neighborhood look … unkempt. Do be a dear and tidy it up while the light is still favorable."

Adrian forced a sarcastic smile. "Yes, dear."

The haggling resumed, punctuated with taunts of "honeydew" and "henpeck."

Adrian put his game face back on, and bluffed, "I do get other collectors you know, I can get a better price by week's ending."

The customer, a man in his fifties and a few battle scars on him, grabbed Adrian's collar. "Is that right? What if I took it right now? You think I can't?"

Adrian dealt with this kind before. He responded, "I have special arrangements with Kazius. He won't take kindly to my absence, or interruptions in the flow of goods. You better leave before one of his spies sees you. There would not be a safe port for two hundred miles. One-eyed Pete would tell you, but he's already dead."

The customer barked, "So Kazius got him, did he? I'll deal with him later. Right now I need safe passage for a trade deal; otherwise I'd off ya where you stand!" The customer shoved Adrian into the counter. "If I see you again, don't count on my good graces anymore, henpeck!"

Adrian replied curtly, "Likewise."

With that, the mercenary left.

Chapter Seventeen
Bargaining Tables

Jonah arrived at West Bend at last, and his request to see the King was denied.

The sentry simply told him, "He is busy all week in council. Our borders have been attacked by dragons. He cannot see you."

Jonah pleaded to no avail, and then decided to poke around in the local taverns. Dragons or no dragons, Oakthorn and Valantir needed help. In the capitol city of West Bend, each quadrant had no less than two taverns each, some as large as Redoak Manor was. One known as the Cider barrel stood out, with posts and beams of oak and ash every twelve feet, with four chambers, at least, three beams wide and four deep. It was a full house tonight. The October harvest festival was a couple days away, and visitors arrived early to get the best sleeping rooms and first dibs on the goods. Northlanders crowded one corner of the place, all wearing fur and leather and eating up venison and brown ale; Eastlanders filled another corner in beige and tan cotton tunics with woolen cloaks, eating steamed vegetables with marinated pork over wild rice, washed down with herbal tea. Another group in woolen vests were laughing over rum and whiskey. Jonah felt twangs of guilt over not letting Bethany know his true history. He had claimed he was an illegitimate child of royalty raised by an uncle who traveled as a cartographer. Jonah was, in truth, the third son of John Saint Noir, and therefore a nephew of the chaos sorceress Lorenna Saint Noir, whose name lives on in infamy. Jonah chose the name Blackthorn himself as he left home ten years ago.

Jonah found an empty table near the Southlanders and struggled to understand what they were saying. He knew their customs, but not their native tongue. A tall, elderly fellow wearing a green tunic with brown trim under a green cloak with blue trim, a long white beard with hints of red, holding an ornately carved maplewood staff joined Jonah at his table and introduced himself.

"In this place, I am known as Lebiced. You have the look of a man far from home, in dire need of some truth or divine assistance."

Jonah interrupted, "No, whatever you're selling, I don't want it."

Lebiced merely smiled in his kindly way, then added, "It may interest you to know you just sat yourself in the middle of a boiling kettle. Neither King nor Prince will hear your pleas. I've been watching them. The council is deadlocked by servants of a dark power who work under our noses. If you poke around too much, you will not return home in time to help your people."

Jonah sat in shock, and quickly whispered, "Who are you?"

Lebiced replied, "I just told you who I am. I can't tell you everything here. Too dangerous."

Jonah asked, "Are you a priest?"

Lebiced grinned. "No. I'm not. Listen, we must leave soon. Valantir cannot wait long."

Jonah reacted, "No more games. I just met you, and ..."

Lebiced insisted, "There is no time now. Those Eastlanders are speaking of a large gathering of mercenaries in Razadur. The Southlanders have already arrived, and more gather every day. We cannot wait for the council. I will see you at the eastern gate at dawn. Good luck."

Lebiced left, and Jonah suddenly noticed the barmaid looking at him. She pointed to the menu on a blackboard. Jonah gave his choice. "I'll have that roast chicken with tomato and garlic. Thank you."

She added, "Anything to drink, sire?"

Jonah considered his options and replied, "I'll have the northern brown ale."

The barmaid curtsied and said, "Very good, sir."

Once Jonah had his drink in hand, he got up to mingle with the Northland Barbarians, who had some laughs at his expense. The biggest one taunted, "The War Trolls of Razadur would see your red armor at a thousand paces and pick you off at five hundred, HAHAA!"

Jonah gave an angry look at the supposed leader of the bunch. The big one taunted some more, "Oooh, we hurt his feelings, where is your army, little boy?"

Jonah slapped down a silver coin on their table hard enough to imprint the varnish on the cedar top. Jonah growled, "My homeland has more of these, for those willing to defend it. Have a good day, GENTLE men ..."

And Jonah returned to his own table. After his meal arrived, six of the barbarians joined him to talk business.

"Is Kazius in a pissy mood again?" the big one asked.

Jonah nodded.

The big one got right to the point. "Kazius commands a high price. He already has the southern creepers discussing a contract with him. Band of cutthroats. If we are going up against them, we want twenty silver coins per belt. We don't come cheap."

Jonah grumbled, "Ten upfront with a bonus after."

The big one shook his head no. "Fifteen, no less."

Jonah sat thinking. "Very well, fifteen."

They shook hands on it and arranged to leave together in the morning.

Jonah's squire was waiting outside and reported the council was outright hostile to Oakthorn. The council got word of the murders of Obsek and Ramus, and believed only their own skewed version of things. The reputation of Kazius made no difference. There was even discussion of withdrawal from the alliance of Westwood and of revoking the treaty. Jonah anticipated why. West Bend already lost two Kings in defense of the five lands. Thomas

Goldlion died in Shadval, and his grandfather Andrew died defending against Izimal in 1490.

There would be no help at all for Oakthorn or Valantir from the council. And there was not enough time to summon allies from Westwood or Xantir. Agama, on the other hand, was just close enough that Jonah thought of the possibility. Jonah was still wrapped up in his thoughts when a dagger missed his face by an inch and stuck in the wall to his right. He looked right and left. Whoever threw it was already gone. As Jonah removed the dagger from the wall, he saw a note attached:

We have a proposition. Meet here at midnight.

"Who in blazes is THIS? No signature, no crest, no name ... nothing!" Jonah complained aloud. "Wake me at quarter of," he told the squire, who nodded and bowed.

That night, Jonah hardly slept at all, tossing and turning for hours before succumbing to horrible dreams of skeletons rising out of the ground and chasing the townsfolk, the screams of women and children everywhere, his own house in flames. Jonah woke violently and tumbled out of the bed onto all fours. He slumped on his side until his breathing was normal again, and his heart stopped pounding in his ears. "By the light, banish these evil dreams and protect my family."

Jonah soon collapsed on his back in exhaustion. He drifted in and out of consciousness until the squire woke him. Jonah grunted and moaned before finally getting to his feet and donning his armor. As instructed, he was in the street at midnight. A beggar approached him, handing him a note that read: "Look above you across the street, and follow."

As he did, Jonah saw the shape of a man on the rooftop, who moved to Jonah's left. He followed. At the edge of an apple orchard in the northern reaches of West Bend, the man stopped and was joined by two others. Jonah halted, and backed away a little. The leader of the three men called out, "No trap, just a precaution. We know the council is infiltrated and corrupted. We are offering a deal. We ask only that you deliver ... (he produced a sealed letter from his cloak, with red wax imprinted with a crest of a crow perched in a black walnut tree) ... this to your baron."

Jonah still did not trust them.

"We are called the Blackbirds, if you must know, but the council must remain ignorant that this meeting ever happened. Goodnight, Jonah."

Before Jonah could blink, he was out cold. He woke up with a headache in the barn next to the orchard.

Next to him was an open cask of hard cider, some of which was spilled on Jonah's beard and tunic, such that nobody would suspect anything amiss. "Clever bunch," Jonah grumbled.

By the looks of things, Jonah had less than twenty minutes to be at the gate. Jonah dragged himself upright and staggered towards the eastern walls. Jonah collapsed again in exhaustion as soon as he got to his horse. The barbarians laughed. Lebiced merely gave a half smile and led Jonah's horse with his own. He whispered to the squire, "He'll be fine in a couple days."

The squire nodded.

* * *

The loud clanging of a club on the bars of his cell nearly frightened Danny out of his skin, and hit his head on the floor tumbling out of bed. The looks on the three neighbors and former comrades in the adjacent cell were the most hateful he'd ever seen. They were soaking wet head to toe, and not slept much at all. A couple empty buckets in the corridor completed the picture. Danny realized what the jailor did last night in retaliation for their misbehavior, and naturally they are going to blame that on Danny as well; he just knew it. The jailor slid a tray of food under the door; it was day old bread and stale cheese with a little tin cup of water. Danny vowed to himself he would not stay in Oakthorn if he had a choice. The jailor stood away from the next door, his arms folded over his chain mail and leather vestments. "You lot going to behave?"

The other three bandits snarled in disgust.

"I'm gonna take that as a no. For that, you get stale crackers on the way to court."

The senior wolf clenched his fingers and growled in rage, kicking the bars of the cell. Danny finished his meal as quickly as he could, and made no sounds whatsoever regarding the quality of his food or lack thereof. Danny then retreated to the far corner and watched the rays of the rising sun coming in the window across the corridor. He was still watching when the jailor returned to say he had a visitor. It was Tyrianna.

Danny was allowed out of his cell, and the leering faces of the three bandits as they made loud whistles and lewd innuendoes made clear why. This was more for the girl's safety than his. Danny did not complain as he was led out the corridor to a visiting room.

"What's this about?" Danny asked.

Tyrianna answered nervously, "I had a vision that you are the key to the future. I don't understand how or why. And ... I won't let the crowd get you."

Danny blushed and smiled. "I'm grateful. It's nice to see you. The decor around here is rather dark and depressing."

The jailor smirked and moved his lips silently mocking Danny's choice of words. Tyrianna ignored him and gave Danny a hug before leaving.

"You'll be okay, promise."

As soon as Tyrianna broke line of sight, the jailor searched Danny for lock-picks and weapons and, once convinced that Danny had none, returned him to his cell momentarily. Danny was still smiling, the fragrance of Tyrianna's hair imprinted in his memory with the warmth of her skin.

* * *

An hour later, the Elves were standing outside the Reeves building awaiting Danny's appearance. The three other bandits were the first out of their cells in shackles, escorted by the honor guards. They filed two doors up the street to the courthouse, and once they were out of sight, the jailor returned for Danny. Today he got a wide berth from the peasants when they saw Tyrianna. Once everyone was seated in the courtroom, the tribunal was called to order.

The mediator general entered the court and began the customary address: "This 27th day of October, Stonehaven Year 1564, is the preliminary hearing for the composite trials of Redmane, Redoak, and Blackwolves. The petitioners and I will determine if probable cause exists to further pursue legal remedy. Counsels for the accused and the regional solicitor may now approach the bench."

They do and confer with the mediator general out of earshot from everyone else.

"Do you have the preliminary witnesses for the five controversies to be adjudicated?" the mediator general inquired.

One counsel for the accused shook his head no. "Sergeant Alex Mill is missing, and the other guard has the fever. Request extension for Redoak versus Blackwolves."

The mediator replied, "Request denied."

"Your honor, Alex is a key witness!"

The mediator general curtly replied, "I know who Alex Mill is. Find someone more reliable. His cowardice would bias the jury when he crumbles under cross examination."

The counsel for Redmane and Redoak meekly bowed his head in acquiescence.

"You have 48 hours to find another witness, while we proceed with the other four controversies." And he banged his gavel for effect.

"Now, are we missing any other witnesses?"

Assistant counsel for Redmane and Redoak nodded yes.

Mediator General Blackhull squinted his eyes and spoke in an irritated, sarcastic voice, "Do you plan on wasting more of my time, counselor? Or should I go fishing while you track down and gather sufficient witnesses to proceed with the hearing?"

The assistant slumped in a placating posture with his eyes toward the floor and responded, "Sorry, sir, we ..."

Blackhull interrupted, "It's 'Judge' or 'your honor' from now on. Or I can fine you for contempt if you like ..."

The assistant stuttered, "N-no, sir, I mean, Your honor ..."

Blackhull forced a sarcastic smile. "Now then, who or what is still missing?"

"The witnesses from West Mill, sir, honor, Judge ..."

"Contempt, first offense. Ten eagles."

The assistant looked aghast, "but, but, but ...."

The judge leaned forward on his bench, staring coldly at the assistant until the counsel backed down. "Extension granted for two cases from West Mill. Proceed to Redmane versus Eledar. Are the witnesses present?"

The counsels nodded yes.

"Bring the first witness."

Counsel complied and brought forth a watcher from the abbey.

"Do you swear on the land, that you shall speak the truth without omission or misdirection, so help you powers above?"

The witness responded, "I so swear it, Your honor."

"State your name for the record, please."

The watcher answered, "Dobbs, Your honor."

"And can you clearly recall the day and time of Eledar's death?"

"It was half past the bell of ten in the morning, on the 12th day of September, Your Honor."

"Location of his alleged killing?"

"The 3rd floor of the abbey, your honor."

"Manner of death?"

"Conrad attacked with his sword."

"Where did he strike the fatal blow?"

"He ran him through and removed his head like he promised he would, your honor."

"When was this promise made?"

"Just before Eledar gave the order to arrest Conrad."

Blackhull stared over his spectacles. "How much time elapsed between the promise and the deed?"

Dobbs began to grow fidgety. "Uh ... less than a minute, your honor."

"Yes or no. Does the second witness concur with the facts as presented?"

The other watcher nods yes.

"Now, Mr. Dobbs, can you explain to me the events preceding Conrad's promise?"

Dobbs showed a look of disbelief and scorn as he added, "The man was insubordinate and out of control..."

Blackhull cut him off. "Mr. Dobbs, the facts, please. What happened between Conrad and Eledar?"

"Eledar was telling Conrad he had to be judged for the murder of Ramus."

Blackhull corrected, "Alleged murder. Can you recall his exact words?"

Dobbs blurted, "Eledar called him a criminal, and it was Conrad's hunting knife they found in the body!"

Counsel for Redmane protested, "Objection! Eledar's opinions are not evidence! Conrad has not been connected by provable fact to the time and location of Ramus's murder."

Blackhull banged his gavel. "Objection carried."

Dobbs gave an angry outburst, "Eledar kept order, and you defend this *maverick* who thinks he is too good to abide our rules!"

The gavel came down again. "Scribe will ignore that statement. Mr. Dobbs, you are in contempt. This is not your jurisdiction. First offense, ten eagles."

Dobbs flew into a rage and leaped out of his chair, swinging a fist at the judge before two deputies tackled him and pinned him, face down, on the floor with both arms behind his back. "Eledar deserves justice! The abbey deserves order! You can't do this!"

The deputies dragged Dobbs out of the courtroom.

"Scribe will register two counts of contempt, and one count of assaulting a judge.

Witness Dobbs dismissed. Court adjourned.

* * *

"Look, this is the real thing, hardly damaged at all. With the helmet on, you could pass for one of them after sunset. I used to live there before I was run out of town by a jealous blowhard and his brother-in-law. I can part with it for 250 gold, whaddaya say?"

The spy shook his head no.

"Kazius won't pay that much, not even to you, Adrian. No deal."

Adrian gave a mock frown. "You wound me. Tell you what. 175 and it's yours. Take it."

The spy countered, "150."

Adrian pretended to be cross. "Oh, alright, 150 then. Here."

The spy paid the sum and put the armor in a potato sack.

Adrian added, "Tell Kazius I may have the boats ready by next week, nice sturdy ones."

The spy answered, "For your sake, let us hope so."

With that done, he left. Adrian pocketed 25 coins, and went downstairs to store the rest in his basement vault. After which, he closed up shop and went to the bar to indulge his love of gambling. With any luck, his wife Mandy would still be doing the wash in a tide pool. Before he found a seat, Adrian was spotted by a mercenary with a dragon tattoo on his left arm, who crowded Adrian into a dark corner.

Adrian asked, "What business have you got?"

The merc replied, "I got juicy intel. It's about the brats. Malsain had to pull out, almost got the entire network exposed after a little murder spree. Now we have to wait for the new buyer to show up."

Adrian hissed, "I knew Malsain was unstable, damn it. Tell no one, we can't have customers making waves."

The merc nodded, "Oh, another thing, double the order on the boats. Kazius wants them delivered south of Shadval."

Adrian's eyes went wide, "Sh-shadval? That's a bad place for anyone alive. No way!"

The merc whispered, "He hates that place, too. I hear his mum died there, but we have word that nothing will happen."

Adrian was not pleased. "Word from who? Kazius hates magic, hates ghosts and undead. Has he lost his mind?"

The merc shrugged. "Somebody up north is helping him for a price."

Adrian frowned. "Oh? For a price? It can't be a firstborn child, his concubines all miscarry, and anybody powerful or crazy enough to go there is not doing this out of charity. I don't like this at all."

The merc paused, then challenged, "You want to tell him yourself you can't deliver?"

Adrian slumped in defeat. "No. Now get lost."

The merc stepped back, "done." And turned to exit the bar.

Adrian forgot all about gambling tonight and got drunk instead. Taunts and insults followed him on his way home.

"Hey, Adrian! My pockets too good for your gold now? Or did you finally get bored with bone tiles? Tell ya what, I'll give ya ten silvers for a night with yer wife!"

Adrian made a rude gesture as he stumbled home, besotted with dark malt. His former gambling buddies followed him and cornered him just outside Alex Mill's door.

"Yer a ruddy faced coward and a leech!"

Alex overheard from inside, and hid under a table in the far corner that was nothing more than driftwood and branches with square nails holding it together. His wife and child were somewhere in town. Adrian balled his fists up and braced himself for a brawl.

"Oh, yeah? You dent and chip your tiles on purpose, you sneak!"

Two of the buddies stopped in their tracks giving a quizzical look at their "leader."

"That true, Sal? You a cheat at the table?"

Big Sal denied it, "No, he's trying to distract you!"

The third man did not believe him, swinging wild as he exclaimed, "You dirty bastard!"

Sal ducked under the swing and returned with an uppercut to the ribs and a head butt, knocking his opponent to the ground. Now the second man punched Sal in the kidneys. Sal staggered to one knee and then spun and grabbed the second in a bear hug and rammed him into the door, breaking it in two and landing on the floor. Alex curled tightly into a ball, averting his eyes in fear. Sal knelt on the floor over the unconscious body as

Adrian snuck behind him and kicked his ribs. Sal groaned in pain, unable to rise from the floor. Adrian closed in for another kick, but Sal caught his heel and jerked it straight up, tumbling Adrian backward on his head. Sal crawled towards the stunned Adrian and began to strangle him, until Mandy and Mrs. Mill showed up, quickly dropping their laundry and raining weakly clenched fists on Sal's head and shoulders, forcing him to block with both arms.

Sal pleaded, "I give! I give! Stop ..."

The ladies kept hitting him and driving him away from the house on his knees, until they had gone two houses down the street, and let him go. The third man came to and abandoned the second. He did not want to hang around for the wrong attention from a Crimson Hood or anyone else working for Kazius. Mandy quickly rounded on her husband.

"You been gambling and drinking again? Losing money as fast as you get two coins to put in your pocket? And you still didn't fix this door like I asked. You never listen to me ..."

Adrian interrupted, "Shut it! I wasn't gambling ..."

Mandy ignored him. "If you were an honest man, we'd still have a nice cottage in West Bend near the orchards with the cow and the goat and ..."

Adrian yelled back, "Shut it already! You beastly nagging shrew!"

Mandy spat in his direction before hastily gathering her wash and then stomping off, leaving her injured husband sitting in the Mill's doorway. Mrs. Mill stepped over Adrian and then saw an unconscious man on the floor, and her own husband still huddled under the table. "Bravely defending the floor, I see ..." she said sarcastically.

Alex whimpered, "In case you forgot, I don't have armor anymore."

His wife Moira laughed.

"Even if you sat in a steel plated stagecoach, Alex, you would find fault with its design and wiggle out of the admission that you are a damned COWARD!"

Alex broke down in sobs again, and Moira had to get far away before she gave in to the temptation to slap him and strangle him. Adrian still sat in the doorway as she left, with a scheming evil grin on his face.

* * *

"Bring the next witness," Judge Blackhull instructed.

Another watcher rose to answer the summons.

"State your name for the record, please."

The watcher responded, "Simon, your honor."

Blackhull instructed, "Describe your account of where and when you witnessed Conrad in the events surrounding Eledar's death."

Simon spoke, "It was in the abbey, after the bell of 10. Eledar motioned for me and Dobbs to arrest Conrad, and before we could lay a hand on him, we were both on the floor, and I heard Eledar fall. Conrad's sword was bloody when I regained my feet, and Eledar was dead."

Blackhull then asked, "And was it still in his hand?"

Simon nodded. "Yes, he never dropped it. I would have heard."

Blackhull weakly smiled. "Thank you. This satisfies probable cause. Redmane versus Eledar and Ramus will reconvene next week at this time. Proceed with the next hearing."

The counsels warily approached, heads bowed. Blackhull shot another withering look over his eyeglasses. "Who is missing now?"

The counsel for Redoak whispered, "None of the guard on duty at the manor gate that day are able to appear, all down with the fever."

Blackhull snarled, "OUT of my Court! Scribe, what other cases are on the calendar?"

The Scribe replied, "Two cases of alleged petty theft, three assaults, a forgery, criminal negligence, and a breach of contract." Blackhull examined the documents a moment and picked one at random. "This one."

The Scribe nodded and called the next hearing.

* * *

Nearby: "What do you mean, Dobbs is being held for trial? He's a witness!"

The deputy folded his arms. "Not after attacking the judge, he's not. You want him out? Gotta pay bail like anybody else."

Arbiter Dhasa scowled, "You *dare* insult me?"

The deputy narrowed his eyes and fixed his gaze level with the arbiter's.

"If you wanna take it that way, that's up to you. But fact is fact. This is OUR jurisdiction. Pay or leave."

Dhasa clenched his fists and left, slamming the door.

"Suit yourself, ya ugly snob."

Chapter Eighteen
North and South

Great clouds of gloom blotted the sun in the barren land called Razadur, whose mountainsides were almost bald of vegetation and scrub, with tiny streams of dark water full of algae and sulfur and iron oxides. The fortress of Eastfall was a dreary mass of slate gray slabs and ironwork, nestled high on a steep cliff next to the iron and coal mines that contaminated the water. The commonfolk depended on rain barrels for fresh water, while Kazius jealously hoarded a hidden spring near the back walls. Razadur's main exports were steel, stone, and gemstones, which was exactly why the shadow Dwarves had prized this remote, barren, unforgiving place, and held on tightly until they were driven out in 1523, retreating north along the Iron Ridge mountains to Zara-Mogai. They had made enemies in the Nation of Vaja and had paid the price for their arrogance. Arius Auguron, the father of Kazius, had claimed this land in 1527 and had abandoned it in 1540. Now Kazius ruled here. His concubines all failed to carry to term, and it was not enough for Kazius to be feared.

Negotiations dragged on longer than expected with the many bands of mercenaries. They could smell the low morale of the Bloodhammers and the Dragonwhip Trolls. The mercs held out for better pay, and Kazius had to give in. He was cornered, because of the accursed sea witch, and her insufferably meddlesome mother.

Something else was wrong, a prickling in back of his mind that made his hairs stand up … it was HIM, that annoying pest who trespassed at will, making mockery of every effort to keep uninvited visitors away from the inner sanctum of Eastfall. Kazius called to him without turning, unable to hide his disgust: "What is your business *this* time, rogue?"

The masked intruder paused, his eyes betraying a sadistic grin, waiting patiently for Kazius to further acknowledge his presence face-to-face. Kazius whirled in frustration.

"I tire of your stupid games. Speak or begone!"

The man, known only as Number Eleven, bowed mockingly, taunting: "Ever the impatient one, who enjoys the table scraps left by his father …"

Kazius lunged in rage, but Eleven had somersaulted over him with barely any exertion at all, laughing maniacally as he did so. Kazius turned to grab him again, but was suddenly engulfed in smoke billowing from the floor, and heard the voice directly above him in the rafters.

"You are getting slower, old man," the agent said in a snide tone.

Kazius bellowed, "WHAT do you want, you infernal insect!"

The veins in his neck were bulging.

"Oh come now, Kazius! My wants are quite simple. You have very little that cannot be had elsewhere," Eleven goaded.

Kazius snarled, "You obviously want something, you prying scoundrel ..."

Eleven cackled, "Flattery will get you nothing, old man. But ... I *am* here to inform you that the fever has failed to cripple the manor and the abbey. We require yet another carrier. You certainly have enough pawns to spare another one ..."

Kazius growled, "Enough of your riddles, *gutter rat.* Who do you mean by *we*?"

Eleven took his sweet time responding, watching Kazius pacing in circles, imagining the hundred ways he could disfigure, maim, torture and kill him. A ballet of devastation.

"Yes, it must be humbling to dangle on a string while the master hides in the forbidden wastes of the North, secure in his frozen citadel, mysterious to the end ..." he said nonchalantly, as if speaking to himself.

Kazius hissed, "Why should I sacrifice another loyal servant? Obsek was ... reliable."

Eleven demurred, "Oh, it's not my decision. You see, without *his* help, you will never get past Shadval. Dreadful things dwelling underground, in the ruins, all that mold and mildew and long dead armies that fell in battle ..."

Kazius looked pale and ashen, which was precisely the effect Eleven had hoped for.

"His terms are not negotiable. Send another carrier or add your army to the ranks of the undead," Eleven said with smug assurance.

The smoke had almost cleared when Eleven leaped down to the window, and Kazius turned only to be blinded by an explosion of light, and sank to his knees choking on the acrid stench of sulfur and magnesium. His eyes watered heavily, as he crawled to the window for air, which Eleven had opened, with no sign of him anywhere. It was a thousand-foot drop over the cliff out past this window, under which the narrow ledge could barely fit a sparrow. This assassin in black leather loved to gloat about his abilities, and rub Kazius's nose in it at every opportunity.

As his eyes and lungs cleared, Kazius shut and locked the window. He then went to fetch a strong drink. He loathed and despised that walking, slinking phantom.

* * *

"I have returned, master," the Father announced on bent knee before the 12 by 36 platform of stone in the center of which the black robed man stood, his face hidden under his hood. This menace was easily six feet tall, and his voice was absent of warmth or sentimentality.

"Where is your sniveling cowardly servant, Toby?" he asked.

Malsain responded, "I sent him ahead to notify you of my situation. The Elves and their allies have managed to expose me. I had to flee before all my work could be undone."

Lord Barton scoffed, "You lie. I warned you about your temper, and Toby is not here. Just as well, I can barely tolerate his presence … You jeopardized the network, Malsain. A very, very lucrative network. What do you bring me in compensation? The worth of a single boat? Do you really think to appease me thus?"

Father Malsain bowed his head low, while his lips curled in rage. Barton turned his back for a moment, and Malsain tensed to pounce on him, just as a wave of Barton's hand sent him flying backward, into the cavern wall.

"You cannot surprise me, werewill. Leave me, and do not return until you have a compelling reason why I should let you live. Go …"

Malsain understood he was outmatched by the Alpha leader and left without comment, giving the evil eye.

"And the girl will be dealt with by … more *talented* help," Barton warned.

* * *

Elsewhere in the north, a masked man in black leather with death in his eyes weaved his way into a maze of tunnels under a mountain, leading him to a furnished cavern chamber of tapestries, ornate furniture, and a throne of gray-speckled black marble, recessed into the wall at the northeast end. Sitting on the throne was a skeletal menace adorned in black-enameled bronze bracers with red runes, a black ring, and a silver ring, a necklace of slate gray stones shaped like fangs, over tattered red rags of silk and slightly rusted chain mail. His eye sockets lit by tiny red smoldering embers under a black crown. His voice was the rustling of leaves and tumbling gravel, colder than the mountain peaks.

"So, D'aarzane, does that clumsy oaf of a king obey my wishes, or must I take additional measures?"

The rogue responded, "He is as stubborn as ever, but reluctantly obeys."

The Lich showed displeasure as the shape of his embers narrowed to half-moons. In a chilling reverb, Arius declared, "Ungrateful stripling! He would be NOTHING without me, NOTHING! And if I so wish, he will be less than nothing, now go back there at once and remind that knuckle-dragging upstart what I will do to him, that I am fully aware of his limitations, in fact ..." Arius removed his silver signet ring and threw it at D'aarzane hard enough to sting.

"Show him the ring and inform him who he is dealing with. Be gone from my sight until he has complied, and while you are down that way ..." Arius handed over a scroll. "Read this and destroy it!"

D'aarzane bowed. "Yes, master," and turned to exit south as a woman appeared from the west tunnel.

She wore a red cloak with brown accents over a yellow robe with orange trim, and decorated with runes of her own. She called out, "Eleven certainly enjoys taunting my brother, Daddy … "

Arius interrupted with an angry glare, "Do not call me that again, I am beyond sentimental rubbish, Winter …"

The woman stepped back a foot, bowed on one knee and replied, "Yes, Father. I had hoped you might have more bitterleaf and angelweed for my powders."

Arius merely pointed to the south chamber in a quick motion of annoyance. Winter bowed again and retrieved her raw materials. While she was carefully sealing her containers, Arius casually mentioned in a quietly sinister tone of forced pleasantry, "There is something else that may interest you …" and waited for her to prod.

Winter hesitated with a worried look on her face. Sighing, she gave in. "There's no need to bait me. I'm not half as bullheaded as my brother …"

Arius mused aloud, "We shall see about that …" He waited again for her to reveal a weakness.

But she called him on it. "Father, is it too much to simply ask? You treat us all like wayward, hungry, thieving runaway children, when it was <u>you</u> who abandoned US."

Arius glared in fury. "SILENCE, witch! You forget your place. I had only <u>one equal</u>, who has been stolen from me by the accursed Elves and their pet humans … and you have not one tenth of her ruthless cunning!"

Winter glared back in challenge. "Because you never trained us, we had to learn completely on our own, under the bitter care and mistrust of Aunt Margo in Thalu, while you vanished from the world of men in search of buried relics!"

Arius thrust out his hand, blasting her into the far wall. Winter defiantly raised up on her hands and knees, a single trickle of blood welling from the corner of her mouth, waiting for her father to speak his business.

Arius stated at last, "If you arrange an accident or illness for the Elder Goldlion, I will allow you to have her ... journal."

So that was the big prize, she realized, this forsaken, unliving thing that was once her father had rescued her mother's diary from the ruins of Shadval all these years ago just to use as another bargaining chip. There were no traces of humanity left in him, and therefore, nothing she could trust.

"Very well ... Father. I shall ... meditate on the best methods of delivery ... "

Arius simply glared in angry half-moons again. He dismissed her with a sweep of his hands, and said not another word. Winter collected her things and followed the same tunnel D'aarzane used.

Chapter Nineteen
Secrets

"Your honor, we have the witnesses for the Blackwolf trials," a counselor announced outside the judge's office.

Blackhull was nonplussed. "Well, it's about time. I can fit you in Monday morning, at the bell of nine. Don't be late. I mean it."

The counselor nodded and bowed, then turned to leave when Blackhull interjected,

"One more thing. Tell your drinking buddy his expense tab is revoked. We are all in fiscal hardship as of yesterday."

The counselor nodded again, with a look of despair, then left.

Minutes later, Arbiter Dhasa appeared.

Blackhull looked up from his desk. "Hello, Dhasa, out of your jurisdiction, aren't you?" Dhasa scowled. "I want Dobbs released. He is needed at the abbey."

Blackhull folded his hands. "Afraid I can't do that. Not without bail. And he is not allowed in my court again. That's not up for discussion."

Dhasa mused aloud, "Suppose I donated ... liquid assets ... "

Blackhull sat back in his chair, mulling, "Dobbs is not negotiable, but I can make concessions on the Eledar case ..."

Dhasa smiled. "Most appreciated. Does 3 bottles suffice?"

Blackhull shook his head no.

Dhasa offered, "Five."

Blackhull nodded. "Now, Conrad is still captain of the Honor Guard, which places him in Oakthorn jurisdiction. If Eledar is in any manner whatsoever guilty of false arrest, the abbey cannot claim jurisdiction over Conrad. You would have to have a reliable witness swear to me that there was no fraud, and have strong evidence that Eledar was sincere in his beliefs that Conrad had no alibi, made efforts to verify the story, and served proper notice ... if these conditions were satisfied, I could move the trial to the abbey under your jurisdiction."

Dhasa fumed. "No! Conrad is banned from the grounds. It cannot be done. And I won't ... betray the ... faith of those who serve Eledar's memory."

"Well, then, there's only one other option, Dhasa ..." Blackhull concluded.

Dhasa asked, "That option is?"

"A trial by combat, in the empty field north of the road to West Bend, under terms of the King, between Conrad and a champion acting on Eledar's behalf. Witnessed and officiated by both my deputies and your watchers, who may not interfere in any way, or forfeit protection of the Itana treaty of 1203. The results of the contest are binding and final."

Dhasa frowned. "I don't like it."

Blackhull responded, "That's your best option, Dhasa, like it or not. If you can't, or won't reverse his ban, it's either my courtroom or the field."

Dhasa gave an evil look and crossed his arms, turning his back.

Blackhull challenged, "How is this going to look for you if your pride undermines the trust of your watchers, Dhasa? Do you *really* think I didn't catch the meaning of your words? The watchers who idolize Eledar do so because they want a 'house' that stands up to termites and hailstones and flaming arrows. I'm not stupid, Dhasa. I know what you want. You want to take his place, and you need their support. I'll give you a fair shake, but I won't break the rules. Now make up your mind."

Dhasa grumbled, "So be it. North field," and shambled out the door.

* * *

A vast storm front of dark, ashen gray clouds rolled in from the harbor, blanketing the land in dreary shadow.

The wind blew cold and sharp like needles, stealing the warmth from Tyrianna's lungs. She stood huddled on a small hill against the elements, forgetting how she got here. Her thin cloak was drawn around her, a feeble barrier against the chill. She shivered and sneezed, wandering towards the forest to the East. The shape of it looked wrong; it should be taller.

As she drew near, the trees were all black, not a single leaf on them. The Elves were nowhere to be seen. A hand settled on her right shoulder, Tyrianna ducked and tumbled clear, only to realize it was Tyrus. Where did he come from, and where were they? Tyrus did not speak; he was staggering and bleeding. One of the outer tines on his trident was broken. Tyrus fell to his knees just as the rain began to fall. The rain washed his skin, and his wounds started to vanish. But he did not rise. Tyrianna turned as something moved in the forest. A wisp of smoke and mist darted in and out of the shadows. A black wraith, with grayish red eyes. It hissed, "Beware the phantom of death. He comes for you, Oracle!"

Tyrianna did not understand. The wraith did not advance on the girl, but kept darting among the trees. Tyrianna tried to follow. She caught glimpses of the wraith as it moved and saw slivers of steel in its translucent hands. The wraith went deeper into the woods, what was left of it. She soon lost sight of him. Lightning flashed overhead among the clouds, and suddenly a low-flying mass of birds, as dark as midnight, swarmed past her head, fleeing the woods as a very large canine in the unseen distance howled at the moon. Tyrianna saw movement again, white apparitions approached her, no more than four feet tall. They were all children.

A little girl clutching a doll pleaded with sad eyes, "Please make bad man go away ..."

Tyrianna answered, "Who? Tell me who he is ... "

The girl just pointed into the woods.

Tyrianna saw no one but the children. They started to vanish also.

"Wait! Who are you? Where are your parents?" Tyrianna called to them.

The girl replied, "My name is Opal ... they can't help. Bad man too scary."

And then Opal was gone. Three children remained. One was more solid than the others. He had a big brown rat on his shoulder. The boy's eyes looked very old; he held the weight of centuries of sorrow inside them. He did not speak, but as he looked at Tyrianna, his eyes brightened. He even smiled. Tyrianna reached for his hand, but he did not accept. He walked right through her and was gone. Another boy and a girl, the last ones, turned away and vanished.

A familiar voice behind her said: "Those were Rod, Alex and Molly. Rod likes you."

It was a full-grown woman, wearing Ravenna's face, but her mother's garments. Her hair was auburn. The woman raised her hand upward, and the clouds began to swirl, opening a window to the starry sky beyond.

"Tell me, who is this bad man, and what am I supposed to do?"

The woman just smiled, and whispered, "You will know."

And Tyrianna bolted upright in a large bed, in the guest wing of Redoak Manor. She held her hand over her heart as she calmed her breathing.

* * *

A woman huddled in her cloak against the cold autumn winds and rain. The sentries at the manor gate allowed her through, as Lady Bethany Blackthorn was related to two of their number, one by birth and the other by marriage. Amanda happened to be walking by as Beth entered the great hall. The two women nodded to one another in greeting, and Amanda took Beth's wet cloak to hang on a hook while Beth sought audience with the baron.

Bravane and his Uncle Alex were conversing.

"The treasury is in the red, no thanks to the looters who exploited Sergeant Mill's meekness and aversion to footwork of any kind …" Alex the Wise opined.

Bravane nodded and noticed Beth, waving her over. "What brings you?"

Bethany bowed and spoke hesitantly, "I don't mean to be a burden, milord …"

Bravane smiled. "Nonsense. Your father was my family, too. What troubles the celebrated cook of the Redmane clan?"

Bethany cast her sad eyes up to meet the Baron's gaze. "I am at wit's end without my husband, I may have to sell my bakery. The abbey has revoked my catering contract without notice, to further punish my brother, and the townsfolk also shun me as an object of malicious gossip. And … I am now with a third child. Our house is in ill repair, I had to dismiss two of the maids as I could not afford them anymore. Nell has graciously offered to work for less and to take a second livelihood to meet her own needs. I shall go insane if this continues much longer …" Bethany confessed, sobbing.

Bravane held out a hand to comfort hers. "I … I had no idea that anything more had been amiss. I am sorry, cousin. I will do whatever I can to help. It will not do to have my grandmother's kin in such despair. Alex, would you bring the promissory notes from the safe?"

Alex the Wise nodded and bowed. "Of course." He turned to retrieve the notes from the cellar.

Bethany still weeped. "I ought be glad of the help, milord, but my heart is sore to be an object of charity … I have nowhere else to turn …"

Bravane held her shoulders and leaned down to meet her eyes. "No more pity, I am buying your contract. And your children will visit here to ease your mind. You will keep your bakery and the house. This I swear."

Bethany hugged him, sobbing still.

Bravane stood limp a moment in mild surprise, and then returned the embrace tenderly before gently backing away, taking her hands in his own. "If not for my cousins, Lady Redmane, I should be insane myself. Trouble not over a favor repaid, fair one."

Bethany still cried, even as she meekly kissed his bearded cheek and shied away to get her cloak. Bethany returned home to see her children and hugged them so tightly that Devi pulled free with great effort.

"What wrong, Mommy?" Little Devi asked.

Bethany knelt down to look her daughter in the eyes. "Mommy is overwhelmed without Daddy and ... the people in town are cold of heart and hard of head ..."

Devi took her mother's index finger in her tiny hand and said, "It okay, Mommy. I go pour hot tea and make better ..."

Bethany gave a weak laugh. "Not that kind of cold, honey. It just means they are cold and cruel to Mommy."

Devi stood tall for her tender age of two with a look of defiant courage. "I make better anyway. Mommy make best food in whole barony, Nell say so. They no find better, dogs smarter than them."

Bethany cried again, hugging Devi. "Oh, sweetie ... "

Jacob tugged at his mother's leg, wanting to be picked up and fed. As Bethany reached down, she saw, once again, how much his eyes looked like Jonahs'.

How she longed for her husband to be home.

* * *

Jonah rode proudly to the southwest gate of Oakthorn, with his squire and his new companions. "Hail, brothers, I bring help for the Elves against Razadur. These men are all with me."

The honor guards bowed and let them pass. Jonah led his group across the south bridge over the Vaniki river, past the keep, and then to the Mariner's Inn at the market square, where they tied their mounts. Jonah showed them inside. "First meal is on me, lads!"

The twelve-plus barbarians wasted no time flirting with the barmaids and ordering their fill of food and drink. The wizard Lebiced simply contented himself with tea and pumpkin bread.

Jonah commented, "No offense to the owners, but my wife makes the best bread anywhere!"

An old peasant nearby frowned and picked up a dinner plate to go sit farther away from Jonah.

Lebiced noticed the look of suspicion and contempt on the man and kept his ears trained in that direction, while discreetly nudging Jonah to take notice. Next to the old peasant, a lone monk, a gaunt, wiry man with sunken eye sockets and sunken cheeks was standing giving a venomous sermon to the commoners: "Not only is the baker financing her brother's defense against Eledar, but the baron and his captain are now pawns of an Elf witch. I tell you the Lawgiver will punish them, and reward his believers that deliver them up!"

Jonah's neck bulged, and he reached for his sword.

Lebiced stopped him with a touch and a whisper, "No, not yet. This lawgiver cult is dangerous. They have pawns in the council of West Bend. We can catch him red-handed soon enough."

Jonah hissed quietly, "What do you know about them?"

The wizard pulled Jonah farther away from the monk and scrawled a note on a spare bit of parchment:

Alphas attempting to recruit Bravane the Elder. Already on the council in West Bend.
I was sent by Xantir to sniff around. Dragons attack the borders of Stonehaven, and the council is blaming the Dwarves of Iglar. Xantir knows better. This smells of Arius.

Jonah's jaw dropped. He was about to say something to the wizard, when the monk called to him directly, in an edgy voice of hypervigilance,

"Hey, you in the armor! Yeah, you! I know who you are! The baker's husband. Come to spy on us? We have nothing to hide, pawn! Unlike your skulking brother-in-law, your insubordinate wife, and your besotted baron!"

Jonah brushed Lebiced aside and drew his sword; he intended to teach this brash monk some proper manners. Jonah snarled, "Hold your tongue, knave!"

The monk retreated a couple steps, and the peasants around him all fled for the door. The barbarians advanced behind Jonah and nudged him to sheathe his weapon, as they surrounded the monk. The gaunt monk produced a dagger, waving it like a wand in figure eights. The tallest barbarian feinted on the monk's right, prompting the man to slash empty air, and another man behind him caught the monk in a bear hug, while two more grabbed his wrists.

"Unhand me, you madmen! The arbiters will make you pay for this indignity! How dare you touch the vestments of the order!" the sickly looking monk protested.

The barbarian's leader, Skorvald, calmly walked up and pried the dagger out of the monk's fingers and asked Jonah, "Mind showing us where the stables are?"

Jonah gave a frown of puzzlement and a raised eyebrow, but did as requested, leading them across the street and past the herb shop to the town stables. The monk, squirming and bucking every step of the way, cried "No! You have no right. Let me go, you base mongrels!

Heathens! Heretics! Foul besotted pigs! Monsters!"

The barbarians then dunked the gaunt monk repeatedly in the watering trough, until most of the fight had gone out of him, and then they just left him on the ground, coughing, sputtering and exhausted.

"I think we'll keep this little trinket where he won't lay his paws on it again," said Skorvald, as he pocketed the dagger in a leather pack. From five paces away, he called to the monk, "In my own land, insulting a man's wife, plus his lord and kin, would find you with your tongue cut out, and you are the most pathetic creature ever to wear a robe that I laid eyes on, monk!" Skorvald spat in his direction to accent his point.

The gaunt monk cast fearful eyes upward as he gained his feet and backpedaled away from these savages in fur and studded leather, turning southeast toward the outer wall, stumbling down the street that curved westward over the south bridge and then northwest to the abbey.

While Jonah's group returned to the inn to finish their meal, the stable hands were quick to spread word of the event, prompting a couple honor guards to get Jonah's version of things at the inn. One of the baron's men shrugged. "Point him out to us later. He sounds like trouble brewing. Inciting a mob is the last thing we need around here."

Jonah nodded. "No kidding ..."

* * *

The monk staggered outside the abbey, clutching his left arm in agony, nearly collapsing at the door, his left sleeve wet with diluted blood. The watchers attempted to help him, but he swatted them away. "NO! Do not touch it! Fetch my pipe from Eledar's study and bring it here!"

Watcher Simon made haste to comply, while Watcher Sean asked with great concern, "How did you suffer such injury, Brother Darmid? Who did this to you?"

Darmid answered with bitter contempt, "A wolf bite when I was young. None of your business ..."

Sean frowned in disbelief and returned to his post north of the front door. When Simon returned with the pipe, Darmid snarled, "Now fetch me a lit candle, quickly! Hurry!"

Simon bowed and raced off toward the altar to comply. Darmid trembled as he held the pipe near the flame, trying to light it. Once it caught, he took a long drag on it and slumped against the wall, sinking to the floor and sighing in a raspy breath; his pupils shrunk to small dots, his arms limp at his sides. Simon waved a hand slowly past his face, and Darmid blinked, following the hand after a long delay. "I'm not dead, you fool," Darmid mumbled sleepily, staring up into Simon's eyes. "Now get me some fresh bandages ..."

* * *

"Bethany! Your husband has returned!" Jonah called out, and his daughter Devi ran into his arms. "Daddy!"

Bethany had tears in her eyes and shuffled her feet tiredly to welcome Jonah home with a weak hug.

"Why the sad face, darling? Is Jacob well?"

Bethany nodded yes.

"Honey, tell me, what's wrong? Where's the maids?"

Bethany broke into sobs. "Gone. No money for them. The abbey revoked my contract out of spite to our family ..."

Jonah was not sure he heard correctly. "What?"

Bethany turned on him with angry tears. "They are punishing my brother and spiting the baron over the funeral he forced them to play host to and spitting on my father's name, and all you can say is what?"

Jonah blurted, "We still have money. I was going to tell you ..."

Bethany yelled, "What? The treasury is empty, and you left me alone with a town gone mad, without knowing we still have money? Where? When were you going to tell me?"

Jonah pleaded, "Honey, please don't be mad …"

She snapped, "Did you know we have another child on the way? Is there enough to feed … who are they?"

Jonah hung his head. "New friends …"

Lebiced tipped his hat and bowed, while Skorvald and his men snapped to attention and nodded their heads once, deep in reverence.

Bethany whispered, "Why was I not warned we had company?"

Jonah groaned, "I was going to …"

Lebiced prompted, "Many pardons, miss. If we might borrow your husband on business a bit longer? The future of Valantir and Stonehaven are in question."

Bethany looked as if her own doom was only minutes away, as she weakly replied, "If you must."

Lebiced discreetly tugged on Jonah's sleeve, and Jonah rejoined Skorvald's group while the wizard had a look at Devi.

"You have a marvelous daughter, Miss Blackthorn. Such wisdom in her eyes." Bethany gave a bare trace of a sad smile. "She gets it from you, I think. I promise your husband will be returned to you safely."

Bethany simply nodded and took her daughter's hand to lead her back inside. Lebiced nodded one more time and approached Jonah. "Your daughter is destined for great things, being descended from Seamus Redmane as she is …"

Jonah blurted, "Pardon me? Do we know you?"
Lebiced smiled. "Not yet, but you will."

* * *

Amanda saw a robed figure approaching and reflexively tensed up to run for help until she saw that the manor guards were unharmed and awake and that the hooded figure was none other than Helen, mother of the baron. It was rare to see her outside the walls of the abbey, and Amanda wondered aloud: "What transpires to occasion your visit, Lady Helen?"

Helen merely gestured for Amanda to follow. In the Feast Hall, Bravane the Younger, Alex the Wise and Conrad the Bold were conversing with Ravenna, Tyrus, and Tyrianna about what little they knew of the trial and how Conrad had not seen Savadi for many days. "It's not like him at all to be isolated this long. I am worried the arbiters are up to something," Conrad confessed.

Bravane the Younger stood up. "Mother! We still have one plate left … "

Helen shook her head politely. She was not hungry. Bravane walked over to give her a hug, and she kissed him on the cheek, before producing a sealed letter with the abbey's crest in green wax. It was a gem with eight rays. The letter was addressed to "Tyrianna." Bravane gave a puzzled frown, as Helen held the letter up in the oracle's direction. Tyrianna looked up from her food, surprised, "Me?

But … who in the five waters is writing to me? Danny? No, he's not in the abbey …"

Helen walked over to the table to present it closer.

Tyrianna broke the seal to read the parchment. Her jaw dropped.

Your dream was a message.
The children are real.
You are the one to help them. Please do not ask why.
You will be called again
to the waters you called home. You must be ready for anything. and must not hesitate to act.
I am being watched, no time to explain.
I dare not reveal my name in event this is intercepted.
but know this, your destiny calls.

"But … who?" Tyrianna asked aloud.

Helen brought two fingers up to her left temple and then motioned straight ahead, into the distance. Conrad declared, "The message is from Andar the Farseer!"

Helen nodded yes.

"And the baron's mother is the least out of place visiting the manor," Conrad added.

Helen nodded again, as Lady Amanda Redoak collected the last scraps of food to take up to her own mother Myra in the Tower. Behind Helen, an honor guard entered the hall to announce nine visitors for the baron. It was Jonah, plus an elderly man, and seven of the barbarians.

Baron Bravane greeted Jonah, "Welcome! How did the meeting go?"

Jonah frowned. "Due to dragons at the northwestern border and a deadlocked council, the king would not see me. That is why these men are with me. They are willing to hire out their services in defense of Valantir, my lord."

Bravane showed shock in his eyes. "So William Goldlion turns a blind eye to Razadur? I find this … unworthy of him …"

Ravenna interjected, "The council was already corrupt when I left home, and my brother cannot see the wider vista of anything … nor have I often had the benefit of being his kin."

Jonah inquired, "Is it true, my lord, what has reached my ears regarding the treasury? I promised these men compensation."

Baron Bravane sighed. "Yes, it is true. We shall need assist from Agama unless Valantir would hire them directly. Were you unable to contact them?"

Jonah responded, "Unforeseen events have prevented me, and this … is for you, my lord."

Bravane accepted the sealed letter and broke it open. After a minute of reading, he spoke, "Why do I keep hearing about this alpha clan? And how can I trust these 'blackbirds' as they call themselves?"

Ravenna spoke again, "I know who they are. They are far less the hypocrites than the council that poisons my brother's ears. I say we make a deal with them."

Bravane cocked an eyebrow. "Perhaps ... "

Now Lebiced introduced himself, "Greetings, Lord Bravane Redoak the Third, great grandson of Bravane the First and Mary Falconeye. I am Lebiced the Wizard, sent from Xantir, the land where Mary was born. And my sister Cedra wedded Mary's brother Ursus, making you and I distant cousins. I came to inform you the five kingdoms are, once again, in peril."

Bravane bowed. "Xantir is held in high regard. Welcome, Lebiced. Why is Oakthorn so important?"

Lebiced answered, "Through no fault of their own, begging the pardon of present company, the Goldlions seem to have lost their courage. Losing Andrew and Reginald to Izimal and Thomas to Shadval, they now cloak themselves in the deeds of the heroic dead, while the living require another leader to step forward. These alphas are fixed on swaying your father to their dark cause, and they may have done so. Of all the men who would oppose the Alphas, you know your father best. So, if I might be so bold, it is your destiny, Lord Redoak."

Bravane shook his head. "No, Lebiced, of all men, my uncle Alex knows him best."

Lebiced bowed, apologizing, "My mistake, although you do carry the bloodlines of several kingdoms. Two of which readily accept you as their own."

Helen bowed as she took her leave from the hall, and now Tyrus noticed that Tyrianna was nowhere to be seen. Bravane offered an explanation, "My mother has never forgiven my father, nor do I."

Skorvald bowed to his host. "No offense, Baron, but if the treasury is empty, my men require some other arrangement. I have already informed Jonah of the opposition we face. Kazius has gathered not only Southland assassins, but eastern clans as well. He will soon make his move."

Bravane gritted his teeth in consternation, "Send word to Valantir, who is our fastest rider?"

Ravenna raised a hand. "I know Valantir quite well. I will go."

Bravane asked, "You are certain?"

Ravenna nodded yes.

The baron relented, "Done. I will have the letter within the hour. Alex, if Kazius advances before the trials are completed, I have to pull all of our security out of there and postpone or cancel the proceedings. What do we tell Blackhull?"

Alex the Wise flatly responded, "The truth about Longbranch and the shameful mockery of a treaty offered by Razadur."

Bravane nodded. "So be it. Let's be done with this foul affair. The dinner meeting is thus concluded. Thank you, everyone."

Chapter Twenty
For Lack of Courage

"Moira! My wife was just talking about you and Molly. What can I do for you?"

Moira produced a sword and scabbard from under her cloak and threw it loudly on the counter.

"What can you give me for it?"

Adrian smiled. "Well, I have to inspect it first, make certain it's not rusted or anything …"

Moira fixed cold eyes on him. "No tricks, Adrian. Remember who saved you from Sal, your gambling friend …"

Adrian chuckled nervously. "Ahh, right … " He inspected the sword. "I suppose I could give you twenty-five gold for this …"

Moira shook her head no.

"Does Alex know about this?" Adrian inquired.

Mrs. Mill shot back, "He's only used it once in his life. I'm doing what I have to because he won't. And your wife Mandy knows about a lot more than just your gambling and drinking. Your name gets around … a LOT. Are you quite sure you want to test a woman's patience, Adrian?"

He gulped. "Ahh, of course not. I believe the fair price for this is fifty. I'll be right back."

Moira put her hand down on the scabbard. "This stays in my sight until I have the coins."

Adrian frowned. "You don't trust me, do you?"

Moira raised a cold eyebrow. "Why should I?"

Adrian slumped and sighed. He returned a minute later, counting the coins out slowly, muttering complaints under his breath about women in general.

"Thank you. Enjoy your day," Moira said as she closed the pouch and turned to leave the shop.

Sal stood in the doorway, blocking her exit. "Well, well, look what the new tenants have," Big Sal taunted.

Moira jabbed Sal's boot with her narrow-heeled shoe, causing him to grab his foot in a dance of pain, uttering a string of curses. Moira slipped out the door and informed Sal coldly, "I know your wife, too, and many of your secrets. Don't test me. I know your favorite whiskey. I know your dog's name and where you sleep. How long would your luck last?"

Sal's eyes betrayed his fear as he backed away from Moira.

After she left, he whispered to Adrian, "That is one crazy bitch …"

Adrian nodded, whispering back, "I may have work for you. Meet me after dark by the dock …"

Sal warned, "No funny stuff, or I twist your head off."

Adrian pretended not to hear, before answering, "Relax. What I have in mind will net a tidy sum for both of us. Trust me."

Sal corrected, "Nobody trusts you, ya dirty rat."

Adrian and Sal burst into laughter and were soon drinking a toast to future business.

* * *

"You sold my sword? How could you do that?" Alex screeched in panic, pulling at his own hair.

Moira crossed her ams, cold fury in her eyes. "Someone had to before the tax collectors returned, unless you wrought some miracle you failed to tell me about?"

Alex Mill paced hysterically on their dirt floor, shaking his empty palms in the air, babbling incoherently.

Moira observed with icy sarcasm, "That some new spell to undo everything you fouled up?"

Alex screamed, "STOP! You are driving me crazy!"

Moira stared him down in sullen silence.

Then Alex sniffed the air. Something was wrong.

"Smoke! Fire! Where's Molly?"

Moira ran to the ladder that led up to the loft. "Molly? Honey, we have to go!"

Molly climbed into her mother's arms, and Moira descended quickly to head for the door. Alex was cowering behind a rickety chair, while two men with makeshift linen masks flanked the doorway with knives in both hands. Moira gasped in recognition; their height and build could not be concealed so easily. She ascended the ladder again and attempted to pull it up after her, but Sal had grabbed the bottom rung. Alex snapped and began advancing with the chair in both hands on the other man. Adrian feinted to one side; Alex lunged, and his right side was wide open to a slashing attack. Adrian drew first blood and closed for an overhead strike when Alex kicked his knee.

Adrian screamed in pain as he fell. Alex now knew who they were. His eyes went wide in shock, and he dropped the chair.

Sal had wrested the ladder out of Moira's grip and was halfway up, even while dodging her kicks to his face. Moira changed her tactics and kicked at the ladder, which teetered slightly before Sal threw his weight against it. He grabbed her foot on her next kick and yanked her shoe off. She threw the other one at him, which drew blood from his cheek.

"Aaaah, you bitch!" He topped the ladder as she launched a double kick to his face. He caught both legs on her next attempt and twirled her on her stomach.

Molly screamed, "Mommy!"

Alex snapped out of his trance and ran for the ladder. Sal kicked Alex in the face, and Alex tumbled on his crown, passing out. Moira lashed out with her nails, but Sal caught her wrist and backhanded her, knocking her out as well. Sal grabbed the wailing child, and soon found the pouch of gold, dragging both behind him, as he crabwalked down the ladder.

"Let's get out of here!" Sal exclaimed.

Adrian gritted his teeth and crawled out sideways on his good leg. He had to leave both knives behind on the floor where they fell. There was nothing else to do but escape.

"Get her to the dock. I'll meet you there!" Adrian called out. He still had the mask on when Mandy spotted him in the street near their house.

"Insomnia again? Had to hide something from me you lying bastard?"

Adrian pleaded, "No, no, I can explain … really!"

Mandy had her fists resting on her hips with a furious scowl of hatred lit by the glow of the lanterns. "You have five seconds, MISTER … " she challenged.

"Sal needs medicine for his sick mother in … in … Stonehaven! But the medicine is outlawed … ," Adrian sputtered.

Mandy screamed, "YOU LIAR! That's it! I want a divorce! First thing in the morning, you greedy, heartless, lying weasel! And don't bother taking the mask off. I can't stand your wretched face anymore!"

* * *

"Wake up! Damn you!" Moira screeched as she slapped Alex. Her husband awoke to a throbbing pain at the back of his head where he had collided with the floor. "This is all your fault! They have Molly! What are you going to do about it?"

Alex winced and then gasped in horror. "No, no, not Molly ... "

Moira slapped him again. "We don't have time for this! DO something! Damn you! Or I will do it myself and haunt you from beyond the grave if I fail, you spineless wimp!"

Alex rose to his knees. "Okay ... just ... give me a minute ..." He clutched his head and marshaled his thoughts.

Moira added, "They took our money, too. We lose everything if we don't get it back. The taxes are due. If you fail this time, our marriage is over, Alex!"

Alex staggered to his feet, clutching a post to steady himself. "I need a weapon ... "

Moira went to the woodstove and brought him the small iron skillet and a carving knife. "There you go. Now kill that bastard if you have to!"

Alex clenched his teeth. "Yes, for Molly and our house ... and, for you, darling ... "

Moira snarled, "Shut up and go!"

Alex obeyed, steeling his nerves for the impossible task ahead, and strode toward the shop in search of Adrian. He arrived to see Mandy ransacking the place.

"Where's Adrian?" Alex called out to her.

Mandy froze in place, slowly turned, and announced angrily, "He is on a boat to hell, after looting all the best heirlooms we had ..."

Alex calmly informed her, "Mandy, he has my daughter ..."

Mandy screamed, kicking the tables over and throwing goblets at the glass cabinets, "Damn you, Adrian! You misbegotten bastard!"

Alex begged, "I have to get my daughter back. Where has he gone? I have to know … please …"

Mandy collected herself. "Some friends of his at the tavern might know … here. You'll need something to pay them …" she said as she gave him a golden cup and a string of pearls.

Alex bowed. "Thank you."

Mandy frowned. "Don't mention it. And good luck sending him to hell."

Alex bowed one more time and picked up his old sword and scabbard as he left. He even whispered to it, "Good to have you back, beautiful."

For once, Alex strode confidently to meet his fate.

Chapter Twenty-One
Blood in the Tree

"Honey?" Jonah called at the doorway. "We can keep the bakery, sweetheart. And still have plenty for raising a third child."

Bethany was quicker to hug him this time, whispering in his ear, "I love you, darling, but no more secrets. Promise?"

Jonah nodded yes and kissed his wife. When he did speak, it was with great sadness: "There is much I have hidden because my past is stained by the deeds of my kin. I adopted the name Blackthorn to start over. Please hear me out. I love you more than life itself and would give all I have to protect you. I would never do any less if I have any choice in the matter."

Bethany drew back. "What are you saying, husband?"

Jonah bent to one knee. "I am not the illegitimate child I claimed to be, nor was I raised by a cartographer. Please forgive my deception. I have pledged my life to right the wrongs of my ancestors. You must believe me."

Bethany's face turned pale with shock and horror. "Then WHO are you? Whose blood is in all of my children? What have you dragged us into?"

Jonah braced himself as if for death. "Your great-aunt Susan and my aunt were mortal enemies in Shadval. Please have a seat, darling. The tale is long and bitterly tragic, and it pains me greatly to tell it."

Bethany clasped her hand over her navel, suddenly overcome with revulsion and tears of rage. "You deceitful swine! How dare you set foot here! All my love and mercy wasted on a nephew of … LORENNA the murderous chaos witch of infamy?"

Jonah sank to both knees, his head bowed in supplication, tears welling in his eyes. "I cannot blame you if you hate me … I-I had … hoped for a chance at happiness like anyone else, to escape the sordid tale of my father's name and legacy … you cannot imagine the torment …"

Bethany roared in defiance, "And *why should I* imagine? You have condemned your children to scorn and ridicule! How could you do this to them, to ME? To my brother …"

Jonah turned his face away in tears, choking. "Will … would you cast me into the darkness then, doomed by things beyond my control, certain to die of sorrow?"

Bethany clenched her fingers, wanting to strangle him, fighting for control of her senses. "You … monster! I … I cannot. Forgive me, Daddy. I cannot … you have put me in the impossible position of hating the … man whose masquerade I have married … how could you kiss me so lovingly before tearing my world apart?"

Devi appeared. "Mommy? Why mad face? What wrong?"

Bethany collapsed to her knees and broke into long sobs of sorrow and rage, still fighting herself, wanting to forget who her daughter was, to forget everything, but Devi was innocent of all these things. After a painfully long pause, Bethany hugged little Devi for dear life. "Mommy is … sorry. Grownups have horrible secrets, baby. The burden of them is too heavy for a child. Many adults crumble under them."

Devi took her mother's hair in her tiny fingers. "It okay, Mommy."

Jonah dared not reach out, resigning himself to the lonely despair engulfing him as his eyes remained cast down to the floor, weeping. "I'm so sorry, Bethany … I don't deserve you. Better I should die fighting dragons than living the shadow of a life without welcome or friend."

Devi pulled away from her mother. "No, don't go Daddy!"

Jonah's arms clung automatically, without thinking, around his daughter, and he broke into racking sobs. His mouth opened to speak, but the words choked and died. He shut his eyes, still weeping, rocking back and forth on his knees, still holding Devi. Bethany saw, at long last, the torment he spoke of.

Jonah, the dutiful soldier, reduced to an infant. She ever so slowly paced to his side and knelt beside him to embrace her daughter and husband alike.

* * *

Helen stopped abruptly in the cloister and, after a moment's pause, smirked knowingly and continued walking again southeast, toward the main stairwell. As she reached the stairs, she turned around with her finger to her lips. As she reached the monks' dormitory, and then a very particular room, Helen closed the door gently behind her, and then motioned with one hand, palm up toward a robed Elf who was staring into the glowing embers of a brazier.

Tyrianna dropped her spell of invisibility and asked, "Are you the one named Andar?"

The Elf nodded yes.

"What do you know about my dreams?" The young water sprite inquired.

Andar whispered, "All our lives are at risk. There is no time to explain. The sundering has started, as you know. The enemies are inside these walls. Be exceedingly careful about who you trust. You must leave before they know I have contacted you. Just remember the children. They are the key.

Now go, hurry ..." Tyrianna turned invisible again, and followed Helen out. Helen froze at the sounds of voices nearby around the corner.

Two men were hissing at each other in subdued whispers.

"You almost got caught stealing again, you fool! I should have disavowed you long ago! You are *this* close to being dragged away in chains!"

The second voice hissed back, "Good luck trying to bring down the Redmanes without me, or sorting through Eledar's archives, arbiter!"

Dhasa snarled, "You forget your place, scribe! *How dare you* speak to me in that tone!"

Darmid retorted, "I serve greater powers than you, old man. They have risen to high positions in Thalu, West Bend, and Korath, and command great legions in the northlands. Any one of them could arrange an 'accident' with your name on it. How many friends do *you* have, old man?"

Dhasa growled and walked hurriedly away, almost bumping into Helen. "Watch where you tread, you mute woman!"

Darmid fled at the reference to Helen. Tyrianna created a distraction by telekinetically ruffling the window curtain at the far end of the corridor. Dhasa turned his head to see who might have overheard, and Helen did not wait for further insults before taking the stairs. Once Helen got to the front door, she grabbed blindly for Tyrianna and nudged her out quite unceremoniously. The young oracle got the impression the abbey was a really bad place to visit.

* * *

"But, honey, are you sure?" Jonah asked.

Bethany nodded yes. "I can accept you, but not the money of your family. Please give it to the people who need it more. Please, husband ..."

Jonah sighed. "For your peace and happiness, darling, anything."

He got on his horse to do business with the barbarians and the public vaults. Lebiced met him on the way, with a sly smile. Jonah cast a suspicious look. "How much do you know?"

Lebiced leaned over to whisper, "I happen to be a friend of Henry the Lorekeeper here at the abbey. He is one of the few survivors of the original order in another land. I think you know which land that is."

Jonah sighed sadly. "Yes, Thalu. A place I hoped to forget. How long have you known?"

Lebiced put him at ease. "Long enough. I know your mother Margo, born of Sirius the son of my sister Cedra. Xantir blood runs in many families. The Redmanes are a proud clan. They remained strong after the great fire and have been excellent judges of character. That's why Bethany picked you, after all. Xantir may not be a signatory to the Westwood Treaty, but we do take interest in the moods of the lands around us. Valantir and Stonehaven especially."

Jonah was dumbfounded. Was there anything this wizard did not know? Or anyone not related to him?

Soon enough, they were at the public vaults.

"I am Lord Blackthorn, I wish to open my storage room today," Jonah informed a young clerk.

The clerk motioned to his manager nearby to approach and oversee business. "Purpose of visiting your chamber, sir?" the clerk asked.

Jonah was slightly annoyed at this. he was perfectly within his rights to decide the fate of his own property. "I have need of my funds. If you don't mind?"

The vault manager arrived and cleared his throat. "We must limit access, I'm afraid. We are under austerity measures. Standard policy."

Jonah challenged, "Limit? The contents of that room are MY family inheritance. By what rights do you deny it to me?"

The manager coughed twice and, in a dry tone, explained, "Under contract, we, the trustees of said property, are allowed to invest a portion, thereof, to foster dividends on your deposits. Presently, said portion is on loan and unavailable. Terribly sorry."

Jonah gritted his teeth. "As primary beneficiary, I am entitled to dispose of MY deposits as I see fit!"

The manager squirmed and muttered, "That right was waived a year ago, under new policies, duly notified by courier to your home, Number Twelve, River Street."

Jonah growled, "I recall no such thing!"

The manager was sweating now. "I, ah, believe your father-in-law signed for it ..."

Jonah clenched his fingers and turned his head to shut the manager out of his vision.

A moment later, Jonah leaned forward with teeth bared, "My father-in-law, Connor Redmane, is now deceased, and I, the rightful owner of SAID property, have not been duly informed by him or you, and if I must challenge it in court, SO BE IT."

The manager backpedaled a few steps. "Ahhh ... that would be ... rather distasteful, perhaps we can discuss a compromise ..."

Jonah was dumbfounded. "Compromise? You think you are doing me a favor? What kind of fool do you take me for?"

Lebiced intervened, "I'm quite sure the manager here wishes to preserve peace and goodwill in this matter, yes?"

The manager nodded vigorously with a nervous smile.

"Let's talk then, shall we?" Lebiced directed.

The four of them moved to a more private room to negotiate. The manager was first to sit at a small table. "Can I have your word that this will be kept in strict confidence?"

Jonah grumbled, "*My* word? What about *your* word that I shall not be cheated out of rightful property?"

The manager placated, "Please, we are not here to cheat you ..."

Lebiced corrected, "Perhaps a gesture of good faith, since words are doing so little to restore peace?"

The vault manager looked to his clerk for support, but he did not receive any, so he looked at Lebiced with his disarmingly warm smile, then at Jonah's angry glare, and finally shrugged in surrender. "Oh, all right … I'll open the room …"

Lebiced whispered, "Thank you."

* * *

"Hello, Bethany? Are you home?" a woman called.

Bethany answered the door, "Rebecca, hi! What brings you? I thought you had that Royal Inn to run. Come on in."

Rebecca hugged Bethany in greeting and continued, "I do have an inn, but business is slow. They started flocking to the Mariner's Inn after that hot-tempered monk began giving lectures there. The entire town has turned on your brother, and I wanted to apologize to him for leaving during his father's memorial when he needed support most. It's just … I'm afraid to speak to him, and I was not prepared for such outbursts and animosity twixt him and the abbey … I'm terribly sorry. I … wish I could have been of more help."

Bethany asked, "What could you have done? I'm afraid the people want blood and tears for their twisted amusement..."

Rebecca answered, "When I heard a rumor about Conrad deserting the baron for some nameless bride offered by Kazius, that was all I could stand. I soured the drinks, and the crowd left early. I'm afraid word has gotten out somehow. Or they drifted on their own."

Bethany concluded, "So they turned on you, too? All to punish my brother … does their indiscriminate hatred ever stop?" Bethany got an idea. "My husband might be of help, if ... well, if expenses are piling up."

Rebecca smiled. "Thank you, but I will manage. It was sweet of you to offer.

Wait! Didn't you have three maids?"

Bethany frowned sadly. "Yes, I had to let two go. I am being punished for my brother's sake as well."

Rebecca wondered aloud, "But if you had to let two go, how can you offer your husband's help? What am I not understanding?"

Bethany confessed, "The source of his money brings me great pain. I ... cannot speak of it. Jonah is not to blame, but ..."

Rebecca prodded, "But?"

Bethany sobbed, "There is bad blood between our ancestors ... please do not ask more of me."

Rebecca embraced her. "I'm sorry. I think I understand. How is your daughter?"

Bethany gave a weak smile. "She is well ... such a bright child. Already inspecting her dollhouse to see how it is built. She has ideas on how to make it a bigger one. Curious hobby for a girl. Maybe she gets it from her grandfather Connor. She does seem to miss him."

Rebecca smiled brightly. "Of course, she does. I've never once heard a bad word about him. And ... the last words I heard him whisper, as I looked in his eyes, were 'good son' ... he heard me confessing what a fine man Conrad had become." Rebecca began weeping.

Bethany wept too, taking Rebecca's hands and clasping them tightly. "My brother has been so very lonely. I'm glad someone fancies him."

Rebecca blushed. "Am I really that obvious?"

Bethany grinned affirmatively, nodded, and laughed before giving Rebecca another hug.

Chapter Twenty-Two
Pawns Advancing

A man in ornate red robes with golden cuffs bearing a scepter of brass and maplewood called out, "The leader barks."

Another man replied from the shadows, "The pack bites, " and stepped into the torchlight of the subcellars. Council member Vamanastral bowed. "Barton's message states we are to allow the witch free access to the passages leading to the royal bath. And not to question her need for them."

The cloaked man in gray mused, "The seal was genuine? You are sure?"

Vamanastral answered, "Quite positive. Embossed on the inside with the clan symbol and his own, tied in red leather. Any who dare to forge his letters are hunted and killed in a matter of days. Even Malsain would not defy him."

The second man bowed. "Then it shall be done as instructed, although I fear the blackbirds already know of this plot against the king."

The council member dropped his scepter in shock. "You?"

Councilman Sandraz grinned. "Yes," and stabbed him.

Two more men emerged from behind storage crates and barrels in the shadowed corners of the room and dragged away the body as it wheezed its last parcels of air.

"Move to phase three," Sandraz instructed the others, "... and seal off these tunnels to outsiders. The chaos sorceress must not reach the king."

Sandraz then hurried to warn King William Goldlion of the plot in motion against him, while his blackbirds cleaned up all traces of bloodshed. It took Sandraz ten minutes to evade chaos spies and agents on the way to the king's throne room.

"Sire, I have news of a plot against your life. One of the council has betrayed you. A chaos witch is involved. There could be other insiders ..."

William wearily nodded his head. "Your news has reached tired ears, taxed beyond all care or comfort by the petty, acrimonious bickerings of the council, the pitiful pleas of the poor, and the malicious schemes of foreign powers. Bother me not with trivial details. Do whatever you must to handle the matter. I leave it to you, Sandraz. I wish to be left in peace."

Sandraz protested, "Sire, they know about ..."

And the King interrupted, "What they know is your concern. My ears still echo with the nonsense of dragons. I cannot believe the Dwarves, under the command of King Gravnar Anvilhammer, have the motive or the means to send such foul creatures against our borders, and the council ... you were there, why am I repeating myself?"

Sandraz cast pained eyes at the floor, nodding once in acquiescence. "Then, by your leave, Your Majesty ..."

William added, "Yes, all fine and good. Be done with it. Where did that wizard go to, anyway?"

Sandraz replied, "I am told he left with Jonah of Oakthorn, sire.

Another threat moves against Valantir as we speak."

William frowned, "Who is it THIS time? The goblins again?"

Sandraz finished, "Kazius of Razadur is amassing mercenaries from all quarters as his father once did. The Elves ..."

William quipped, "Yes, yes, I know. Scores of them died alongside my father in Shadval. My mother became regent when I was three. I cannot forget, not even if I drained entire barrels of the darkest Dwarven ale, the strongest Elven wine and ..."

Finally the king's wife Lissa Firebird spoke, "Be not so bitterly obsessed with the shadows of your tormented past, my husband. Sandraz has patiently heard the story before. Can you not be kind, as befits a loyal ally, William. He has been helping above and beyond his station."

The king merely grunted in exasperation as Sandraz bowed stiffly in forced courtesy before turning to leave in angry silence. Queen Lissa gave William a cold stare of disbelief, "Darling, your ill temper is clouding everything and shall soon snuff out every flicker of joy in the land if this continues. Come take a bath with me …"

William grumbled, "Now?"

Lissa took his hand and tugged. "Yes, now. Before you drive away the last real friend you may ever have."

The king sighed and allowed his wife to lead him away from the throne.

* * *

Outside the city gates, beyond the sight of the sentries, a lone man kept to the shadows of the trees. "I demand to know who in the nine hells dares to summon me with this cursed threat of blackmail!" he called to the edge of the water.

A woman stepped partially into the light, her hooded cloak still concealing her face. "One who knows what REALLY happened at the waterfall those many years ago, before you were forced into exile," she said with an air of authority and sneering satisfaction.

The man growled, "Did Helen put you up to this, you witch?"

Winter finally stepped fully into the daylight and drew her hood back, "Your wife? No, Helen has nothing to do with my purpose here. No, my business is within the capitol, and you are going to see that I get in without delay or hindrance."

Bravane Redoak the Elder bared his teeth in a snarling protest. "You ask much, whoever you are!"

Winter displayed a wicked grin. "You'd like to know, and when I tell you, I expect full co-operation … "

Bravane the Second restrained his fury as he declared, "Preposterous! It will take more than your silence and discretion to bend me to your treachery!"

Winter grinned even more, taunting, "Oh, yes, you will bend because, not only do I know about your sons, I am the mother of your grandson! Fail me, and you will never lay eyes on him, but prove useful, and I may restore your legacy. And you must choose before nightfall."

Bravane stammered, "Impossible. My son has no heir …"

Winter laughed. "He is ignorant of it. He was stone drunk like _your_ father! Amazing that he finished at all …"

Bravane the Elder fell to his knees, stunned. "I … yield."

Winter smiled. "I commend your intelligence."

* * *

"Heed the words of one who served a keeper of order. I tell you that Conrad sold out his baron for a dark-skinned bride promised by Kazius, and it was Conrad's sister who brokered the deal. I heard them whispering in the dark by the riverbank the night before Ramus was murdered by his hand! And then he dared strike down Eledar for exposing the truth! Yet his baron forgave him and shields him from justice! But no longer. For on the morrow, he must answer in a trial by combat! He will die painfully. I promise you. Then you will see the justice of the lawgiver who watches from above!" Darmid exhorted the crowd inside the Mariner's Inn.

The peasants cheered in drunken zealotry, raising mugs and voices in unison.

Jonah saw enough; his anger would not be swayed this time. "ENOUGH! You rabble- rousing snake. You will answer for the crime of endangering the safety of the barony, by inciting such riots as this!" Jonah shouted as he drew his sword and strode forward.

The peasants fled from the seething anger in his eyes, trampling each other in their haste for the door.

Darmid flashed an evil grin. "You were lucky last time, betrayer ..."

Before Jonah could blink, Darmid's hand thrust forward, releasing a throwing dirk that struck Jonah's collarbone, drawing blood, and Darmid advanced with a dagger in the other hand.

Jonah was suddenly dizzy. "I know who you serve now, snake," he mumbled as he ducked to the right of Darmid's lunge. Jonah misjudged his own stride and grabbed at Darmid's left arm to keep from falling.

Darmid howled in pain and dropped his dagger. Jonah found his vision blurring and slumped to one knee. Darmid grabbed Jonah's collar and headbutted him, making Jonah drop his sword. Other honor guards were filing into the inn to investigate, and Darmid decided to flee through the window overlooking the riverbank. One of the men caught Jonah by the armpits as he fell and saw the discoloration around the shallow cut to the collarbone.

"Summon the physician! Jonah has been poisoned! HURRY!"

And hurry they did; Jonah was second in command under Conrad. None wanted to be the bearer of bad news. James arrived minutes later and examined the throwing dirk on the floor.

"Quick! Fetch me the ashes from the fireplace over there! You! Get water and whiskey! You! Get a clean rag, and you ... hold his head up. Keep him elevated. You, get Savadi or Helen! Go!"

Jonah's last spoken word as he faded out was "Bethany."

* * *

A chill wind blew from the north, against a lone man paddling in a stolen canoe, with no compass to steer by, over the Winding Sea that separated Mojara from Agama, Stonehaven, and Valantir. He had very little luck at the tavern, and, therefore, no idea where Adrian was going.

Alex Mill had thrown caution to the wind and given chase anyway. The shortest crossing of the sea was over seventy miles. Alex the Meek knew not the patterns of the stars, nor the currents, and did not even plan for food and water. After long hours of paddling, his arms became lead weights that burned with every effort to move them. His vision blurred with fatigue, his throat dry for lack of fresh water, he slumped backward in the canoe, and his boat drifted at the mercy of the sea. Exhaustion overtook him, and he faded into a dark, dreamless slumber for many hours. He awoke in a strange subterranean cavern on a sandbank, adorned with crystals that gave a golden-hued light, and the rocks here were covered in seaweed and moss.

"How did I get here?" he whispered, though he was alone.

His pilfered canoe was standing on end, leaning against a rock wall to dry out. He must have lost the paddle; it was nowhere to be seen. At the far end of this cavern, he saw a vast pool of calm water. He could smell the salt in it. He struggled to speak, to call out to whoever was near, but again, his throat was too dry, he could barely speak or even swallow.

He searched the cavern and found a tunnel, which sloped upward gradually.

After a couple twists and turns, the tunnel opened into another chamber, a vast room with more pools of water, columns of white marble at one end, in what looked like a temple. A small table of polished stone to the right had an altar cloth over it, with seashells and pearls and brilliant blue lustrous gems. Alex Mill approached warily. Behind a column on the left was a silvery pitcher, full of water. He looked closely and was overcome by thirst. He drank without thinking. The cool, clean mineral water was the best he had ever had. He sighed with relief and explored the temple. And was soon dumbstruck to see the backside of a very tall, naked woman with flowing red hair, facing a short pedestal of granite with a recessed basin of water, in the middle of a semicircle of small stone benches.

"You are the third mortal to visit here," she said without turning.

Alex thought of running, but where could he go?

"Be seated, one called Alex."

He dared not refuse, such was her tone; though calm and neutral, it carried authority. The woman strode to a far bench and retrieved her white tunic with yellow accents, donning it gracefully, not out of modesty, but to put her visitor at ease. She turned to face him, finally. "You seek two men, who have already delivered their goods, plus your daughter, far east of here. You would have died at their hands. Sal alone is stronger and has no fear of combat. While you, would hesitate, and be the first to sustain injury. Your wife would learn of your death and follow your footsteps to her doom, leaving your daughter alone without family or friend, at the mercy of men who forget the meaning of the word. And now, you wonder why a goddess would bother with such things as one family of ordinary mortals with such humble origins as you have. I will tell you. The longevity of immortals leads us to complacency, boredom, and discontent. We forget what true courage is. Love decays into mere jealousy and obsession, and our true passions grow dull. Your courage in the face of overwhelming odds, contrasting your lifetime spent in fear, reminded me of someone … "

Alex the Meek gulped. "And who would that be?"

"A man named Kaedrus Moondreams from the nation of Mojara, whose home is now cursed, by me. He was named for visions that appeared to him in the moonlight, and all that remains of him now, is his daughter. OUR daughter. He spoke of things people wished not to hear, of past, present, and future. He saw through their falsehoods, their petty facades, and for this, they despised him. He was lonely among them. And I, too, was lonely, out of neglect. My sons grew up craving more power and have turned to violence. I provide nothing of what they seek. But in each other, Kaedrus and I were happy while he lived. And we had a happy child, until ... the day Kazius Auguron of Razadur sent men, under the pretense of tax collection, in search of enchanted weapons rumored to belong to Kaedrus. By your calendar, it was the year 1551. The memory poisons my daughter ... and now yours will suffer if you fail. You must return to the surface and enlist help. You cannot prevail alone."

Alex feared to ask, but had to know. "If you can foresee so much, then how ..."

Syrene finished his sentence, "How could Kaedrus be harmed and murdered? My jealous husband had intervened, distracting my attention, while Kazius made his move, misled by rumors. The item he sought belonged not to Kaedrus, but to me. This is why a mortal was entrusted with my daughter's safety. Her half-brothers care nothing if she lives or dies, and my vindictive, power-mad, and jealous husband would happily see her dead. You should leave before he decides to pay a visit."

Alex's eyes popped wide open in dreadful shock, and he wasted no time running for the canoe down the tunnel.

Chapter Twenty-Three
Decisions

"Why is this child here? This was not part of the bargain, Adrian," Kazius hissed in contempt and rage.

Another voice from north of the bay called out, "Quite correct, errant one. It was I who made arrangements for any orphans that needed a new home ..."

Kazius turned to the man in black robes and red trim. "And who are you to meddle in my affairs and mock the leadership of Razadur?"

The tall man in black responded, "You are ignorant of my influence because I wished it so, son of the Augurons. Your tongue is ... too careless to entrust my secrets to. And ignorant you will stay ..."

Kazius drew his sword, ready to lunge, but a motion of the man's hand held him frozen.

"This is exactly why you are unfit for the secrets I wield, o tempestuous orphan. The loss of your mother in Shadval, the abandonment by your power thirsty father, such pain it brings you, weakling," Barton sneered.

Adrian dragged the bound and gagged little girl to Barton and kneeled with one palm open, while Sal kept his mouth shut and stayed near the boat. Barton dryly observed with a tone of sneering contempt. "Yes, your greed is legend, merchant. Why else would you appear? Your eyes betray your suffering, whelp. Your wife knows your sins. And again you flee from your past, how predictable.

Here," the leader of the Alpha clan scoffed as he tossed the bag of coin to Adrian.

"Ah, yes, the rogue. Come on out where we can see you, assassin, " Barton turned his head as he spoke to the treeline fifty feet away.

Agent Eleven complied in his best imitation of nonchalance, "I bring word to Kazius from the power I serve."

Barton just laughed. "Yes, of course, you have been ordered to spoil the great secret you cherish keeping from him. It shall be amusing to watch. I release him thus …"

And Kazius fell to his knees. "Insolent magician! You shall rue this

insult!" Kazius barked indignantly.

Adrian backed away and departed with Sal in the boat.

Barton just crossed his arms. "The boasts of overgrown children do not frighten me, Kazius. Do try to be original once in a solar cycle …"

Agent Eleven had a cold look in his eyes, as one who arrived too late for dessert, and weakly tossed the signet ring to a startled Kazius who demanded, "What is this about? Has my sister gone mad or did some jealous lover finally take a blade to her?"

Agent Eleven grinned with satisfaction under his mask, savoring the last bit of pleasure he was going to have with Kazius. "Your sister has other business, *pawn*."

Something about the tone set Kazius off again, who lunged at Eleven with his sword. The rogue rolled underneath and sprang back on his feet for the next attack. Kazius swung wildly, as D'aarzane backflipped beyond reach. Kazius charged again and again, until he slipped on wet sand and fell on his face. Barton levitated the bound and gagged child and left the others to fend for themselves. The army of Razadur just stood there, fearing both the wrath of Kazius and the ruins of Shadval to the north of the bay.

D'aarzane taunted once more, "Pathetic, old man. You were never a match for me, ever. But I will tell you anyway … the ring you recognize as the Auguron crest is from none other than the one who created you!"

Kazius propped onto his elbows and knees, his eyes wide in horror. "No, it cannot be …"

The rogue grinned again. "Yes … he has gained power over the undead and even over dragons. And he need never sleep again! He is the one the Elves fear! You poor lamb …"

And then Kazius saw a fog rolling in from the north, billowing from a small cluster of trees west of the ruins in the distance. His mouth opened to speak, but his voice failed him. From within the fog, a figure emerged, tall, skeletal, clad in armor and rags. The half-moon embers in his eye sockets expressing his malice and cruelty. The army of Razadur dropped their weapons and ran in terror ... as Arius conjured a dust storm from nowhere, blinding them and causing them to trample each other to death in their panic. Kazius recoiled in terror as his entire army was reduced to a dozen stragglers. The mummified features of his father flashed a sepulchral grin of grayish teeth, and the Lich's voice, akin to rustling leaves and tumbling gravel, sounded, "Obedient servants are such a rarity these days. I thank you for your contributions, *pawn*. You may return to the castle you pride yourself in ..."

And Arius waved his hand again, causing the bodies to rise, one by one, as stiff, clumsy, unblinking mockeries of life.

Kazius quickly ran to the boats, kicked them loose of the sand, and jumped into the last one.

The stragglers of his army ran into the water to grab hold of a spare boat and flee with him. Two of them were mauled and eaten before they could clear the shallow surf. Arius turned to D'aarzane. "Your next assignment requires souvenirs from down below ... some of them should still be functional.

* * *

"The lady is my new personal attendant. I will vouch for her. Let us pass," Bravane the Elder declared at the gate.

The taller sentry replied, "New orders, sir. All visitors must be cleared by Councilman Sandraz or by Councilman Adam Walter Coppergrass, there is a plot against the king, we have to insist on the removal of all weapons."

While the shorter one gestured for them to reveal and surrender all such items. Bravane snarled, "For pity's sake, who is going to invade here under cloud of dragons? Get a grip, man ... does Sandraz wish me to face a dragon bare handed?"

While Winter used her wiles: "Search away, handsome. I won't mind," she purred suggestively.

The shorter man eagerly accepted the invitation, taking his time feeling her clothing and contents.

Bravane rolled his eyes. "Hades, woman! I don't have all night."

Winter just winked at him as the sentry moved around in front of her, and she brought her right hand down swiftly on the man's neck, leaving a tiny red puncture from her ring ... the guard froze instantly and slumped over, while the other sentry turned to run, calling for help as Winter lifted the downed man's crossbow and loosed a bolt right in the taller man's back.

"Now you've done it, witch!" Bravane protested.

"Shut up and bind this one behind the tree line. Hurry!" Winter hissed back.

As Bravane complied with her strategy, Winter tossed away the crossbow and ran under the gate, calling, "Help! Intruder at the gate! He tried to kidnap me!"

Bravane the Elder heard and cursed under his breath as he ran deeper into the woods. "Treacherous whores … wench deserves to hang for this … the wicked bitch … I swear on all my fathers she will rue this day …"

Without even thinking where he was going, he found himself circling north to his old hunting grounds, just west of the waterfall where he constructed his hermit cabin, where he had lived in exile until joining the council and attempting to live among people again. Every year, on Donald's birthday, he returned to the cabin to pay homage to the son he lost. The loss of which almost made him murder the younger one in a fit of insanity. He was thwarted in his effort by Conrad that day. Conrad, the nephew of Helen through her sister, was also the great nephew of Bravane the Elder's own mother Susan through her brother Seamus. Bravane the Second was overcome with grief and rage to do such a thing, and when Helen found out, she drove her husband out under threat of revealing his great shame. He regretted his actions each and every single day that he lived. To lose his family, thus, almost drove him to take his own life. He wanted to, before a voice in the water stopped him. A woman called to him in his own mind, which was surely driven over the edge of insanity to see a woman's face in the water talking to him. She said he was destined for better days ahead and would redeem himself. The voice was so certain then; she gave him strength. He never heard the voice again and wondered if it was ever real. That woman with the red hair, more beautiful than any he had ever seen. Yes, he must have been mad.

* * *

Baron Bravane Redoak the Third took a seat facing Mediator General Blackhull, who looked over his spectacles at the baron. "I heard about Jonah. I'm very sorry for his family. What can I do for you, Baron?"

Bravane had trouble speaking, every time he parted his lips, more grief choked him up. So Alex Redoak spoke on his behalf. "We may need to pull the security detail from the courthouse if Kazius invades Valantir as expected, and thus delay the trials."

Blackhull mused, "Ahh, now <u>there</u> things get complicated. The abbey does have some jurisdiction in the matter and had agreed to trial by combat. Conrad was scheduled for this morning, but the champion acting on Eledar's behalf has already fled because he is the same man who attacked Jonah. This puts me in a bind. The matter has to be settled according to evidence, of which we have so little. What am I to do then? The town is clamoring for blood, and I need compelling proof to quiet them down."

Alex Redoak cleared his throat and challenged, "Tell me, Magistrate. What business does a monk have with poisoned daggers? Tell me how that is not proof of evil intentions ..."

Blackhull conceded, "You do have a point.

This calls for a new investigation. Of course, the abbey will be quite displeased, but I have no other choice under the current circumstances."

Alex responded, "Thank you. We will keep you posted, and hope to catch the true villains."

* * *

Elsewhere in the Blackthorn house: "WHY? Why us? Why, Jonah? WHY?" Bethany wailed in rage, despair, and sorrow, as Savadi and Helen did their best to tend Jonah's comatose and pale mortal shell.

Conrad could find no words, and just held his sister close as she pounded her fists on his breastplate in utter helplessness. Even Devi was no comfort now, as she hugged her mommy's leg for dear life. James returned from his errand and reported, "I requested use of the abbey's library and other resources, but Arbiter Dhasa refused to grant it. The crotchety old bastard ... perhaps the Elves would know, but I fear the delays will be Jonah's doom."

Conrad spoke in a resolute tone, "Then we take Jonah to the Elves. get the horses. We leave within the hour."

James stayed behind with Nell to look after Bethany's children, and the others departed after leaving a message for the baron.

* * *

"Where do you live, miss?" the sentry asked.

A middle-aged, but strikingly attractive woman replied, "I'm visiting my uncle, Arthur Kenneth Clayton, but he was not here to meet me ... he is dreadfully absent-minded sometimes ..."

The sentry told her, "You wait here. He is a busy man."

As the man faded from sight, Winter displayed an evil grin as she whispered, "Yes, do toddle along, fool ... " as she began exploring the market sector in search of someone. But the man she expected was nowhere to be seen; the shadows of the sun turned clockwise by about 40 degrees since she arrived, and daylight was soon to end. Winter preferred not to deal with ruffians so far from home for fear of exposure. "Curse that councilman! Where is he?" She began to size up security around the wealthier merchants, looking for weaknesses. And then she spotted a small child exploiting one of those weaknesses, a break in their field of vision near the cart with the silk scarves. "He must not rate his own men, " Winter said to herself.

A voice behind her said, "No, he does not."

Winter flinched, and then berated the man, "Took you long enough. Where is Vamanastral?"

Arthur explained, "He is missing. We suspect his cover was blown, and the blackbirds got him. Now let's leave before someone sees you."

"Did they break the code? Others are at risk ..." Winter whispered as they turned a street corner. Arthur kept silent until safely behind the doors of his own manor.

"They must have, but changing the codes now will alert them. We don't know who we can trust anymore. Malsain has been exposed, too. The whole syndicate network is in peril. We have more than just blackbirds to worry about.

The centaurs up north are hunting down the poachers, and the pirates are in trouble, too, one of their new recruits went berserk. Some guy named Garzon. They say he is death incarnate with a battle axe. Everything is falling apart around us. Your father is going to pop rivets when he hears about it. We don't dare tell him. Certain death if we do. You pretend I never told you. Promise me."

Winter shook her head no. "He would torture me in spite of the blood curse, and he is already insane. Use your head for once, Arthur. You know I cannot make that promise. I will only tell if he asks. The rest of you are on your own. The less I know of your business, the better for both of us."

Arthur nodded. "Yes, you are right. I've cleaned up the guest room for you. You are lucky the sentry never asked about our relatives. I was not expecting you."

Winter finished, "Cannot be helped. You know how insidious my father is."

Arthur nodded again, and he showed her to the room upstairs.

* * *

"Trial of Blackwolves versus Redoaks and Ramus now in session," the magistrate declared. "You are charged with trespassing, kidnapping, murder, blackmailing, and larceny in the five kingdoms joined by the treaty of Westwood. How do the Blackwolves plead?"

The counsel for Danny rose to speak, "Daniel pleads guilty conscience and wishes asylum in return for sharing critical intelligence."

The other three Blackwolves jumped from their seats to take vengeance. One was grabbed by the collar and slammed, face first, into the floor. A second got elbowed in the throat, and the third vaulted himself over the intervening deputy, only to be brought to his knees, clutching his head in agony by the tuning fork effect of Tyrus and his trident. Tyton Umbral watched with amusement from the audience.

The next sound was a banging gavel and the irate mediator general barking: "Order! Restrain those three properly and we will resume court proceedings."

The three other blackwolves were thus wrestled and shackled to their chairs, over their many vulgar protests. "Court has considered your plea, and will conclude the decision at a later date after hearing testimony. How do the <u>other</u> accused parties plead?"

The leader of the gang strained against his bindings to lean forward. "Not guilty! That traitor blackmailed us into working for Kazius and ..."

The gavel sounded again, "Order! The short answer will suffice. Call the first witness."

The regional solicitor spoke, "Prosecution calls Amanda Redoak to the stand."

Her father Alex held her hand tenderly as she stood to approach and gently let go.

Amanda stared at the floor as she passed the counsel's tables.

An assistant to the mediator general recited the oath to Amanda, "Do you swear on the land, that you shall speak the truth without omission or misdirection, so help you powers above?"

Amanda raised her right hand and answered, "Yes, I shall."

The solicitor extended his upturned palm toward the witness stand. "Please have a seat."

Once she was seated the solicitor began, "If you could describe to us, the time and location of your ordeal and who was involved."

Amanda gathered her will, not accustomed to speaking before a large crowd. "It was the twelfth day, last month. I was seized from within the front gates of Redoak Manor by those men (pointing)."

One of the bandits was about to protest when a hand clamped around his neck. It was the same old deputy he had mouthed off to in the jail. The de facto leader coughed once and fell silent in fear. The deputy smiled and let go.

The solicitor continued: "And the time of day?"

Amanda answered: "It was early afternoon, bright daylight. One of them followed me to the gate with ale in his beard, and then another one put a sack over me."

Counsel for Blackwolves stood, "Then you could not possibly identify all of them ..."

Blackhull banged his gavel. "Out of turn, counsel. Save it for cross exam. Solicitor, proceed."

The next query was more focused. "Please enlighten the jury to the details of your captivity."

Amanda rubbed her brows before speaking. "I remember being tied to a tree, and I was gagged. I saw their faces by the campfire, five of them. Laughing themselves hoarse over their escapades and red wine."

The blackwolves squirmed in their seats.

"Told ya we shoulda blind ..." one whispered.

"Shut up weasel!" the leader hissed.

Counsel for the Blackwolves hit them both over the head with a rolled up parchment. Magistrate Blackhull made a comment with a sarcastic barb in it, "Gentlemen, if our style of justice is too boring for your liking, perhaps you would prefer the arena I hear so much about in your former base of operations ..."

The gang leader gulped. "Uhhh ... that won't be necessary ..."

Blackhull smiled before calling the defense counsel forward. "You may now begin cross exam."

The counsel nodded, "Is it not true you were upset by the disappearance of Conrad that day?"

Amanda blurted, "Of course I was, what does ..."

Blackhull interrupted, "Get to the point, counsel."

Defense cleared his throat, "Yes, Your Honor, I was about to do so."

Blackhull gave an incredulous look over his spectacles.

The defense continued, "Witness admitted she did not see all five during her abduction, and could have been handed off ..."

Amanda snapped, "The man with ale in his beard was there at the campfire, and their body odor was unmistakable. It was the same men, I tell you!"

The defense challenged, "Describe please, for the jury, how you recognize their body odor ..."

The solicitor objected, "Defense is badgering the witness!"

Blackhull frowned. "Counsel, please refrain from your theatrics and cheap character assassinations. First warning. Continue."

The defense asked, "How does a jury decide a man's identity based on smell? It's preposterous ... "

Amanda screeched, "They all smelled of red wine, ale, sweat, and venison, and had not bathed for many weeks!"

The solicitor smiled while defense looked as if his favorite dinner had burned black.

"No further questions, Your Honor."

Blackhull prodded, "Solicitor? Proceed."

The prosecution asked, "What other characteristics could you identify on them?"

Amanda paused. "Well ... the one who punched me had a wolf's head tattoo on his left bicep; they all do. A solid black one."

The solicitor smiled again "That will do for now. Next witness ... thank you, Miss Redoak."

The de facto leader was unshackled to allow him to approach the bench. The assistant recited, "Do you ..."

The bandit blurted, "Yeah, yeah, let's get on with it ..."

Blackhull removed his spectacles and leaned over the bench. "The fine for contempt is ten eagles. Do you wish to pay or comply with the formalities?"

The bandit leader scowled, "Comply ..."

Blackhull sat back and instructed them to start over.

"Do you swear on the land, that you shall speak the truth ..."

The bandit gritted his teeth at these words. "Aye, I swear on this forsaken ..."

The gavel sounded again, "Two counts of contempt, twenty eagle fine. Get this man out of my court!"

The old deputy grinned as they put the shackles back on and escorted him out.

"Next witness, please ..." Blackhull prompted with irritation.

The solicitor called Danny forward, who took the oath without further drama.

"Let's start with your account of the twelfth day in question. Who was there?" the prosecution asked. Danny avoided eye contact with the other wolves, "The five of us had split off from our original dozen to cause trouble in Oakthorn.

Kazius told us to kidnap a noble, and the Lady Amanda was convenient. I was the one on top of the wall with the scaling rope."

The solicitor prodded, "Please detail the five present that day."

Danny continued, "Myself, the two men at the table, plus one who died in Valantir, and the one dragged out in shackles."

Next, he was asked to verify Amanda's other testimonies. Danny showed his tattoo, and verified that yes, red wine, venison and ale had been their staple diet for their entire mission, with occasional mushrooms and nuts and berries when game was scarce (which was often).

"Now, can you tell us why kidnapping a noble was so important to Kazius?" the solicitor queried.

Danny answered, "I never questioned his orders before I became sober. I was like them, only cared about the money and getting drunk. But I can give you what I do know …"

The prosecution nudged, "Please enlighten the jury."

Danny gathered his courage. "Kazius cut us loose because we failed to finish our task and because I told him things he already knew about a girl with a bounty on her head, that the Elves knew who she was. And Kazius was always a sore loser. He stinks at chess, lousy pawn structure …"

Defense protested, "How is this relevant to the day of the twelfth?"

Danny interjected, "Your Honor, forgive me. I am getting to that."

Blackhull smiled, "Please proceed."

Danny picked up his narrative, "I'm explaining the character of the man who sent us here. By evidence of the petty things he chooses to punish, including games of chess with his general. He would toss the entire board across the room after losing, which was often because he relied too much on his knights and his queen; his bishops were always blocked in by his pawns, and his rooks too. Kazius is not adept at multi-pronged attacks. But General Axegrind is, and so was the father of Kazius. I hear stories about him, Arius, I mean. Diabolical, insidious, evil man."

Blackhull prodded, "This is an interesting story, but please tell the jury how this applies to the kidnapping."

Danny nodded. "Okay. So Kazius relies on brute force. He's arrogant. He ordered the kidnapping, but I don't think he planned it. He does not have that sort of mind. He's being used. Somebody else is pulling the strings. And he was extra edgy when he kicked me out."

Blackhull sighed, "Relevance, please. The short version first."

Danny tried to comply, "Right. Short version. He was really mad, more than usual. The camp did not feel right. Axegrind was demoralized, too. They had a major setback, and he took it out on me ..."

Blackhull cut him off, "The jury and the Lady Amanda do not seem enlightened by this ..."

Danny tied it together, "I was trying to say, the kidnapping may not matter to Kazius, but to someone else. It's not his style. But he gave the order. He certainly doesn't accept orders from Axegrind, so it has to be someone else, from outside Razadur.

Kazius is a pawn himself. That's what I'm saying."

The regional solicitor groaned. "Possible. However, that is outside the scope of the trial. We are no closer than before to remedy or restitution for Redoak, nor to a suitable verdict on the Blackwolves. Both of whom are fast asleep ..."

Blackhull grinned. "Asylum granted, lad. Court adjourned for lunch."

Light snoring could be heard at the defense table.

As Danny passed the outer barrister, Tyrianna hissed, "I'm never speaking to you again!"

* * *

"His tracks turn north here at the riverbank, toward the Dragon Ridge mountains. Look ..."

Skorvald pointed at the ground. His band of barbarians saddled up again and gave chase, certain the ill-mannered monk was less than half a day ahead of them. A reckoning was due for the attack on the man who hired them only hours before the gutter rat laid him low.

They rode slowly among the sparse tree cover, alert for any signs of ambush or booby traps. They reached the foothills by nightfall and set camp to rest the horses.

"I thought we were to meet with the Elves in Valantir," said one of the men.

Skorvald chimed in, "This monk skulks like a spy. I wager he is helping the enemy. We have a chance to smoke him out and expose their plans. I say we take it."

The men gave a wrinkle of the lips and nodded in agreement.

As they settled down, Skorvald wrinkled his nose in revulsion as he caught whiff of a biting and pungently bitter odor. Northeast of their campsite, he traced the scent to a sheltered hollow between some large tree roots, one wide enough for a small framed man to curl up in it, wherein Skorvald discovered a clump of ashes. The monk's tracks were visible here also.

"Our quarry has a profound weakness for opium. Now we know he will squeal most eagerly for lack of it!"

Immediately the men feigned mockeries of a stripling begging for mercy, competing for who could make the most convincing facial contortions and hand gestures, and laughing well into the night, after draining a pint of mead and eating the last of the cornbread and smoked salmon.

* * *

Faraway in Valantir, Jonah fell off the bed and vomited in great convulsions, waking Bethany out of her inadequate sleep. She was pale with exhaustion and worry, and weakly smiled in relief, that Jonah was awake at last. Ravenna was there, too, after negotiations on behalf of Stonehaven for material aid, and one of the sentries by the doorway went to summon the others. Helen, Savadi, Conrad and several Elves arrived to witness Jonah's slow recovery.

"Please, I'm a wreck right now ..." Jonah wearily pleaded to his observers.

Bethany caressed his hair in her fingers and rained kisses of gratitude on his forehead. "I missed you more than water and daylight, darling husband ..."

The Elves mopped up his mess, and his visitors bowed or waved as they turned to leave the room, all save Bethany who hugged Jonah tightly for many long minutes and helped him back into bed to tuck him in.

"Love you, too, darling," Jonah mumbled in his sluggish state as he drifted off to dreamland once more. And Bethany tucked her head over his shoulder, drifting off right behind him.

* * *

"Are you insane? Why would I march into Mojara and ... allow my father's murderers to finish the job?" Tyrianna blurted in defiant rage.

"They won't because they will not expect any of this. I will collect the fee, Your tall friend here will collect you from their clutches, and the agents of Mojara will collect flowers on their graves. The barony will gain necessary funds, and Kazius will feel torn between objectives when the news reaches him, and it will. He is already demoralized. He cannot wage a campaign on two fronts," Tyton explained matter of factly.

"You are going to trust the word of a thief in the courtroom? " Tyrianna challenged.

The guildmaster of the Obsidian Owls replied, "I don't need to. Danny is not the only living witness to the flaws of King Auguron of Razadur. I know his ways and weaknesses."

Tyrianna shot back, "Oh? You have some source who escaped detection all these years within his ranks?"

Tyton smiled. "Yes, I do. I have my own networks in many lands."

Tyrianna huffed in disbelief, "You are still mad. There is nothing that would bring me back to … the place of his death …"

Tyton turned his head ever so slightly, to catch a glimpse of a man down the street who appeared to be starving and cold, but was hanging on every word relating to Mojara.

"Ahh, Alex Mill, are you not?" Tyton asked rhetorically.

The man nodded weakly, his eyes wide in fear.

Tyton beckoned with his index finger for Alex the Meek to approach.

Alex did and fell on his knees, "Please, if you can, I … I cannot find my daughter Molly … I will give anything … "

The name Molly hit Tyrianna like a bolt of lightning, her jaw slackened and her eyes bulged. She stared at Alex, the grown man, and saw within him the features of Alex the child in her vision. The faces were unmistakable.

"What? What have I done? Do I know you? " Alex begged.

Tyrianna's eyes glazed over, and the glow of the moon returned within them, and Tyrianna then screamed in agony, buckling to her knees, "Nooooooooo! Stop it! Leave him alone!"

She saw motion in the darkness of some faraway basement, a tall man in robes towering over a small child, and Malsain's voice whispered, "This is our secret, boy ... your service is for the good of the flock ..."

Tyrianna curled into a fetal position, shaking with fear and despair as if locked inside the child. Tyrus knelt over and sheltered her from onlookers as she babbled incoherently. Alex stared in fear, dumbfounded by Tyrianna's bizarre behavior, "What ... what happened?"

Tyrus hissed as he turned his head upward, "Just give her room. She's an oracle."

Alex stammered as he backed away, "O-o-oracle? Y-you mean, like the lady in the cave?" Tyrus stared him down, "Cave? You have seen Syrene?"

Alex the Meek whimpered, "I-I don't know her name, just, she had red hair, and mentioned some guy named Kaedrus ..."

Tyrianna's eyes popped open. "Faaaaatherrrrr, nooooo!" just before she began gagging, and rolled onto her knees to vomit.

* * *

"The prosecution now calls Darren Whitepine to the witness stand."

Darren rose to approach.

The assistant recited, "Do you swear on the land, that you shall speak the truth, without omission or misdirection, so help you the powers above?"

Darren nodded, "I so swear it, yes."

The solicitor motioned toward the chair, waited for Darren to sit, and asked, "Can you please state your position and duties, for the benefit of the jury?"

Darren responded, "Yes, I am a vault-keeper for the settlement of Falcon Ridge, the only town where humans and Elves co-exist within Valantir. I oversee the safety of our records and deposits."

The solicitor nodded. "Thank you. Now, can you identify any of these men?"

Darren replied, "Yes, all four of them belonged to a larger group of twelve bandits. Two of the dozen were wounded and apprehended right away. But the others escaped with many of our twentieth anniversary coins."

The solicitor prompted, "Can you explain the importance of these coins?"

Darren continued, "Certainly. The year of minting was Stonehaven reckoning 1560, commemorating the twentieth year since the tragedy of Shadval. We learned much later, that these same coins turned up at a murder scene in West Mill. The robbery of our vaults and the murder are only ten days apart. Valantir expresses their regrets to the family of Ramus."

The solicitor bowed. "No further questions at this time."

Blackhull motioned for the defense to approach.

"In those ten days, could the coins, yes or no, have changed hands from the bandits to other men?" the defense queried.

"Well, yes, but ..." Darren stammered.

The defense continued, "And once the bandits left Falcon Ridge, you could no longer account for any of their activities?"

Darren responded, "Now look here ..."

Blackhull directed, "Answer the question, please."

Darren was downcast as he answered, "No. No, I could not."

The defense asserted, "So, the coins are what we call, mere circumstantial evidence, and don't really prove anything."

Darren contested, "Wait a minute now ..."

The gavel sounded. "Order! Stand down, counsel. The jury decides on the evidence, not you! Scribe, strike that last remark."

The defense frowned. "Your Honor ..."

Blackhull snarled, "No more theatrics. Clear?"

The defense hung his head. "Yes, sir ... Your Honor ..."

Blackhull simply gave him a warning glance over his spectacles.

The defense backed away. "No further questions."

The solicitor stepped forward again. "Is there any other information you can give us on these men who robbed a treasury?"

Darren shook his head no. Solicitor called the next witness. An innkeeper from West Mill stepped forward.

The assistant recited the oath again, and the man nodded yes.

"State for the record, please," Blackhull prodded.

The innkeeper said, "Yes, I swear to give the truth."

Once he was seated, the solicitor began, "Please tell the jury why you are here."

The innkeeper replied, "I run a small inn near the place where Ramus died. These fellas paid for a room in the coin of falcon whatever. They smelled of venison and red wine, no mistake."

The two Blackwolves at the table made sour faces.

The prosecution continued, "Were they at your inn the morning of the murder?"

The innkeeper answered, "They certainly were! And split right afterwards. Never saw them again until this here trial!"

The solicitor had one more question, "Was there anything else that set them apart, anything unusual?"

The innkeeper mused, "Well, aside from weird tattoos and speaking to each other mostly in hand gestures and code words, no, not really."

The prosecution prodded further, "What kind of code words?"

The witness, puzzled, answered, "Well, they often talked about 'the bastard' and 'the sucker.' I don't remember much else. I did have other customers to pay mind to, ya know."

The solicitor nodded. "Thank you. No further questions, Your Honor."

The defense rose, "At what time did you join these men in drinking?"

The solicitor stood back up, "Objection! Defense is leading the witness!"

The gavel sounded once more. "Sustained. Defense will cease casting innuendo and leading this fellow by the nose. First warning. Don't test me, it will cost you."

Defense paused. "Did you have any drinks that night?"

Innkeeper replied, "If you mean did I get drunk while on duty, the answer is no!"

Defense pressed on, "When was your duty over?"

The witness scoffed, "I had a half-pint after cleaning up. They were already shut tight upstairs by then. I never had any other dealings with that lot!"

Defense pushed, "But the drink may have affected your memory."

The innkeeper barked, "I know what yer tryin' to get at. My memory is just fine, sonny! It takes more than a half pint to muddle my head!"

Blackhull smiled. Defense backed down, "No further questions ... Your Honor." The mediator general looked at the solicitor, who shook his head no.

"Next witness, please, " Blackhull announced.

Chapter Twenty-Four
False Friends

"How does that overbearing, pompous slave driver expect me to prove myself when the Alphas all shunned me and deny my rightful place among them? Curse you, Barton, and that little Toby as well. I'll show all of you! Everyone shall fear Malsain and bow before me! You stole my work, and I will destroy it all before I let you take credit for it! The orphanage, the church, the grooming of the young prince ... it was all MY work, you monster!" Malsain was near starving in dirty torn robes, wandering the mountains, and now, he gave in completely to the werewolf, tearing the last of his clothing to tatters and howling his rage at the forest below as he ran on all fours toward Korath again. Far in the distance, the lone hunter heard the howl and packed his bag for Valantir.

* * *

"The throne room is out, too many witnesses and sentinels. Same goes for the kitchen and bedchambers.

And the blackbirds are on high alert. If any of this is tied back to me …" Arthur complained.

Winter patted his cheek in a patronizing gesture. "It's the risk we all took, Arthur … "

He swatted her hand away. "*Some* of us prefer to have a pleasant retirement, you know …"

Winter chided, "Stop being such a child. It's unworthy of the Alphas."

Arthur retorted, "How would you know? The only reason the Alphas tolerate you is your father. Your … abilities … rub the Lawgivers the wrong way. You are too obvious about them. You would blow their cover."

Winter stuck her tongue out. "Like I care about their petty concerns. Now be a good sport and tell me where the king is vulnerable."

Arthur sneered, "Just like that? Stick my neck out like a sodding fool? With no promises of protection? I think not …. "

Winter dropped her chin and rolled her eyes up at him in a look of annoyance. "Oh, do be realistic. I'm the most reasonable living Auguron you will ever deal with. My brother would pull your tongue out, and my father would make you beg for death. Either help, or explain to HIM why not. He had no patience in life, and his … state … has only made him worse."

Arthur fumed, "Curses, woman! Must you be so blasted right so often?"

Winter smiled cruelly, "Flattery ill becomes you, Mister Clayton …"

Arthur hung his head in exasperation. "This is more in Clark's league ..."

Winter sighed. "I'd rather not go to him. He should have been hanging from the gallows by now. He's as bad as my father. A self-aggrandizing deluded maniac who spits on every creature he cannot buy for a pet."

Arthur added sarcastically, "Those are his good qualities. "

Winter paced back and forth. "I don't want him involved. I have no leverage on him. And my father likes him too much. No, it has to be you, Arthur."

He sighed. "I was afraid you would say that ... "

The chaos witch smiled again. "That's because you're a smart boy."

Arthur snapped, "Stop patronizing me. It's most annoying!"

Winter conceded, "Such a hard habit to break, but seeing as how I require your assistance ... very well. Perhaps we can exploit the dragon situation."

* * *

"Ludicrous, there is no such thing as dragon repellant! This woman is trying to trick you, sire!" Sandraz proclaimed.

Clayton interjected, "My niece is well-versed in medicines and potions. If anyone can create such a thing, she is the one to do it!"

King William Goldlion commanded, "All of you, GET OUT, your senseless, catty bickering tires me!"

Clayton pleaded, "But, sire …"

William repeated, "OUT!!!"

Clayton bowed and said no more, followed by Winter and Sandraz.

"I swear, Clayton, if you are up to something, I will expose you and your guest, and you will pay dearly!" Sandraz declared as he turned to take the west corridor.

Clayton gave a sour look and continued south to the courtyard. "Irritating, self-righteous busybody …" Clayton mumbled under his breath.

Winter purred, "Now, Arthur, he can't prove anything.

He …"

Clayton put his hand over her mouth as they rounded a corner. "Shhhh … save it. Ears," he warned.

As they cleared the courtyard and passed the fountains and the lion statues, he whispered, "We found the body. Vamanastral is dead. He was left in the sewers.

They know. He was in on the plan."

Winter blurted, "But my father sent me to you as the backup. Who else is involved?"

Arthur concluded, "Has to be high command among the Alphas, such as Barton. Nobody dares defy Barton, you know that … "

Winter grumbled, "Something is wrong. We are being played."

Clayton conceded, "I hate it when you're right …"

Chapter Twenty-Five
Travels

Bravane the Elder was gathering firewood for his cabin when he saw the hoof-prints of seven horses that passed through not long ago, several hours at most. The depth of the prints and the stride patterns suggested riders, searching for someone, perhaps himself. He dropped his firewood, and packed up some things from the cabin, and traced the prints back toward their source. As the hours passed, he concluded their origin was Oakthorn, not West Bend.

They were not hunting him after all. Instinct told him they would pass this way again. He slowed his pace to gather edible plants and look for clues to the identities of the riders. A couple boot prints told him they wore leather, not plates, and then, "Sandal prints? Who wears sandals this far from ... the abbey. That should be an interesting tale .... "

Unbidden, his thoughts turned to his wife Helen and his brother Alex and whether they would forgive him or not. His heart had been unbearably heavy for years, and he wished to be free.

* * *

"Now?" the youngest man Vithgar IsenBeorn asked, peering over an outcropping of rock.

Skorvald shook his head no. "Wait until after he lights his pipe and inhales. Then he is most vulnerable. Do not forget he used poison on Jonah."

The others grinned at his impeccable logic. They waited many long minutes for the opportunity to present itself, and rushed in when Skorvald made the hand signal. Darmid was helpless in their grip again in mere seconds, and Skorvald tore the pipe from his grasp, and held it aloft in triumph as he teased Darmid with it.

"You dirty rascals, give it back ..." Darmid moaned piteously.

Skorvald laughed. "Us? Rascals? You have quite the nerve, after all you have done! What do you say to that, men?"

Four of the barbarians all mocked Darmid with long faces and puppy dog eyes, and whimpering as they squatted on all fours.

This infuriated Darmid, even in his sedated state. "You DARE mock the scribe of Eledar! You unwashed cretins shall pay dearly!"

Skorvald waved the pipe high over his head. "In a couple hours, prideful one, you will be begging for this and telling us everything we need to know! Go ahead and tie him up, lads."

Darmid struggled weakly from hunger and dehydration and the effects of the opium, and was no match for their brawn on his best day.

They gagged him for good measure and removed all of his coin pouches, his silver goblet, and his blades. Then Darmid was slung unceremoniously over the saddle of a horse. He stared at Skorvald with hate in his eyes, who tauntingly bulged his eyes and pretended with obvious sarcasm to quiver in his boots.

They walked the horses back for many miles until they passed a meadow. The flowers had all withered, and the trees had shed their leaves. But there were still starchy tubers and other roots to be dug up for food. The barbarians camped a short while and roasted the vegetables for sustenance. Darmid wriggled in his bindings and tried to speak. The men mocked this, too, until Darmid gave up the struggle.

After eating and letting the horses forage a little, Skorvald gave the signal to mount up and ride. In a couple more hours, they encountered Bravane the Elder, who waved them down as they approached. "Are you riding to Oakthorn?" he asked.

Skorvald replied gruffly, "Perhaps. Who needs to know?"

Bravane bowed his head. "I have a message for the baron. He knows who I am."

Skorvald looked closer. "Supposing I believe you, why should we take you?"

Bravane cast his eyes to the ground. "No reason at all, other than the future of Oakthorn may depend on it. If I were any other man, I would not care. But his blood is my own."

Skorvald looked him over again, concluding, "We shall see," and waved the youngest man over to accept a passenger.

* * *

"A friend of mine says chamomile tea is good for the nerves, here ..."

An old man offered a cup to Tyrianna. Tyrus looked suspiciously, ready to grab the cup.

"The Elves have nothing to fear from me, and neither do you," Lebiced added.

The girl hesitantly accepted the cup while propped on one elbow and sipped at it.

Tyton observed, "That staff is proof enough to me, only the elder wizards from the free republic of Xantir have such symbols carved in their sticks. "

Lebiced smiled, and Alex Mill said nothing. A weary Tyrianna sat up in the bed within the guest wing of Redoak Manor, still reeling from her visions and flashbacks that were hopelessly jumbled together. She looked at Alex the Meek, and saw in his eyes, that he had blocked his memory of the priest. Alex had done the only thing his mind could handle. The experience yesterday was almost more than Tyrianna could handle.

Tyton politely excused himself. "I shall return later. I have other duties requiring my attention."

When the rogue was gone, Tyrus spoke up, "I still don't trust him. There's nothing stopping him from keeping the coins for himself."

Lebiced mused, "Nothing, you say? I suspect he does serve some higher purpose than merely himself. Hidden his mind might be, but he cares not what people think of him.

Only the arrogant and the wise can claim such an attribute, and I see no posturing on his part, he sees drama as a waste of his energy. No, I think his motives are quite sound. But we will see, won't we?"

Tyrus wrinkled an eyebrow, "Interesting ... "

Chapter Twenty-Six
Messages

"Has the jury reached a verdict?" Blackhull inquired. The foreman responded, "We have, Your Honor. We, the jury find the four Blackwolves on the counts of kidnapping, armed robbery, and endangering public welfare, guilty. We find three of the blackwolves, on the charge of conspiracy to commit murder, guilty."

Predictably, three of the Blackwolves attempted to flee, again. The old deputy had already clamped his hand on the leader's throat, and the other two were felled by clubs to the head. While Danny awaited judgement, Blackhull chimed in, "By the provisions in the treaty of Westwood, and in the interest of expediency, this court hereby declares that the three men, for the offense of conspiracy to murder Ramus, shall receive no less than fifteen consecutive years hard labor in the mines. For armed robbery, no less than ten."

Danny hung his head in defeat.

"For the count of kidnapping, no less than seven years. For public endangerment, no less than three. You shall, therefore, serve thirty-five years." And down came the gavel.

Danny lost hope, having been forsaken by Tyrianna, and now this.

"Take them away, bailiff."

Danny was left alone. When the other three were beyond earshot outside the courtroom, the magistrate spoke again, "Mister Daniel Darkmoon, you are given the lighter sentence of ten years community service. We will negotiate later."

Danny sighed with relief and fell to his knees.

* * *

"Behold, I bring an orphan, rescued from the clutches of the Elves, drugged on her way into slavery!" said Toby.

A peasant asked, "What happened to Father Samuel Malsain, why did he abandon us?"

Toby answered, "Alas, Malsain has become ill, and he entrusted me to put his affairs in order until he returns. But his faith in the lawgiver remains strong. He also confides his great fondness for his children, and hopes you will take comfort in this."

The peasants just stood there confused, somehow that did not sound like Malsain, but nobody was brave enough to speak up. They simply looked at each other and shrugged. While Molly could barely stand up, her eyelids heavy with fatigue, and her skin pale from malnourishment. In her delirium, Molly saw a woman in the mist among the trees away from the crowd, or the shape of a woman. It looked as if she was made of moonlight. She saw the lips moving, and a voice inside her head spoke to her, "Your parents love you, and they will find you. Do not lose hope. They are far away and looking for you. Stay strong, little one." Then the mist faded, and the vision was no more.

* * *

"How dare they abandon their duties to the abbey!" Dhasa fumed. "I want them back here at once! Do you hear me?"

Dobbs and Sean bowed.

"Yes, Arbiter, as you wish."

Dobbs asked, "What about Darmid, Father? He is missing as well."

Dhasa scowled, "Darmid is another matter. I'll decide about him later. Just get Savadi and Helen back here!"

Dobbs bowed eagerly. Sean simply nodded his head forward.

"We will not fail you Dhasa," Dobbs promised, as Sean merely bowed again.

They promptly left to get horses from the town stable across the river. Lorekeeper Henry overheard from his table in the reading room, got up to fetch another book, and placed a silk ribbon inside it after leafing through to a very specific page, and replaced the book on the shelf. A young apprentice waited for Henry to go upstairs, and retrieved the book to hide it within a false book jacket before placing it in a pile for the scribes. The apprentice then returned to his duties cataloging archives.

Much later, a scribe took the pile and retired upstairs, knocking twice on Andar's dormitory door before leaving the book on the floor. Farseer Andar waited a few seconds before answering and picking up the book. He thumbed directly to the silk ribbon and opened to the page detailing the wedding of Bravane Redoak the Second to Helen Aristodemos in 1531. "So ..." Andar spoke aloud before catching himself. In his mind, he reached out to a nun in the cellars, his beloved Sasha, a ward-keeper and half-Elf. "Dhasa has plans against Helen. What transpires in the cellars, love?"

Sasha returned the thought: "The wards are nearly exhausted. They could fail at any minute now. I have not been able to restore them after losing an apprentice to the fever. Arius continues to probe our defenses. He knows we are weakened. It is sheer luck the wards did not already collapse. Dhasa's assistant still watches me like a hawk, as always."

Andar messaged back: "Eledar's ghost still wanders upstairs. And Dhasa seems ignorant of the girl; her abilities are growing stronger. I misjudged some of the signs, but now they are unmistakable. I felt a great calamity to the east near Shadval ..."

Sasha finished his sentence. "You told me this, love. I know."

Andar added, "Be careful."

Sasha replied, "Always," and turned her full attention back to the wards.

* * *

"Baron, there's a man at the gate who says he is your father," a herald reported on bent knee.

Bravane the Third snarled, "What in Hades does he want now? Haunting my nightmares is not enough? Zounds! The nerve to return here!"

The herald asked, "Should we send him away then?"

Bravane assured him, "No need. I shall send him away myself! Go fetch my battle axe."

The herald gulped. "Yes, my lord … as you wish …" and nervously hurried away, as Baron Bravane strode to the front door.

His father was pacing nervously at the gate, chewing on his knuckles.

The son yelled, "By what right do you return here after trying to drown me as a child? Or did unmitigated gall summon you here?"

The Elder Redoak bent to one knee and pleaded, "I have done a horrible thing, and if I had the choice, I would not be here. I have news which concerns us both. Please hear me out."

The son laughed. "News? What could possibly be so important to me that only you would know?"

The father sank to both knees and touched his head to the ground. "I did not believe it either. A woman claims you have a son."

The baron was stunned in wonderment. "How is that possible? I never ..."

And then he knew. The dream, plus vague remembrances of a diplomatic visit, and more than his usual drinks. The son did exist; that was the missing part of his life. The baron felt his strength ripped from him as he grabbed the bars of the gate to steady himself.

"Who is this woman?" he asked.

The father realized, "She never gave me her name, we ... parted company under ... drastic and violent circumstances. She is plotting against the king."

"WHAT? This *mysterious* woman with no name is plotting against my king? Have you ANY idea how this looks for me? Pardon my saying so, but you need to do better than that! You have to take me to find her, *now*!" the baron exclaimed.

The Elder Redoak begged, "I cannot. She falsely accused me of trying to kidnap her. I had no time to explain ..."

The baron concealed his face behind a clenched hand. "Zounds and Hades, man! TWICE now, you ruin my life in the blink of an eye! AAAARRRRGHHHH!"

The baron kicked blindly, colliding with the shin of a gate sentry, who buckled to the ground, gasping and wheezing in pain. The herald had just returned with the axe and froze in the doorway, staring into the front courtyard. The baron saw him and just waved his arm in a backhand sweep, signaling the man to go back indoors. He turned toward the gate again, fingers clenched in fury. "You! Has Ravenna delivered the message yet?"

A guard nodded yes. "She is still in Valantir, my lord, and has not returned."

The Baron commanded, "Send a courier and tell her I have need of her diplomatic status. NOW!"

The guard snapped to attention, saluted, and bowed. "As you wish, my lord."

The Baron just now noticed the guard on the ground and regretted his rash action. "Take this man to the blackthorn house to see my physician James."

The one remaining guard complied most happily.

To his father, the Baron said, "Get up. May as well get you a decent meal … Father …"

* * *

"What do you plan to do now?" Arthur asked. Winter gave her weary reply, "We have to finish it, any other action ensures the wrath of my father and of Barton both. I still don't understand how Barton wields as much power as Arius. Everything about him feels wrong.

Somehow he does not belong here."

Arthur sneered, "The Alphas derive substance and form from Barton. What you speak is heresy. Say what you like when we are done with the deed, but if you drag my name into it, I will deny you."

Winter grumbled, "Then let us hope they do not ask too many questions about our delays."

Arthur laughed. "Men with such ambition and power not asking questions? Elven plum wine would rain from the sky before that happens!"

Winter had an odd look in her eye concerning the Elves, but said only, "We would welcome such a thing for what they can do when angered ..."

Arthur nodded in agreement and began thinking aloud, "Did he give a deadline?"

Winter sunk her head. "We have two more days, no more.

Some other plan depends on it."

* * *

"Hello, brother. Ghosts of the past brought you back?" Alex Redoak queried.

Bravane the Elder groaned, "Yes, one could make such a claim ... you seem as smug as ever about my troubles ..."

Alex countered, "Only because our ruined father knew where to find you, and you adapted too little too late. Enough about that. What brings you out of exile?"

Bravane the Second quipped sarcastically, "Oh! The same thing that drove me out, a *woman* ..." and took another bite of chicken from his plate.

Alex took his time to mention, "Helen won't be speaking to you, unless she breaks her vow of silence."

Bravane paused. "Oh, that's right. I heard about her sister. But figured I was the last person she wanted a letter of sympathy from … Summer was a kind woman …"

Alex taunted, "Yes, Conrad's mother. You remember Conrad, don't you?"

Bravane snapped, "Don't start *that* again. You think I have not regretted that day? I had nearly done myself in were it not for a voice that stopped me …"

Alex wrinkled an eyebrow in disbelief, "Oh? And why did it not speak sooner?"

Bravane frowned. "I know not. Before that day, I had no belief in spirits, gods, or fairies, and now I can no longer dismiss them so easily … "

Alex let the matter drop. "Well, it's good to see you mellowed out a bit."

Small talk about cold weather and crop yields followed, punctuated by more food and drink.

* * *

"I demand you release me at once! You will all pay for this indignity! When Dhasa hears of this — and he will — you are all dead men! You hear me?" Darmid protested bitterly.

Skorvald and the deputy both laughed.

The deputy responded, "I don't think so, mister. Your thievery has caught up with you. All those bad loans to cover your opium habit, stealing from the abbey and the treasury both. It's only a matter of time before we find your supplier. Somebody had to cover your tracks, and nobody is happy with you. No, you are going to rot in this cell, knave!"

Skorvald crossed his arms and grinned, silently daring Darmid to dig his own grave with more threats and empty boasts. Darmid tugged at his manacles in vain, scowling with death in his eyes at the Northlander. He grumbled vile curses under his breath and began to sulk in bitter silence. And then a visitor showed up, concealed completely within a black robe with a deep hood, approaching Darmid's cell. The man held up one gloved hand before Skorvald could speak, and whispered to Darmid, "Confess now and I may grant mercy."

Darmid stammered in panic, "No, you said I would be rewarded for helping the arbiters! You promised! I was loyal the entire time!"

The man in the robes teased, "Did I really? Are you sure?"

Darmid sobbed. "You have to keep your promise! The pain ..."

The robed man beckoned to the deputy, who brought the cell keys, allowed him inside the cell, and locked it again.

Darmid broke down. "No, please, Barton. I did everything you asked. I swear it!"

The robed man laughed and tossed his hood back, revealing Tyton Umbral in his rogue's mask. "Confession accepted, Alpha. You may open the door again, Deputy."

As the old man returned, Tyton strode toward Darmid and ripped both sleeves from the scribe's arms, causing Darmid to howl in agony. His left arm had open sores and horrible scars on his bicep, with blisters and black ink from a botched tattoo. Darmid whimpered, "Please, my pipe, the pain is unbearable."

Tyton grabbed the left arm to turn it in the lamplight and examine closer, as Darmid wheezed in submission. "Look here, " Tyton instructed the deputy. "It's a bad rendition of a wolf head, with inferior ink, probably black walnut, causing his allergic reaction, over an older tattoo of a viper, which makes him a midnight viper infiltrating the blackwolves, but if he thought I was Lord Barton, that means he is also in the Alpha Clan, who tend to forego telltale signs of their identity. How long has he served Eledar?"

The deputy shrugged. "Do I look like a monk?"

Tyton sighed. "No, I suppose not." The deputy bowed. "Thanks for your service. The magistrate will be pleased."

Darmid spat, "Vile cretins! Barton will fix all of you!"

Tyton poked his arm, causing Darmid to convulse in agony and cease talking. Tears ran down his cheeks as he sobbed again in helpless surrender. Tyton and the deputy left the cell, and Skorvald gave a satisfied, cruel grin. "Nicely done, cat."

Tyton merely bowed slightly, not letting his eyes off the barbarian.

* * *

An Elven messenger arrived in Valandrassil, the capitol of Valantir, barely able to speak. "The undead of Shadval are upon us ... their numbers ... have grown ... and Arius is among them. He deflects all of our spells. We could not hold the border cities, two of them are over-run. We must summon help ... or all is lost!"

Andrath then announced, "Send the call, and prepare to retreat north to the temple if Valandrassil falls. May the forest protect you!"

The scout nodded and bowed, and was on his way. To another Elf, Andrath commanded, "Herald, bring my spyglass!"

* * *

While in the western border city of Pineval, Dobbs and Sean arrived with Dhasa's edict for Savadi and Helen to return to the abbey. Dobbs flew into a rage at the sight of Conrad. "Murderer! I will see you hang in the name of Eledar!" He drew his sword and charged on horseback, directly into a volley of arrows from the trees. Dobbs dropped his sword and slid in slow motion to one side in his saddle, and then fell to the ground, wheezing away his last minutes of life.

Sean put both hands in the air. "I yield!"

The Elves took Sean into custody and led the horses to be tethered.

"Things are not looking well for the future of the abbey," Conrad commented to his kin and the Elves.

Bethany replied, "After everything the arbiters and their flock have done to us, what dim ray of hope could possibly pierce such a fog of delusion and gloom?"

All fell silent in contemplation.

* * *

"Friar Toby, the beast has returned, it attacked the orphanage ..." a frightened peasant reported.

"*Whaaaat?* He's going to ruin everything! No-oooo!" Toby exclaimed in an uncharacteristic tone of authority.

"Friar?" the peasant begged in fear.

The short man known as Toby melted and shifted into the shape of none other than the taller form of Lord Barton. "I thank you for your service, but your usefulness has ended, human."

With that, Barton raised his hand as if clawing the air, and the poor peasant was levitated with great speed into the stone ceiling, his short cry of panic reverberating through the chapel, ending on its highest note at impact as he lost consciousness, followed by even more rapid impact with the floor, his life oozing over the marble tiles.

Barton snarled, "Now you DIE, Malsain, this I promise!"

* * *

South of the orphanage, two children hid in the stables with the horses. Molly and Carol had been guided here by a voice in the mist, and they did not question it. All the others were dead or dying, and visions of Malsain's savagery played in Molly's mind. Bodies thrown everywhere with broken necks, slashed throats, things beyond her worst nightmares. Molly's tiny heart felt as if it would burst in fright. Carol had gone numb with shock. Somewhere out there, Malsain was still on his rampage. He had entered the orphanage through the upper windows and struck down everything that moved. Everything but Molly and Carol. If not for the lady in the mist, they would have died. Molly prayed the lady would return, but nothing happened. Only the breathing of the horses and the sound of Molly's heartbeat broke the silence. Despair enclosed Molly's world with emptiness and crushing abandonment; she tried to hide it, but the tears could not be denied.

Chapter Twenty-Seven
Fickle Dice

Kazius staggered, wide-eyed and delirious, into his castle, babbling nonsense, "All lost ... meaningless ... we have no future. I have no children. There is no hope ... the end has come ... all is dust ... and darkness."

Behind him, Axegrind and nine other survivors marched with stone faces and heavy eyelids, intent on reaching the kitchens. Axegrind stopped to splash himself at the nearest rain barrel. The others followed suit. All except Kazius, who grabbed a wine bottle from an old man's fingers. The old fellow weakly protested in a grunt of resentment and walked away before any troops could surround him. Kazius popped the cork and drank greedily as he continued to stagger and rant his discontent and gloom, saying, "Worthless concubines, cursed land, and, that ... that THING ... hateful eyes of death ..."

Axegrind paid him no attention. The wheels in his head were still turning. "If we play the girl against the undead, we can force a confrontation with the goddess, perhaps wrest the dagger from her … with the right pawns in play," Axegrind mused softly.

Kazius was too far away to hear. The other nine survivors saluted Axegrind and pledged themselves to his leadership.

* * *

Amanda screamed, "Whaaat? You accepted custody of Daniel? That … THIEF … is responsible for …"

The baron cut in, "And his former cohorts tried to kill him twice already, before they were dragged off to the mines. I think that is proof enough of his intentions …"

Amanda screeched, "It could be a trick! Did you forget that Kazius never waited to hear the outcome of his treaty negotiations? Or that some power ordered him to kidnap me? I don't have the luxury of forgetfulness, cousin …"

Baron Bravane the Third snarled, "Enough! It was MY decision, and you will not bend me from it this time!"

Amanda turned on her heels and left in bitter, smoldering silence.

Alex Redoak overheard on his way in and responded, "Tread carefully, Baron. You still need us, especially against the Abbey. Dhasa is livid over the search and seizure of Darmid's belongings, including unfinished copies of books and scrolls that Eledar had requested before his demise. You should also know that Tyrus and Tyrianna have left the city. And listen to this — Tyton instructed his guild to accept Conrad as their leader until he returns.

Bethany's Co-op manager Rachel told me when she could not find any of them at home."

The baron was incredulous. "Whaaat?"

Alex explained, "Tyton submits articles to the Co-op via courier. His mastery of herblore rivals even Savadi. This gave him the cover of business as usual. You did not know that?"

The Baron harrumphed sarcastically, "Obviously not … must have been drinking that day."

Alex Mill arrived just then, falling to his knees and begging, "Please forgive me. I just want to find my daughter. I'll do anything. I swear …"

Alex Redoak raised an eyebrow. "Well, I believe him. I've never known him to lie. Only dodge anything remotely dangerous … interesting about daughters being involved."

Mill pleaded, "Please, I never intended for anything to happen to Amanda."

Uncle Alex offered an idea, "Why not have Danny help him find his daughter? It will keep him out of Amanda's hair and still honor the terms of his sentence."

The baron shook his head no. "I cannot turn him loose unsupervised. No."

Mill begged again, "Please, my wife and daughter mean everything to me!"

Uncle Alex asked, "Where is your wife?"

Mill shrunk away in shame. "M-mojara …"

The baron's uncle crossed his arms. "Really? Safe and sound? You left her alone in a land that pays tributes to Kazius, is the rumored capitol of crime, and you expect me to believe she means everything to you? Understand this, Mister Alex Mill, men capable of kidnapping children are not nice people. You have to meet and conquer the fears that haunt you, or you put your daughter in greater peril than she already is. You have to be stronger than the kidnappers expect you to be. Now, GET UP!"

Mill jumped involuntarily, quaking. "Y-yes, uh-understood."

Uncle Alex mused, "Would the wizard Lebiced be willing to supervise them?"

The baron thought aloud in a melancholy tone, "Maybe."

* * *

"What is the meaning of this, Axegrind? I wished not to be disturbed," Kazius mumbled angrily as he pulled away from two of his concubines in the bedchamber.

General Axegrind gave an evil grin. "We have other plans for new leadership, starting today."

Kazius rushed for his axe, and two Bloodhammers intercepted him, grabbing his wrists and dragging him to be bound in leather cords. "This castle is my birthright, you treacherous toads! I built this army! I made all of you! Unhand me at once!!!!" Kazius protested vehemently.

Axegrind smirked. "Gag him as well and take him to the arena ..."

Kazius struggled ferociously against his bonds and captors, head-butting the man on his right, and kicking the shins of another, before a hammer-fist blow to his back knocked him flat on the floor. The press of many bodies upon him stole the air from his lungs, making him helpless and mute. Kazius stared with eyes of death as he was carried ignominiously in his nightshirt, bound and gagged, through the halls of the castle past several dead sentries and out into the daylight. The subjects smiled for fractions of a second, before returning to their standard gloom, as they well knew that Axegrind was just as bad.

The concubines all took this as an opportunity to escape, since the sentries were so few after the infighting. They stole through the shadows of the corridors, pausing at every corner. All but one, who parted ways at the inner door of the front lobby. She was determined to save he monarch. The other women rolled their eyes and let her go. Bernice had always been the loyal one, even to those who proved unworthy. While Belinda, the rebellious one, was, oddly enough, the favorite of Kazius; he liked her fire. Almost as much as he enjoyed extracting compromises from her. But Belinda would not miss him. Today she was free. Leaving the city was just a matter of time. Her will and her wits would solve that.

* * *

"I apologize for the sedative. It should wear off soon, after we have collected the reward," Tyton whispered to Tyrianna who moaned in delirium with her hands bound by silk scarves.

The outlines of ships at Dexia Harbor in Mojara were becoming visible. Tyton paused for several minutes to apply more herbal salve to his arms and shoulders, which were still burning from his exertions with the paddle. Below the canoe, the submerged Tyrus could also see the ship hulls in the distance and slowed his pace to follow farther behind. The dockhands looked incredulous.

"The sea witch? Is that really her? How did a nobody like you pull that off?" one of the dockhands asked.

Tyton smiled, his dark face betraying no malice. "That remains my trade secret. I am told the dockmaster has the reward?"

The men nodded yes and pointed the way to the office.

Tyton bowed. "Thank you. I regret to say, however, I believe I was followed."

Almost on cue, Tyrus emerged from the water, trident in hand. The men were so intent on Tyrus that they did not have any warning of Tyton jabbing their necks from behind with his tensed fingers. They dropped like wet noodles. Tyrus wasted no time binding them below deck on one of the ships. Tyton found the office with little problem. But the delays in paperwork were formidable.

"You need to sign here, here and here ... and wait while I check in with the boys... " said the overweight dockmaster.

Tyton quickly sized up the contents of the office, including the location of the hidden safe and the desk compartment where the dockmaster kept his weapons, such as a flintlock pistol, a crossbow and a saber. Tyton decided to empty the powder from the pistol, remove the flint, and then play the rest by ear.

* * *

Tyrianna began to stir; the sedative was wearing off, and the risk from a second dose was too great; it would upset the clock. Tyton took a bandana and gagged her, before she ruined the plan. Then he signed the papers as "Ivan." He had just finished when the man returned.

He picked up the parchment and asked, "Ivan what? You have to give a longer name."

Tyton answered, "Goodhill. Parents died in the great fire of '33."

The dockmaster accepted his word. "Orphan, huh? Tough break. Well, let me go get the coins."

The dockmaster had a cocked pistol in his hand when he returned, "Now tell me what happened to my boys outside on duty. Ivan ..."

Tyton was a blur, ducking and rolling under the man's aim, and hooking the man's left knee with one foot while kicking his right knee with the other, toppling him backward like a dead tree, and sending the pistol flying. The man curled up in pain, clutching his shattered knee. "You bloody devil! You will never get the reward now ..."

Tyton just kicked him in the chin, went straight to the safe, and tumbled the lock in a single minute. Tyrus entered the front office just as the safe opened. Tyrus undid Tyrianna's bindings and looked her in the eye as she became lucid.

"Where is he?" Tyrus asked.

Tyrianna nodded toward the room where the safe was. As Tyrus entered, Tyton tossed him the bag of coins. "You can take the whole sum. Give half to the baron, take a few for yourself, and give the rest to Conrad. I have family business south of here. I hope you will forgive my secrets," Tyton said as he bowed and left.

Tyrus stood there dumbfounded. After Tyton left, Tyrus said to Tyrianna, "Perhaps I misjudged him after all."

Tyrianna felt compelled to take the documents with her for some unexplainable reason, and in the next moment, a sudden look of fright came over her. "Tyrus, we have to go back to Valantir, right now!"

* * *

"Arrows have no effect on them, Lord Andrath," a panicked Elf reported.

"Ready swords! Take their heads! Charge!" Andrath ordered to the ranks.

They braced themselves for death as they did so and fought valiantly for hours. For each undead they felled, more appeared, until, by day's end, the fallen of both sides numbered in the hundreds everywhere surrounding the main trunks of Valandrassil.

And as the Elves retreated north to regroup, Arius swept his arm in a semicircle toward the freshly dead, replenishing the numbers of his own servants. "THIS is for Lorenna!!!!" Arius cackled as he concentrated his formidable will on the base of the smallest tree, causing it to wither and blacken with mildew. It creaked and groaned under the weight of the platform, causing nearby trees to twist and bend before sections of the platform came crashing down with broken branches and split trunks. Thus came the end of Valandrassil, the third city to be conquered in two days. Arius then directed the undead westward, toward Pineval and then Oakthorn. He swore the humans would also pay.

He would finish off the Elves on his way home.

* * *

Andar the Farseer screamed, "NO! The unsleeping menace has sacked Valandrassil!"

Outside Andar's room, Dhasa overheard, sporting an evil grin. "Yes, now

you will spread the word, defeating the morale of those who still resist my efforts to bend their knees to my wishes. You will all regret your actions. I will make an offer when the menace arrives and join with him to gain the power and respect that should have been mine long ago," the arbiter thought aloud.

Dhasa had forgotten about Henry the Lorekeeper, who spent more and more time in the dorms as his years advanced. And old Henry might be, but his ears still heard. He searched his shelves for a particular book, turned the pages until at last he saw the one in mind, and placed another silk bookmark. And then waited for Dhasa to be gone.

* * *

"Barton will have our heads when he finds out the network is crumbling between the berserker and the centaurs! They are unstoppable! Where do we go?" asked a blond-haired skinny pirate named Gimp.

"We flee back northwest to the islands and make a stand there. That Garzon is a demon, I tell you. He's as strong as the tides and then some! Cut the ropes! Quick!" said the rusty auburn-haired Captain Ramrod.

Away in the distance, the berserker named Garzon felled pirates by the half-dozen in great sweeps of his massive gray metal battle axe, cleaving bones and sabers like twigs. Garzon was six foot nine, and built like a grizzly bear, his axe adorned at the haft with a skull emblem, and the bracers on his arms had never even been dented, nicked or scratched, such was their composition. It did not take long at all for the pirates to completely lose morale and run for their lives from this gargantuan behemoth of a man. Scores of pirates ran for the ships. Many arrived too late, and chose to risk the sharks rather than go back to shore.

"Go ahead! RUN! I will find you and make you pay for what you've done!" Garzon roared from the coast of Izimal.

This was where the syndicate trail had led. Izimal was second to Mojara in its corruption and filth, manifest in slave trade, opium smuggling, and piracy. And somewhere out there was a small Bazadani girl, stolen from her parents and from Garzon's adopted tribe.

* * *

"We desire to speak with Jonah. Is he among you?" Skorvald asked the Elves.

A sentry nodded his head. "Indeed he is. Are we expecting you?"

The barbarian leader answered, "I thought the woman Ravenna had delivered the news."

The sentry blushed. "My apologies. Right you are. Follow me."

A runner came up behind them as they ascended the spiral stairs. "Valandrassil has fallen, and Arius is headed this way!"

Skorvald responded in shock, "Arius? This was not what we signed up for. His infamy reaches everywhere. Our price just doubled."

The sentry gave a disgusted look but said nothing. This was Andiri's decision to make. Up they went to meet with the Elves and greet the Redoaks. Skorvald thought it odd to see a human monk meditating inside a wooden cage, and he opened his mouth to speak before thinking aloud, "No."

Finally, they met up with Conrad, Jonah, Bethany, Ravenna and the others, while Helen and Savadi were elsewhere, studying Elven medicine.

Ravenna spoke first, "I just received a summons to return to Oakthorn on urgent business, but it is good to see you. Pardon me." And away she went.

Skorvald informed Jonah, "My men and I split the funds as you requested. Why did you wish your donations to be anonymous? Does it have much to do with the abbey? We caught the assassin, by the way."

Bethany gave a slight nod to her husband, and Jonah replied, "Indeed. It does concern the Abbey. Those lying snakes supply the people candied falsehoods which they prefer to a bitter truth. They would eagerly believe I am trying to bribe them, rather than realize they are already fooled."

The Elves motioned for everyone to join the council on the next platform, and they relayed the news along the way.

Andiri bade to them, "Eat well. Our time is short. The sundering has not unfolded as we expected. Arius himself leads an army of undead, as we speak. Valandrassil is in ruins, so is Korval and another border city. Many of our survivors have fled north to make their stand within the temple. We shall all need our strength in the days ahead. A toast to friends and allies."

The assembly raised their goblets. "To friends and allies!"

The next few hours were spent discussing strategy and tactics.

* * *

"Arthur! Which fires are the least watched? I know what we must do!" Winter exclaimed.

"The kitchens, the wall torches, all but the feast hall and his bedchambers," Arthur replied.

"The kitchen will not do, and we must still slip past Sandraz ... I should never have let Father talk me into this." Winter sighed bitterly.

Arthur gave a tired response, "A bit late, you think?"

Winter snapped, "Do hush, you simpering toad."

Arthur remarked sarcastically, "Oh, I forget! I'm no match for Clark or Barton or Arius, or even Malsain."

Winter laughed. "Yes! That's it! That is how it will be done!"

Arthur scratched his head, "How what will be done?"

Winter corrected, "The less you know, the better for both of us, Arthur," as she jabbed him in the arm with her fingernail.

"Ow! How am I to cover your tracks if I'm kept in the dark?" Arthur protested.

Winter smiled. "Improvise."

Arthur threw his hands in the air. "Oh, such help you are!"

Winter left the room, and her giggling echoed in the corridor.

Chapter Twenty-Eight
Dark Deeds

Molly had never stolen food before, but here she was, hiding in the stables with an apple and a loaf of bread between her and Carol, the only survivors of Malsain's rampage in the orphanage. And she had just been caught by the stable boy on his rounds. "You have to give that back, or I'm reporting both of ya to the royal court!" the young lad insisted.

Molly pleaded, "We cannot. We will starve. Please don't."

The boy crossed his arms. "Where's your parents? They can't feed you right?"

Carol shrank into the corner of the stall, afraid to go anywhere.

"No, please, we will die," Molly explained. "Bad man broke into the orphan house. All dead now. He is still out there. A lady told us to stay here."

The stable boy refused, "No. If they find you here, I'm out of a job. Now get lost!"

Molly had no choice, as the boy snatched the bread from her hands. Molly pushed hard with both hands, causing him to hit his head on the gate to the stall, and little Molly had to drag Carol quickly as she took the loaf back on their way out.

The boy stirred a moment later. "Hey! You! Thieves! They stole food from the market!"

Carol was screaming hysterically, making them easy to follow.

Molly had to shake her. "You have to be quiet or they catch us, and then wolf come get us."

Carol nodded vigorously; she did not want Malsain to get them. They ran and hid under wagons, behind barrels, between old ladies and monks, and behind drain spouts. Molly just knew they had to leave town but had no idea where to go. They spotted a drunken old man climbing onto his wagon, and saw a way out. Anywhere was better than Kozos right now. They ate on the ride to wherever he was going. And it was a long, bumpy ride.

* * *

"Do you see by this cloak that caught in the brush, that the Elves have done this? They made war on our children and killed our chieftain! They must pay! Our truce is over!" announced a Dabani tribesman.

"Over here!" declared another. "I found the bow! Clearly of Elven design! He has fled into the mountains!"

The first man responded, "We will have the trials for a new chieftain, and then go teach the Elves a lesson! The men in black robes do not honor our gods, but in the Elves, we now have a common enemy, we will meet them in Korath and make council. Trials begin at first light after we bury our chief. Tonight we make weapons!"

The tribe went straight to work on flint spearheads and kite shields of animal hide, glue, twine and willow branches.

Far to the north, on an outcropping of rock, D'aarzane pocketed a borrowed spyglass and smirked under his mask. "Excellent. Master will be most pleased."

* * *

Tyrianna and Tyrus arrived too late, the south of Valantir had already been ravaged.

Broken trees were everywhere, fallen platforms and broken bodies, including a few Elves, all minus their heads and in states of advanced decay. Tyrus knew at once what happened. "This is a necromancers work. These Elves were already dead and then reanimated as servants. This is the unsleeping menace they spoke of."

Tyrianna gagged and threw up. These had been her friends. She had thought Kazius to be truly evil, but this was so much worse. Forced to fight their former comrades, it was nearly unimaginable. Tyrianna wailed and sobbed in her grief, inconsolably. There was nothing for Tyrus to do but wait in silence and keep vigil against any new signs of hostilities. And in a distant cave, the image of Tyrianna rippled in the waters of a scrying basin. Tears ran down her mother's face, mourning the complete and final loss of her daughter's childhood that could no longer be prevented.

"Would that I could have spared you this knowledge, dearest one," she spoke to the basin. "Some things, even I cannot do."

* * *

"The pain is killing me! I'll do anything! I must have my pipe!" Darmid begged and sobbed, desperate for relief from the throbbing, stinging, and burning pain in his arm, and the aches in his entire body. "You have to give it back! Pleeeease ... the pain!" The deputy grinned, "Is that right? You'll confess everything you know?" Darmid sobbed. "Yes -- I can barely think. It hurts, so just give it back ..." The deputy brought the pipe as promised, and Darmid took a long drag on it. "Now, about that confession ..." the deputy prompted.

Darmid just stared into empty space with bloodshot eyes.

The deputy waved his hand in front of his face, to no effect. Darmid did not blink or move. The deputy stepped closer to examine him, and Darmid suddenly bit his neck, making the deputy scream and convulse as Darmid brought his hands up and wrestled the deputy under the chain of his manacles to pull it taut and strangle him.

Minutes later, as the body lay twitching, Darmid lifted the key ring from the deputy's belt, and removed his restraints.

"Barton would kill me if I confessed. Can't have that. No, sir ... he'd wait until the last minute to give the barest whiff of my medicine, and then beat me to a pulp ... he's cruel like that ... lucky for you to have a quick death. Farewell, Deputy."

Chapter Twenty-Nine
Memories of Home

The outer walls of the palace in Korii, the capitol of Mojara, were much taller than Tyton remembered. It was the year 1531 when last he visited, as a boy of fifteen, trained in arts that people twice his age could only dream of, abilities that even warlords and bandits would envy if he allowed them to be discovered. It was in this city that the Midnight Vipers recruited him to work for Arius. And now, thirty-three years later, the smells of the spice market were exactly the same.

And the dancing girls, almost the same. None of them compared to Sidhuri, his first love. And his first heartbreak. Duty came first, then and now. His greatest regret and sorrow in life.

Tyton was the inside agent that helped the people of Vaja almost completely destroy both the Whispering Tiger gang of their own land and the Blackwolves, who originated in Razadur. And now, he had returned to call in favors. He had three half-siblings through his mother's second marriage, many cousins, and many temple brothers, all scattered throughout Vaja, Mojara, Izimal, Agama, and even Talos.

"Can I help you, sir?" a tanned merchant with a curly mustache and pointy beard in a silk vest, cotton robe and turban asked Tyton.

"Ahh, yes, a business partner is arriving in a few days and sent me ahead to get a map for his expeditions. Many stories from his uncles of lost cities," Tyton answered.

The merchant smiled. "I think I can cut you a good deal, sir, and do hope to meet your friend soon!"

Tyton followed the man through a tight alley of vendor carts full of silk scarves, cotton tunics, incense, spices and perfumes; it was nearly overpowering. At the end of the narrow alley, another one ran right and left, with the merchant taking the left turn, and then right, and finally arriving at his shop.

"I was watching the dancing girls perform. I should like one of them to entertain my son on his birthday," the merchant explained.

Tyton smiled and followed his cue. "Your son is turning sixteen?"

The man beamed with pride. "Yes, soon he will become an apprentice to a craftsman, a cousin of mine, and he will earn fortunes to impress any woman he chooses! He even has my looks!"

Tyton forced another smile and allowed the merchant to indulge his vanity.

"Your wife must also be proud, to have a fine son," Tyton said with practiced diplomacy.

"Oh, yes! Beautiful woman! But, alas, fate had other plans for us … it pains me to speak of it," said the merchant.

Tyton nodded politely. "Of course. Many pardons for my careless assumption."

The merchant changed the subject. "You have a wise business partner, to choose a man who knows our customs well. The maps are over here."

Tyton perused at leisure. The merchant pried, "Your friend? Would I know his name?"

Tyton nodded slightly. "Perhaps. His father is the one financing his expedition. Do you accept foreign coins?"

The merchant smiled, "Clever man. Of course, I do, if it is in gold or silver."

Tyton smiled. "Good. Nikolai will be pleased, if the exchange rate is fair."

The merchant frowned. "You wound me. Of course, I am fair."

Tyton added, "That's Nikolai from the Aristodemos family."

The other man almost fainted. "Aristodemos? You should have told me! Always proud to do business with such a noble family! Come, come, we shall fetch the scales right away!"

Tyton smirked. As a boy, he would have boasted of his relations first and demanded special treatment with far less effectiveness.

* * *

"So good that you have returned, Master. Your congregation has been worried about you!" the servant Toby said to Malsain as he entered the balcony over the altar.

The wereform of Malsain just snarled in annoyance as he sniffed around for other human scents. When Malsain's back was turned, Toby transformed back into Barton and, using both hands, mentally shoved Malsain flying into a stone pillar and let him drop thirty feet to the tiles. Both were cracked from the impact. Malsain roared in bestial rage, looked up at Barton, and recognized the threat. Barton and Toby were one and the same. Malsain leaped onto the nearest pillar, only to be repelled again into the next one by Barton. Malsain realized something else — there was a reason why Barton never used silver. It must somehow affect Barton, as well. Neither one could exploit that weakness, nor could Malsain get close enough to do any damage. So Malsain fled in defeat, planning to exact revenge some other day.

* * *

"Wait! I sense great evil ahead. We must turn north!" Lebiced warned.

Danny and Alex heeded his advice and veered the horses left from the main road, into Valantir. In the distance, they began to see movement among the trees.

Stiff, awkward movements of the undead. Alex panicked and spurred his horse into a full gallop; the other two gave chase right away. Low branches smacked Alex Mill about the face, stinging his ears and forehead until he dared not look where he was going. He soon fell off the horse, and the horse kept going.

"You cost us a fine horse, and maybe our heads for your foolishness, Mr. Alex Mill," Lebiced said bitterly. "Now get up, move!"

Alex the Meek swung a leg over the saddle in a very uncomfortable spot and groaned every time the horse jumped over a tree root or fallen branch. Hours later, after they were certain there was no pursuit, they stopped to rest the horses and gather food, since the original plan of meeting with the Elves in Pineval and resting there was shot. Alex could barely walk and moaned incessantly.

"Let that be a lesson to you to always mind your surroundings," said the wizard.

Alex nodded weakly and said nothing.

Danny then realized, saying, "Wait. If those undead are out in force, who is leading them? That cannot be Kazius."

Lebiced answered, "Quite right. it is not Kazius. It is the Lich that was once the father of Kazius, seeking vengeance for the loss of his wife Lorenna Saint Noir, the chaos witch born in Thalu, north of the Dragon Ridge Mountains, to Jack Saint Noir and Irena Mollenbeck in 1517. She died in Shadval in the year 1540, within sublevel four next to their foul altar devoted to the darkest powers of five pantheons. The Elves paid dearly in Shadval. And it is my hope that some have sheltered within the temple in their last line of defense."

Alex moaned. "And Oakthorn? Who is going to warn them?"

Lebiced mused, "I suspect one of the monks already knows. Hopefully he will find a way. If not, the men on the walls will sound the alarm. The Redmanes and Redoaks were no fools when they built the town long ago."

Alex Mill could not sit comfortably on anything, so he curled up on his side instead.

"We should not remain here much longer. Our pursuers, if we have any, need no rest," Lebiced warned, more for Alex Mill's benefit than Danny's.

* * *

"How dare you bring ruin on Eledar's reputation! Stealing from the treasuries and murdering a deputy? You are not welcome in these walls any ... urrrrrk!" Dhasa gurgled as Darmid stabbed him. "What ... have... you ... done ..." the arbiter wheezed as the poison took effect.

"You are a bloody bore, Dhasa. You have no appreciation for my real profession. You really thought I was going to be a scribe for the rest of my life? Fat chance! Now be a good neighbor and hush up," Darmid exclaimed in a sneering tone as he shoved at Dhasa, who fell to the floor, limp. Darmid wiped his blade on Dhasa's robes and then searched Eledar's old room.

"Ahhh, there you are," Darmid thought aloud, as he found the lapis pigment that he used for Eledar's documents. "The one thing they did not seize … insufferable deputies … I shall run empty of coin soon thanks to them." Darmid cursed as he sealed the pigment in a small jar. "Unless someone nearby pays their scribes better than you did, you old prune!"

* * *

"As I told you, Vamanastral is dead because of some chess gambit being played by Barton and my father, and if the blackbirds keep poking around, all of the Alphas are at risk, including you, Clark. We tried to advance our pieces to control the center, but Sandraz has blocked us at every turn. So, in desperation, I came to you," said Winter.

Clark Russell Whitetree smirked. "It is unlike you to reveal your plans or seek my help. Nor is it like a desperate woman to make no offers of compensation or trade or any mention of what I stand to gain, which means you are attempting to use me, Winter. Whatever I might do will doubtless be scrutinized by Sandraz and leave me exposed. No, I think not. Your game is up, Miss Auguron. Good day."

Winter frowned. "Pompous ass!"

Clark rebuked, "I do not recall asking your opinion. You are dismissed. Go."

Winter stomped out of the room and slammed the door before flashing an evil grin as she turned a corner to the next corridor.

Clark summoned one of his servants and whispered, "I want Arthur and Winter followed. Alert me to whatever their schemes are. And use the utmost discretion if you value your life."

* * *

"Sasha, dearest ..." Andar signaled. "Dhasa is dead. And Eledar's blue pigment is missing.

This makes Darmid suspect yet again."

Sasha returned the thought, "Perhaps for the best. Henry left a page marked where Arius betrayed the original order in Thalu. Dhasa could have been planning to do likewise."

Andar then willed, "There's more. Helen and Savadi have not returned, nor Dobbs or Sean. They are still in Valantir, and Arius will be at our town gates in a day or less. This is worse than I imagined."

Sasha comforted him, "Even though the barrier wards have failed, Arius is divided. He is not bringing his full abilities to bear. Something distracts him. We may have hope yet, love."

Andar closed with: "Let us pray then."

* * *

"I should have stayed in Stonehaven. Moving here was the worst mistake of my life," Moira confided. "The tax men seized our house; your bastard husband stole my daughter, and my own husband … I dare not imagine what happened … I have lost everything … <u>how</u> do you survive here?"

Mandy patted Moira's hand. "After two years of living with a gambling, lying, greedy, cheating husband and getting exiled from Oakthorn, West Bend, AND Agama, surviving is a piece of cake. Not that it helps you at all."

Moira gave a split-second, dry half-smirk, and then sighed in melancholy, burying her face between her arms on the table, weeping. "It's not fair, my poor Molly."

Mandy rubbed Moira's shoulders a short while, and then returned to her housekeeping in the home Adrian had bought. Strangely enough, ever since Adrian had fled, the house had stopped falling apart. Mandy had her suspicions about why, but did not like to think about such things.

Chapter Thirty
Call to Arms

A horn sounded at the eastern gate of Oakthorn, followed by "Undead to the east! Hundreds! Bar the gates!"

Suddenly the peasants stopped their gossiping about Conrad and fled to their homes, dropping anything that slowed them down, unless it had two legs. The REAL threat had emerged and put the lie to their idle slander. News spread quickly, and the last remaining arbiter of the abbey, Dharana, was not pleased with anything that was beyond his authority and control. He was already outraged over the missing watchers Sean and Dobbs, chasing after Savadi and Helen, and they had not even arranged Dhasa's funeral yet.

"Why was I not warned about these undead? Why has Andar hidden this from me?" he demanded.

Henry offered the opinion, "Perhaps the death of Dhasa was a greater concern ..."

Dharana rounded on the old lorekeeper. "Dhasa was a petty man with petty ambitions. The undead are the greater concern!"

Henry bowed and gave a placating smile. "Of course. Please forgive me an old man's folly."

Dharana scowled. "Too late for that. Now go rally our defenders, and there will be no talk whatsoever about Eledar, Darmid, or Dhasa henceforth."

Henry interjected with a bowed head, "We have yet to perform his ceremonies."

Dharana gave a frown of exasperation. "No other exceptions, my station has suffered enough slander ..."

* * *

"Has Axegrind sent you to taunt me, woman?" Kazius grumbled. "No, my liege, I begged him for mercy, and he granted this one visit. I could not abandon you. And to hear you are to fight in the arena ... there must be a way to appease him," Bernice presumed.

"You suppose wrongly that Axegrind will allow an insincere apology to outweigh his ambitions. There is no way," Kazius said with resignation.

Bernice pleaded, "But ... you could die!"

Kazius flatly replied, "Yes. I might even welcome it. My life has been cursed from the beginning."

Bernice cried, "Please don't say that! We could escape ..."

Just then, the sound of bodies hitting the floor startled them, and outside the bars stood D'aarzane. "Oh, how touching! The slave girl wants to elope with her master," he taunted sardonically, with a sadistic grin under his mask.

"YOU!" Kazius spat with revulsion.

"Yes, none other. I've come to see how you handled the change in command … I had no idea you'd sunk this low," the assassin replied with sarcastic delight.

"Liar, there's always something more you want from me, so speak and be done with it, vermin!" Kazius snarled.

Bernice cringed behind Kazius in the cell, shaking her head no.

"Ahh! How refreshing, so predictable, Kazius. I'd sit down for tea with you, but your selection is so boring," D'aarzane goaded.

"Insufferable toad! I'd pluck your eyes out, if I could, and feed them to the crows! What do you want?" the former monarch of Razadur hissed.

"Well, since you asked so nicely, I've come to make a deal. Your little blond lost kitten can come along as well," the assassin explained snidely.

Kazius growled with teeth bared, "You smug bastard!"

D'aarzane smiled. "I think the story of a slave liberating her master would make a wonderful sonnet."

Kazius grabbed handfuls of straw from the floor and threw them at D'aarzane through the bars. The assassin raised his eyebrows in mock surprise. "My, my, my, such fire! Too bad you don't harness it better. Arius had plans for you. After all, you make a much better puppet than Axegrind. He sent me next door for a little errand, which went quite nicely. Thank you for asking …"

Kazius just growled, fixing eyes of death on D'aarzane.

"I think perhaps Izimal or Mojara would be a nice change of scenery for you. Shall we?"

Kazius spat, "Don't expect any gratitude for this … PAWN!"

The assassin frowned, crossed his arms, and turned his back to leave.

"Wait! Where are you going? The shift changes in half an hour!" Kazius demanded.

D'aarzane paused, looked over his shoulder, then stooped to grab the keys off a body, and tossed them just outside the bars, his final taunt for the day.

* * *

Belinda and the others managed to bribe, seduce, and charm their way out of Black Falls, and were headed south along the coast toward the lake that separated Razadur from Vaja.

Fishing in the Dabani Gulf kept them reasonably fed and crafting jewelry from seashells gave them bartering items. This was the limit of their skills, and they would need more to secure their independence. Belinda knew this. She remembered bitterly, being sold as a young woman. She was once a Blackwolf, in the days when they were still rebels against the rule of Dwarven exiles.

In 1522, the wolves were almost exterminated before switching sides. Belinda was the only known survivor who had stayed a rebel and had kept her tattoo hidden under her armband. The traitors captured her and sold her to save themselves. For this, she would not forgive them. None of the younger women would understand the things Belinda had seen. How men were such selfish and cowardly creatures. The remaining Blackwolves and all the Bloodhammers above all others.

* * *

"Lord Whitetree, the witch has been oiling the lamps in the hallways. What do you wish to be done about it?" asked a servant.

Clark snarled, "Avoid those hallways. Do not interfere. I don't want anything traced back to me. Make whatever excuses you need to. That is all. Thank you."

The servant bowed. "As you wish, sire," and left the room.

Clark muttered to himself, "Yes, you are definitely up to something, Winter. Do not ever think I am ignorant of your specialties."

* * *

"A woman has arrived to see you, Baron," reported one of the honor guards.

"Yes, let her in … no, wait … I will greet her myself. This is urgent," Bravane the Third replied.

Minutes later: "Ravenna. Good to see you. I need your …"

The druidess answered, "Yes, I know. Something about my brother in peril. As much as I wish to help him, the undead are at your gates. They swept through Valantir just as I left. Is it truly wise to leave the barony without their leader? You have a weighty and urgent choice to make, and I shall hope that, whatever you do, you are crystal clear about your motives. Any deception whatsoever will come back to haunt you."

The baron gulped; she was right. The memory of his brother Donald already haunted his dreams. "I must consult my uncle, then. I have always trusted him …" the baron thought out loud. "Can you wait here?" he asked.

"Not long," Ravenna informed him.

"I shall be as quick as fate allows me then," the baron declared.

"Few mortals can claim to know the fates, Baron. Even oracles are hard pressed to comprehend them. I have consulted many. Do not think to hand off your duties to them," Ravenna warned.

The baron bowed, thinking to himself, "By the powers, she is a sharp one."

* * *

"Yes, I will gladly aid you against the Elves who murdered your chief. I need only a couple days to assemble the people and detail what must be done. You have my word," said Father Barton to the Dabani tribe.

"Good. We wait two days, then make war. Elves pay for their audacity," said the new leader of the tribe. "We need only to hunt food in the forest until then."

Barton nodded. "Of course. I will advise the royals to suspend the tree-cutting."

With that, they shook hands and sealed their agreement.

Chapter Thirty-One
For Love of Family

Molly and Carol were lost. They had run away from the old man who was abusive when drunk, and wound up heading east out of Korath, across a river, into a vast open land of misty valleys. They passed a small shed with shiny black roof tiles and heard a piercing mechanical birdcall and it gave them a fright. Molly spoke, "Can you feel it? Somebody watching us..."

Carol said nothing, being scared out of her wits. They did not see any windows or doors on the shed, which was strange. The walls were a solid gray. Then there was a hiss as a door appeared in the wall and opened, revealing a man in a white tunic with red trim and a flowing orange beard framed by shoulder-length hair of the same color.

"What brings you, and where are your parents?" the man asked.

Molly sensed something about him. He was different; all the other adults that Molly met had fear or anger hidden in their eyes. This man showed none at all, which, in its own way, scared Molly because it could only mean that he was very powerful, or maybe had no emotions at all. She had no words for this, of course. But she blurted, "Parents are lost, very far from here. We had to run from bad wolf." Molly dared not reveal more.

The man smiled, "Well, let's get you some food, and find your parents later." He led them away from the shed, and the door closed behind him. Molly was very uneasy about this, but she was also starving, and the promise of nourishment won out. They passed a garden which was torn up and dormant for the approaching winter season, and entered a tall glass house with trees on the inside, and many types of vines and vegetation. Molly had never seen such a thing. The man paused to pluck a few tomatoes, pick a few leaves of funny looking skinny lettuce, and other edibles, and he sliced them all up in a polished wooden bowl before serving them. They ate without complaint. The salad was actually sweet. Carol finally said, "Thank you."

The host smiled warmly and bowed. "Welcome."

* * *

"I have to know. Do I truly have a son or not? It gnaws at my insides every day ..." said Bravane the Third.

His uncle Alex advised, "What will you tell the people? Will you have a barony left if you leave? They already accuse Conrad of desertion, betrayal, and worse. Your future hangs by a thread, unless ..."

The baron snapped, "Unless what? Tell me."

Alex the Wise responded, "If you were stripped of title by reason of insanity. They know about your drinking binges and your nightmares. It is the only ruse they would believe."

The baron protested, "No, there has to be another way …"

Alex prompted, "If there was, I would gladly suggest it. Forgive my saying so, but there is no time to waste. You must make a decision."

Bravane thundered, "My son is out there. I can feel it! I hear his cries in my dreams, now stand aside. Damn you!"

Alex frowned. "Then it is done. GUARDS! Take the baron and remove him from the manor. He is to be banished along with his father until such time as he regains his … composure. You are henceforth banned from these grounds under penalty of public disgrace."

Bravane reached for his sword as Alex stepped back, and two guards intercepted."You cannot be serious. The birthright is MINE."

Uncle Alex asserted, "I am serious. I wish you a safe journey, but you cannot stay here in such condition. Confiscate his weapons until he is outside the western gate. Do what you must to see him safely out."

Bravane the Younger waved his sword, with teeth bared, exclaiming, "No! This is madness!"

The guards encircled the baron, flanking him and taking their time to avoid harm. Bravane slashed in one direction, and then the other, missing. Amanda appeared in the doorway, "Father, what is the meaning of this?"

The baron froze. His cousin Amanda was the last person he wanted to see this. He lowered his sword in surrender and dropped it on the floor.

Alex told his daughter, "I shall explain later. We have a town to defend."

As they reached the western gate, however, they could plainly see the undead encircled the entire two and a half miles of the outer walls.

Alex whispered to one of the men, "Sewers, south tunnel underneath the tannery. Follow that to the very end, re-lock the gate when he is safely gone. It should only be three miles long. Go."

Alex Redoak then took command of the defenses on the wall. One by one, the Lich Arius was seizing the minds of the defenders, and turning them on each other, while the undead battered the gates with an uprooted dead tree. Time favored the Lich, and Alex knew it. He sank to his knees to pray.

* * *

"The king has fallen ill and a quarter of his men with him. A plague is upon us," concluded councilman Emil Jacques Fleur, starting a cacophony of hot debates among the council.

Three chairs sat empty, King Goldlion's seat at the head of the table, Bravane the Second's, and Vamanastral's, while the other ten pointed fingers at one another with wild accusations and other nonsense.

"This council is no place for a woman!" spat Councilman Whitetree.

Darla Mae Copperhill retorted, "Why? Is your mistress losing her touch? I have every right to be in the seat my brother once occupied!"

Basil Penrod Blake quipped, "I find the council to be a terrible bore without Darla," as he smiled at her.

Clark shot back, "Oh! Of course, you two lovebirds find this amusing!"

Sandraz shouted, "ALL of you, shut up! This brings us no closer to dealing with the dragons or the rumors of undead in Valantir. We have actual business to attend to!"

Vaude Krantz spoke next, "Quite right, Sandraz. Would be a shame for the city to realize they can actually manage quite well without us ..."

Clark sneered, "Oh, very funny, Vaude!"

The others fell silent for a minute before another round of bickering led Sandraz to call for an early break.

* * *

The first snowfall of the season arrived in Valantir, prompting the lighting of extra candles and torches within the temple where the refugees had taken shelter.

"Scouts and farseers have confirmed Arius has moved on to Oakthorn, and wears down the defenses even now. Facing him on open ground is suicide. He is stronger now than Lorenna ever was. Many family lines were broken in Shadval, including our greatest mages," said Andrath. "A new enemy marches from the east. Our truce with the Dabani has now failed. Our doom is upon us," he sighed with melancholy.

Conrad snarled, "So that's it? Stand here and wait to die? NO, I will not! I'd rather die in battle than meekly accept the yoke of slavery that Arius surely has in store for us!"

The hunter from Korath spoke next, "Arius is not the only problem. The Malsain werewolf has fanned the fires of hatred. I've seen the spell my people are under. They follow him without question. There is no hope for them. They will bleed for his cause and his mad ambitions."

Skorvald chimed in, "We must strike quickly while we still can, even if only to buy time. They will overwhelm us no matter what we do."

Tyrus nodded in agreement.

Jonah added, "I stand by Conrad and Skorvald. Let us do some damage!"

Andrath challenged, "And what will you use against a Lich? You would have no defense against his magic, and it could take years to find his canopic jars that contain his life essence. How long can you hope to last?"

Conrad barked, "This maniac is ravaging my homeland! My sister's children are still in there! The longer we wait, the faster our future is taken away from us! I swore an oath to that land, and I still stand by it! Have you no enchanted weapons that would aid us?"

Andrath soberly pointed out, "Those, too, lay within Shadval. What you ask is dangerous. The surface and the sub-levels of Shadval are full of every undead you can imagine."

"Time is wasting, then. We ride tonight for Shadval!" Conrad announced with finality.

Jonah, Skorvald and the Barbarians raised their fists and cheered, and Tyrus merely nodded in agreement. Lebiced stepped forward. "Andrath, old friend, we shall require a map if you have it."

Andrath sighed. "I know better than to try to talk you out of this."

Lebiced gave a sly smile.

Alex Mill begged, "But my daughter is out there! I have to find her!"

Danny prompted, "True, although Kazius has never been on the selling end of slavery, I have an idea who might know ..."

Lebiced raised an eyebrow and said with a tone of concern, "Are you quite sure, Danny?"

Daniel Darkmoon answered, "Well, no. But I have to try. Adrian has made quite a few enemies. Someone out there will help."

Lebiced then warned, "Be advised. Your old name must be cast aside."

Danny nodded, "Rather figured that."

Andrath called a scout to escort them safely as far as the mountain pass. Danny bowed, and Alex Mill gave a weak smile. The company would part near the border.

* * *

Bravane the Elder and Bravane the Third mounted up outside the sewer grate hidden behind the middle falls of the western fork of the River Vaniki, translated as "Vein of Water." A twelve-foot drop lay just ahead, and neither man had attempted this in a long time.

"Age before beauty, Father," taunted the younger one.

"No, no, vanity before wisdom, I insist," said the elder.

"Together then. On the count of three," said the younger.

"Aye," his father replied.

They steadied their breathing, bracing themselves.

"One, two ... THREE!"

And through the waterfall, they jumped on horseback into the river. The guards above then locked the grate behind them. As they emerged onto the narrow bank downstream, the younger said, "You remember the trail leading up from here?"

The elder nodded yes.

The younger added, "It's not visible anymore. The weeds have choked it. The treasury has been low for years, and I had to decide between this and repairs to the mansion."

His father grumbled, "Well, at least they can't see it either. Let's go."

* * *

Alex Redoak felled yet one more mind-controlled honor guard and seized his longbow to lob a flaming arrow at the dead tree trunk battering the gates. It lodged itself firmly next to an undead, who caught fire in seconds, and distracted Arius. The Lich summoned a gust of wind to blow it out, but only succeeded in toppling the trunk, crushing one flank of undead beneath it, with the arrow sticking straight up. The embers relit, and the flailing undead in flames caught others on fire. Arius now turned his full attention to Alex, knocking him flat with a lightning bolt. Alex fell fifteen feet to the street behind him. His eyes blinked in panic as his heart went into cardiac arrest. The defenders fled the wall and retreated in two directions, southward to the keep, and north to the mansion, every man for himself. James, the physician, was the last civilian to enter the mansion gate before it closed, right behind Nell and Bethany's children.

Bethany's neighbors John and Amber were trapped outside with all the other peasants.

* * *

The fortress of West Keep was now burning rubble; the soldiers of Stonehaven were bloodied and bruised or dead. The dragons closed in for the kill and then suddenly veered off.

"I don't understand. Why did they stop?" said one injured defender.

"Who cares! Now help me rescue some of these poor lads under the wreckage," said another.

A third said, "Did you see the look in their eyes? It was like they just woke from a deep sleep. Maybe the Dwarves did control them, like the council said."

A fourth added, "Rubbish! The council can hardly agree what day of the week it is. I don't believe a single word from their lips ..."

The first replied, "Maybe you're right ... they did have a weird look in their eyes."

The third added, "Maybe, with the dragons gone, the king will recover."

The fourth one scoffed, "Was no dragon that made him sick, happened soon after that Redoak fellow vanished. There's a connection there, I tell you!"

The second piped in, "Hey! Talk later! We have work to do here!"

The others grumbled, but did their job of lifting stone and lumber off the bodies of the trapped and the dead.

* * *

"*What?* My father is out there, and *you just left him* to die?" Amanda screamed in rage as she slapped the guard so hard it stung. "Let me through! Damn you! That's an *order*! Do you understand?" she commanded.

None of the guards dared to challenge her. As she squeezed through the gate and forced her way through the crowd, John and Amber caught her attention.

"We know where he is! We can help!"

Amanda nodded. "Lead on, then!"

Minutes later, as they approached the eastern gate where Alex fell, they froze as they saw the figure of Arius outside, telekinetically ripping the dented gates from their mooring, making the stone foundations crack and groan.

"Quick! Help me pick him up!" Amanda shouted.

John and Amber snapped out of it and hurried to wrap some rags around the smoking hot armor and drag Alex away from the gate. As they passed the market square, Amanda seized and cleared a vendor cart and directed them to put her father on it. A loud clanging in the distance heralded that the gate was breached.

"Hurry!" Amanda prodded.

As they got closer to the north bridge over the river, they could still see the crowd of peasants outside the manor. Amanda yelled for them to clear a path, but they ignored her. Then she called to them, "My father just risked his life and limb protecting all of you, now stand clear!" A select few stood aside, others still refused. "Let us pass! Damn you! Guards, do something!"

The men did not budge. The fear in their eyes said everything. Fear of the crowd, fear of Amanda herself, and fear of the Lich off in the distance.

"My kin have defended all of you time and time again, and now you turn your unworthy backs on us after gleefully slandering our names and cheering for rabble-rousing rat droppings! Hades take you all, you miserable cowards!" Amanda spat in disgust as she led John and Amber past the manor toward the abbey.

A smaller crowd was gathered there, attempting to gain access, but the doors were locked.

"Arbiter, hear me! My father, Alex Redoak, requires medical assistance! He has risked everything defending the barony! Open this door! I know you are in there!"

The door did not budge. The watchers within looked at each other and shook their heads. Dharana had given orders to deny entry.

"Curse the lot of your kind! Arbiter, mark my word! I will never forgive you!" Amanda promised. She then directed John and Amber to take the cart and her father to the courthouse.

Oddly enough, very few people thought of this place as refuge. Magistrate Blackhull ordered the deputies to allow them in.

"Are there any physicians here?" Lady Amanda pleaded.

The mediator general shook his head no. "None, Lady Redoak."

Her father Alex was starting to look pale; his eyes had been vacant for awhile, and there was neither breathing nor pulse. Amanda cried hysterically at the end of her wits, "Nooooooo!"

What she saw next, made her doubt her sanity, a woman materialized before them inside the lobby, in a white and silver gown, wearing an amethyst pendant on a gold clasp, and sporting long tresses of flowing red hair, her eyes glowing white. The woman waved her hand over the form of Alex the Wise, and a pool of light shone down on his body.

"None who witness here may tell of it, for I shall not visit again. But you will henceforth be safe here from the unliving. I have spoken," the woman said in a high baritone.

Then she was gone, and Amanda fainted. Nobody dared speak for minutes afterward.

Amber was the first to hear Alex Redoak breathing. "John, he lives!"

Blackhull and the deputies sighed with relief and went back to other duties.

* * *

Rebecca pulled aside several peasants to follow her to the inn.

"Fire and water will be our last defense against the undead. Hurry! We have to get the bottles to the north bridge before they swarm over it! Who is with me?"

Desperation outweighed any misgivings they had about her loyalties to Conrad, and they accepted her leadership without protest. Rebecca directed one peasant to collect rags, while handing bottles over the bar, praying they had acted in time to save the western half of the barony.

Elsewhere, inside the Abbey, Andar confronted the last arbiter, "Don't be a fool, Dharana. If we don't help soon, there will not BE an abbey or a barony left to defend! I saw that future, and Arius himself laughed as he ripped you limb from limb! After you offered him an alliance! Are you mad or just stupid?"

Dharana backhanded Andar and ordered the watchers, "Place this dog under lock and key where he belongs!"

Andar did not wait for them to move, but launched into a flying sidekick, catching one in the plexus, and as he landed, swept the arbiter's feet out from under him, and then rolled into a ball under the second watcher's lunge, rebounding up into a handstand double-heel kick right under the chin. The second watcher fell down for the count, while the first gasped, catching his breath.

Andar then struck the rising arbiter in the throat with a ridge hand, making Dharana cough and sputter, before a chop to his collarbone took him down. The first watcher struggled on one knee to grab Andar, who sidestepped and smashed his face with an elbow. Once the watcher was down, Andar called out, "Henry! Now or never! Arius is advancing to the south bridge!"

Within seconds, the entire Abbey was locked in battle between the faction loyal to Eledar's memory and the faction that hated Eledar. Thus began the long-predicted sundering.

Farther south at the lower bridge, the Obsidian Owls had gathered lamp oil and lit the bridge as the undead started to cross. What few of those undead reached the western bank were savagely beaten or decapitated in short order by the thieves' guild. The peasants under Rebecca's leadership at the north bridge launched their bottles with flaming rags, and denied passage to the undead there. Arius was not pleased.

The half-moon embers in his eye sockets narrowed even further to tiny slits of flickering rage as he raised his skeletal arms toward the river from his position at the western edge of the market square, and six peasants defending the north bridge suddenly turned into stone, while a gust of wind threw three defenders on the south bridge into the river. Arius waved his skeletal hands yet again, and wagon after wagon flew one by one from the square, dropping into the river, eventually damming it up and creating a new bridge over which Arius strode to the western bank, heading straight for the Obsidian Owls Guild headquarters. Two apprentices and a veteran let loose slings and arrows which Arius swatted aside with ease before obliterating the thieves and their base of operations in a huge fireball. Defenders at the north and south bridges ducked for cover from the wrath of the Chaos Lich ravaging the town without mercy.

* * *

In the heavy gloom of Shadval's perpetual bluish-gray fog, Conrad, Jonah, Skorvald, and several of his Northlanders from the kingdom of Frost Pillars all struck down wandering ghouls and skeletons among the withered trees and rubble at the surface level of the ancient Dwarven compound. Orange fungi and dark green moss and lichens dotted the cracks and pits in the cobblestone walkways, and the stench of mold and rotted flesh which permeated the ruins made Tyrianna queasy. Lebiced and Tyrus flanked her on both sides. Their Elven scout warned them, "The entrance is close at hand. I must caution you that the great battle here long ago collapsed many underground passages, navigating the tunnels may prove daunting, even for one who escaped this forsaken pit."

Lebiced added, "Valantir emptied this place once called Modar, now known as Shadval, of Dwarven exiles in 1475. The people of Vaja had driven the exiled Dwarves out of Razadur completely in 1523. Razadur changed hands in 1527 upon the return of Arius, whose Chaos allies used to trade here with the exiles. Those exiles and Arius himself now operate out of Zara-Mogai in the north. Kazius reclaimed Black Falls in Razadur sometime after 1540."

Tyrianna made a disgusted look at the mention of Kazius' name.

When the scout spotted the doorway leading down to the sub-levels, he recited a blessing over a flask of oil and applied it to all of the weapons in the party, "This will last but a few hours. Let us make the best use of them."

Conrad took point down the stairwell with Lebiced, Tyrianna, and Tyrus behind him, with Skorvald and Jonah protecting the rear flank. Below the second landing, the light became perilously dim, and Lebiced drew forth a translucent white orb and intoned an ancient verse that made the stone emit a pale glow. The wizard then led their descent into the dangers before them.

At the third landing, they heard hissing below, Lebiced whispered to Conrad, "Ghouls have keen smell. We have been discovered. Everyone stay on your toes."

Tyrianna felt her stomach heave. She leaned over the side with only a second to spare.

Skorvald sighed. "This is no place for children ..."

At which Tyrus snarled, "She is no child, and anything that threatens her must reckon with me first, Northlander."

At the fourth flight, the stairs opened into a corridor running right and left. The left passage was collapsed and full of blackened corpses, scorched stone, and a coating of transparent gray slime. Tyrianna retched again.

Skorvald whispered, "Let us pray you are up to the task, ocean dweller ..."

Jonah hushed him and pointed down the hall to the right, which ended in a sharp turn. The soft hissing of multiple throats around the corner was unmistakable.

Conrad whispered, "I count a dozen or so. I will lead the attack."

The others nodded. Captain Redmane charged ahead with a bear growl, which startled his prey and his allies alike, as his sword rang against bone and flesh in arcs and spirals of fury, rending arms and necks like so much ripe fruit. The last ghoul panicked and scurried away on all fours with inhuman speed.

As the echoes of Conrad's frenzy died down, the party rounded the corner to see his handiwork. The pale gray flesh of the enemy had the same texture as the stone walls and bled a watery gray mucus. It carried the same odor of contagion that Conrad detected the day of Obsek's death.

"Curses! These ghouls are the source of the plague!" Conrad exclaimed. "The fever that took my father, nearly crippled our town, my sister, and threatened all I hold dear! Arius and Kazius will PAY! This do I swear!"

Even Tyrianna was awed by the intensity of Conrad's anger toward Kazius. While Conrad himself was now hell-bent on completing the quest, no matter what it cost him. He was hot on the trail, and by the powers above he would see it through. The corridor branched ahead, one fork running straight, the other turning left. Ahead, the hallway led to a crater of rubble below. The party had to turn back to the other passage. A new fork ran right and left. Twenty paces right, the hall was blocked by debris, and twenty paces left a doorway led to more stairs.

Conrad tried the stairs, and nearly fell to his doom below the second landing, losing his sword as he clambered for a foothold on the collapsed stairs. Conrad growled like a beast, as he searched the depths to no avail. The drop was steep, and the bottom beyond the illumination of Lebiced's stone.

"Curse these exiles and cult fanatics," the captain mumbled bitterly.

Conrad drew his hunting knife and marched back to the blocked passage. For twelve minutes, the party labored to clear the path, and found a door to the right. More stairs going down. They proceeded with great caution, and arrived at the second sublevel.

"Which way?" Conrad asked the Elf.

The Elf responded, "That way," pointing right.

Twenty-five paces right, the hall forked left and right yet again, and Conrad felt the hairs on his neck rise and braced his shield in front. Three dozen undead squeezed into the corridor from both sides, fitting three abreast in front of Conrad, who ducked low with his shield raised, slashing at the thighs of ghoul and zombie, while Tyrus impaled one on Conrad's left on the trident. Tyrianna freaked and yelled with a voice not her own, no longer aware of what she was doing, her eyes glowing like white flares, and a white fire rose inside the undead, coming out their eyes, ears, and mouths, reducing them quickly to ashes. Tyrianna collapsed afterward into an exhausted sleep.

Skorvald spoke, "The girl is most strange, but I retract my words from before ..."

Tyrus gave a grim look and said nothing as he picked Tyrianna up off the floor. The Elf led the way this time, turning left beyond the smoldering ashes, taking another set of stairs down after forty paces.

On their way down, he said, "Sublevels three and four will be the worst of them all. The greatest casualties of Shadval mounted here."

Conrad just grunted. "And once again, they will have an angry Redmane to reckon with!"

* * *

Bravane the Elder and the baron were halfway to the capitol when Ravenna appeared on foot in front of them.

"Your trail was not easy to find, else I would have caught up half an hour ago," she declared. "Pray that there will be a barony left to return to; it did not look well when last I saw."

The baron nodded, "It would pain me more to abandon my son, but do not think I made this choice lightly. I shall later be glad to hasten the demise of the foul Augurons and their lapdogs in payment for their treachery."

Ravenna was not impressed. "Begging pardon, but you are ill-matched even for the werewolf who has lent his labors on behalf of their allies. None of us would last ten minutes against the Lich Arius in single combat. One rash move would seal your doom."

The baron opened his mouth to speak and quickly changed his mind. And the Elder Bravane helped Ravenna up onto the saddle behind him. The remainder of their journey was a calm before the storm.

Chapter Thirty-Two
Unholy Alliances

"Who dares enter the audience room of Emperor Axegrind unannounced?" a regal voice called from his throne to an old man whose very touch felled the guards with a crack of electricity.

"My name is no concern of yours, *mortal*. We have a mutual interest, you and I. Her name is Tyrianna."

Axegrind looked incredulously at the old man. "Supposing I believe you, old man, why does someone with your ability need me to be involved?"

The old man gave an evil grin. "Consider the girl's suffering to be payment exacted from an unfaithful wife who bore her into this world. Right now, the goddess is preoccupied with all that happens in the five kingdoms up north. Tyrianna is unconscious in the bowels of Modar. Oh, I forget! You know it as Shadval."

Axegrind frowned. "How am I to trust you if you would betray your own wife?"

The old man grinned even more. "Ahhh, how black your own heart is, _General_. If you choose to waste the opportunity, I will find others willing to seize it. And I shall help them take your place. It matters little who steps forward. I care nothing if you trust me or not."

Axegrind thought hard for long moments, and then nodded, "Very well, I shall see to her capture and torment or something better. It will be done."

The old man laughed. "I know what you are after. You seek the same blades Kazius did. And two of them are nearby. One the goddess keeps, and another is in the Elven temple. I would have told someone else, but he is much too … unstable."

Axegrind smirked. "Indeed. Father and son both. I appreciate your … generosity. Thank you."

The old man grinned again. "And I welcome your ambition."

Then, in a flash of pale silver, the old man vanished.

Axegrind immediately summoned his men and said, "Ready two hundred troops to ride by sunset. Tell them simply that we are hunting a fugitive. Dismissed."

The new monarch of Razadur then opened the iron room to don his best armor and weapons.

* * *

"Look, I just need a small loan to finance my business. My credit is good, Kazius himself knows me. We're buddies and cousins!" pleaded Adrian to a leathery skinned old broker.

"Then you are behind on the news, sir. Kazius is no longer in power. If you mention that name once too often, the new monarch might throw you in his arena to take his place. Wherever he has got to, he is not in Razadur. I can tell you that right enough. Now stop bothering me," said the old guy in a silk turban.

Adrian and Sal left in despair.

"It's another night of fishing for dinner for us ..." Adrian mumbled sadly.

Sal replied, "I told you not to gamble our payment from that guy, but no, you had that greedy look in your eye again! Your luck has run out, and if you do that again, I won't help you anymore, you big idiot!"

Adrian kicked at the pier and stubbed his toe before hopping madly on one foot and falling backward into the surf. Sal burst out laughing. "You'll freeze by nightfall if you don't get some palm bark going. Let's go, idiot."

* * *

Andar and Sasha broke loose from the battle inside the abbey and left the north door just in time to see Arius destroying the houses on Oak Street next to the smoking ruin of the thieves' guild. They joined hands and exerted their combined will in a telekinetic force burst, which caught Arius by surprise and tumbled him backward into a tree. As he stood back up, he mentally ripped timbers loose from the rooftops of several houses and hurled them all at the couple. Andar took the brunt of the volley to shield Sasha, and he was struck unconscious.

Sasha gasped in horror at the blood from his forehead, and Arius cackled. "Your precious Abbey is next, Elf wench. And I will make you watch helplessly in abject fright! Your wards have failed, and you have no hope alone against me!"

With those words, he cast a lightning bolt at the abbey, causing parts of the altar to catch fire. Sasha desperately willed a torrent of water from the river to smash Arius against the outer wall, which damaged him and put the fires out. Now the Lich was furious and hunted her like a starving wolf as she ran north in panic past the library. More lightning bolts followed, striking the houses on Maple Crescent, having just missed Sasha. She attempted to shelter within the Reeves' building, but a fireball hit the door before she could reach it, singing her clothing and hair. Arius then caused several windows to shatter, raining shards of glass all around her, and drawing blood head to foot from many cuts and scratches. Arius was intent on making her suffer. Sasha willed another torrent of water to hit the Lich, and even dislocated his jaw this time. Arius snarled in vile hatred, "Insolent wretch, I will break every bone in your body for this!"

The next thing to be thrown at Sasha was a lamp post, which hurtled too fast to dodge. Sasha felt her left leg break on impact then fell sideways. She dragged herself on her elbows toward the courthouse in agonized groans, certain she was about to die.

Arius took his time to gloat, "Perhaps it would be more fun to watch the zombies pull you apart after they cross the dam. This is what your defiance has bought you, wench!"

Sasha kept crawling on her elbows, dragging her useless leg behind her, struggling against the pain that was sending her into shock.

Arius levitated another wagon from across the river, and kept it spinning aloft over his head, taunting Sasha as he savored her fear and torment. Sasha finally reached the steps of the courthouse, and Arius hurled the wagon then, which careened off the pillars, instead of hitting Sasha as Arius intended. He levitated the scraps and tried again, but as Sasha made contact with the door, an eerie white glow surrounded both the courthouse and Sasha, and shone from her eyes as well. The wagon scraps rebounded off the field, and a shock wave of white force blasted Arius and all his minions clear from the city, splintering all but Arius against the trees in the forest. A dome of light now covered the barony, and a voice sounded on the wind in a whisper, "None who witness may tell of it. I have spoken."

* * *

In the desert, a lone figure in beige and white rags carried a dark canvas shoulder bag full of only he knew what. His dark natural complexion marked him as native to this land. Ahead, over the next sand hill was a band of men betrayed by the odor of their tobacco. They were Crimson Hoods, tax enforcers for Razadur. The lone figure crept low to the ground and held a knife in his teeth as he skirted around the low end of the hill.

One of the hoods spotted his bag in the distance and summoned the others to fan out in a search pattern. The stranger rose up behind one of them, one hand jabbing his neck, and the other liberating a dagger from the victim's belt to hurl it flawlessly into another Crimson Hoods' throat. Three more men responded to the sounds of felled bodies with blades flashing. Another toss of a knife reduced that number yet again. The last two closed in certain of a kill now that the stranger was empty-handed; their swords raised overhead. The stranger feinted right and dodged left with such speed they could not react before he seized the right hand and weapon of one to sever the right arm of the other in a down stroke, and then with a single horizontal arc, both throats were cut.

The stranger then wiped the blades clean and emptied the men's pockets. He found their orders:

Bring the girl. Alive.
Twenty bottles reward.

"That sounds like Axegrind, not Kazius," Tyton mused. Something in this turn of events bothered him. Tyton retrieved his bag and continued Eastward after piling the bodies. "Why is Axegrind after the girl?" he wondered.

* * *

"Remember, the Elves can turn you against each other; do not allow them to speak, and if humans are helping them, they must be subdued for questioning. I will do the questioning myself. Let us teach the Elves a lesson! We march for justice!" exhorted Lord Barton with a trace of an evil gleam in his eyes.

The Dabani tribes drummed the hafts of their spears on the ground in rhythm, with murder in their own eyes. With that, they advanced toward Valantir from Falcon Pass.

Syrene watched the scene unfold in the waters of her scrying bowl and scowled, "So, you walk the Earth again, demon. The order that banished you was too merciful. No matter what name or body you cloak yourself in, you cannot hide forever. Your days are numbered, evil one."

* * *

As the honor guards cautiously scouted the perimeter of the city under a heavy gray sky to assess the damages, they found a sobbing monk on top of the west wall. It was Darmid.

"The pigment … my opium … not fair …" he mumbled.

His pigment jar was broken on the stairs, his pipe was empty, and he was still quaking in fear of the undead.

As the men returned him to his cell, they found the dead deputy. The guards immediately beat Darmid to within an inch of his life and tied him to a post so tightly that he had difficulty breathing. The rest of their duties were much more discouraging. Many houses in the middle of the west side were burnt to charred embers, and not a single window on the east side was left intact. Broken pottery and dead animals littered the entire market section. A few scattered peasants had tried to defend their homes, but they had been overwhelmed, strangled, beaten, and even bitten savagely. A dearly bought and bitter victory, such that morale ebbed very low. And a long chill winter was still ahead.

Lady Amanda was in charge until her father regained his strength. While little Jacob cried, and Devi begged to see her mom, who was not here. Nell and Blackhull and Rebecca were all distributing soup, and a few widows wailed on the north bridge where their loved ones were turned to stone.

The abbey had casualties, too. All of the apprentices were dead, several watchers, many scribes, a librarian, the alchemist, and the last arbiter. Andar and Sasha were both in critical condition, over which James devoted the majority of his waking hours. The entire barony was beset with gloom.

Outside the barrier, Arius raged with vengeance against the barony, trying to break the shield. Fire, lightning, and force bolts all failed to penetrate the dome. Finally, he skirted around the perimeter, and in his last act of spite before retreating north to his fortress, he blighted all of the pumpkins, beans, and squash that were not yet harvested.

* * *

In the corridors of the third sublevel of Shadval, Jonah dropped his sword in a weak parry of rushing skeletons and ghouls, and took a hard blow to the shoulder where Darmid had poisoned him in Oakthorn. Conrad drove the enemy back on one side of Jonah, and Tyrus let loose on the other side in berserker fashion, impaling undead and smashing them sideways into the walls, activating the trident's powers while the target was completely unable to dodge the disrupting sonic attacks, shattering bones and causing their eardrums to explode. Zombies, ghouls, and mummies all fell in helpless writhing heaps before his wrath, until a vampire held the Myrmidon's mind in its merciless will, to be broken only by the now-awakened Tyrianna, her eyes lit like the sun. "Get away from him, you monster!" she screamed as her force wave blasted the floating predator backward, and as she raised her hands higher, the corridor caved in, sealing off the vampire from the party, and crushing all the undead still in front of Tyrus.

Her eyes now blazed orange, and a faint glow surrounded her hands as she turned in Conrad's direction, under her gaze scores more undead erupted in white flame from the insides.

Tyrianna had her teeth bared like a snarling wolf. Lebiced backed away from her, alarmed at how quickly her power was growing. But he said nothing.

Skorvald laid to rest two of his men, the oldest and the youngest, that had been overwhelmed at the stairwell leading into the third level.

"Grandfather of my wife, honorable Elmund and brave cousin Vithgar, may your deeds be recounted in the halls of the Valkyries, comrades."

Lebiced put a finger to his lips and pointed to the next turn in the corridor, past Conrad, and soon enough, the others heard more hissing in the distance. Conrad picked through the bodies of the fallen from the great battle long ago and discovered a sword of the same weight and reach as the one he lost. It was clearly Elven craftsmanship, and then, on the body, he saw his family crest of a red bear in a black circle with a gold border. This was Susan Redmane, the baron's grandmother. Conrad knelt in reverence, before taking the scabbard.

Then a voice whispered to him, "Son of my nephew Connor, linger not. The sundering is not over. You must return by water. The roads are not safe."

And then the voice was gone.

Conrad stood quickly, and with new resolve, he charged down the passage leading right, his newly acquired sword flashing in deadly arcs through the enemy ranks. Their numbers were many times greater than the last group of ghouls, and Conrad began to reel from the stench; his aim suffered, and he had to backpedal to stay clear of their clutches. As they rounded the T-corner they were quickly obliterated by Tyrianna.

"Thank you," Conrad nodded to the oracle.

Tyrianna did not respond; her face was taut with murderous rage, and only the destruction of these foul denizens would appease her.

* * *

"You have some nerve crawling back here after the mess you made, ERIK. I should have you slain where you stand, you arrogant pig!" said a dark-skinned priestess in black silk robes, flanked by assassins in a dimly lit cloister.

Tyton bowed and kneeled. "You see before you a much older and wiser man than the rash child I once was. There could be no greater regret or punishment than my losing your sister Sidhuri. I have paid many times for the pride of a foolish young boy."

Nikita was not impressed; her arms remained crossed, her scowl full of hatred. "I am the senior priestess now. Since your mother died last year, your two sisters live in other lands, your brother is on assignment, and your nephew is too young to intervene in a debt of blood."

Tyton spoke again, "Hear me, Nikita. I loved her deeply and had not the wisdom to prevent what happened. Her words haunt me to this day in every waking hour."

Nikita barked, "Liar! You broke her heart and destroyed her!"

Tyton whispered, "It is no lie. I have never missed her birthday once. Every year since her death, I have burned plates of food before an image of her cast in silver. This very one ..."

Nikita fell silent as he presented a tiny silver figurine in her sister's likeness. Nikita quickly snatched it from his hand, and looked it over.

This one detail seemed to be true. It did look like her sister at the age of fourteen. Nikita snarled, "You must then prove yourself, in the trials by combat, and are forbidden to use your shadow jumping." Tyton nodded and turned toward the corridor that led to the testing grounds.

* * *

A contest between a bandit and a petitioner was going badly for the man who wanted to join the gang. He was skilled in combat, but did not have their speed and dexterity, which counted plenty in the bo staff duels. Kazius kept landing in the mud. Bernice shielded her eyes whenever he took a blow. The leader of the Black Scorpions camp, Mosallah Halad, finally clapped his hands twice to signal an interlude. "You have the fire, but not the focus, boy ..."

Kazius grit his teeth and clenched his fingers, wanting to strangle the man, knowing that to do so would be his own death.

The chief continued, "The mind and heart are the compass and the ox. If your compass is off, the ox gets lost. You waste your energy and attention. Try again."

Kazius snarled and got back on the log. He blocked high and low with more control now, but his offense still suffered, his intention too obvious. The overhead strike most of all; the bandit he faced parried with ease and swept Kazius's feet out from under him. Kazius dropped his staff and clung to the log awkwardly. More bets were taken by the audience on the outcome of the match. The adversary grinned wickedly as Kazius retrieved his staff. He clambered back up, and set his stance before attacking overhead again. His opponent parried the blow perfectly, but was taken off-guard by the thrust to his foot and hobbled in pain just as Kazius finished with a sweep. Kazius scored his first point.

"Thirteen to one," the leader announced, as he declared the first match over. "Next round tomorrow."

Bernice sighed with relief and helped Kazius bathe. For once he was glad of her company.

Chapter Thirty-Three
No Rest for the Weary

Tyrus and Tyrianna were now on point, with the Elf navigating right behind them. Here at the fourth sublevel, the burnt corpses of the war dead were everywhere.

"Lorenna's handiwork, I wager," said Conrad, struggling against the horrific odors.

Jonah turned his head in shame. Lebiced lightly rested a hand on Jonah's shoulder and winked in sympathy as he walked past him, down the corridor toward another T-fork. The scrying bowl of Syrene began to darken and turn red, as Tyrianna turned the corner ninety feet from the Chaos Altar. At sixty feet, the water turned pitch black. Just then, Syrene's husband appeared. "Why do you persist in aiding these petty and feeble mortals? They rebel against us, squander their short lives, and breed like vermin."

Syrene glanced at him with disgust. "You would rebel if your places were reversed! How are you really so different from them?"

He exploded in rage, "HOW DARE you! Insolent whore!"

His first action was summoning a tidal surge to flood the cave and smash her decorations and pottery to shards, which cut Syrene viciously. Her wounds slowly sealed up as she defiantly stood herself upright, and she teleported away from her deranged husband.

"FACE ME, you bitch!" he roared as he, too, teleported.

Tyrianna clutched her head in pain as she stood thirty feet from the altar room, a cavernous round chamber with four doorways. She could approach no closer, and she heard, impossibly, the troops on the surface. Before anyone could react, she roared at the ceiling, her fingers clenched like giant cat paws, and with her eyes glowing bright red, she caused the ceiling of the altar room to collapse with a great rumble, taking all the upper levels with it, opening a great pit above and sealing the chamber forever. Axegrind leaped clear from the tremors above, clutching at tree roots that stuck out from the edges of the sinkhole, and a few dozen other men did also. Hundreds fell to their doom. As the undead made their move, filling in the corridors southwest of the altar room.

Tyrianna let loose again with a new power, dancing tendrils of red fire snaked around the undead, igniting what hair they had left and the rags they wore. Conrad was overwhelmed by the stench and his stomach heaved.

Lebiced assumed command. "This way! Look for the caverns!" as he strode northwest past the stairwell they had just exited.

* * *

Lady Amanda, John, Amber and a couple court deputies had finally removed Alex Redoak's armor, and he was blistered and burnt all over, just as his wife Myra had been in the great fire of 1533. One deputy left hastily to summon James, the physician. Magistrate Blackhull gave a pat on the shoulder to Amanda. "The boys got word we owe a debt of gratitude to your father, and other brave souls today. We will help what little we can."

Amanda broke into sobs, but dared not hug the mediator general. Amber held out her arms, and Amanda melted into them. The insanity of the last forty-eight hours ran down her cheeks for several minutes as Amber stroked her hair. When James finally arrived with Nell, Devi, and Jacob, his assistants had also brought the injured Sasha and Andar inside the courthouse.

* * *

"Halt! Who goes there? By order of the queen, no one goes in or out until positively identified and deemed worthy of her trust, yield or turn back!" a sentinel barked at the approach of three figures, two of them with horses.

A woman replied, "Tell Queen Lissa Firebird that her sister-in-law has returned, and these men are my guests."

The sentinel looked at her, astonished, and dropped instantly to one knee, bowing. "Lady Ravenna! Forgive me.

We have not seen you for many moons! I regret to inform you, your brother has died of illness, milady."

Ravenna frowned. "When? Tell me everything!"

The sentinel shook his head. "It is not safe to speak of it here, Lady Freebird."

The druidess, thereupon, hissed, "Take us to my sister quickly then. We are on urgent business from Oakthorn."

The sentinel led them through the courtyards, and once past the gilded lion statues by the fountain, he whispered, "Sandraz will want to see you, milady. I can say no more."

Ravenna nodded. "Thank you."

The two Redoaks and Ravenna proceeded to the throne room. Lissa welcomed her sister in a tearful hug. Ravenna stood silent a few minutes before asking, "How did it happen, Lissa? I must know."

Lissa wiped her cheeks as she answered, "He fell ill, along with many servants after a woman arrived claiming she could repel dragons. The council cannot reach an accord on what to do. I am losing my mind. There is no one I can trust anymore … except you and Sandraz."

Ravenna mulled over the implications, then asked, "Have you put up a reward for information? Certain members of the council would sell their own mothers."

Lissa then noticed the Elder Bravane and spoke to Ravenna, "Are you certain these men are vouch-worthy?"

Ravenna nodded yes. "They have their faults, but they are on our side, Your Majesty."

Lissa looked Ravenna in the eyes and, after a moment of searching there, accepted her word. Then Sandraz arrived, and his eyes went wide upon sighting the Elder Bravane.

Without thinking, Sandraz moved to attack and subdue, but was intercepted by the Younger Bravane, his wrist held fast in the strongest grip Sandraz had ever felt.

"Hold, young one. Perhaps you can tell me the importance of this letter." Bravane the Younger held out the message that was given to Jonah.

Sandraz silently read the words, pretending he had not seen them before. He then asked, "How did you get this?"

Bravane huffed in annoyance, "It was delivered to me by Jonah Blackthorn and a wizard. I am the Baron Bravane Redoak the Third, of Oakthorn. Who are you?"

Sandraz finally gave his name, bowing.

Ravenna added, "Time is short for all of us. It is urgent we decide on a course of action without the interference and espionage of the council and their foul schemes. Shall we convene in a more secure setting?"

Sandraz saluted Ravenna before turning on his heels. "Follow me, good sirs and madams..."

* * *

"So, the two of us are looking for work, and for a man named Adrian; he owes us a great debt," said the man who called himself Wayne Blackmoon.

The fruit vendor looked around cautiously and whispered back, "Don't mention that name too loudly. There's evil folk in business with that swindler. But there's plenty of work rebuilding what some wild deranged beast destroyed. My wife hears that ..."

Wayne interrupted, "We will take it. Who do we speak to?"

The vendor harrumphed at Wayne's haste. "Since the father is away on business, ye have to talk ter the royals at the castle over yonder. Now off with you!"

Wayne and Alex the Meek departed, glad to avoid idle gossip.

Alex Mill mumbled aloud, "You think the beast is still out there? What if ..."

Wayne stopped him. "Alex, do you want to find your daughter or not?"

Alex stammered, "O-of course, I do ..."

Wayne finished, "Well then, beast or no beast, it's your duty to protect your daughter and bring her home."

Alex slumped his shoulders. "You sound like my wife..."

Wayne shoved Alex to the ground. "You coward! You think Adrian or Kazius is going to hand back your daughter if you just ask nicely or give them two silver coins? NO! They would laugh at you and beat the stuffing out of you, and then make your daughter Molly suffer ten times more! Either you stand up and do what needs to be done, or crawl away and hide in fear for the rest of your miserable life. I know what these men can do. I know how they think, and if you show fear, they will OWN you. Now get up!"

Alex crawled in panic, trying to get away.

"I'm about to reconsider and leave you here alone. You want your daughter to be tortured by these people?"

Alex shook his head no.

Wayne prodded, "Can't hear you, Alex. What was that?"

Alex squeaked, "N-no ..."

Wayne cupped his ear. "Can't hear you!"

Alex replied with annoyance, "Said no."

Wayne shrugged his hands high. "Forget it. I can't help you. Go home if you dare ..."

Alex finally yelled, "NO! I can't!"

Wayne cajoled, "What's in your way then? What stops you?"

Alex whimpered, "My wife would ..."

Wayne punched him, knocking Alex to the ground. "Wrong answer! Get up and tell me again why we are here!"

Alex crawled away again. Wayne stopped speaking and just walked away. When Alex realized this, he froze, trembling with indecision. Wayne was walking back west, toward Valantir, and Alex felt his chest tighten, gasping for air. The fear was closing in from all directions, like a swirling fog, causing Alex to shriek as if he was a small child. He collapsed into a fetal position, muttering,

"D-don't leave me h-here ... p-please ..."

And then, a voice thundered inside his head, "Alex Mill, GET UP!"

He bolted upright as if a wasp had stung him. It was the voice he heard in the cave, the red-haired goddess. She was nowhere to be seen, but there was no doubt about the message. Alex ran to catch Wayne, who had a two-minute lead on him. Alex ran harder, panting and stumbling, but he kept running. After three more minutes, he closed within earshot. "Wayne! WAIT!"

Wayne stopped, turned around, and said, "So, it speaks at last."

* * *

When Tyton was finished with his meditation, Nikita snapped her fingers from her overlook position in the testing grounds arena. Five men encircled Tyton's position. Nikita spelled out her additional conditions, "You will proceed blindfolded and must answer my questions until all five men are down, or until you are incapacitated. Refuse, and you will be forever exiled. Fail the test or answer falsely, I will strip your rank within the temple to a first-year disciple. This is my decree. The terms are absolute."

Tyton gave one cold nod of the head in acknowledgement and was presented with the blindfold. He put it on. Next, he heard the draw of weapons and tracked the steps of a man behind him. As his first opponent lunged forward with an overhead strike, Tyton ducked into his swing and flipped the man on his back as Nikita asked her first commanding question, "Tell me her last words!"

Tyton faltered, caught by a right cross from the next opponent. As he tumbled back into a crouching position,

Tyton's voice sounded faraway, full of anguish, and replicated Sidhuri's tone. "I will always remember ..."

His third opponent caught him in the ribs with a truncheon. Tyton barely rolled with it.

Nikita asked, "Remember what?"

Tyton replied with a forlorn undertone, "The love we shared."

Tyton rolled away from the kick of the fourth and caught the foot of the third, toppling him. He heard the first standing up again.

"What did you tell Sidhuri that broke her heart?" Nikita barked.

Tyton somersaulted over a wild swing by the fifth man before answering, "It is bad luck for us to remain together. You will ruin my cover."

Three men rushed him at once, and Tyton sidestepped to his right as he swept the feet out from one.

Nikita screeched, "Why did you take that assignment?"

Tyton replied flatly, "The Whispering Tigers had to be dealt with."

Tyton went on the offense, catching a man in the throat with his right elbow, and spun backward into the stomach of another with his left elbow.

Nikita asked, enraged, "But why YOU?"

Tyton answered, "I was the best and youngest, the least suspected by the tigers."

Another man launched to choke Tyton, but was felled by a shoulder throw. The next man swung a punch and missed. Tyton ducked perfectly and palm heeled his plexus.

Nikita kept pressing, "Wrong answer, ERIK. Try again!"

The last opponent threw his truncheon and missed, followed by Tyton's double crescent kick, taking him down for the count.

Tyton spoke with finality, "I was a proud youth then, but I <u>was</u> the best operative. Just not the wisest."

Nikita frowned. He satisfied her terms, but she still hated him for it. Tyton ripped the blindfold off and tossed it unceremoniously in her direction. Nikita hissed, "You are still scum."

Tyton corrected, "WAS. Erik died in heart and soul when Sidhuri departed this life. Only his body survived. I would trade all the wisdom since that day to have her alive in my arms again. My torment is that it cannot be so. Your hatred consumes and blinds you, Nikita. As surely as my ego destroyed what was most dear to me then ..."

Nikita growled, "You DARE! Insolent dog!"

The next senior priestesses intervened, "He speaks justly and humbly, Your Eminence. The council moves to reinstall Erik to full rank. And exempts him from further reprisals by you. We beseech you to abandon your vendetta."

Nikita stormed off in silence to her private chambers. Tyton bowed to the speakers of the council and proceeded to visit his mother's old room.

* * *

"Open the store house and feed these people. I am assuming command," Lady Amanda Redoak announced to the honor guards.

The men hesitated until Blackhull chimed in, "Do as she says before the people riot. I don't have enough deputies left for that. We'll deal with the abbey later."

The men finally bowed and saluted and turned their eyes away from Amanda in shame. Rebecca was on hand to assist them, and the people around her showed a reverence for the bar maid-innkeeper they did not have before the close call with Arius and the undead. Only a small handful of the Obsidian Owls had survived, and they stood among all the other hungry townsfolk. Soon, the healthier folks were helping pass out rations of nuts, flour, and dry beans. The food reserves emptied in a single night to Amanda's great despair. "We must get supplies from the abbey and relocate before the worst of winter begins. We cannot last here with the crops ruined."

* * *

Alex Mill found himself in a wide valley at a lakeside covered with fog, and Wayne was nowhere to be seen. The moon was up, and the pale light that reached the ground did little to reveal his path. The stars were all hidden from him, and the frogs had fallen silent. Something was out there in the dark, prowling for him. Alex spun nervously at every breeze, with his sword held out at arm's length. A terrible voice called out, "Are you lost, my child? Have you come here to accept your place among the sheep?"

Alex dropped his sword and ran blindly toward the mountains, and he could hear something leaping about on all fours behind him.

"Accept your fate, boy, the many must serve the few, now STOP!"

And a great weight landed on him, full of claws, fangs, and fur everywhere. Alex turned his head to see, and his voice failed. His eyes opened wide as saucers in abject terror as he saw the tattered priest robes it wore. The claws flashed in a red arc where his head once was, and Molly awoke screaming, "Daddy!"

"Nooooooooooooooooooooo!"

Chapter Thirty-Four
Finding One's Place

"Where has Mother been all this time?" an underfed adolescent demanded of his jailor.

The hooded man in a gray tunic answered, "None of your concern, whelp. The priesthood needs her more than you."

Rod scowled and paced, mumbling, "The priesthood indeed; everyone knows she is no priestess."

The jailor barked, "Keep it up, boy, and you'll get another twenty lashes in the yard. Now shut up!"

Rod clenched his fingers, and his eyes rolled back in his head. His mouth opened, as if in pain but making no sound, and his body stumbled into the cold stone wall for support, while a sound akin to rustling leaves and the soft patter of many tiny feet filled a faraway corridor, followed by the echoes of screaming guards, and the jailor left his post to investigate. He need not have bothered; a great swarm of rats was headed straight for him, and his eyes went wide in horror; he was cornered. His scream rose and cut off on a high note as the mass of brown rats engulfed him and brought his doom. Within a minute, the swarm dispersed, save for one, who scurried into Rod's cell. Rod sat against the wall, catching his breath as the rat scampered onto his shoulder.

"Hello, Wilbur," Rod whispered. He began giggling as the whiskers tickled his face, and he fell onto the floor. Wilbur leaped off, and Rod spoke to him, "Keys, Wilbur. Fetch."

And the rat bit the cord on which the keys dangled off the corpse of the jailor, chewing through the leather. Wilbur returned with the keys, and Rod fitted the correct key on the third attempt.

"Good boy, Wilbur," Rod whispered reverently.

Now he was free, and also scared. Where would he go? This was the only home he had ever had, after all. Winter kept him on a tight leash, never allowed him to see the world outside the castle. In a sad tone, Rod instructed, "Lead the way, Wilbur. Show me where the food is."

* * *

Kazius crawled onto the log for what seemed to be the hundredth time, bloodied, bruised and sore all over. His arms felt like lead, and his eyes had circles of fatigue. His opponent finally spoke, "There's no sport in this anymore. You have spirit, but this line of work is not for you. Find another job, Zed."

Kazius's fingers went slack, dropping his staff into the mud and a drooping, tired body shambled away, wearing the weight of the world on his back. Bernice did her best to cheer him up, but his eyes barely flickered. His long face just hung there, draining the happiness from all around him. Bernice could not bear to see him this way and cried, "What can I do? My heart is breaking to see you thus, my lord … please come back …"

Finally, his sad eyes met hers, and his walls slowly crumbled. He sank to his knees and held her waist tightly, burying his head in her lap, choking on his tears until the pain of holding it all in became too much. Her hands stroked his hair as he sobbed away the things he had no words for.

"What am I?" he pleaded in despair.

"You were a king of men, and now a man, one that I still love …" she replied.

He had no words to answer her; they died on his tongue. He just slumped to the ground as she leaned over him, kissing his forehead.

* * *

"I <u>must</u> go back! My children need me!" Bethany spoke with uncharacteristic authority.

The Elves could not convince her otherwise, and finally relented to send a small escort with her, in addition to Savadi, Helen, Sean, and the horses that bore them into Valantir.

"May the safest road be open to you and fortune smile on your return, Lady Blackthorn," Andrath said with a bow of the head.

She replied, "May your happier days soon return and be multiplied. Live well and wisely."

And then the white gates of the temple were unlocked to let her pass from their last refuge. Andrath watched between the bars as they were shut again. Bethany and company faded into the trees and the western foothills under a dark and cloudy sky.

As evening drew near, a scout arrived, "Sire! The Korathians and Dabanis are marching for war. They are but two days away! I counted eight hundred of them, led by a priest."

Andrath sneered, "Malsain ..."

The scout answered, "No, sire, twas not Malsain, but another. Even more sinister in appearance, if I dare say so."

Andrath motioned a herald over, "Summon the council. Assemble them in one hour."

* * *

"I owe you an apology, Alex," said Wayne. "My anger was at my father, who is long dead.

If you will pardon a bitter truth, you are a lot like him. His cowardice caused his death. His liver failed when I was but a boy of seven. He drank too much. Never dared to speak up against wrongdoing, no matter who suffered, for how long, or how badly. Kazius is but five years older than I, and his father abandoned him the same year I was born. I fell in with the Blackwolves to survive. It was that simple."

Alex said nothing as he hung his head staring at the ground.

Wayne prompted, "Nothing to say when a man reveals the scars of his past that still bothers him? It is a bit rude of you and cowardly, unfitting of a man whose daughter looks up to him."

Alex squirmed and fidgeted nervously, his lips convulsing as contrary thoughts contested each other to be formed into words.

Wayne nudged, "SPEAK! Damn it!"

Alex muttered, "I-I'm sorry about your dad ..."

Wayne looked Alex full in the eyes. "What else?"

Alex floundered, "Uh, what year..."

Wayne answered, "Fifteen-forty, the year of the battle of Shadval. And how can you know if the question you fear to ask is too intrusive, unless you do something to find out?"

Alex squirmed again. "Umm ..."

Wayne finished the thought for him. "You cannot. And therefore must ask. I fear that you will die the same as my father, Alex. A lonely man afraid of his own shadow. Pushed around by every bully there was, even children who were smaller and weaker than him. Your daughter deserves better. Because if you run or die, her world will be forever desolate and scarred. You are the one that must decide the legacy you leave to her, Alex, not me, not your wife, not the lord of the land, nor even the gods of the earth and sky. You, and you alone. Your job, your duty, your responsibility, YOUR decisions. And, here we are..."

They were now at the gates of the castle in Kozos.

* * *

"Lady Blackthorn, if the undead are still about ...." one of the Elven escorts cautioned.

"If I must die protecting or avenging my children, so be it! I will defy anyone who says nay!" Bethany declared, with an icy tone that left no doubt she was deadly earnest.

And on they rode, past the trail of occasional mangled bodies, both Elf and animal. And one unfortunate undead seemed to have been decapitated by a bear, whose tracks turned north away from the staggered prints of the zombies. Bethany smiled, thinking of the bear, and her brother's nickname. The heirs of James Redmane would not go quietly.

* * *

After many encounters with the undead and a final showdown with a vampire, the party had, at last, emerged from a labyrinth of caverns underneath Shadval, to find a cove facing the bay on the easternmost edge of the winding sea. Lebiced had a bulging canvas saddlebag with many metal objects poking out the open end, and he also carried a shield among the new acquisitions. Conrad walked hesitantly and was aware of the world seeming to spin around him, disorienting him even as he leaned against the walls to steady himself.

Lebiced concluded, "The fever. I might have known … we are going to require the Elven lore yet again."

Conrad mumbled, "No, road … not safe … must … find boats."

Skorvald huffed, "Already delirious, just what we need."

Tyrianna then spoke in a voice of certainty, akin to her mother's voice, rather than her former meekness, "No. He is correct. Many new enemies have taken the roads through Valantir. The aura of his ancestors are on the sword he now carries. He has received guidance from spirits before the fever gained strength."

Even Tyrus was looking sideways, unsettled by the rapid transformation of the oracle's powers and personality. Jonah took one of Conrad's arms over his shoulder, and they searched the cove, but no seaworthy vessel remained. All had been severely damaged long ago, and repairing these boats would take weeks they did not have to spare.

Tyrus volunteered to search around for better crafts. "I am the fastest swimmer. I shall not be long, if anything useful is within several miles."

Since the ruins above had collapsed, the original path back to the horses and provisions had been cut off, and everyone was down to the last two days' worth of rations. The only hunters among them were Conrad and Skorvald, and Conrad was in worsening condition.

Thus it was a great relief when, hours later, near sunset, Tyrus finally returned with two canoes in tow. "We are in luck! These two crafts still float, and were abandoned to the south of here, at the borders of Razadur. Two of us need not be in them. The rest should fit inside."

Jonah helped Conrad climb in, and the others boarded after. Then Tyrianna had a vision again, clutching her head in her hands. "The children cry out. I cannot help all of them ... Alex, Molly, Jacob, I cannot be everywhere ... I cannot choose between them ... I cannot ..."

Once again, the old personality had surfaced, the one Tyrus knew best. Lebiced gently suggested, "To choose none is to fail all of them. And only you know which ones have most need of you."

Tyrianna's mortal persona felt her torment and indecision lessen, and stood upright as she responded, "Yes, the one who is alone in a strange land. It is her then. Away to the east ..."

Lebiced added, "Do not forget that Father Samuel Malsain dwells that way, and other men who helped his cause ..." as he removed from his robes a silver dagger. "There is a man who will need this. His name ..."

Tyrianna, the rebel goddess, emerged again with her commanding voice. "Yes, I know the one you speak of. But I follow my own path, old man."

Lebiced backed away, unwilling to provoke her temper. And thus the company split awkwardly, with Tyrus avoiding any eye contact with Tyrianna. He was afraid for the first time in years. It was his duty, and that alone, which held him to follow where she went, turning toward the Iron Ridge Mountains to seek passage beyond many days' journey south of the Falcon Pass. While Conrad shivered in cold sweat, his hands icy cold, and his brow hot to the touch. His eyes were unfocused and fatigued, and his speech slurred beyond recognition. Jonah rowed all the harder in an effort to reach a safe port before his brother-in-law was beyond all help, despite the wound on Jonah's shoulder.

* * *

"So, tell me, why have you returned after all of your long years in exile? Nothing you do is random. I know you too well, Erik," said a senior priestess and friend of the family.

Tyton Umbral braced himself. "Once, our order drove the Dark Dwarves out of our lands, and out of Razadur as well."

The priestess nodded. "And now you seek to repeat this action against a new enemy. What you ask would be bold even for Nikita."

Tyton added, "She knows not the evil plots in motion between Razadur and Zara-Mogai. The Chaos Lich Arius has gathered allies and infiltrated many lands. We may already be too late. The Alpha Clan, the Syndicate, and the Chaos Cults are all behind this. I pried some of the information out of a low-level agent myself. Barton is planning something."

The priestess bowed and warned, "You have yet to earn back the trust of the order, Erik. Your idea is certain to be rejected. I can promise nothing in this matter. Whatever wisdom you have gathered. You will have great need of."

Tyton brought his palms together and gave a slight bow. The priestess left his mother's room, and Tyton returned to his meditations.

* * *

"Who leads the abbey now?" Lady Amanda demanded of the apprentice who opened the door.

"The lorekeeper has seniority, madam," the young lad responded.

"As acting deputy mayor of the barony, I need to speak to him. This cannot wait," Amanda instructed.

The apprentice bowed in fear, "Yes, milady ..." and scurried off to summon Henry.

Blackhull sniffed the air and commented sadly, "The embalmers have been busy."

Henry arrived a few minutes later with his arm in a sling. "A bit worse for wear, I'm afraid. Don't mind the arm. How are you, Lady Redoak?"

Amanda nodded her head politely and spoke, "Also a bit worse, but have no time to worry about it. The people require provisions for a journey westward. We cannot last through winter here after what Arius has done. Have you anything to spare?"

Henry answered, "We may. Shall we go look?" Amanda followed him inside, with two honor guards behind her, and Blackhull left to resume his duties at the court house.

* * *

Kazius awoke to the sound of a roving hyena. Bernice bolted upright and dashed behind a palm tree. Kazius looked the scavenger in the eye, and his lips curled in rage. The hyena hesitated and sniffed in their direction and then backed away to turn around and leave. Kazius stamped loudly after and yelled at it for ten seconds to speed up his departure. And once the coast was clear again, he climbed the tree to fetch more dates for their breakfast. Great looming shadows of doubt still hung over his head, but he would not allow Bernice to go hungry. Bernice could see a change for the better in him since yesterday, and she hoped it would last.

Chapter Thirty-Five
Royal Pains

"I cannot mention names here, in the event we are overheard, but, we are beset by enemies within and without these walls. The dragons have retreated; nobody knows why. But the council is still debating new security details, to search every wagon and saddlebag for dragon eggs, dragon blood and magical devices. The king would never have allowed this," said Sandraz in the southwestern storage room of the subcellars.

Queen Lissa said nothing. She was still in shock and mourning; it was written on her long face. Bravane the Elder nodded; he knew the council well while his son looked distracted by other thoughts.

It was Ravenna who spoke, "I wish to speak with the witnesses to these dragon attacks. I have a hunch I need to verify."

Sandraz bowed. "Of course, Your Ladyship. I will send the message myself."

Ravenna shook her head no. "The council must not know of this. I need you to divert their attention elsewhere, Sandraz."

He bowed again. "As you wish."

* * *

Mandy and Moira were rudely awakened by a flash of light in the middle of the house, and a high baritone voice telling them, "You must leave now and never return here. There is no time!"

Mandy squinted to make sure her eyesight was working. There was a tall woman in savagely torn white robes with long red hair, who dared set foot here without invitation, telling HER to leave her own house!

"Who do you think you are, bitch? Did Adrian tell you that I am his wife?" Mandy snarled.

Syrene summoned a huge gust of wind to accentuate her reply, "Fool! Did you ever wonder how Adrian acquired this house so cheaply? Because it was cursed! Ever since the Crimson Hoods murdered Kaedrus Moondreams, the father of my daughter!"

Mandy gulped, as the eyes of Syrene began to glow. Mandy's jaw went slack and her eyes wide, before whispering, "Oh … shit!"

Moira was the first to bolt and run, gathering what little clothing and gear she could grab in a hurry. Mandy staggered as if drunk, doing a slow, stupefied repeat of Moira's actions. No sooner had she exited the front door than another flash of light heralded the arrival of a huge, bearded old man in full-scale armor, brandishing a huge broadsword. He bellowed, "There is nowhere you can hide, Syrene! Now you die!"

Mandy dropped everything and ran in stark terror until she could run no more and had lost all bearings of where she was.

* * *

"The unrest in the south is exactly what Arius wants. How long are you going to ignore the signs, Doug?" asked Queen Margo Falconeye.

"I'm not ignoring anything, but I will not offer my neck on the block, Mother," Prince Doug Saint Noir answered. "Even if I am the son of Lorenna's brother …"

Margo slapped him. "You know full well why I married John. He was not like the others. The Alphas knew he did not have their ruthless streak. He could have been redeemed, if he had the backbone!"

Doug whined, "We can't all turn out like Jonah, the ever so noble exile …"

Margo slapped him again. "Jonah went with my blessing. He obeys his heart, unlike you … and your base cowardly politics! Now leave my sight!"

Doug turned and stormed out with a scowl of smoldering jealousy, whispering, "If not for the blood curse, brother …" and clenched his fingers such that his knuckles blanched.

Margo watched him leave, and then spoke to the painting of her late husband, "Four children, John, and two of them never had hope. They needed someone to look up to, a father they could be proud of. We all needed that from you. We failed them, John. YOU most of all. We needed your love and more, and your fear may have doomed us all."

* * *

"As the queen is still deep in mourning, it falls to us to arrange King William Goldlion's funeral," Sandraz announced to the council members.

Councilman Clark Russell Whitetree sneered but said nothing, and Councilman Arthur Kenneth Clayton was fidgety and sweating. Franz Leon Croix gave a dirty look to Bravane Redoak the Elder, and Bravane gave one back. Bitter debate ensued in a matter of minutes over the details of the invitation lists, the selection of who would deliver the eulogy, should the king's five-year-old son, Prince Mark, be allowed to witness, and what is the Queen Regent going to do about the dragons. Finally, Sandraz motioned to adjourn the council. Bravane supported, as did Darla Mae, Basil, Vaude, Morgild, and Adam Coppergrass. While Clark, Franz, and Emil opposed. Arthur abstained. The motion carried. Sandraz was in a foul mood all evening, more frustrated than ever with the political bickering that Clark seemed to relish and exploit. Lady Ravenna Freebird found him in the courtyard, throwing daggers at target dummies.

"I have verified my hunch. The dragons veered off precisely when Arius brought all his attention to bear on Alex Redoak, about the time I was leaving. Two men witnessed the expressions in the dragon's eyes. They went from unfocused to fully awake just before turning northwards. Arius Auguron was the hand behind this, not the Dwarves of Iglar. You know what this means, Sandraz," she said.

"Indeed, I do. We are being played. I need to expose the Alphas very soon. We discovered proof that Vamanastral was among them; the others are more difficult. But I would start with Arthur Clayton. He had a foreign visitor just before the king became ill. A woman."

Ravenna promised, "If Arthur was part of the plot to kill my brother, I will have his head on a pike."

Sandraz smirked, "That is the Lady Freebird I remember so well. We have missed you."

* * *

"Bring the beggars and fetch some wine, one cup only. Do hurry along," Prince Adam Silverlane ordered in his nasal tone of disdain and pity.

Thus the servant returned to the outer hall to admit Wayne and Alex the Meek and lead them to a side room with a brass inlaid maple desk with a speckled gray marble top. There the Prince examined his nails, and, for a full minute, took no notice of the men awaiting his decision.

"Oh, there you are," he finally said.

Alex Mill began to stare at the floor.

Prince Adam took offense. "You are to look me in the eye and bow as befits my station, citizen."

Alex bowed awkwardly, and Wayne simply nodded his head, saying, "Greetings, Your Highness."

Adam Silverlane smiled lukewarmly. "That's better. Now, as for your request, we do have work to be done repairing an orphanage. Since you have no tools, you will earn them, and you shall henceforth be forbidden to leave until the repairs are complete. That will be all for today."

The servant appeared again to give the prince his cup of wine.

As the two men left, Alex whispered in panic, "What a mess! What a mess! OOOF!"

Wayne had elbowed him. "Say that one more time, and I will vanish in the night without you, Alex," Wayne whispered back.

Alex gave a sad puppy look and nearly whimpered.

Wayne gave a sharp kick in the rump. "Stop slouching! You're lucky you never met Kazius. He'd kick your teeth in for doing that! Now walk like a man. Damn you!"

Alex straightened up a little, but his eyes still scanned the ground nervously, and his shoulders were limp. Wayne spun about to block his path. Alex gulped and shut his eyes, wincing.

"Do you want Molly to be a victim like you? You want her to live her life in fear? Do you?"

Alex stammered, "N-no ..."

Wayne slapped his chin. "Chin up," then his arms, "Shoulders back," then his belly, "There. Now start acting like her protector."

Alex blinked and said nothing. His face was deadpan.

Wayne circled him twice, evaluating his posture, and said, "That's a start. Let's go find some food."

* * *

Lady Amanda Redoak stopped at the doorway of the baronial mansion, crying inconsolably as she touched the outer wall one last time. Worst of all was leaving her parents behind. She had pleaded and begged for them to come, but they preferred to be secluded out of sight in the tower, away from the common folk who could not see past their ruined features.

The long march began. Amanda and all who followed left by the western gate of Oakthorn, leaving behind a small number who stayed at the abbey who were too weary for the journey, or felt their chances were better here. Amanda no longer took any joy in food, and felt as if she were already dead.

* * *

"I have nothing more to offer. I cannot fish. The dates are nearly gone. What am I to you now but a broken man cast into the wilderness, a ruin of what I once was?" Kazius asked in a spell of despair, staring into the firelight.

Bernice began to cry. "Not again, my lord, not again. Please come back. Do not give in to the whispers of doom and darkness. Not now, not when you have a child growing..."

Kazius was thunderstruck. "What? How can that be? I have been cursed with impotence all my life..."

Bernice nearly choked on her words. "Nay, my lord, there was a woman who put things in our tea, all of your concubines. But she does not reach here. We are free of her here. We can be happy at long last."

Kazius fell on all fours, stunned; his eyes wide in shock. "Winter..." he spoke, at last, in rage. "It had to be her! I'd skin her alive if not for ..."

Bernice pleaded, "No! She is not here now. I am. Please stay, and protect your unborn child. Please ..."

Kazius felt great pressure in his temples and neck as his pulse pounded like war drums within. He struggled with his own words. "The Lametree prophecy and the Auguron inheritance, that is what she is after ..."

Bernice gasped. "What prophecy, my lord? You are not making sense ..."

Kazius fought to calm his breathing, "My sister, Winter, knows of a prophecy about a child of some Lametree heritage. My family has hunted them down to stop the prophecy. A child who would usher either peace on Earth or complete dominion over it. And Bazadani tribes far in the south have hated us ever since. We ... killed ... many ... Lame trees."

Bernice could not speak; she doubled over in tears. And finally Kazius went to her and stopped short. His fingers clenched, feeling an impulse he was ashamed to admit to. He could end it with a single motion. But then, his child ... what if they could be happy? He could start over.

"No! I have no legacy anymore! Only sand and dust and starvation! No!" He thought out loud as his control slipped from him and despair closed its tentacles about him again.

And then, in the distance, he heard cries of absolute panic intermingled with death screams. The Black Scorpion camp that he had tried to join lay that way. And without thinking, Kazius grabbed Bernice close, whispering, "Keep quiet. Stay close. I need to know what is happening out there."

Thus they crept carefully toward the sound of a violent struggle, and off in the distance, backlit against more campfires, a huge man with a battle axe was cleaving every bandit in sight by the half dozen whenever they swarmed him. Soon, they all fled for their lives. And one nearly tripped over Kazius and was about to speak when Kazius punched him in the throat to silence him. A second punch to the gut took him out of action. Behind a palm trunk was as close as Kazius dared approach. As the fighting died down, along with most of the bandits, the great hulking bear of a man sniffed the air.

"If you have information, out with it!" the huge man demanded, looking right at the trunk where Kazius hid. Kazius knew there was only one sane choice.

"Yes, I have information. What do you wish to know?" he called back.

The large warrior approached, coming two paces closer. "Where have this pirate scum taken the children?"

Kazius replied, "I am not with the pirates, but I might know who is."

The man stepped closer. "Speak or taste my wrath!"

Kazius gulped. "I know a man … Adrian … he is one of the people who sells children to the Syndicate. A Father Malsain in Korath is part of it. Malsain is either a buyer or a middle man. That's everything I know, I swear …"

The large warrior scratched his chin. "I believe you. You may live. What is your name?"

Kazius stuttered, "They, they call me Zed."

The large man harrumphed, "Zed? What kind of name is that? You lie."

Kazius slumped and corrected, "Yes, yes, I was once known as Kazius Auguron, I am king no longer. I am now a beggar. You can kill me if you wish, but spare the girl."

Bernice cried, "My lord, No! Please, spare him!"

The large man grinned wickedly. "At long last, an Auguron is at my mercy!" He laughed. "Here of all places, many leagues from his home in Razadur! To what do I owe the pleasure?"

Kazius crawled out from behind the trunk and rolled onto his back, facing the stars above. "I was overthrown by General AxeGrind. He leads Razadur now. I was … liberated … by a man I hate, who works for … the most wretched evil to walk this planet…"

Garzon stepped closer again, "The name, I need a name. Speak."

Kazius whimpered, "Arius, my… father… now a chaos lich. I don't know the agent's name. He enters without a sound and goes wherever he pleases."

Garzon scratched his chin again, pondering what to do with Kazius. It would be a terrible shame to lose a good source of information.

* * *

As the scale armor-clad angry old bearded man entered the house, the ancient curse laid on it caused the doorframe to collapse on him, distracting him long enough for Syrene to throw a stoppered vial at him, which broke on his face. Green acid ate away at his eyes, faster than he could regenerate, making him scream in agony.

"A gift from the mining shafts, and the mortals you so despise," Syrene declared just before teleporting behind him, and sinking a resin-coated dagger into his neck, which rapidly turned his veins purple and paralyzed him. "The curse has just proven to me that you were somehow involved in his death, after all of YOUR affairs and neglecting me for hundreds of years!" Syrene protested to him as she pried the broadsword from his unmoving fingers. Next, she ran him through with it, then stepped back, and caused a chasm to divide the house in two, yawning wide under his feet and sending him hurtling deep underground. "Your mad hunger for power, prestige and unquestioning worship has long ago consumed you, and now … good-bye, evil husband!"

With those words, she set the house on fire and sent burning timbers after him and sealed the chasm above him, as the last echoes of his screams faded away.

"It is done," Syrene whispered as tears ran down her face. She sank to her knees at the spot where Kaedrus died, touching the disk of white marble inscribed with his initials, and curled into a ball, sobbing.

* * *

Lady Bethany feared the worst when she saw the wreckage of the eastern gate ahead under a strange dome of light. She prodded her horse into a full gallop.

"Lady Blackthorn, wait!" cried the Elves.

Lady Helen followed right after her.

The honor guards who remained at the gate, stepped aside to let them pass. Bethany took in the horror at the market square, including the ransacked Co-op, and as she arrived at what remained of her house, she wailed, "Noooo! Not my babies!"

Bethany's Aunt Helen Aristodemos drew to a halt behind her and, breaking her vow of silence, said, "They may yet be alive. Yes, I feel it. Let us go find my late sister's grandchildren."

At the North Crossing, they saw a scorched bridge topped with several statues of horrified peasants. Bethany wondered what it meant, giving them a perplexed look.

At the mansion, all seemed normal, except for the reduced number of men on duty. The guards saluted the women and bowed.

"Your children are with Lady Amanda seeking refuge. Where is your brother Conrad?"

Bethany dismounted and demanded, "Refuge? Where? Why?"

The guards related all they knew, including the blight of the last harvest, the many betrayals of Darmid, the quest of Bravane the Younger, and the tragic scarring of Lord Alex Redoak.

Helen, in turn, related the quest of her nephew Conrad.

"He is too late, Lady Helen. Arius has fled North. We fear he is preparing another assault. We can only hope the dome will last."

Bethany nodded and strode toward the mansion, saddened at the emptiness that now pervaded it, and found her way to the tower where Alex and Myra stayed.

* * *

"You buffoon! What if these men are spies? You just let them walk out of here like that?" King Nathan Silverlane chastised his son, Prince Adam.

The young prince protested, "I forbade them to leave. They are bound until they finish repairs."

The king snarled, "Now I have to double security around the orphanage on account of these two worthless peasants! And the coin will be out of YOUR inheritance!"

Adam countered, "You forget we are short of labor, since many have marched to war on ..."

Nathan yelled, "I have forgotten NOTHING, you insolent mockery of a Silverlane! I will dangle you from a tree for the wolves if you talk to me like that again!"

Adam turned his back to sulk in bitter silence.

Nathan muttered to a guard, "Tell Queen Marcy I have cancelled his birthday."

Adam grabbed a candlestick and threw it randomly at the fireplace, with his lips curled in rage.

Chapter Thirty-Six
Regrets

"Summon forth the Ivory Colossus and make ready to defend the temple, archers to the second level terrace, shields and pikes to the front. Mages inside," Andrath ordered his sentinels.

The sentinels bowed, and his herald ran inside the sanctuary to relay his message.

Andrath looked up to the sky and saw storm clouds gathering in the south. He then recited an Elven prayer for better days ahead, before donning the last of his armor and strapping on his scabbard and helmet. "Let the bards sing that we fought bravely. And may history forgive us for the blood of innocents."

* * *

"Yes, I saw a man such as you describe. He boasted he is good friend of Kazius. I send him away. He wanted loan for his business. I refused. He went that way," the old merchant said, pointing east.

Garzon gave him a silver coin, and the three unlikely companions went searching the coast, until hours later, they found two hungry men with empty fishing nets. Sal was fatigued and did not realize the size and number of their visitors when he said, "Go away! We have nothing to share ..."

Garzon picked Sal off the ground by his throat and made clear his intentions. "We seek information. If your information is no good, you both die. Where are the children?"

Sal pissed himself. And Adrian tried to run for it. Garzon slammed Sal into the palm tree and left him for Kazius to deal with. Adrian was a surprisingly fast runner for his short stature and what remained of his girth from weeks of undernourishment. But Garzon had the superior stamina, and within minutes, Adrian collapsed from exhaustion.

"Tell me where to find the children, or I twist your arms loose."

Adrian gasped, "Syndicate ... has them ... it's too late!"

Garzon yanked Adrian's left arm, dislocating his shoulder.

"Ahhhhhhh ... God ... no ..." Adrian groaned in agony.

"Tell me where, or I do this all day," Garzon exclaimed.

Adrian began hyperventilating, "Korath. It runs mainly out of Korath, at the orphanage, but the network is everywhere ..."

Then Garzon dragged Adrian by the collar, back to the others.

"Wait! What are you doing? I gave you the information. Please let me go ..." Adrian begged.

"I bring you along, in case we need hostages," Garzon answered.

Adrian cried, "Oh, God, no! Please! Noooooooo!"

* * *

"There's no pass here! We need to go back!" Tyrus shouted ahead.

The wild creature that was Tyrianna merely turned around to look at him. Once again, her eyes glowed like the moon, and she willed them both into the air, levitating over the mountain ridges toward the border of Korath and Razadur. Men below cowered in abject terror of the girl they had been ordered to apprehend, and Axegrind himself knew he was hopelessly outmatched against her. He shoved, with great annoyance, at his men to keep marching toward home.

* * *

A band of Crimson Hoods spotted a lone female wandering in the desert sands, who appeared [and was] very lost.

"Well, this is our lucky day, boys!" the leader of the gang declared.

The woman stopped and wagged a finger at them. "I'm warning you. My husband knows Kazius, and you will be in BIG trouble if you try anything!"

The Crimson Hoods all laughed so hard they could barely stand upright.

"Lady," one spoke as he wiped his eyes, "Kazius is old news, sweetheart, a has-been, a wash out, we don't work for him anymore. And the new guy, he don't care what happens to YOU, if you're any friend of Kazius. So, sweet cheeks, it's just you, and us."

Mandy screamed and ran for all the good it did.

* * *

"A man named Tyrus said to bring this to the baron and to Conrad to divide between them," said Lady Bethany as she revealed a bag of gold coins. "Can you keep this safe here until they return?"

Lord Alex the Wise nodded yes. Bethany dared not say more, with all the tragedies that had befallen Oakthorn and the horrible scars that Alex bore for defending it.

Alex could read her expression of concern. "Do not mourn for me. I did what had to be done. I have no regrets. My daughter said your neighbors, John and Amanda, helped save me. I wanted to thank them."

Bethany bowed in mixed reverence and sadness. "I will remember that, if I should see them. I'm very sorry …"

Alex Redoak held a hand up, "No pity. Just make sure Amanda is safe. That is all we ask. Tell her we love her and wish for a safe return in better days."

Bethany cried, "Yes, I can do that. Thank you for all you have done."

Then, having no more words to say, she hugged Alex and Myra farewell and went on her way.

* * *

Jonah collapsed in pain; his shoulder could not tolerate anymore exertion and gave the oars to one of the Northlanders, who said nothing. While Conrad was burning up and hallucinating, Lebiced and Skorvald glanced over occasionally from the other canoe.

Conrad mumbled, "No … no more food for you … you ate the last of my bread already …" And then he faded out again.

Skorvald spoke up, "We should take to the road and return to the temple."

Lebiced argued, "Not without swift horses, nor against the new enemies that the oracle spoke of. We may yet find an island near the border of Stonehaven and Valantir, south of Oakthorn. Some Elves may have escaped the Lich's notice there. Keep rowing."

* * *

"Rod is on the loose, and we can't find him. Winter is going to have our heads for this," one guard predicted.

"I pity the idiot who helped him get out," said another.

"Yeah? Well, I heard the screams that day … was no single person capable of scaring the crap out of the poor sods like that. Tore the buggers to shreds, head to toe, and I saw teeth marks on their leather. Wasn't anything human did that, I tell ya," said a third.

"What would anyone want with him? Scrawny, underfed kid and all," said the first.

"That's not our job to know why or who. Just find the little brat!" corrected the third.

The guards fanned out again, unaware Rod had overheard their every word from the storm drain.

* * *

"Please! I beg you! My family needs asylum here. We are all dead if you refuse," said an old blind man.

"What will you give in exchange that we do not already have, old man?" demanded Nikita.

"Promise me they will be safe. I do not have long to live. I overheard men discussing a contract. I am a wanted man," he replied.

Nikita hissed, "Why should this concern me?"

The old man whispered, "The contract is for the new leader of Razadur. He is hiring assassins, and the Creepers told his men that, yes, they would discuss terms and prices."

Nikita huffed in disbelief, "How does a blind man know who is who?"

The man chided her, "For one who blindfolds her students, it should be obvious. Their heartbeats, their strides, their types of tobacco, the foods they have eaten, the sounds of their voices, their dialects and accents, the words they use ... now promise me."

Nikita dismissed him, "They are none of my concern, old one. Do not waste my time any further."

The blind man frowned, "May your lesson burn deep in your heart, and your karma be swift."

Nikita hissed, "Get him out of my sight at once!"

When Nikita was alone in the audience chamber, Tyton Umbral sauntered in.

"YOU! You have no place here. Be gone!" Nikita snarled.

"He speaks the truth, Nikita. Did you not know? The leader of the Southland Creepers was the youngest son of a Whispering Tiger. You have lost your touch," Tyton said flatly before leaving.

Nikita threw a brass bowl at the door just as he closed it. "I still hate you, Erik! Never forget that!" she yelled to empty air.

* * *

The first wave of Dabanis and Korathians had been completely decimated by the Elven archers, and Barton hid behind a tree with a single arrow in his arm. A Dabani asked to treat him, but he declined. "You lead the others! Forget about me. Go!"

As the tribesman rejoined the front line, Barton removed the arrow without flinching, not a speck of blood to be seen on him.

"Vanquish or die. I win either way, mortals," he hissed with an evil grin.

Moments later, a great gust of wind tore the shields away from the Dabanis and tumbled the tribesmen like balls of cotton. Barton whimpered, "Oh, no!"

He was then held fast by glowing white chains around his neck, torso, wrists, and ankles, and his human shell dissolved.

"Behold! The true face of an evil chaos demon, mortals. He has tricked you all," said the high baritone voice of Syrene.

The Dabanis prostrated themselves before her, and the Korathians stood in disbelief.

Syrene held aloft the arrow. "Tell me truly. What kind of mortal does not bleed when struck by this arrow? NONE. Behold, N'Tar'byss, whom you called Lord Barton, or Friar Toby, or Gunnar Mollenbeck. The leader of the Alpha clan which controls the ministry of the Lawgiver, who has sold your children to the Syndicate for the pleasure of wicked men, who has never loved you. He would have fed on your hatreds, your fears, your violence, while you bled and died for his agenda."

A tribesman stammered, "But we saw the bow that killed our chieftain!"

Syrene conjured an image of it in midair. "This one?"

The tribesman nodded vigorously.

Andrath walked forth to examine the image. "This bow was stolen from the ruins of Shadval! This triple-leaf pattern died out with the family that crafted it! The bow is covered in mildew, and who has seen the arrow it launched?"

The demon opened his mouth to speak, and Syrene quickly added another chain between his teeth, much to his chagrin. Two men stood to confess they had seen the arrow.

Andrath added, "I tell you that no Elf uses a rusty arrow! See for yourselves!"

He tossed his quiver on the ground for them to examine. Next he laid his bow on the ground, which had the single-leaf pattern on the tips.

The Dabani leader crawled before Andrath with his head bowed. "Please forgive us."

The demon shook his head no with fear in his eyes.

Andrath asked, "Will you take our hand in friendship again?"

The leader nodded and rose to shake his hand. The demon felt wracking pains and shook his head mutely, "NNNNN, NNNNN!"

Syrene spoke to Andrath, "One more task remains. I require the silver lance you keep."

He motioned his herald to fetch it. The demon shut his eyes and doubled over in terror and agony. Syrene raised a hand in the air, and gold light shimmered all around, causing steam to exit the pores of the pitiful creature. His eyes bulged wide, and his pupils shrank to pinpricks. He quivered in a great seizure and struggled to break free, to no avail. The Dabanis looked down on him, and as they pitied him, his body shrank further to skin and bones. The chains held fast, and when the herald handed Syrene the lance, the demon wailed one last time, "NNNNNNNNNNNNN!"

With a cold and blank expression, Syrene spoke, "Goodbye, demon." She thrust it with great force through the demon's torso into the ground, causing him to discorporate into red light, and a great orange shockwave was seen for miles around.

"Leave the lance where it is, and seal it off from tampering. He was banished centuries ago in Zara-Mogai, and somehow, Arius, while still a mortal some years ago, was tricked into setting him free. Now I must rest. Fare thee well," Syrene said sadly as she phased out of sight.

The Dabani leader asked, "Why must a god rest when our children still cry for justice?"

Andrath whispered, "She once loved a mortal and lost him in great tragedy. I sense she is still in mourning."

The Dabani man bowed his head and said, "We weep alongside her."

* * *

"You ask far too many questions about the orphanage. The king will be most angry," said Peter, the foreman.

Wayne grumbled, "A man named Adrian kidnapped this man's daughter, and I have been tasked to help him. Have you not a shred of compassion for the children?"

The foreman looked at the floorboards in shame. "This is a bad place for you. I'd keep moving in your shoes. And keep quiet about what I told you."

Wayne shook his head and returned to work on repairing locks and latches. While Alex the Meek hammered away at door frames and support beams. Awkward silence pervaded the rest of the day.

* * *

"What? No, I cannot go back to Korath! King Nathan and his queen would have my hide tanned and quartered!" Adrian protested vehemently.

Kazius asked indelicately, "Did you cheat or swindle him somehow, Adrian? Did you?"

Adrian dodged, "Why are you in league with ... him?"

Garzon smiled and said nothing. Sal avoided all eye contact and walked like a beaten dog, while Kazius answered, "I have my reasons, you kidnapping swine. Not your business why."

Bernice also said nothing; she did not trust these men. As well she should not.

Chapter Thirty-Seven
Karma

Sister Helen and Brother Savadi divided their duties between the abbey and the courthouse, preparing medicines and tending the wounded, including Sasha and Andar, while Watcher Sean was training new apprentices. The entire barony still had an empty feeling, with more than half the population relocated for the lean months, or dead and buried. What few men remained of the Owls Guild, either patrolled the sewers of Oakthorn or helped the refugees forage for food near West Bend, while Lady Bethany rode out to catch up with Amanda. Scaffolds were everywhere as two-thirds of the buildings were under slow repairs, and the sunlight was dimming each day.

* * *

Moira looked northward mournfully at the waters from the pier where the fishing boats docked, as she absentmindedly repaired the nets for the family who took her in. Somewhere out there, her husband had probably drowned, and her daughter most likely lay at the mercy of wicked men. Moira was numb to everything now. Her existence seemed hollow and utterly meaningless. She wondered why she bothered living, and had no answer. While knitting nets and cooking for someone else's children without joy, without pay, without anything of her former life, she felt dead already.

* * *

"Nikita, I think you should come see this …" said one of her top assassins.

He led her down several streets of beat up old shacks with dirt floors and holes in the roof and walls, riddled with starving old people and naked children under failing roof-beams, and garbage piled against the buildings, and finally, at a particular intersection, there lay nine dead bodies. All slashed ear to ear by professionals, and three gashes on each cheek, including the blind man who requested asylum.

"You are the first I have shown this to. I thought you should know."

Nikita scowled. "Do not tell Erik…"

Her words cut short. Her command was too late. Erik stood on the roof across the street from them. He said nothing because he had no need to. In the next instant, he vanished. Nikita brought her hand over her face in despair and consternation.

"Damn him!" she protested, before snarling like a wounded cat. "Can we pin the blame on Erik?" she asked.

The other shook his head no.

"Everything was fine until he returned!" she lied to herself, and wanted to believe. She kicked at animal bones from the meals of homeless people on the way back to the temple and cursed Erik's name every other minute.

* * *

"What is the meaning of this? I've done nothing wrong! Get out of my house at once!" demanded Councilman Arthur Clayton.

Sandraz and a half dozen royal guards were combing his dwelling, looking for clues.

"You sheltered a woman here, a foreigner, at the time King William fell ill, and I *will* get to the bottom of this, Arthur," said Sandraz.

A guard returned from another room to summon Sandraz. "Found something, sir."

In the guest room, a small leather pouch had fallen under the bed. Inside were padded silk pouches, glass vials, and metal canisters with crushed herbs and powders inside.

"She must have left in a hurry, Arthur. Are you going to talk, or do we pin the contents of this bag on YOUR good name? I see some opium in here, and no idea what these are," Sandraz gloated.

Arthur hung his head and said nothing.

"Very well. Take him away, gentlemen."

Outside, another guard motioned Sandraz toward the outer wall of the castle. A dead guard leaned against the upper battlements with puncture wounds at every weak spot in his armor, and the dagger was still in his shoulder. The guard's sword was still spotless, not even a nick on it, same for his shield and his armor plates. Sandraz had never seen this kind of handiwork. The assailant was inhumanly fast and cruel, and it chilled Sandraz to think of how anyone could ever hope to defeat this new enemy.

"Well, she obviously had help getting out …" Sandraz muttered in a somber and anxious voice.

* * *

"We wish to resettle here, the lawgivers are very powerful in Korath, and would punish us severely for speaking ill of their leaders. And our king does not care a single copper-pence about his people," one of the humans confessed.

Andrath replied, "Falcon Ridge is not far from here. You would be welcomed there."

The man bowed. "Thank you," and then to the hunter, he said, "I am sorry I ever doubted your word about Malsain. Forgive me."

The hunter shook his hand, saying, "Done."

They all waved farewell to the Dabanis, who moved southward to avoid Falcon Pass and Korath and seek a path home over the Iron Ridge Mountains.

* * *

"Wait! My leather bag! I must have dropped it. Those powders are hard to replace!" Winter complained in distress.

D'aarzane casually ignored her. They did not like each other, and made no secret of it. And both knew that any bloodshed between them would draw the undying wrath of Arius. Winter regretted the errand of killing King William Goldlion and wondered, even now, if her mother's diary was worth all the trouble. It held many of the answers to Winter's tormented past and memories her mother left nowhere else. The rest of the ride home to Zara-Mogai was dominated by sullen silence and gloomy skies.

* * *

"We need food and rest and must go ashore," said Skorvald.

Lebiced sighed, "Yes, I feared we would."

Jonah's left arm hung limp at his side, and he collapsed on the beach.

Skorvald helped one of his men carry Conrad above the high tide mark, and all who were able, busied themselves with setting camp and foraging for tinder and food. Lebiced found a few wild carrots and dill weed. Skorvald caught some trout and salmon, and one other dug up some wild garlic. Jonah felt useless and ashamed, while Conrad mumbled to thin air, "No, North is THAT way, now go ..."

* * *

Alex the Meek was fetching some lumber from the basement, when he recognized a closet door … and dropped his lumber while his eyes went wide in horror.

"Noooooooooooooooo! Stop! Leave me be!"

The odors came back to him, the dark shadow of Father Samuel Malsain towering above him in the pale light of a single candle, the sound of that horrible voice, all the memories he had locked away in the cobwebs of his childhood. Alex was overwhelmed, shaking and shivering like an autumn leaf spiraling to the ground. Scores of workers came to investigate and did not understand what they saw.

Alex was balled up between his dropped lumber and the closet door, with no other creature to pin blame on.

Peter the Foreman showed up, "Oh, cripes, I recognize you now. You are Alex the Meek, one of the choir boys. We need to get him out of here, or the king will have our heads. Help me lift him up. And get some cold water to snap him out of it. Easy now …"

* * *

Farther south, common folk swarmed at the approach of Tyrianna and Tyrus.

"The Elf witch has returned! Get her!"

And as they threw objects and stones at her, everything bounced away from an invisible bubble. And as Tyrianna lifted a hand in their direction, the wind tore the objects from their grasp. Tyrus worried that the young water sprite he once knew was not coming back. The people fled, except for a young child who had hidden in a barn. The boy tried to follow without being noticed, but that was quite impossible. Tyrianna turned in his direction. "Why does my appearance fascinate you?"

The boy answered, "They say you're a witch, but you don't look like the stories they tell. They have hairy noses and big warts, but you're pretty."

The oracle weakly smiled. "So ... honest humans still exist here? Good. Do you know of a girl named Molly or a boy named Alex?"

The boy displayed a sad frown. "No, my friends are all gone to the academy. This is the season that all the seven year olds are taken. I only get to play with animals now. Next year it will be me."

Tyrianna inquired, "Where is this academy?"

The boy pointed northeast. "It's five miles east of the orphanage, and nobody ever comes back out. The king runs it himself; he's a big bully."

Tyrianna flashed a wicked grin as she declared, "I know how to handle bullies."

The boy saw her eyes change color, and ran away in fear. Tyrus stood aghast; the gentle soul he knew seemed forever gone.

* * *

"Where in the world is Gunnar Mollenbeck? And why am I never informed about his errands?" Arius demanded of the Alphas and the Chaos Fanatics.

"We do not know, great one…" said a middle-aged man with a brown beard.

Arius the Chaos Lich repelled the man into a stalagmite. "That's not good enough!"

Another replied placatingly, "We were taught not to question our superiors, and he is second only to you and Barton, as you know, most powerful of the Augurons …"

Arius roared, "GET OUT! Begone from my sight, you simpering baboons!"

They dropped all their books and scrolls to flee with expedience.

* * *

Lady Bethany finally saw what she was looking for, dismounted, and ran, yelling, "Devi!

Jacob! Mommy's here!"

She scooped up her children in her arms and hugged them for dear life, kissing them repeatedly.

The walls of West Bend were just on the horizon. Lady Amanda welcomed Bethany with a weak smile of relief.

Nell informed her, "They asked about you every day, milady."

Bethany weeped. "I missed my babies so much!"

Rebecca walked over to greet her, as did John and Amanda, and they exchanged tales of all that happened in Oakthorn and Valantir. They told of the betrayal of Arbiter Dharana, of Lord Alex's bravery, the downfall of Valandrassil, everything but the courthouse and the goddess.

"I'm so glad you survived," said Bethany.

"Good to see you again, Lady Bethany," said the couple.

Bethany did not mention Jonah's errand, and nobody had asked, yet.

* * *

"Imagine, the great Erik, the master of masters, his job regarding the Whispering Tigers was never completed," said Nikita with venomous sarcasm.

"You <u>know</u> what happened, Nikita. I was recruited into another gang, based in Razadur. It was an opportunity to spy on a more dangerous enemy. One that I had inside knowledge of through my mother," replied Erik.

"Oh, of course, your evil half-brother who married the chaos witch ... was your family reunion pleasant?" Nikita taunted with naked malice.

"Still blinded by ego, Nikita? That family of nine is on YOUR head, not mine. You could have easily given them asylum; it was well within your authority. Why didn't you?" asked Erik.

Nikita hissed, "My decisions are not yours to question, Erik! You forget your place!"

Three senior priestesses from the council entered the room once occupied by Erik's mother.

"No, Nikita. It is *you* who have abused yours. Erik is right. We lost a valuable witness and wasted an opportunity to seize an advantage over the creepers and tigers. Your ego has cost us all dearly, Nikita. The council moves to strip your title and expel you from both the order and the temple, effective immediately."

Nikita growled and launched into an attack instantly, and Erik shadow-jumped to intercept with an elbowed uppercut to the jaw, knocking Nikita to the floor and giving the others time to react with weapons drawn. Nikita grabbed for a lantern and broke it against the wall, setting the draperies on fire. Two of the priestesses tried to contain the fire, while Nikita sped past the third, slashing her throat. Erik sighed with remorse, just before throwing a kris dagger between Nikita's shoulder blades, staggering her attempt at escape. She crawled in debilitating pain, clutching at furniture to get up.

Erik blocked the doorway. "I'm sorry, Nikita, more than you know."

Nikita collapsed, and wheezed her last minutes on Earth. "I envy you one thing, and one thing only, that you will see Sidhuri before I do."

Chapter Thirty-Eight
Tipped Balances

"Begging pardon, Your Lordship. Had to let him go. He was unfit for work around spiders and creepy crawlies. The lad had a breakdown right in front of me. He needed quiet work, such as the clerk's office," said Peter the Foreman.

King Nathan Silverlane slapped him. "The man is a suspected spy, and if his actions cause me any trouble, I shall hold YOU responsible!"

The foreman backed away and bowed. "Yes, Your Majesty. May I go now?"

The king barked, "GO, and I'm reducing your pay."

The foreman gave a sad look, but dared not speak. He bowed as if at a funeral, and then shambled out.

* * *

"Darling, what were your parent's names again?" asked Alex the Wise as he examined a contract.

"Morgan and Julia, why do you ask?" replied his wife Myra.

"A bounty was collected in Mojara by an Ivan Goodhill. What do you make of that?"

Myra looked puzzled, horrified, and outraged as she answered, "There's no Ivan in my family, and none of my relatives would do such a thing!"

Alex spoke soothingly, "Honey, I'm sure there's a good explanation for this. It's okay. I'll ask Henry about it."

Myra stayed cold and aloof for two days afterward.

* * *

The snow had fresh tracks in it, and the short statured leader of the gang pointed to the hoof prints.

"You boys are new here. These marks are heavier in front than a horse. The centaurs have found our traps again and ripped 'em up. Plus some human that works with them. The network has a bounty on all of them. Seventy-five gold each, dead or alive, " said a dark-skinned Dwarven mercenary. "Don't let them get the drop on you, or it will be the last mistake ever. Fan out and keep quiet."

As they delved deeper into the foothills and pine forests of the Icefang Mountains at the borders of Vostiok and Nordranaya, they fell, one by one, over the next few hours, to the sniper shots of a woman in arctic fur and leather known as Rachel LongArrow, who had heard them conversing and plotting from her hidden perch in the trees.

Much later, when only the Dwarf and one bandit remained, they found themselves in a cleft that dead ended against a vertical rock face, and the centaurs cut off their escape.

"I forgot to mention how clever these bastards are," said the Dwarf begrudgingly, as he lowered his weapons.

* * *

Two canoes pulled up to the island of South Watch, and the Elves recognized Lebiced, but not the others. Lebiced quickly introduced everyone, and Conrad was taken to the healers' platform.

"Remarkable that he is still alive at all. No one has ever taken such a large dose of this pathogen. Where and how was he exposed?" asked the senior healer.

Skorvald replied, "The lowest levels of Shadval, cleaving his way through dozens of ghouls. Where else?"

The healer stroked his chin. "This explains much. He was angered instead of panicked. Both taxing on the immune system, but somewhat different chemistry at work. All the other victims we know of ..."

Skorvald waved his hands. "These things are beyond my grasp. I am no healer."

Lebiced pulled him aside. "Now that we have a few hours to spare. I managed to salvage a few things from our journey down there in the ruins, which was our main purpose, after all ..."

* * *

Adrian cast a lustful glance at Bernice from where he was tied to a tree, and Kazius saw the wicked grin on his face. Adrian kept looking, blind to Kazius sneaking around his side, until the blunt impact of his knee met Adrian's jaw and knocked a tooth loose, followed by a right cross to the same jaw, and a left hook to his plexus.

"Don't ever do that again, if you want to live, vermin," Kazius warned.

Adrian did not understand how he got on the wanted list so quickly, and just blinked at him stupidly, spitting blood. "Wh-why yew do thaht? Thot we were friends …"

Kazius backhanded Adrian for good measure. "Not anymore, greedy swine."

Just then, Garzon emerged from the surf, hauling a net with a big swordfish wriggling inside it, until the huge, bearlike man tossed it over his shoulder, smacking hard onto the sand. Adrian just stared, thinking to himself, Right. don't make that guy mad.

Sal shrunk his head away with his lip quivering in fear.

* * *

"I can't do this, Wayne. The nightmares keep me up for hours. I can't face HIM again. I just can't!" Alex the Meek cried.

Wayne shook his head. "Then Molly is already doomed, Alex. You will never be free of him, and many other children may suffer because YOU are a fucking coward. Molly deserves better. Your wife deserved better. And I'll tell you something else. I used to be afraid of Kazius. Can he still hurt me? Yes, he could. Everybody gets hurt. Nobody lives forever. But I'm not going to hide the rest of my days out of fear. I gave my testimony. Three men are now where they deserve to be … in the silver mines doing hard labor. If not for my part, and the Lady Amanda, they could still be free to kidnap more people. I hear Conrad took out some bandits, too. If not for him, you could be dead yourself. You ever think of that? That because someone had the courage you lack, did things you refuse to do, you are still breathing, and you can't even thank them or learn from their example! You disgust me."

Alex just cried and curled into a ball again, while Wayne threw his hands in the air and walked away.

When Alex Mill went looking the next day, Wayne was gone.

"He vanished into the mountains up north yesterday, lad. You're too late," said Peter the Foreman.

Alex whimpered, "No, no, no, this can't be happening."

The words "too late" echoed in his head like church bells.

"Nooooooooooooo!"

* * *

AxeGrind was in a foul mood, and even the Blood Arena did nothing to appease him.

Only when a messenger reported that both the Southland Creepers and the Whispering Tigers had agreed to negotiations did he show a sign of satisfaction.

"Good. It is time to destroy Valantir and Stonehaven, once and for all. Then the girl will have nowhere to hide, no one to help her, and she will be utterly demoralized ... go arrange the meeting location. Dismissed."

* * *

Dale Woodman heard a knock at the door of his remote cabin on the outskirts of West Bend and answered, "What do you people want from the 'bastard commoner' now? You deny me the ..."

His words died mid-sentence, and his jaw fell slack; he dared not believe his eyes. "Ravenna?"

Her reply was, "Yes, my love, it is I!" And she kissed him full on the lips with all the years of longing and separation, and it was still not enough. There was only one thing that could intervene between them.

"Mother!" Young Dane exclaimed with joy as he strode forward to hug her.

"Dane! How you have grown! I missed my baby!" She ruffled his hair and turned back to Dale. "How is my son getting along?"

Young Dane groaned sheepishly, "Mother ..."

His father, Dale, answered, "He takes fancy to some ladies already but has trouble mustering the courage to speak ..."

Dane protested, "Dad!"

Lady Ravenna added, "Tell me everything! I missed you both terribly ..."

Dale changed the subject, "How are your niece and nephew taking the loss of your brother? I know you did not get along much, and I can't say I miss him, but he deserved a better ending ..."

Ravenna turned somber. "I have not spoken with them yet. Let us not speak of it now ..."

Dale asked, "Why did you go away?"

Ravenna sank her head gloomily, and Dane took his cue to give them privacy.

"My brother had men hounding my every footstep and conspiring to keep us apart. You know that. And you know why."

Dale pressed on, "We could have gone far away. I don't care about the legacy or the crown. I just wanted YOU. I have hated taking their bribes, but I had nowhere to go without you. You tore my heart out when you left."

Ravenna begged, "Please stop. I was being driven mad. I'm sorry I hurt you, darling. You have no idea ..."

Dale said, "Then show me."

Ravenna's response was to yank his shirt off and push him onto the floor, raining kisses all over him.

* * *

Henry the Lorekeeper arrived at the baronial mansion with a few books and charts at the request of Lord Alex the Wise, and they met in the baronial library.

"So Bethany received this bag from Tyrus after his return from Mojara, which happens after the message granting leadership of the owls to Conrad. If this were a random name, and the odds make this unlikely, what I am about to show you would be incredibly, astronomically improbable. Follow, if you will. Myra is the last Goodhill in this area; her parents died in the Fire of '33. The name Ivan originates in the northern regions, where none of the Goodhills are ever found. Take Arius, for example, who was close to the original Emerald Order in Thalu. Arius led the Bloodhammer raid of 1533 wherein the Goodhills died. His father's name is Ivan, born in 1483. Ivan's mother, Elaine, flees Vostiok after her husband was killed in the rebellion of 1491. Ivan fathers Arius in 1513 by Helga, who dies during childbirth, and a second son, Erik, is born in 1516. Erik's name vanishes from public records in 1529. Assumed dead. Now take this together with the fact that no record of Tyton Umbral exists before 1533. I believe there is a missing link in there. And get this, Umbral is the maiden name of Ivan's second wife. This cannot be mere coincidence. What this means, we do not know yet. But this is not random."

Alex sat there, dumbfounded. "But why now? What is the message? I do not understand."

Henry replied, "The answer to that is somewhere between 1529 and 1533. About the time when a gang known as the Whispering Tigers were almost exterminated from Vaja. I do love mysteries, and I fully expect we will solve this someday soon!"

Lord Alex Redoak shrugged. "I will leave this in your able hands then, Henry. Thank you."

Henry answered, "My pleasure, Lord Alex, dear fellow, my pleasure! Thank YOU."

Chapter Thirty-Nine
Cold Revenge

"You know full well I can't give you that information. It's a fate worse than death if and when the alpha leader discovers who betrayed him. Do your worst, bitch," spat the Dwarf.

Rachel kicked him onto his back, while tied to the chair, and dragged him toward the east wall of the cave, where the sun was melting snow above them. Then she kicked the chair again, onto its side, such that the ice cold water dripped in his ear. Then she broke off an icicle and poked him with it in his tender parts.

"AAAAaaahhhhhh … oh, you will pay for that, girly…" he threatened.

Next, she broke off the sharp end and rubbed it smooth, before jamming it in his nostril. The sensation of brain freeze set in very quickly.

"GAAAAAAAAaaaaaaaaa! Take it out! Take it out! I'll talk!"

Rachel smiled. She let him flail, scream, and suffer a minute longer to break his will further. His breathing was rapid and shallow as he volunteered what she wanted. "The drugs are run by Winter herself, and the slave market is controlled by Malsain and Barton. Gunnar handled the fur and ivory. Arius and his agents handle the gems. You're no match for any of them, girl. You'll die begging for mercy," he stammered.

Rachel then gave him a dagger in the heart. "Take the other as a hostage," she said to the centaurs.

* * *

Tyrianna saw the engraved brass plate with black enamel on it, which announced to the public that this was King Nathan Silverlane's Iron Hand Academy.

Tyrus grumbled, "I already dislike this man, taking children from their parents and housing them here like animals in a barn."

Tyrianna replied, "Go see if you can find anything at the orphanage. I will look here."

Tyrus started to protest, "But ..." and then remembered, this is not the Tyrianna he knew anymore. "How will I find you?" he asked.

She replied, "I will find YOU. Now go."

Tyrus had to hide his trident somewhere, and thus he put it in the lake north of Kozos, before returning to town and collecting some extra clothes from the church, while Tyrianna entered the academy invisibly.

In a large two-story dining hall, she heard a man lecturing the children.

"I know that many of you are new here and might be wondering why your king would walk among children of such humble origins. I will tell you ... because you are the future of this land! And we feed you very well here. You may wonder about that as well. We feed you better than your parents did because they starved you to convince the tax collectors they were poor. They hide their riches from the kingdom, and someday you will help right this wrong. Some of you will become tax collectors, and be richly rewarded!" said a man in a fur-lined cloak, wearing a gold crown, a gold ring inset with a large ruby, bearing a gold scepter. The words "tax collectors" echoed in Tyrianna's head, conjuring images of the Crimson Hoods who killed her Father Kaedrus in 1551. Objects began randomly falling off the tables, and buckles came unfastened on the guardsmen who flanked the king, causing them to stumble and fall, and the children laughed.

"Stop laughing!" barked King Nathan.

Next, the ruby popped out of his ring, and Nathan grabbed after it in complete panic as it bounced and tumbled on the floor. Drapes fell from the curtain rods, lanterns went dark, and Tyrianna added to the confusion by punching guards in the darkness, provoking them to fight each other.

Pandemonium ensued.

"Who is doing that? I order you to show yourself!" the king announced with an edge of anger and fear in his voice.

"You cannot order me to do anything, old man!" said a high baritone voice. Tyrianna then levitated him twenty feet in the air. "I can come and go as I please, and do whatever I wish!"

The children ducked under the tables.

The king started pleading, "I can make you very rich! Put me down and we can talk about this like reasonable people."

Tyrianna laughed. "I already have power. Why do I need riches? You amuse me, mortal."

Now the king pissed himself. "What have I done to you? Please put me down."

Tyrianna stood silent and let him squirm.

"Who are you? Why are you doing this?" he begged.

"*Men like you caused the death of my father!*" Tyrianna screamed, enraged.

King Nathan now understood that his life hung by a thread. He was at the mercy of a demigod.

"Pleeeeease don't hurt me!" Nathan whimpered in tears.

Tyrianna asked, "Why? I have no trust in the words of tyrants, bullies, and greedy mortals! Why should I spare you, old man?"

Nathan whined, "Everyone has a price. Name it. Name it and it's yours."

Tyrianna waited a moment.

"Tell me what you want from me." Nathan cried.

Tyrianna then gave the command, "Release the children. Let them return to their parents. And you will stop stealing their food from their families. Fail in this, and I will return without mercy."

Nathan gulped. "But, but, but ..."

And Tyrianna let him drop three feet before stopping his fall.

"Okay, okay, okay! It is done. They can go!"

Tyrianna prompted, "Your WORD, old man, on ALL of these terms !"

Nathan sputtered, "Yes, I agree."

Tyrianna continued, "SAY IT."

"The children may go free and ... and keep their food," he said mournfully.

"Remember my warning, old man," Tyrianna said as she let him drop to the tables.

The children rushed out of the compound and ran home. Tyrianna then floated out, still invisible.

* * *

"Tell me! Where is my son?" Winter demanded.

The guards fell to one knee, and one of them spoke, "We found signs of him stealing food, but we don't know exactly where he is."

Winter slugged him hard. "Who is the bumbling idiot that let him loose?" she screeched.

"He's already dead, Your Ladyship," said another.

"Show me the body or join him!" she ordered.

They led her through the caverns of the dead to the south of the city, to the newest coffin and opened it.

Winter did not recognize what was left of him. "How did he die?" she asked.

"Rats, Madam Auguron," answered the first.

"Burn it," Winter said.

The guards stood puzzled.

"This idiot does not deserve memorial services. BURN it!" Winter hissed.

They complied in great haste, as they knew her many dark moods.

"I am going to visit my father, and when I return, I expect for Rod to be back in his cell! Fetch my horse," was her last command for the afternoon.

* * *

"Arthur, you're in this up to your neck. Who are you protecting? Your career is over when this goes to the tribunal. Now talk! Damn you!" barked Sandraz.

Arthur just looked at the floor.

"Very well, you leave me no choice but to freeze your accounts, turn your house inside out, and pursue charges of conspiracy to murder the king. You're finished, Clayton. Good-bye," Sandraz said with exasperation. "Return him to the dungeon."

* * *

"Who are those men on the next rise? They are not pirates," stated Garzon.

Kazius took a look. "No, those are tax collectors for AxeGrind, and they have a captive."

Garzon warned, "You wait here. Do not follow until I say so."

Adrian taunted, "Kazius taking orders?"

Kazius kicked Adrian's knee for that, and he dropped like a stone, wailing and groaning. While Sal had gone mute for days, Kazius watched as Garzon openly challenged the Crimson Hoods to combat, and they drew swords and daggers, then fell back and ran as Garzon displayed his enormous battle axe. Garzon cleaved two of them as they ran, and threw the axe into a third, and three more got away. The captive was a woman, bruised and bloodied all over, and barely breathing. Garzon retrieved his axe, then cut the woman's bonds with a borrowed knife, and carried her back to the others. Adrian turned his head to hide his face. Kazius realized, "You recognize this girl, don't you, Adrian?"

The woman stirred and spat in Adrian's direction, just before collapsing again. Kazius taunted with a sinister grin and a gleam in his eye, "You will be at her mercy, SWINE."

Adrian tugged at his bonds to no avail. Garzon knew how to tie a knot. Bernice walked over to tend to the woman's injuries, and Garzon tied Adrian and Sal to a tree once more.

Chapter Forty
Changing Fortunes

"The aura on this helm, interferes with outsiders reading your thoughts, which will be very useful against Arius ... and it appears it would fit you perfectly," said the wizard from Xantir.

Skorvald tried it on. "Aye, it does indeed. May it prove enough to avenge my comrades in battle."

Lebiced cautioned, "Not by itself, it won't. To face Arius in single combat would be foolhardy. A lesson not lost on the Elves who fought Lorenna. The chaos elders are crafty, cunning and powerful, never underestimate them."

Skorvald clapped one fist to his breastplate and bowed before turning away. Lebiced returned to the healers' platform to check on Conrad. The Elf had a grim look on his face as he spoke, "His body is strong, but his spirit does not return. He has lost hope, which none of us can give him. He must be seen by those he holds most dear and by one who loves him. There is nothing more we can do here."

Lebiced nodded, then went about in search of Jonah, whose shoulder was mending slowly. "Let us pray for a happy reunion at home, it is time for us to go. Conrad requires things that are not found on this island for him. Come."

The word "home" conjured thoughts of Bethany and his children, and Jonah said, "Yes, I am ready to see home."

* * *

At long last, the gates of West Bend were visible to the refugees of Oakthorn. Lady Amanda, Lady Bethany, and everyone were gladdened by the sight. They had only lost two people to exhaustion and predators. But as they got closer, they saw all visitors were being searched head to toe. Amanda went ahead, demanding audience with someone in command.

"Under the military emergency clause of 1301, " the sentinel began.

"I know how your system works, Sergeant. I am the Lady Amanda of the Redoak Mansion, and acting deputy mayor of Oakthorn, and I demand to see the king!"

The sergeant replied, "That is impossible. The king is dead. The council voted five to four in favor of invoking the clause, therefore, all visitors must submit to a thorough search for any and all dragon eggs, dragon's blood, claws, scales, spikes, horns, and ..."

Amanda interrupted, "I will not submit, and I will not subject my people to this nonsense! And I wish to file a petition!"

The sergeant groaned, "The queen is not to be bothered right now, so move along ..."

Amanda stood her ground. "We will be camping by the southwest corner and will remain there until this matter is settled!"

The guard protested, "You can't do that!"

Amanda shot back, "Yes, I can! And unless you are fully prepared to violate the Treaty of Westwood ..."

At these words, the guard walked away, muttering under his breath, "Only thing worse than arbitrators is a woman ..."

* * *

Tyrus looked around carefully at the orphanage, hauling supplies and trying to blend in when a smaller man ran from the clerk's office and collided with him, falling backward. Tyrus stared at him.

"I didn't mean it! I'm sorry. Please don't hurt me!" begged Alex the Meek from the floor.

Tyrus lifted him back to his feet with one hand. "I'm not here to hurt you."

Alex took a second look at him. "You were at the Elven temple with the girl ..."

Tyrus nodded. "Yes, and now we are here, seeking answers to her visions. Where were you going in such a hurry?"

Alex looked away.

Tyrus prodded, "I am bound by oath to the girl, but you have nothing to fear from me. You may speak."

Alex sighed. "I found records of my daughter Molly, and … and …" Tyrus tilted his ear closer, "Go on." Alex cried, "I can't face Malsain again … he … he …" and his voice cracked. Tyrus tapped Alex under the chin with two fingers. "Look at me. We are seeking the children. Will you help for Molly's sake?"

Alex whimpered, "I'm scared to …"

Tyrus answered, "All men know fear. Do you wish to master it one day?"

Alex stuttered, "H-how? I don't know …"

Tyrus finished, "You must act. You must break the chain of your past, and begin a new chain. Each day is a link. How you live this day is up to you."

Alex stood in silence, other memories dancing before him; his wife Moira handing him the skillet, Wayne correcting his posture, Mandy telling him to go send Adrian to hell, the smiling face of Lebiced, and an image of Molly in her mother's arms minutes after being born, so tiny and so precious, at which Alex cried, "Yes … yes, I will help."

* * *

"You let the children go? Our dynasty depends on that academy! You must tell the lawgivers, so they can deal with this spirit or witch, whoever she is …" said Queen Marcy to her husband Nathan.

He answered, "Who would help? Barton is leading a militia. Malsain is on some sabbatical, Toby has vanished, we are not protected from heathens anymore …"

Marcy mused, "What about Razadur?"

King Nathan snarled, "They would be no more effective against an invisible spirit or witch than we are …"

Marcy thought ponderously for a minute, pacing in circles, and then exclaimed, "The alchemists! Certainly they may have an invention for this …"

Nathan went to summon them at once.

* * *

"There's a chill wind and many dark clouds from the east. We need to get Conrad to shelter before the storm reaches our position," declared Lebiced. "Let's make for the western side of the bay, and take cover within the trees."

Skorvald and Jonah nodded in agreement.

Conrad continued to babble, "No, you can't borrow my fishing net …"

Jonah whispered a prayer with a tear in his eyes, "Powers above us, grant me that my brother Conrad will live …"

* * *

"Yes, you heard correctly. I will pay seven hundred and fifty gold eagles upon proof of his demise, and Mother must not know of this arrangement, EVER. I will add a bonus for your discretion, and great pain if you bungle it," said Prince Douglas Saint Noir.

A man in a black cloak answered, "The blood fangs will see it done."

Doug hissed, "Now go before you are seen."

They exited at opposite ends of the alley between the spiced apple tavern and the candle shoppe. The candlemaker's youngest brat pulled away quietly from the window and snuck out the side door.

* * *

In the bustling crowds of the city markets of Cranali, Vaja, Tyton spotted two very familiar women, and followed thirty paces behind them. Someone else was following the women as well, on the other side of the street. Tyton tucked his head low to get lost in the crowd as he moved to intercept. As the women zigzagged through the many vendor carts and tents, Tyton drew close enough to size up their tail. A skinny man in beige robes hid several knives in his belt and had not seen he was being watched. As he moved to corner the women in an alley, Tyton delivered a double chop to his neck from behind, just short of a killing blow. The adversary slumped, unconscious, to the ground, and Tyton dragged him behind some baskets. The women turned to see what the sound was, but there was nobody there. They quickened their pace in the other direction, and there was Tyton in their path.

"Erik! You should have told us you were still alive!" said Narjali.

Laksmi concurred, "Instead of all these riddles that Mother was famous for ..."

Tyton bowed and nodded his head. "Good to see you, too." He quickly hugged his half-sisters, and then led them away from the alley.

* * *

"I miss my daddy," said Molly with downcast eyes and a tone of despair.

"Can you tell me how you got here in case he is looking for you?" asked her host Thomas.

Molly answered, "I was taken in a boat, then over sand, then through a forest, then ran from bad wolf, hid in a wagon, ran from mean old drunk, crossed river, ended up here ..."

Thomas frowned. "Well, that's not much for me to go on. What is your daddy's name?"

Molly looked afraid to answer and hesitantly told him, "Alex. Mommy calls him bad names sometimes, but he likes to be called Alex."

Thomas stroked his beard. "And how would I know if I ever found the right Alex?"

Molly asked, "Is Meek a bad word?"

Thomas laughed, "Well, that depends. It could be. I will ask a friend of mine if he knows where your dad is."

He left Molly another block puzzle to keep her occupied while Carol watched butterflies inside the great glass dome. Thomas went back into the shed with the hissing door and no windows, that was only 12 feet tall, 8 feet wide and 18 deep. Molly knew there was not enough room for normal people to live in it, and she was never allowed inside it.

* * *

"Well, okay, since he vouched for you in an upbeat mood, we can use a strong hand like you here. Just don't cause any trouble. The king is easily angered, and I've already done all I can afford on behalf of Alex," said Peter the Foreman.

Tyrus bowed. "Thank you. I appreciate your gesture of faith. I shall not forget."

As he turned to rejoin Alex Mill downstairs, Tyrus heard a whisper over his shoulder: "There you are. What have you discovered?"

Tyrus whispered, "Not here. Outside."

At the bottom of the stairs, they met Alex Mill, and Tyrus motioned for Alex to follow quietly. Once beyond earshot of the orphanage, Tyrus spoke, "The mortar around the windows has been painted to hide bloodstains. There was a massacre in this place. Most of the records have been destroyed or hidden away. The locals talk of a beast, but cannot agree on what kind."

Tyrianna mused, "Hmmmmm ..."

Alex jumped at her voice. "Who is that? Where are you?"

Tyrianna answered, "I am hidden out of necessity. My reputation here is most unflattering. Curiously, I recall Ravenna speaking of Malsain, the werewolf. Is he the beast they speak of?"

Alex fainted on the spot.

"We'll ask about it when he comes to," Tyrus advised.

* * *

"Why is there no news from the pirates and poachers? Have Barton and Gunnar taken leave of their senses and moved their operations? You spineless slugs have thirty seconds to tell me why two of our markets have dried up!" Arius warned, with a tone of malice more sinister than usual.

The oldest man stepped forward. "There are rumors of new enemies..."

Arius levitated the old man and turned him upside down as he interrupted, "I don't want rumors. I want results!"

The old man gulped. "Two savages and a herd of centaurs are cutting our ranks like grass ..." just before Arius impaled him on a stalagmite.

"I will not tolerate failure! Find Gunnar, find Barton, and bring me the heads of these … beasts and savages!" roared the Lich in a violent rage, sending his minions scrambling for cover again.

Just then, Winter arrived. "Greetings, Father. William is dead as you instructed …"

Arius just glowered and tapped his skeletal fingers on his chair.

"I hoped you would be pleased, Father. What is wrong?" Winter asked.

"Hope is for weaklings, and EVERYTHING is wrong, wench!" Arius snarled.

Winter bowed and backpedaled. "What is thy wish then?"

Arius sulked for long moments before answering, "I wish my enemies to die, beginning with the centaurs; perhaps then, you will be worthy of her memoirs …"

Winter bowed again to hide her displeasure, gritting her teeth and then spun around to leave. "I will investigate … the possibilities," she declared as she walked away with hatred and disgust in her eyes.

* * *

"I thought Uncle Alex was in charge! What happened?" Baron Bravane the Younger asked.

Sandraz replied, "You had best go see Lady Amanda and ask her that. Meanwhile, my attention is required at council, that jackal Whitetree is taking over …"

Bravane bowed as Sandraz left. "What foul fortunes, this madness has no end!" Bravane the third complained.

* * *

Conrad found himself in a land of mist near a mountain and knew this place had some meaning or purpose to it. A white figure in robes of nobility approached and held out her arms.

"Mother?" he asked.

The figure nodded yes and motioned with a sweep of her arm to follow.

She led him to a castle archway past a bent and battered iron gate, and here was strange place he had never been. They walked past towers and storm drains to a secluded garden, and through a veil of smoke people appeared and vanished with no notice of Conrad or Summer.

"They do not see us," she whispered in his mind.

One woman was kneeling and harvesting herbs while ignoring the cries of a young male fifty yards away, as a bullwhip cracked again and again.

"Why are we here, Mother?" Conrad wondered.

Summer simply pointed to the lad in chains, and time stood frozen as they approached closer. The whip suspended in midair as it recoiled off the exposed skin of the boy's back. As Conrad walked in front, he saw in the young man, features of Bravane the Younger's jawbone, brow ridge, the same ears, and eyes as old as time itself, filled with sadness and despair.

"How is this possible? And what has he done to deserve this?" Conrad asked.

More silence. The strange woman appeared again to chastise the boy. "Never question my activities again! Your grandfather will do far worse to you!" she said.

Conrad attempted to intercede, but everything faded into the mist before he could.

"Wait!

Mother! Don't go!" he cried as he woke up. "Nooooo!"

* * *

The sound of a falling body outside awakened Tyton Umbral instantly, and in the darkness, he was without equal, even when unarmed. With a single thought, he moved from one shadow to any other in visual range. The intruders fell one by one in seconds from his deadly counteroffensive. A quick inspection of their gear and uniforms told him everything. This was a combined assault by the Whispering Tigers and the Creepers. Nearby, Laksmi and Narjali, plus their family, Narjali's son Nikolai from Agama and Laksmi's husband Febennin from Talos, their children Mahani, Sarnos, and grandchildren Emiri, Navi, Andrei, and Olivia, awoke to the carnage in their third-floor suite at the finest inn this city had to offer.

"Erik, what happened?" Narjali asked.

Tyton explained, "There is no time to explain now. We are not safe here. These were enemies of Mother's and mine, seeking revenge. You must go quietly and quickly, take only your bare necessities. Now."

They complied. Tyton recited a silent prayer over the body of a fallen temple brother on the balcony, and then he quickly descended the outside wall to secure the ground exit. More enemies appeared with the first rays of the sun. Tyton tore into them with borrowed weapons, and fought as if he was a predatory wild cat himself. They tragically underestimated him after all these years and fell like shredded rag dolls.

The family arrived at the door just as the last body hit the ground. Tyton handed his nephew Nikolai a map of Mojara and pointed to the city of Korii. "A merchant friend there will help you. Tell him the expedition was postponed by the illness of an uncle and grandfather."

Nikolai looked at his uncle with an expression of confusion, but took the map and nodded.

Tyton's relatives mounted their camels and waved farewell.

"We hope to meet again soon under better circumstances," said Nikolai.

Tyton bowed. "May the Blessed One grant us the luxury one day."

With those words, he vanished into the shadows of the dawn, and sped on his way to the temple.

"The gangs have joined forces. We need to find out what they are up to," he reported to the sentry on duty at the front door. Together they summoned the council and started breakfast.

Chapter Forty-One
Agendas

"You were the courier for Tyton, yes?" Bethany asked one of the surviving Obsidian Owls.

He nodded. "Yes, I was. Have we met?"

Lady Redmane-Blackthorn answered, "Rachel ran the Co-Op for me, so yes. I have an errand for you."

The man hesitated. "Of what nature?"

Bethany assured him, "The people are low on food. I need you to gather walnuts, acorns, and anything edible to feed them. Has Tyton passed on any of his herblore to you?"

The man nodded again. "He made a point of instructing us on a minimum of three edible mushrooms, two of which are local to these lands."

Bethany smiled. "Good. Might you start foraging now?"

The man agreed, bowing before he left.

Lady Amanda appeared to announce, "I'm glad you're here. A bit of food will be good for their spirits. The guards are on edge and overstepping their authority every hour.

I can't get word to the queen or anyone. They expect us to be fifty feet away from the walls even when the rain comes down; it's preposterous. I never knew the capitol of Stonehaven was so badly managed ..."

Bethany retorted, "You have never had the tragic occasion to meet Arbiter Eledar the Unforgiving ..."

* * *

"I want to know everything there is to know about these centaurs. How many agents have they killed? Where they roam? Who they know? What they eat? Where they sleep? And I want it in great haste, Dwarf," said Winter Auguron in her snide tone of annoyance.

"Beg pardon, miss. That ain't an easy job," answered the short, dark-skinned brute.

"I don't recall asking what you thought of the task, but I will remind you of the things I am capable of if you cross me, and that my father will do worse," the queen monarch of Nug Za snapped.

The Dwarf bowed unhappily, knowing this errand could mean his death. "Yes, milady ..." he grumbled, and shuffled away.

His thoughts dwelled on his brother, who had never reported back from his bounty hunt.

* * *

"Thank you for telling me," said Queen Margo to the boy. "Take this, and tell your father to seek refuge in the Frost Pillars northwest of here," she declared as she handed him five gold coins. "I will pursue the truth of your story soon enough."

The boy bowed and tucked the coins away before running home.

"I have long dreaded this day, John," Queen Margo spoke sadly to the painting of her husband. "More than I dared admit ..."

* * *

"Did you find Daddy yet?" Molly asked after Thomas reemerged from the shed.

"Yes, I did. He is somewhere in a land named Korath, not far from here, across the river you told me about. But the Bad Wolf is roaming there also. You would be safer here until the wolf is gone."

Molly cried. "But I miss my daddy! I miss Mommy, too. Please take me home!"

Thomas wanted to help, but he was sworn to secrecy, and his burden grew heavy on his heart. "I wish I could, little one. I wish I could," he confessed.

"You have to! I had bad dream about Daddy and wolf. You have to take me home!" she insisted.

Thomas could bear no more. "Can you promise to keep a secret?" he asked.

Molly replied, "What kind? Mommy says secrets are dangerous ..."

Thomas paused, sighed, and answered, "Yes, they are. Many burdens are dangerous, and this one must be kept safe from bad men who seek power and control. These machines must never fall into the wrong hands," as he finally relented to admit her into the shed.

* * *

A man in torn rags explained, "The lawgiver has healed my wounds after the beast attacked me. But I am still weak from my ordeal," said the priest to a peasant who found him while feeding the chickens.

The peasant inquired, "We were told you were on sabbatical, Father. We did not expect to see you again so soon? Have you returned because of the Elf witch?"

The wickedness in Malsain's eyes betrayed his greed. "Are there any bounties on her?"

The farmer replied, "Yes, the new monarch of Razadur has just posted one for five rubies if dead, ten alive. But she is stronger than ever they say. She moves objects with her mind and turns invisible. She even threatened the king!"

Wheels turned in Malsain's head. "And where is Lord Barton?"

The man answered, "He has marched on Valantir; none have returned. We do not know what has befallen them, Father. I am sorry."

Malsain chose his words carefully, "None must know I am here. The enemies of the Lawgiver are many and have grown bold. We are being tested!"

The farmer bowed, "We can hide you in the barn, then. In the hay loft."

Malsain flashed a wicked grin. "Yes, the barn."

Chapter Forty-Two
Lessons

"We have reached a decision. Several, in fact. First, that, given your inside knowledge of our many enemies, you are the best candidate to lead a campaign against them. Second, that you are the best qualified to fill the vacancy of high priest, and therefore nominate you. Third, the continued threat of Razadur must be remedied. Do you accept the role?" asked the council chairwoman.

Tyton bowed humbly. "I am honored, and answer yes."

The chairwoman nodded and concluded, "We will conduct ordination at sundown, and deal with our immediate enemies before sunrise. May the Great Mother bless our efforts."

The council ended session and within the hour, conducted Nikita's ceremony.

A senior priestess intoned, "Farewell, sister. May the gods have mercy on you in the next life and beyond, and guide you back into wisdom. Speed thee on thy way, and remember us with kindness. So say we all."

* * *

Off in the distance, behind the tree line, a loud rumbling was getting closer. A cloud of dust was rising in the forest, and the ground trembled. Conrad then saw the stampede of animals coming straight at him. He turned to run, and suddenly he could no longer feel his body. He watched from above as a great bear led the stampede. His namesake, a red bear.

Voices echoed in his head, voices of panic, and one of comfort. "Son of my nephew, learn well the woods, the stars, and the wilds. Our ways are bound to them. The ways of Xantir were in us and are now in you. You will understand soon enough."

Conrad, much like his cousin Bravane, traced family bloodlines from Agama, Xantir, and Stonehaven. And he awoke once more, confused and disoriented, but no longer delusional. The fever was finally fading.

* * *

"I have news, milady. One of our … business partners have seen the enemy. He sent a bird not long ago. They number three dozen centaurs, plus a woman and a prisoner. They were moving south from Icefang, toward Kozo-Makan to the east," declared the Dwarf.

Winter Auguron responded, "I want a bounty on them. Tell our eastern friends I will pay fifty gold per head, including the prisoner. But bring the woman alive, I want to question her ..."

The Dwarf bowed. "Consider it done."

His boss sneered, "Only done is done. Now go!"

* * *

"I can't fight a werewolf! Are you crazy?" Alex protested.

Tyrus admonished, "Perhaps you would have preferred fighting ghouls and vampires, or hundreds of goblins, or trolls with ballistas, or will you abandon your daughter, dishonor your rank among the honor guards and be remembered as a coward on your gravestone?"

Tyrianna produced the silver dagger. "This was given by a wizard for YOU, Alex Mill. Take it and use it to fight for your daughter, or I will tear you apart myself."

Alex dared not refuse. He trembled as he took the blade, and his eyes scanned the ground in shame. His allies then departed on other business.

Alex prayed, "Please let Molly be safe."

* * *

"Oh, really? If we were to take this matter before the queen, it is YOU who would be countermanded. What kind of fool presumes to know my sister-in-law better than myself? I don't care what the council says, you let these people in NOW!" said a furious Lady Ravenna to the guards.

They avoided eye contact with her thereafter and moved about like weary old men as they complied with her edict.

Lady Amanda whispered, "Thank you," as she passed Ravenna, who nodded ever so slightly in response. The people of Oakthorn were glad to finally be afforded decent shelter from the cold. The grass was still damp from a misty rain the night before, and their cloaks and blankets were both completely soaked. Lady Bethany headed straight for the food vendors to negotiate terms and prices with Nell and Devi beside her and Jacob on her hip.

* * *

"These ... are our copies of public documents from around the world, updated every month by friends of ours. I'm not allowed to tell you how, and these ... are digital maps of this world showing mineral resources, primary trade activity, travel routes, population density, level of technology," said Thomas as he pointed at floating rectangular lit panels on an underground crystalline wall.

"What is tick-knowledge-ee?" asked Molly.

Thomas ruffled her hair. "It's a fancy word for what kind of machines people make and use, little one."

Molly inquired again, "So, is my daddy on a map?"

Thomas replied, "No, there is a limit to what kind of devices we can have out in the open. But we do know he is in Kozos, the capitol of Korath, where King Nathan Silverlane runs an academy and an orphanage. And some fellow named Wayne was there with your dad."

Molly inquired, "So why are we here instead of Kozos?"

Thomas sighed. "Because the bad wolf is also out there, and I need a special device to protect us from him. It is not finished yet."

Molly finally relented, "Okay."

* * *

"Yes? What is your report, herald?" Emperor Axegrind inquired in a weary tone of exasperation.

The herald bowed down on one knee, "We have lost contact with most of our tax enforcers, many Crimson Hoods are missing. Rumors are spreading of a bearlike berserker with an axe bigger than yourself, and one witness found the work of a professional killer, who erased his tracks and hid the bodies very thoroughly. If not for the citizen's dog, we would still be unaware. The Blackwolves would be no match for him on their best day. Other accounts have come in about the old man you saw. He has vanished in a disaster that destroyed the house of Kaedrus. We are still waiting for word from the meeting with the Creepers and Whispering Tigers."

Axegrind displayed a sour look and grumbled in annoyance, "Leave me be. Return when you have better news. Dismissed!" To another servant, he said, "Raise the taxes, round up another dozen prisoners for the arena, and put a pig on the spit. That will be all for today."

* * *

"As I told the Father, Lord Barton has marched on Valantir and has not returned or sent any word of what transpired. Why does a stranger to these parts ask?" queried the farmer.

D'aarzane spun faster than the man could even blink, and the farmer fell dead with his throat slit.

"Cannot have you giving a warning to Malsain or anyone else," the rogue whispered.

He dragged the body behind the chicken coop and covered him in straw, then wiped away the tracks.

"Now we shall see what hides within the city," he hissed with a sadistic grin.

D'aarzane then became a blur of motion approaching the city proper. The wind from his passage made eddies of dust and straw for miles. He was inside the castle gate before anyone could see him.

One sentinel looked around, sniffed the air, and shrugged. "Must be a storm brewing tonight."

The rogue gained the rooftops with ridiculous ease and prowled for the most promising and approachable sources of information; vendors and nosy peasants, especially if they reeked of alcohol. One such fruit vendor was closing up for the night and imbibing his own pear wine.

"Whatcha need? Plenty of pickles and jam, and my wife made the apple cobblers ..." the man mumbled as D'aarzane sauntered into view.

"I have taken a vow of charity. Father Malsain said it would do me good. Allow me to help you with that cart," the rogue said soothingly with great practice.

The vendor was charmed without knowing what happened. "Thank you, sir. Very kind of you. Where ye from?"

D'aarzane fidgeted as his thoughts churned.

"From over the mountains, here to visit a cousin. He was going to introduce me to Barton ..." the rogue explained, but something in his tone bothered the vendor.

The old chubby fellow wrinkled his eyebrow for a quarter second, before D'aarzane added, "I fear I am unworthy of his presence ..."

The vendor struggled to find his words. "Well, the wife says, 'Beware of strange folks.' You never know who has the greed, but you ... I suppose you're okay," he said before taking another gulp from his bottle.

D'aarzane bowed to hide an evil grin. "Your wife is most perceptive. You should be glad of her concern for your safety."

As they wheeled the cart through the streets, the old vendor answered, "Oh, yes, resourceful woman. She taught the children everything they know ..."

D'aarzane yawned. He had to pick one who grew more boorish with drink, he thought ruefully.

As they turned a corner, D'aarzane cursed, "Confounded cobble stones!" as he clutched his foot, pretending he stubbed it. The old vendor stopped to look, and the next instant, D'aarzane snapped his neck. "Boring fool ..." the rogue hissed as he gathered pickles and jam into a sack, and then emptied the pear wine over the old man before smashing the bottle against the wall and repositioning the body and tipping the cart over. Then the assassin emptied the old man's pouches and removed the wedding ring. One sentinel approached to see what the noises were, but was too late; the killer had vanished, heading westward.

* * *

A woman was running barefoot over cold sand in the dark, stumbling whenever her foot hit scrub or bark, and behind her was a gang of evil men with lanterns and torches, taking their time in pursuit, and laughing whenever they heard a yelp of pain or panic. The lady fell flat on her back after colliding with a tree, and the men circled for the capture. She felt a hand on her wrist and another on her throat, and suddenly bolted awake screaming, with no memory of her rescue. She saw the dim embers of a dying fire nearby, and the silhouettes of people roused from their sleep against a backdrop of stars in the night sky. Mandy crawled away as quietly as she could, but a large shadow sped past and blocked her path, but did not touch her or even speak. A huge axe hung on his belt, and Mandy stared in horror, thinking her life was over. Her tongue no longer worked. A familiar and sarcastic voice about fifty feet behind her grumbled aloud in her direction, "Thanks for ruining another night's sleep, you nagging wretch."

A look of recognition and hatred stole over Mandy's features. "You vile, wretched, steaming pile of camel dung! What band of pirate scum have you taken up with now, you cheating bastard?" she spat in Adrian's direction.

Garzon bellowed in laughter. "HA! Your lust and ambition have marked you, merchant! The bloodsucking pest has been granted his just reward! Shall we leave you alone in your accounting of past deeds o' greedy one?"

Adrian's voice squeaked in terror, "Noooooo! Don't leave me alone with her! I'll give you anything you want! Pleeeeease ... anything but that!"

Sal just sat there, as mute as ever, his eyes not even acknowledging anything was happening. A thin sliver of dawn was showing on the horizon, behind the distant mountains. Kazius just smiled. He was quite satisfied with this turn of events for once. Mandy tried to size up exactly what her situation was, and her face betrayed her confusion and bewilderment. She began to see but not understand. Two men were tied to a tree, the largest one stood just out of arm's reach, and another was propped on his elbows next to a woman. Mandy was lost and outnumbered by strangers, the Crimson Hoods were nowhere to be seen, and she caught a whiff of smoked fish nearby. Hunger won out. Mandy crawled back toward the dying fire to feast her malnourished and aching frame. And said no more for the entire day.

Chapter Forty-Three
Word and Deed

"The potions are ready, sire," a Dwarfish alchemist reported to his king.

Nathan grinned with malice in his eyes, "Goooooood ... prepare the search immediately, and teach that Elf witch a lesson! None may mock the crown with impunity! Now go!"

The servants bowed and left on their errand. Half of the king's guards were summoned to the task, and peasants everywhere left the streets and shuttered their windows as the witch hunt began. The foreman at the orphanage saw the horses and footmen approaching, and summoned Alex the Meek inside to safety, while Tyrus fled north to retrieve his trident. A small company detached from the main force to pursue the Myrmidon. Tyrus mustered everything he had to evade capture, dodging maces and swords, dismounting two adversaries, and capturing one horse in the process. As the lake became visible at the bottom of the valley far ahead, he rode hard between the vineyards and the forest, on a narrow path sloping down toward a riverbank, and a single lane stone bridge. Tyrus waited until the last minute to swing his left leg over and brace for the jump. He dove off the bridge as the men drew closer. Nathan's men broke into two teams, combing north and south of the river, believing that Tyrus would surface any minute. The minutes dragged on, and their frustration rose, such that they began yelling insults and threats at the wilderness, at each other, and the stranger they lost. At the lakeshore, one man spotted a wake in the water, just as Tyrus emerged near a rock and struck his trident upon it while pointing at them. They all buckled in pain, clutching their ears, and dropped to their knees.

Tyrus wasted no time racing into their midst, felling them with blows to the head and stomach. As one attempted to remount his horse and escape, Tyrus slammed the pommel on the ground, and the tremor sent the horse into a panic and dragged the man to his death. Elsewhere, the search for Tyrianna continued.

* * *

Jonah gathered more wood for the fire as Skorvald went hunting. Conrad was not yet in shape for a hunt, and foraged for nuts and berries instead. Lebiced walked beside him in silent contemplation. Conrad paused once in awhile, straining to hear something, but detecting nothing and then shaking his head. Lebiced observed, "Perhaps what you search for, the ears cannot find. The voices of the forest reach other senses. Just as the voices of your ancestors seem to be from nowhere and everywhere. A great many of my peers in Xantir are taught this. It is not unexpected that you experience this now. You are learning the path they were on. It is your destiny and heritage, after all. It's in your veins."

Then Conrad gasped and stumbled, dropping to his knees.

"What did you see, Conrad?" the wizard asked.

Captain Redmane answered, "I felt a great emptiness, tragedy has befallen Oakthorn, we must reach it tonight … something is very wrong …"

Lebiced corrected, "First you must eat and take rest. Get your strength back. Then we will do what we can for Oakthorn."

Conrad relented.

* * *

"You will tell me who killed my brother, or face the wrath of your chaos brethren after I pin the betrayal of Vamanastral on YOU, Arthur! I can and WILL turn your own family against you and make your life a living hell. Would you rather wait here, deprived of rest and food, and find out for yourself or wise up and tell me?" Ravenna demanded.

Something in Ravenna's voice and the rage in her eyes convinced him he had no choice, and he finally confessed in sad defeat, "Her name is Winter. Her father Arius will chase me to the ends of the Earth when he finds out I cracked. If Lord Barton does not rip me apart first ..."

She was not finished yet and slapped him for good measure. "Where do I find her, vermin?"

Arthur whimpered, "In the northern reaches of Zara-Mogai, the border city of Nug Za ... for all the good it does you. Nobody returns from that land."

Ravenna kicked him in the shin for spite before leaving. Arthur writhed in pain on the floor cradling his leg. All the guards bowed as Ravenna passed by; she had achieved what nobody else could manage — finding Arthur's weakness. Lady Ravenna met up with Lady Amanda and Bravane the Younger as they were exchanging their news of events since the day of the undead attack on Oakthorn.

"I am most grieved that my uncle has suffered so ..." Bravane the Third offered in sympathy.

Amanda clasped his fingers lightly. "I hope you find your son, cousin."

Ravenna turned to Bravane. "I need to straighten up some council matters, after which we can go search for this woman and your son, if you are ready. It is a dangerous road to her city."

Bravane nodded yes. "I cannot rest until the emptiness is made whole again. I must find him and my legacy or die trying."

Ravenna nodded in respect and went about her other duties.

* * *

Belinda awoke to another late autumn freezing morning in the tiny fishing village north of Seaside Bluff. Her three companions were still sleeping. Young Kendra had a lazy smile on, as her eyes twitched in the middle of a dream. Kendra's older sister Krisa snored lightly, and poor Layla moaned in pain from another nightmare. Belinda bent over to stroke Layla's hair, until the moaning diminished. Unbidden, memories of Belinda's only son surfaced, a boy stolen from her when he was but three years old, her forever tainted lost son ever since, his mind molded by the warring factions that sprang up after Arius's defeat in Shadval. Belinda shut the images out at once, a single bitter tear running down her cheek. Her boy did not exist anymore, in his place now was a bloodthirsty tyrant worse than Kazius. The son she once loved was just a tormented memory. A cruel jest that plagued Razadur and all the surrounding lands. And as Layla woke up, Belinda looked like a stranger, her eyes distant and stone cold, more than usual. Belinda remained aloof the entire day.

Chapter Forty-Four
Homecoming

After his long ordeal, Conrad gazed at last upon the walls of Oakthorn in the distance, and raised an eyebrow at the dome.

"What sorcery is this, Wizard?" he asked Lebiced.

The old wizard replied with concern, "The dome itself poses no threat to us, but I have a feeling things are not well with the town, and that Arius was responsible."

Skorvald nodded in agreement.

Conrad bolted into a run, thinking only of his sister, his niece, and Rebecca. Jonah was right behind him. Minutes later, wanting for breath, Conrad sank to one knee as he began to see the broken windows of the east end past the southwest gate.

"By the gods, no! Let them be safe, please!" Jonah prayed aloud, and Conrad whispered the same sentiment.

In a few moments, they strode cautiously toward the gate, swords at the ready, when Conrad heard the voice again. "Son of my nephew, have no fear. They are well.

Your sister has taken refuge in West Bend. Rebecca has also done so. But speak with Alex and Myra before you go." And then, the presence of Susan Redmane was gone.

Jonah gave a puzzled look as Conrad announced, "Let us go see Alex the wise."

Jonah protested, "What did you see? What happened to my wife? My children?"

Conrad assured him, "They are not here, but in West Bend, I am told they are safe."

Jonah sighed, "Thank heavens."

The rest of the party soon caught up, with Lebiced at the rear. The southwestern gate was intact, and opened before them by the slow efforts of haggardly exhausted men still in the grip of great melancholy and grieving for a broken town and lost relatives. Conrad saw why when they entered, several trees to their left near the abbey were charred black, a mass of wagons lay rusting and molding in the river, and a curious lack of livestock in the market area hinted at terrible sorrow.

Lebiced spoke, "It is as I feared. Arius did indeed breach the gates and set his undead to their nasty work."

Even Skorvald despaired at the damages to the inn, the market, and the stables. But for a few people here and there, the town seemed desolate. Repairs, if any, were clumsily slow, now even more so with the growing presence of winter. And the light dusting of snow upon the grass was like summer in Skorvald's land far away, where his vocation as a mercenary began the night his wife and child were stolen from him little more than a year past. Ever since, Skorvald and his band had financed their effort to reclaim their loved ones from the Syndicate and the customers thereof. Not in his wildest dreams could he imagine how closely his own blood and his destiny was bound with his present companions. Soon he would learn just how much.

Peasants in passing gave a sour look at Conrad even now, after the truth of Darmid's treachery and the diabolical evil of Arius could no longer be credibly denied. Their stubborn pride and their die hard envy would not relinquish old embers of bitterness and unfounded suspicions. The expressions on their faces were not lost on anyone, Lebiced, least of all, who gave them hard and unforgiving expressions of his own. Lebiced was born in the time of Bravane Redoak the First, and James Redmane stood side by side with them as a young lad against the armies of Izimal under the tyrannical zealot warlord Abazad Hakeem Ebn Brakaan in 1490, and witnessed with his own eyes the signing of the Westwood Treaty that reunited five kingdoms. He was no dewy eyed child with illusions about legends, heroes, or men, he knew the Red Clans as friends and neighbors for the greater part of his ninety-three years. For all but the last years of Brent's life, he, too, was a friend. More than that, through his sister Cedra, Lebiced was blood-related to two generations of the Falconeye lineage, including Queen Margo, the mother of Jonah. The Redmanes and Redoaks were his distant cousins through marriage. Thus the prejudices of ignorant people against Conrad was an affront to his own flesh.

They arrived, at last, at the North Bridge leading to the baronial manor and passed the statues of fear-stricken peasants set there as examples to all of what Arius did to any who opposed him. The baronial gates opened, and weary guards greeted Jonah and Conrad with weak smiles that betrayed their dim hopes and their exhaustion. Inside, they turned toward the tower where Alex the Wise and Myra stayed. The door opened in response to Conrad's knock.

"Alex! What have they done to you?" Conrad exclaimed in shock, unprepared for the sight of his ruined face.

Alex Redoak sighed. "Twice I have saved victims from the evil of Arius, and twice I have paid for doing so. Now the both of us stay hidden from the eyes of men. What brings you today?"

Conrad and Jonah entered, and the rest stayed on the stairway.

"Susan told me to speak to you, before we left for West Bend," Conrad informed his cousin.

Alex lit up in recognition. "Yes, you do look different since your journey eastward. Much else has changed.

Bravane is in exile. It was the best way to allow him to seek his son. And my daughter Amanda is now deputy mayor. It may interest you, that Tyton left you in charge of his guild, what remains after Arius destroyed the Guild Hall. And ..." Alex paused, turning to extract a small bag from its hiding place. "These were also given to you."

Conrad hefted the bag of coin. "By whom?"

Alex answered, "Tyton instructed third parties to deliver it, unaware of your quest."

"If the Guild Hall is no more, where do I find them?" Conrad inquired.

Alex told him of the sewer patrols, and then shook his hand. "It was good to see you. Give our best to Amanda and Bethany."

Conrad bowed and left, and the others followed behind him in double file.

Conrad paused at the baron's stables, and sadly remembered he was parted from Bill in Shadval.

"You all go ahead to West Bend. I have some business here before I join you," Conrad ordered.

Jonah clasped Conrad's arm in farewell, and then mounted a horse. Conrad waved good-bye and turned southwest toward the abbey. The charred trees with their light dusting of snow looked much like the dream world he had visited with the ghost of his mother.

As he got closer to the abbey, he could, at last, feel her presence while fully awake. Conrad wept and fell to his knees. All the turmoil of the past year came rushing through, and Conrad did not resist. He needed to let it through and find his catharsis.

Chapter Forty-Five
Sins of the Past

"Clay, keep your shield up! Benson, your swing leaves you wide open for a counterblow, tighten up that posture! My nanny can fight better than that!" shouted a young lad in chainmail wearing the tabard of the Iron Hand Elite Corps.

"That's the last straw, Corbin! I've had all I can stand of your smug face and your wagging tongue! I wager you can't beat me bare handed, ye bastard!" growled a red-faced Benson.

"Your training is done when I say it is, you two pence yapping runt!" Corbin yelled back in disgusted tones.

Benson lunged, grappling Corbin's torso, and landing on top, rolling in the mud of the academy courtyard near the archery range. Corbin hooked a thumb under Benson's jaw and forced his head back until Corbin's leg could reach up and catapult Benson backward into the air. Benson clambered back onto all fours and lunged again, as Corbin spun out of the way and landed a hammerfist blow on Benson's back. As Benson rose to his knees, Corbin kicked his hindquarters. The other lads were now taking bets on the final outcome. A mud-caked Benson drew a knife out of his boot and lunged again. Corbin leaned to one side and tumbled free, then closed the distance before Benson could recover.

With one hand on each wrist, Corbin headbutted Benson and then brought his knee up, hard and fast. Benson dropped his knife and doubled over, groaning, coughing, and sputtering. Corbin collected the knife and kept it. "Everyone dismissed," announced Corbin.

"The word … is … out … you … only got … junior trainer … position … on account … of … being … the king's bastard and have been … his … favorite … all along …" wheezed Benson in a fetal position.

Corbin kicked him in the gut. "You shut your mouth! Or I'll have you in leg irons!"

Benson spat blood and rolled onto his other side and laid there, mute. Four men in brown robes appeared and nudged Corbin away from Benson, while one whispered, "We overheard, and we see an opportunity for a strong lad like you, with your command abilities. The church of the Lawgiver needs you for a special occasion. Are you interested?"

Corbin hissed, "Does this tabard look like Motley? Do ye take me for an addle-headed old fool? This high and mighty church of yours rather frowns on bastards, yeah? Furthermore, what bloody use have I for such a church?"

The one man stormed off in silent rage, while his elder strode forward to Corbin's side as they neared the barracks. "What we mean to say is, we see a political opportunity, and you are far more able than Prince Adam for what we have in mind. He lacks sorely in leadership qualities and diplomacy, as well as your gift for hunting and combat. We want someone who can hold this kingdom together. Don't think too long on this; the opportunity will not last. Time is short. We will hear your decision at sunset by the orphanage. Don't be late."

With that, the men left. Corbin wondered why they happened to be inside the academy to begin with. With an exasperated heave of his shoulders and dismissive wave of his arms, he went to have a drink at one of the inns. Elsewhere, in a tunnel known only to King Nathan and his most trusted allies (which Malsain never was).

"What if he talks and exposes our plan?" asked a newly ordained brother of the Alphas' inner circle.

"Then at sunset or soon after, he will have a most unfortunate accident. Now keep your tongue still or you might join him," said the elder. "I did not rise to Alpha Minor simply because of Malsain's temper, nor should you forget that," he concluded. "Meanwhile," he added, "you can make yourself useful by investigating the cabin on Pine Slopes. I hear someone is repairing it with borrowed tools. Don't bungle it like the last group did."

"As you command it, Father Sandhaven," said the apprentice.

* * *

"The devices are all set, Your Majesty," announced one of the alchemists.

"Good! We will set the bait, and hope they do their job," replied King Nathan Silverlane.

"They will, sire. I will be certain of it," answered the Dwarfish alchemy guildmaster, who was wearing goggles that appeared glossy black.

"No one else is to know of this plan. NO ONE. Not Adam. Not Marcy. NO ONE. See to it!" ordered Nathan as he turned to leave and set the plan in motion.

Minutes later, King Nathan barked at Prince Adam, "The spies you allowed to go at will have stolen work tools, and one has left for the mountains, and I told you this would be subtracted from your inheritance, you insufferably self-indulgent, lazy, pretentious, insolent, obnoxious, mangy bitch!"

Adam Silverlane scowled and sneered, "You are one to talk about indulgence, Father. I heard about the bastard Corbin that you promoted all the way to junior trainer at the academy. For <u>shame!</u>"

Nathan backhanded Adam across the room. "How DARE you take that insolent tone! UNLIKE you, the spoiled effeminate snob with less meat on his bones than the underfed orphans fresh off the boat, who dallies about with other pretentious windbags and mama's boys who could not lift a sword let alone defend the kingdom with one! You are nothing but a liability! I should have drowned you or left you to the wolves at the first sign, even if you ARE Marcy's own blood! Your uptight prissy bitch of a sister, Minerva, has more sense than you! How the two of you could have any of the Auguron genes is beyond me! Minerva or Corbin should take the crown, not a mewling whiny rug rat who would greet thieves and invaders by sulking and throwing weak, impotent words at them!"

Adam finally snapped, "I hate you!" and threw a candlestick that Nathan easily dodged.

In seconds, Nathan closed the distance and slapped Adam hard enough to draw blood. "Then it's mutual, you half-witted clod of a son, who can't catch a fish or hunt a duck to save his sorry hide!"

As Adam grabbed for another object, Nathan just shoved him hard into the wall. Adam stumbled onto the floor, choked with fear and shock. Nathan gave a disgusted look, said no more, turned away, and slammed the door shut. The overall message was hard to mistake.

Adam would be disowned in spite of his mother's protests. Oh, how the peasants would laugh for the rest of his life.

* * *

At one of the inns of Kozos, that familiar haunt known as the Falcon's Perch, to be precise, the walking butter roll of an ugly old woman was ranting, "The Elf witch must have overpowered Father Samuel Malsain and scared Toby away, too. I told ya she was trouble, didn't I now? But whoever listens to old Karina but my nephew? Or my sister Kitra? Ye'll be sorry now, the lot of ya! The Elves have killed Father Barton, too, I reckon, the high lord of the Lawgiver church hisself, and they won't stop there. No, they won't be satisfied until they destroy our homes and drive us into the sea! And what has King Nathan done about it? Nothing!

Because he's too busy fathering bastards and cleaning up after his lackwit son who spent too much time on Marcy's poison tit!"

The crowd cheered and roared in agreement, clapping the bottoms of their mugs and flagons on the tables.

One of the male drunks blurted out, "He woulda fathered one on the Elf witch if he could. I seen him secret away a redhead somewhere last year, with his paws all over her parts from the wagon to the dungeons ... he passed by where I had stopped to water the bushes ... that horny devil never stops. Marcy will skin him alive when she finds out."

Several women hearing the utterance of those words lost their balance with looks of horror, and thereupon was a crash of crockery and tin cups in every corner of the inn. Then the din began, dozens of conversations sprang up again, with wild predictions of who would strike first, admonishments over the royal scandals, gossip about Corbin, gossip about Adam, boasts about who made the best pies, the best wine, or who caught the biggest fish; more of the evening business as usual.

Karina could tell her moment was over, so she left for home to plant another seed another day. Her drunken nephew Kurt followed, protesting, "Better if I had made a proper lady out of that Elf witch, instead of her acting high and mighty and makin' a sodding fool outta me ..."

Karina soothed, "Now, now, Kurt, you worry your head over a lady with better breeding and manners than that evil vixen blathering about dark times and champions and other nonsense."

Kurt whined, "But, Auntie, they all turn their nose at me and laugh ... none a' the girls worth an owl's hoot want me for anything but the bill."

Karina scolded him, "Ye oughts be chattin' up the girls in church, not the taverns, where yer liver will turn to stone like your father's did, boy!"

Kurt groaned. "Yes, Auntie."

* * *

Prince Adam peeked out the keyhole of his door, and he saw his least favorite sentries, the most loyal to his father Nathan, Sir Gregor the Cruel and Sir Bothun the Brave. The walls felt suddenly confining and unbearable to him. He had to get out. In desperation, he lit a candelabra and knocked it into the window curtains before crying for help as the smoke began to spread, and the fire gathered strength. The two sentries stood rigid and apathetic for minutes before the smoke seeped out through the cracks. Then they reacted swiftly, raising alarm and opening the door. Adam tried to rush past them, but both sentries gripped his scrawny biceps like steel traps and dragged him down the hall into one of the opposite guest rooms on the second floor until they could ascertain what Nathan wanted done.

Seconds afterward, other sentries were racing back and forth, beating out the flames and relaying buckets of water. Queen Marcy emerged from her meditation chamber to the sounds of the commotion and immediately recognized which room the smoke was coming from and, without a moment's hesitation, ran to interrogate about her son's state of health. None of the sentinels in the halls could answer where he was.

"That is wholly unacceptable! I *demand* to know this instant, exactly who was on duty when this happened!" Marcy screeched with venomous disdain and contempt.

The men stumbled over themselves in an effort to discover and provide the names, fearing with their every nerve her notoriously volatile temper.

Marcy pulled aside one of her own men, the queensguard, and whispered, "Lugnai, I want you and Lochar to learn what my husband is up to. There was a look in his eyes these past few days which I found unsavory and unseemly. If anyone asks, you are searching for Adam or sending a message to my young Minerva. Do you understand?"

Sir Lugnai the Savage nodded and bowed. "Yes, Your Majesty... perfectly."

Marcy revealed a cruel smile. "Good," she said before politely dismissing her loyal servant to his duties, while she prowled the halls for easy prey, such as the dull-witted Sir Jorna.

She found him pacing at the foot of the grand staircase, muttering to himself, "Who's he think he is, anyways? I … oh, hi, Marcy."

The queen simply frowned and squinted her eyes in rage and exasperation. Sir Jorna knew that look and gulped. "Bothun went to see Nathan, some important question, very urgent, that's all I know, that's all they tell me … please don't hurt me."

Marcy's voice was a hiss colder than the mountains, "And *where* is Sir Gregor, then? He is nearly always on my husband's business."

Jorna blurted, "Second level … east wing."

Marcy relaxed her frown by a small degree and hissed, "See? Was that so hard, Jorna? You may stand at ease now. *Thank* you."

Jorna looked downcast, like a scolded puppy. Marcy snapped her fingers as she ascended the grand stairs again, and another knight, Sir Cernach, answered her summons. One look between them conveyed the queen's angry determination to seize control of the day's events and Cernach's eagerness to enforce it.

* * *

Margo Falconeye, queen regent of Thalu, the mother of Douglas, Richard, Jonah, and Roxanna, steeled herself for the unwelcome task of correcting a great wrong and discouraging further plots from hatching. "Douglas, you are hereby accused of conspiracy to murder Jonah. How do you plead?"

The prince spat, "You would take the word of a rug rat over your second-born son? There's no proof! The little brat is lying!"

Queen Margo continued, "Do you deny your hatred of Jonah and offering coin to the Blood Fangs for the murder of my youngest son?"

Douglas spat again, "Yes, I deny it!"

Margo forced herself to stand strong and coldly replied, "You lie. You have always lied. The poison of your aunt Lorenna runs deep. You have one last chance to beg forgiveness and confess. I have been far too soft on you all these years."

Douglas refused with a string of curses. A nod from Margo, and the two knights who brought Douglas in chains forced him onto his knees. Douglas growled in disbelief, "What? Are you actually going to kill me without trial? You can't do that!"

Margo frowned. "No, death is too good for you. Too swift and merciful. No, Douglas, you are to be humbled. An ungrateful and treacherous toad such as you have become must learn and share in the suffering of those he holds in contempt. Hold him fast. This will be over soon ..."

Douglas struggled in vain to escape as Margo fetched a poker from the fireplace and held it in the braziers. "What are you doing, you madwoman? The Lawgivers will hear of this, and the other groups who despise you! You are making a terrible mistake!"

Margo chided coldly; his insolence had burned away all her remorse, "They already despise me, Doug, and my greatest mistake was not intervening sooner when Lorenna lived here. Richard has followed her to the grave, and so has your son. I'll not allow her evil to continue to fester and grow anymore, and may John forgive me for what I must do."

With those words, she strode from the brazier to face Doug one more time.

"I now sentence you to roam the streets as a beggar. There will be no reward for feeding you, and no punishment for turning you away, one protection and one only shall you have. You are not to be broken or bloodied by any peasant or noble but me, and from this day forward ..." She announced as she seared his eyes shut, "You are not my son anymore."

Douglas screamed and passed out. Margo tossed the poker at the fireplace and turned her back to Douglas.

"Take him to the dungeon for one night and release him tomorrow. That is all the mercy I shall give."

The knights bowed and did as she commanded.

"I shall deal with the Blood Fangs later."

After they left, Margo finally collapsed by the window, sobbing. "Damn you, John ! That's three you lost to your wretched sister."

* * *

"I have missed you, Mother, so very much. Father was not the same without you," Conrad confessed under falling snow near the abbey.

A disembodied voice replied, "Connor is not at rest. His spirit is in disquiet. His body is infected, and is becoming a ghoul as we speak. You must give him rest before you leave."

Conrad could not believe what he had heard.

"What? No! I …" he stammered, almost choking. He wondered why not someone else; the town had other defenders. Why him of all people, and of course, he knew why. Conrad was the yardstick of courage in this place. There was no one else up to the job. Cursing his luck and the name of the Augurons, he mustered his nerve and his rage for the onerous task ahead. "By all that is holy, Kazius, Arius, and the rest of your sorry lot, I will make you pay! On my honor and my life, I so swear it!"

With those words, he marched southward, toward the gates, and then to the graveyard to await the rising of his father's mutation.

* * *

"I'm sorry, ma'am, but those words are forbidden here by order of the council," said a dull-looking knight in the marketplace of West Bend.

"I can't say a simple 'light bless you'?" exclaimed Lady Bethany Blackthorn.

"Correct. The Lawgivers have taught that deviance from their ways is heresy and treason, and you get two warnings only. After that, you will be fined and thrown in the dungeons," answered the knight.

"Preposterous! Is your council run by morons? What does the queen say about it?" challenged Bethany.

The knight said, "The queen is secluded away from affairs of state, and Sandraz has been handling the king's funeral arrangements. They were unable to participate."

Bethany fumed, "Amanda will hear of this! I will not be ordered about by some council of strangers in Motley!"

The knight just stood there, his expression blank and devoid of comprehension. It wasn't his duty to question the council.

Bethany strode off in seething fury.

* * *

Two knights entered the orphanage on business, and ordered Peter the Foreman to accompany them. Alex Mill was organizing documents when they appeared, and once he noticed they were keenly interested in *him*, his nerves betrayed him, and the papers tumbled from his grasp. "What have I done? Did Adam send you? I can put these back in order, and fix the doors, and whatever you need me to do, please ..." Alex begged to no avail.

Sir Skavund the Unremarkable and Sir Vornadin the Serpent closed upon him, grabbing his elbows and dragging him forcefully from the room.

"What's the meaning of this? I'll do anything the foreman or Adam or the king need. Please, why are you doing this?" he pleaded again.

Finally, Sir Skavund replied, "You are deemed guilty of espionage by the king, and you will be tried accordingly."

Alex stuttered, "N-no, you must be mistaken. I'm looking for my daughter. I'm no spy. I was raised here by Kitra Cooper in the orphanage after my parents died. The foreman knows me. Tell them, tell them who I am."

The foreman sighed. "Sorry, lad. The king is wroth with me already. I dare not do more … I'm truly sorry. You're a good man, Alex."

Alex Mill struggled in vain to break free. "Stop! I'm not a spy! Please!"

The knights ignored him.

* * *

Lebiced broke the silence as the party journeyed from Oakthorn to West Bend. "My great-grand niece Roxanna speaks rather highly of you, Skorvald. What brings you so far from home?"

Jonah's eyes registered shock as he nearly fell off his horse. Lebiced had just named his sister!

Skorvald was also taken aback. "You have known me this whole time and said nothing?"

Lebiced smiled. "I have found it useful to observe first before speaking. I trip over my tongue less that way."

Skorvald made a sour face before relenting. "Well, if you must know, my wife Astrid, my daughter Carol, and several other relatives were kidnapped by the Syndicate pirates and sold into slavery. My son, Avnand, is dead. My brother-in-law Vithgar and his grandfather Elmund, we lost in Shadval. Sigurd here is Roxanna's husband. His father Dagnar, and this is Jonak, and Gormund. Also with us are cousins Grimhorn, Dolf, Durgane, Jornath, Balnir and Beren. Roxanna's money has run dry, and I have had to hire us out while hunting the Syndicate and seeking our loved ones. I had not realized a wizard of Xantir was related to Roxanna."

Jonah inquired, "And how do you know Roxanna of Thalu?"

Skorvald answered, "By her husband Sigurd, the son of Dagnar, son of Elseba, the daughter of Jomund, who was my paternal great-grandfather."

Dagnar and Sigurd gave a salute.

Jonah finally confessed, "Well met, friend of Roxanna. I am her brother."

Skorvald laughed, "THAT Jonah? Ha-ha, well met, friend! And now we understand the story behind the money. I do not envy the bad fruit in your tree."

Jonah winced, "You could say that …"

For the remainder of the journey, Lebiced regaled them with stories of the Westwood Treaty, the battle of Koso, the cult of the Lawgivers, and how they have dominated the human kingdoms, and Jonah grew quite bored with the account.

* * *

"The tracks are a couple hours old. Their pace has not changed. We are slowly gaining on them. Keep going! Move!" Tyton Umbral informed his temple brethren and sisters.

Ahead of them were an ancient enemy and its spawn, the older band of outlaws known as the Whispering Tigers, and an offshoot band known as the Creepers. Last known to have negotiated a contract for services to the new ruler of Razadur, self-styled as Emperor Axegrind. A contract Tyton planned to terminate. For many hours through day and night, the chase continued northward, toward the ruins of seaside bluff. Over grassland and desert plains, past a remote oasis, and over bare rock, they ran without rest.

On the second day, both the ruins and their targets were visible on the horizon.

"Two minutes rest. Liquid rations only ..." Tyton wheezed. "When we engage, one prisoner only. Kill the rest on sight."

* * *

"Kill me if you want, but please get me away from her!" Adrian pleaded.

Garzon simply raised an eyebrow, then responded, after a pause, "Is her opinion so painful to your ears, o greedy one? Or the truth so baneful to your existence?

Your request is denied. You are a useful hostage and informant. And your suffering is well-deserved. So … too bad!"

Kazius chuckled within earshot.

"*You* stay out of this, you traitor! YOU got me into this mess!" Adrian accused Kazius.

The exiled former ruler of Razadur corrected, "No, you did this to yourself. You agreed to do business with the Syndicate as I did, and with my father's zealots. You fell in with the worst of the worst, and now you blame ME for being caught? You presume much, SWINE!"

At long last, Sal spoke again, "I told him not to gamble all our money, stupid ass …"

Adrian snapped, "Gods kill me now! I'm surrounded by backstabbers and cruel fiends!"

At these words, Mandy leaped at him while his hands were still tied behind his back. "I'll show you who the real fiend is, you lying bastard!" And her nails dug deep, drawing blood from him while trying to strangle him with all her might.

Garzon picked her up by the collar of her shirt and held her at arm's length with one hand. He gave a word of caution to Adrian, "It is unwise to anger her, oh greedy one. More foolish words from you, and I may allow her to abuse you however she sees fit. Am I understood?"

Adrian gasped for breath and looked up into those hard, relentless eyes. He felt true fear then, in all its nakedness. He gulped twice and nodded vigorously in the affirmative.

Garzon pressed, "The words, foolish one. Say it."

Adrian began to cry, "Yes, yes, I understand." Adrian remained silent the entire day afterward.

* * *

"Do you deny that you traveled through Valantir to get here?" barked an irate and rude King Nathan Silverlane.

Poor Alex Mill stammered, "No, I did, but I'm searching for my daughter!"

King Nathan gave a sneering and disgusted look and snapped his fingers. "Search him!"

Sir Bothun the Brave and Sir Ulmadast the Round obeyed, and within minutes, produced the silver dagger that Tyrianna had given Alex.

"I demand to know at once why this dagger was in your possession, Knave!" commanded Nathan.

Alex was now frightened out of his mind and his tongue would not work. Nathan backhanded him and drew blood, causing Alex to cower in fear, begging, "Please, no! It's to save my daughter from the werewolf ..."

Nathan laughed maliciously. "Is that the best chicken manure you can conjure, knave? A werewolf? Truly?"

Alex nodded. "Th-there's records, i-in the orphanage, o-of a massacre ... it was him. The werewolf, he tore them in pieces ..."

Nathan did not laugh this time but shouted, "What business did you have going through the records? That was not what you were hired to do!"

Alex cried. "B-but the basement gives me nightmares … m-memories of F-f-f-father M-m-malsain …"

Nathan mocked him with cruel sarcasm, "Oh, the *poor peasant* has nightmares in order to beg off a job that's too hard for him … and I should order construction of a new hall, and call it Nathan's House of *Charity* …"

The knights laughed.

Alex cowered even more.

"LOCK him up! I can't stand this mewling simpleton!" Nathan ordered.

Alex cried and whimpered as they dragged him to the dungeons.

Chapter Forty-Six
A House Divided

Stuart led a select few Lawgivers into the mountains as instructed by Father Sandhaven and searched for the cabin where this Wayne character was supposed to be. The youngest of them, Otto, blurted out, "This place looks familiar … Malsain sent a couple of us here months ago …"

Stuart admonished him, "Shut up! This ain't no social visit! Now button it!"

Otto gave a sad puppy look and whined, "Jus' cuz I'm the youngest, doesn't give you the …"

Stuart punched him before he could finish his complaint. "If this fellow overhears you and this little walk in the woods goes sideways, I will tell Sandhaven all about it! Now button it, ya runt!"

Otto kept to the rear of the party after that, and thirty minutes later, he vanished from sight.

Frederic asked, "Hey! Where's Otto?"

Stuart hissed, "Who cares? Whiny brat's a liability. Now keep your voice down, moron!"

Wayne heard something in between the axe strokes while splitting firewood on the stump. He continued as if nothing happened, but his ears and eyes were probing the forest to the east. And his instincts, honed by solitude, told him danger lurked nearby. Less than a minute passed before he saw movement behind the trees, and he braced himself for action at a moment's notice. Stuart and Frederic did their best to avoid detection, but it was too late for that. As Stuart got close to the cabin, Wayne let the axe fly, and it struck its mark full in the chest.

Frederic dropped all his gear and ran with such panic that he slipped on a patch of pine needles and collided with a tree, then tumbled unconscious another twelve feet downhill. Wayne searched the body of Stuart and the dropped gear for clues to their purpose and identity. Stuart wore a cross about his neck and had some black powder plus oiled rags and flint, which pointed to attempted arson. Wayne remembered the condition the cabin was in when he found it. The fate of the previous owner was unknown to him. Wayne picked up Frederic's gear then dragged his limp body to a small sapling, and tied his hands with the rags. Wayne then scooped some snow into a bucket and dumped it all on the kid's head.

Frederic sputtered and said, "What? Stuart, we have to …"

His words choked off at the cognizance of his situation.

Stuart's body lay where it fell, with the axe still lodged in it, and the stranger who flung it stood over Frederic who was tied to a tree completely at the stranger's mercy. The man spoke, "Your friend is dead. Why do you trespass here with intent to burn my shelter?"

Frederic lied, "It was his idea! I didn't want to!"

Wayne clicked his tongue. "You are a horrible liar. Why then, did you both have oiled rags and black powder? And how many miles from town are you? This is a long way to go on a lark, someone planned this, and you're not smart enough to be that one. You can talk, or freeze here by morning. I promise you, it will hurt worse than anything you have ever endured."

Frederic stammered, "You wouldn't. You can't do that …"

Wayne raised an eyebrow. "No? You sure about that? Not even to someone who would have eagerly burned me alive? How would a stupid lad like you know? You know nothing, whelp!"

Frederic began to cry. "I don't wanna die! Father Sandhaven ordered us to do this! You have to believe me!"

Wayne corrected, "You have it wrong. There is no reason for me to trust what you say, and another man would have kicked your teeth in. You are a stupid, naive boy taking orders from evil men, whoever they are. I've never heard of Sandhaven, means nothing to me."

Frederic was dumbfounded, how could anyone not fear Sandhaven or know who he is? Unless … "Ye must be a spawn of the Fallen One, come to destroy us all!" Frederic blurted before anything resembling wisdom could stop him.

Wayne retorted, "Oh DO shut the hell up, you moron!" before landing a right cross and knocking him out.

The lad woke hours later, shivering cold to the bone with a sore jaw and a single blanket tucked around him, still tied to the tree, and Stuart's body collecting crows. The axe was not there anymore. Frederic leaned to one side and threw up.

* * *

Eastward, the party marched across the sandy coast of Mojara, ahead were the palm trees that marked the Croc River on both banks, and a tiny fishing village to the north by the sea. A lone woman was sobbing in the shade of the palms, for reasons known only to her. Garzon approached first, "Tell me the nature of your suffering, and I will tell you if I may help."

The woman looked up, and her mouth hung open as her voice ceased to function. This was bar none, the largest man she had ever seen, easily four to five times the mass of her lost husband. He could snap her neck with a single hand if he so wished.

"I intend no harm," he assured her.

"I -" she started, before she recognized someone behind Garzon, no, THREE familiar faces, two of which she hated. "Mandy!" she called out to her friend.

Adrian whined, "Oh, GREAT! This is just perfect! Could it get any ..." a single warning glance over Garzon's shoulder silenced him.

Mandy ran forward to greet Moira in a tight embrace of relief.

At last, Moira spoke again, "My... husband ... has gone to rescue our daughter. He left weeks ago, I fear he is dead. I have no money to pay you."

Garzon smiled, "Fate has smiled on you, for I also seek after missing children. Where has your husband gone to?"

Moira answered, "He went north across the sea. That's all I know. He may have even drowned. Nothing has gone right since the diplomat's visit in Oakthorn."

Kazius turned to hide his face at these words.

Garzon noticed and commanded, "You there, what hast thou to do with the place called Oakthorn exile?"

Kazius hung his head in shame and walked as if on the edge of starvation toward Garzon and Moira. Slowly, he began, "My father, through his agent, manipulated me into sacrificing my emissary and ..."

Moira gaped in shock. "K-Kazius? Why is he here? And who are you?"

Garzon replied, "He is overthrown and exiled, and a useful informant. I am Garzon from a land far south of here. And these are ..."

Moira gave a look that would curdle milk, "I know *who* they are ..."

Garzon laughed again. "Your reputation precedes you, o greedy one!"

Adrian did his best to hide his face in disgust and embarrassment. "Bloody wonderful. Let's have the whole community invited to the reunion ..." he complained aloud sarcastically.

Sal gave Adrian a hateful slanted eye, and turned his back. Adrian's love of gambling, after all, was the reason for their predicament. Bernice was behind Kazius with her hands on his arms, saying nothing. Moira could tell there was something between them, a bond, a trust and affection. Their body language and familiar proximity revealed that much. Instinctively, Moira trusted Garzon, and with Mandy there, her only friend in this land, her despondence had lifted. She would go with them, in hopes of finding her husband and daughter, and of one day rebuilding her life.

* * *

"These Lawgivers have gone too far, I tell you! I was warned I cannot say a simple 'light bless you' anymore. Please tell me we can do something about these, these... tyrants, bullies and zealots!" Lady Bethany Blackthorn pleaded with Amanda, the acting deputy mayor of Oakthorn, who was also a cousin.

Amanda sighed in exasperation, "I wish I could. The council will not hear me or see me, or allow me a seat, and not even Bravane can get anything on the table. It's out of my hands. I am sorry, Beth. They are worse than I feared. MUCH worse. Lady Ravenna is our only hope in this. The queen has all but ceased to exist since the death of her husband. We shall go and appeal our complaints about this council of snakes."

Bethany let out a sigh of relief, and off they went.

* * *

"Raj, there's movement behind us. Someone is following our tracks," reported one of the gang members.

"Everyone take cover in the ruins and prepare for battle! GO!" answered Raj.

They all hurried to do so, knowing that their pursuers were most likely their ancient enemies, the Temple Assassins of Kali. Whether it was Nikita or someone else who led them, it did not matter. Today the old scores would all be settled. Raj knew this day would come, but he did not plan to die.

No, he had vengeance on his mind and his father's honor.

* * *

"Let me go! I have to find my daughter! Let me out!" Alex Mill pleaded until he was hoarse.

Jailor Ognar the Terrible and all the others ignored him.

When Ognar finally took a break for his meal, a female voice from an adjacent cell whispered, "Most of the orphans were slain by the werewolf, I'm afraid. What was your daughter's name?"

Alex wheezed back, "Her name was Molly. It's all my fault she was taken."

The woman replied, "You must not blame yourself. I hear Molly and her friend Carol managed to escape. A kindly monk told me."

Alex brightened at these words. "She's alive and well?"

The lady answered, "Perhaps. All I know is they have left town without a trace. To where? I cannot fathom. I pray for them. Carol is my own daughter."

Alex wept. "Thank the gods. Thank *you*. Never have I had better news. Would that I could repay you."

The woman smiled. "Perhaps someday you may. My name is Astrid, wife of Skorvald F'jornung from Frost Pillars far to the north and west. You are?"

Alex told her, "Alex the Meek, orphan of Korath, and now a man with no home out of Mojara."

Astrid hissed, "I hear someone coming ... pretend you don't know me or anything I said."

Soon, Alex also heard. The footsteps were even louder than Ognar's. Astrid knew each one. This was none other than Jailor Gerundin the Glutton. The rotund man arrived with a jangling of keys and announced, "Time for the weekly bath, sweet-cheeks. You know the rules."

Gerundin seized Astrid and spun her around to attach her manacles while pressing her against the wall. Alex heard the sounds of struggle and could not help his flashback. Again, he was a small boy in the basement of the orphanage at the mercy of Malsain. The taste of his sweat made him gag. Alex the man threw up in his cell.

Gerundin mocked, "Don't like our food, eh? Too bad, runt!"

And then the clanking of chains told of poor Astrid being dragged off to another part of the dungeon, beyond earshot of Alex. Korath was worse than he remembered. His parents died when he was only five, and after that, he was under the care of Kitra Cooper, a cruel woman whose husband died of cirrhosis years before. Kitra ran the orphanage for Malsain, and when Alex was almost a grown man, Kitra's own daughter Vanessa helped Alex and Moira escape to the westlands. Alex never imagined that anyone could be worse than Kitra, but Adam and Nathan and the jailers definitely were. And Malsain himself had no equal. Korath was a corrupt kingdom, no question. And there was nothing he could do, as Tyrus was on other duties when Alex was dragged out, and there was not another friend within miles of here. Alex despaired what the point of his life was.

* * *

"Where is Alex? I'm concerned about him …" Tyrus inquired of Peter the Foreman.

"King Nathan sent for him, thinks he's a spy, and wasn't too pleased about the tools that Wayne took off with either. Nothing I can do, lad," the foreman answered with a sadness in his voice. "These are very bad times, especially for nosy strangers in these parts. Unless ye fancy making enemies of all the knights, ye best forget that poor fellow."

Tyrus did not even blink before declaring, "Honor will not allow that, sir. I will not abandon him to his fate while I have the means to do something, no matter how small."

The foreman shook his head. "Gods, you're a stubborn one. Good luck to you. You'll need it aplenty. A word of advice, and you didn't hear me say this, understand? You can get information the easiest from Sir Jorna the Dull, but don't be too obvious about it."

Tyrus bowed in acknowledgement and returned to his duties to avoid raising suspicions too soon.

A whisper behind him announced. "Nathan has a bastard son named Corbin, and that ugly, old woman from the inn is plotting some kind of rebellion. We can use this to our advantage."

Tyrus objected, "No! That is a bad idea. Gossipy old women like her are dangerous, and not to be trusted. No matter who wins, being associated with her kind is distasteful. I will not tarnish my honor thus, and neither should you."

Tyrus could hear the exasperation in Tyrianna's breathing. In his mind's eye, he could see her arms crossed and her grumpy frown with the hard eyeball. A light breeze betrayed her departure, still invisible.

"Stubborn girl," Tyrus intoned.

* * *

A scraping sound in the dirt grew louder until a bony hand with some of the flesh torn away broke the surface near the headstone of one Connor Redmane. Followed by another hand from the unmarked grave of the diplomat from Razadur. And yet others from the town who fell to the fever. Conrad waited, sharpening and oiling his sword, which steadied his nerves. Obsek was the first to poke his ugly face above ground. It was a ghastly sight with the worms and bugs tunneling through the flesh, and those horrible grayish eyes. Conrad felt his disgust and rage rising, and he tossed aside the whetstone. Now he inspected his sword held out straight with one edge upturned. When the Ghoul of Obsek was still waist deep in the ground, Conrad struck the head clean off in one horizontal stroke. He hesitated next to Connor, his hand trembled, and with tears in his eyes, pleaded, "Forgive me."

Conrad screamed his rage at the injustice of it as he swung at Connor, who grabbed at the blade before the stroke could be finished. It pulled at the sword, wrestling for supremacy. Conrad yelled again as he kicked at the jaw, snapping the mandible off the head, and the shock of the blow tore the sword free of Connor's grasp.

Conrad raised it again and took the head off on the diagonal. Now his rage burned like wildfire, the adrenaline coursing through him in battle frenzy.

Two more ghouls were felled before they could clear the ground, and the others began to surround him. Conrad hacked off legs and arms until their numbers were too great, and he had no room to swing. He elbowed one, kicked another, and then felt many hands closing about his ankles, pulling him down. This was not how Conrad hoped to die, and for the first time in many years, Conrad knew the icy grip of fear.

"Gods help me. There's too many!" he yelled.

Then the dome, which covered the barony, began to shimmer and expand outward toward the graveyard. As it enveloped whatever ghoul it touched, they burst into white flame and crumbled to bits.

They backed away with what little haste they could muster, giving Conrad his opening to retrieve his sword, and he dove into the dome to get free of them. One by one, they burned away, and when the last ghoul fell, the dome shimmered one last time and dissolved. A high baritone voice on the wind called out, "Conrad, you alone may hear this, your destiny lies in Xantir and with the blood ties of your ancestors. Fail to go there, and Arius will win. I have spoken."

Conrad shook his head. "Great. Just *great* …"

* * *

A swift kick in the rump roused a groggy kid from his sleep as the blanket was yanked away, and a familiar voice announced, "Time to go, moron. We are leaving."

Frederic looked up with bleary eyes at the stranger with his wood axe propped over his shoulder. Last night was no dream, and the ravaged corpse had now been torn apart by wolves. Frederic heaved a watery bile, and moaned piteously.

"Your leader should not have sent such a green kid on such an evil errand. Blame him, not me. You forced my hand," the stranger declared.

Frederic had no strength to argue; all his muscles were cramped from the cold. Even when his bonds were untied, he could barely move. The stranger spoke true when he said the cold would hurt worse than anything the boy had ever known.

* * *

"OW! By the preserver, that fucking hurt!" blurted one of the Whispering Tigers from his concealment in the southmost part of the ruins of Seaside Bluff, in a narrow twelve by twelve foot tower nearly flattened by cannonball fire from some long ago battle and overgrown with moss, ivy, and lichens.

"Damn spiders!" he moaned as he stamped his foot on the floor after brushing the thing off his sleeve.

"Quiet!" The Southern Creeper Guildmaster Raj hissed from the adjacent eighteen by eighteen foot wreckage to the east.

A couple others stifled their outcries as they felt the bite of millipedes and fire ants, while one ventured too close to edge of the bluff, lost his balance, and fell screaming to the rocks below, which also disturbed a flock of crows among the pine trees, who took to the sky and revealed their position.

Raj whispered, "Curse the luck of this bug trap! And curse the temple! Dirty animals ..."

Southward on the sloping plain, Temple Leader Tyton Umbral and company saw the crows take flight in the early dawn's light, and noted the position. Tyton gave the silent signals to fan out and flank the ruins. His orders were otherwise unchanged. They were to take only one prisoner and kill the rest on sight. Brother Vidur led the eastern coastal flank on point, with his longbow at the ready, while brother Bhadran took point on the western flank with a chakram in hand, and Tyton closing the center at the South. The two Whispering Tigers in the south tower ruins had a clear fifty yard shot at sister Amala in Tyton's group, but they both missed due to letting their skills grow dull. The crossbowman shot too high from the recoil, and the other gripped his longbow string at a bad angle, shooting the arrow too far left. Tyton responded with two rapid shots of his own longbow, and both bandits fell dead. Raj saw from a westward facing hole in the wall, as they crumpled. He could not see the enemy yet, but he could almost smell them. He motioned to his men Sanjay and Manara that enemies were near, and to cover the east and west approaches to their position.

Brother Vidur, Sister Vasanti, and Brother Jai all kept to the shadows under cover of the pine tees, along the east end of the bluff, and advanced unseen while scouting for targets of opportunity, while Bhadran, Vedanga, and Shankar scurried behind sparse cover of small shrubbery along the southwest corner of the ruins. Facing the shrubs was a north-south long axis, thirty by sixty foot, cobblestone market space long vacated and overgrown with tall weeds, moss and ivy.

Bhadran flattened to the ground as small rodents fled his vicinity; his two companions followed suit. Three arrows whizzed overhead from somewhere in a three story twelve by twelve tower north of the market. There were but four structures with any appreciable walls left, all adjacent to the eastern half of the market area, with the towers enclosing the long ends. Approaching the southeastern corner of the abandoned market was Tyton's team. Tyton confirmed the kills in the ruined tower, while the other three scouted for more enemies. From the eighteen by eighteen structure next to the tower, Manara fired his crossbow and struck sister Amala in the left shoulder, inches from her heart. Prasad and Bodhan reacted, releasing two arrows in unison, both striking Manara in the torso. Raj and Sanjay fled to the east in the shadows cast by the rising sun and the pine trees. Manara stood frozen in shock, and slumped to the floor like some marionette whose strings were cut one by one. Prasad took Amala's right arm over his shoulders and helped her take cover behind the rubble of the south tower.

Brother Bodhan covered their retreat and was then struck in the thigh by an arrow from the north tower. Bodhan caught the next one that would have punctured a lung. He clenched his teeth as the leg wound flared up, and as he ducked for cover, he reported, "Some of them are using scorpion venom ... I think their most fortified position is the North Tower."

Tyton nodded grimly. He already regretted pushing them this hard on the chase. They were all exhausted. "I will scout the southeast building next to us, when it is empty, move our team inside and take defensive action there," Tyton instructed.

The next instant, he melted into the shadow of their sparse cover and reappeared in the shadows of the other building. Only one dead body with two arrows in the torso showed any sign of the enemy. Tyton waved for the others to follow. Prasad provided cover, dodging two arrows and returning one, which glanced off the side of a slit in the tower wall. No further injuries were tallied.

Brother Vidur, Sister Vasanti, and Brother Jai saw two figures break for tree cover from the northwest of their position and crouched down low to observe before giving chase. When it was clear that only two had fled, Vidur motioned for the others to run them down, while he scouted the eighteen by thirty-six building in the middle of the ruins. A rotted wooden snow fence encircled part of the building and the southeast corner of the walls was completely leveled. The second story of the northeast corner was heavily damaged, and no movement could be seen within.

One crossbow bolt launched from behind the staircase going up, and grazed Vidur's bicep as he twisted out of the way. Vidur returned fire and missed, embedding the arrow in the vertical risers, before retreating to cover of the trees again. Tyton heard the sounds, and from cover of the eighteen by eighteen wreckage to their south, also fired on the crossbowman, hitting his left shoulder. Four crossbow bolts and one arrow answered Tyton's attack. Two sped past him, and three hit the wall between them. So now he knew their numbers. There were five or six hiding in there. Tyton readied his two triple bladed (right-angled) katars, and shadow-jumped to the last known position of the injured crossbowman.

The southern Creeper named Naveen fell dead before he could scream with his throat slashed and bowels cut. Tyton vanished again as more arrows cut through empty air. Two more men on ground level fell, one to double puncture wounds to his kidney and heart from behind, and the other to slashes in his femoral and carotid arteries.

Three men remained, all on the upper level. Tyton waited for their morale to disintegrate. He could hear them beginning to hyperventilate; they had definitely heard the bodies fall. Tyton scanned intently and … there, a heartbeat, directly above him. One more time, he melted into the shadows and took the main target from behind in the lower vertebrae and slashed the throat of one on his right. The last man on the left loosed an arrow and struck Tyton in the left bicep. Tyton lost his grip on one of his katars, still buried in his victim. Tyton threw the other with his good right arm, sinking it in the last man's trachea. Tyton snapped off the feathered end of the arrow and pulled it through. The venom was already burning.

Vidur reentered the building as Tyton was binding his wound. Tyton whispered, "Bodhan says they have men in the North Tower, and some use scorpion venom. Can you see any of them from here?"

Vidur peeked quickly around the edge of the broken wall and shook his head no.

"Help me up. My arm is going numb ..." Tyton hissed.

Vidur took his right arm over his shoulders, and Tyton nodded to the building south of them.

Bhadran's group attempted to scramble behind the distant cover of the cherry tree at the northwest corner of the abandoned market, but a volley of five arrows from the tower met their effort, two missing Bhadran and Shankar, and three hitting Vedanga. He fell dead with his eyes wide in shock. There was no more cover beyond the cherry tree for another twenty feet, point blank range from the tower. Bhadran gripped his chakram for an overhand throw, peered around the east side of the tree, and as one arrow whizzed past from the second story, he took his aim and let it fly. A scream from the tower told him he'd hit something. A severed left arm and a longbow fell to the ground. Now the adrenaline-fueled battle fury was upon Bhadran, and he rushed into the open with his sword drawn, a wide back-slanted curved Adya Katti blade; a hail of arrows rained down, many missing, and some he expertly deflected or cut with the sword. Bhadran spun with his back to the wall adjacent to the southward facing door, panting. Shankar stepped to the side of the tree, drawing fire as he aimed his bow, one missile pierced his thigh, and Shankar let loose his own, finding another mark. He retreated behind the tree again, and tended to his leg. Bhadran tested the door latch, which broke off from years of rust. He gambled that the hinges were also weak, and mule kicked the door in, the ground floor was empty. Ducking low on the stairs, he crept forward, scanning.

Bhadran met no resistance until the last ten steps to the second story, where another arrow launched at him, which he also deflected before reversing the sword into a spear tossing position and sent it squarely into the ribs of one enemy. Bhadran closed the distance before he fell, using him as a shield against the others. He ran at one with the sword still protruding through the body, impaling the second man, then removed his sword to parry a dagger thrust from the third. Bhadran then ducked and spun around behind him, slashing the man's calves and knee tendons. The enemy's legs gave out, and Bhadran finished him off with a cut to the throat from behind. A door closed above on the third level, and an arrow launched from the stairs, grazing Bhadran in the thigh. Bhadran ducked under the stairs for cover, as one more grazed his cheek.

A scraping noise from outside raised Bhadran's suspicions, giving him a split second to react to an object thrown into one of the arrow loops before it exploded in a blinding flash and billowed smoke covering the escape of the last man inside. When the smoke cleared, Bhadran saw the rope swaying outside the arrow loop. Two men had gotten away. Bhadran retraced his steps to the cherry tree where the wounded Shankar had laid flat on his belly to avoid being seen or shot at. Shankar reported, "They fled west, toward Razadur. I have not seen our brothers."

Bhadran decided aloud, "Time to regroup."

Shankar nodded in agreement.

Vasanti and Jai were the only ones unaccounted for when they all met in the eighteen by eighteen structure, and Amala was the worst off. They confirmed twelve enemy kills, and the loss of Vedanga in the open.

"So ... there's four enemies on the run, and one building left unexplored. Plus, we are all exhausted. The wounded can stay here. Vidur, I need you to lead the assault on the last building. My arm is currently useless," Tyton told them.

Vidur nodded and bowed.

Thus Tyton, Bodhan, Amala and Shankar stayed put, while Vidur led Prasad and Bhadran on their mission. Using the eighteen by thirty-six building as cover, they approached the target zone. The last eighteen by eighteen structure northeast of the abandoned market had two fully intact walls blocking visibility both ways. Vidur decided it was best to stick together rather than split up, and led them toward the east side of the building.

As he peered around a gap in the east wall, four crossbow bolts and two arrows greeted him, one piercing his right forearm, and another grazing his brow. He spun against the wall, and whispered, "Half dozen. Hit them hard!"

Bhadran peered around, dodging everything they launched, and let his chakram fly again, which caught one full in the chest. Before another volley could follow, Prasad appeared to loose two arrows in succession, missing his first target, and hitting the second between the eyes. Prasad took cover as the remaining four fired. Vidur tended to his wounded arm and then drew two throwing dirks with his left hand. Bhadran was now outside the northeast corner of the structure with no chakram. Prasad launched another arrow blindly into the building, and a grunt of pain issued from the west wall. Bhadran drew his sword and charged from a gap in the north wall.

As the enemies turned to aim at Bhadran, Prasad took out two more. The wounded man along the west wall fled for his life, dropping his crossbow. The leader followed suit, leaving the structure empty of opposition. Bhadran retrieved his chakram again. That was four more confirmed kills. Vidur felt his reflexes growing dull, and his arm succumbing to paralysis. The Whispering Tigers were notorious for that type of poison. Prasad and Bhadran helped him back to the others. Tyton then ordered the last two able-bodied temple brethren to give chase and find brother Jai and sister Vasanti. They left with what energy they could muster.

Chapter Forty-Seven
When it Rains …

Adrian awoke to the sound of distant thunder over the winding sea to the northwest and saw dark ominous clouds over the horizon moving eastward.

"Ohh … SHIT! This is NOT good! Guys? Get up. There's a really big storm heading this way …." he moaned in a voice of dismay and resignation.

Garzon pulled out two glass marbles and a hollow reed of bamboo from somewhere in his loincloth, and had a look at the cloud mass. The clouds were dark and flat at the bottom, and their humps rose very high in the middle, moving fast with flashes of lightning above and below. "You are correct, greedy one. It is a storm," Garzon taunted with a wide but sly grin.

Adrian snarled, "You think this is *funny*? What kind of fiend are you?"

Garzon smiled and said flatly, "A man with no humor is a perfect target, too good to resist.

Now, unless you desire to be buried in sand for a hundred years, we need to move."

He woke the others and nudged them eastwards.

Adrian panicked. "What do you mean buried for a hundred years?"

Garzon shook his head in disbelief. "Are you so new to deserts, greedy one? Those clouds bring rain and cold air, these race downward, displacing dry sand and creating sandstorms. We must hurry toward the foothills of the Iron Ridge."

Adrian whimpered piteously. Sal just grunted, while Kazius guffawed cruelly at Adrian. Moira wondered with a perplexed look what kind of circus she was caught up in.

* * *

Tyrus worked late one night, and Peter the Foreman left him the keys to close up when the cleanup was done. Tyrus was very thorough, and just before locking up, took one of the monks' robes from the closets, knowing that the orphanage was connected somehow to the Lawgiver cult. He folded it neatly into his shoulder bag, and closed up as promised. Outside, that familiar young female voice whispered, "Some drunken knights were boasting about Alex's pleas to be released from the dungeon. I think I know where he is."

Tyrus taunted, "Do you sleep invisible, too?"

Tyrianna huffed, "As if I would tell you!"

Tyrus rolled his eyes. "Fine, but be careful. I have a bad feeling about this."

Tyrianna mocked him, "Oh? Are you an oracle now?"

Tyrus grumbled, "No, it's called experience and intuition. I hope you live to acquire them someday ..."

The girl left in angry silence again.

Tyrus complained aloud, "You lose all composure when I abstain from speaking, but gods forbid, I should ever protest the impetuous, young oracle invoking the same prerogative ..."

In answer, a gust of wind from nowhere stirred up the fallen leaves at his feet outside the orphanage and then faded.

* * *

Sister Vasanti and brother Jai both hid under the fishing pier to avoid being seen by the targets they followed to the village. If either of the enemies knew they were here, hostages would be taken and slain. Jai only got one glance at their faces many hours ago, but was very certain that it was Raj of the southern creepers, and his righthand man, Sanjay. Vasanti went into her trance, seeking answers to their problem. Her dreamstate melted away her surroundings in a great mist, and from afar, she saw gray faces in pain; most of their brethren were injured and poisoned, only two of them able to give chase. She saw them on the trail of four more enemies. Vasanti opened her eyes and announced to Jai, "Vidur and Prasad are on their way, and we lost Vedanga. We will be outnumbered yet again." Jai gave a grim nod of acknowledgement.

* * *

"Sire, we received word of more attacks on the Crimson Hoods. Previous losses have made peasants in nearby lands bolder. We are losing revenues, and there is now talk of the Syndicate pirates raising prices on the transport of slaves and cargo. The vault will be emptied within two years if this continues. What shall we do?" asked a low-ranking Bloodhammer.

Emperor Axegrind snarled, enraged, "Then institute a new tax on all the water barrels within the walls of our town, raise the penalties of desertion, late payments, and open defiance, and bring back the prima nocturne. AND, I want three more hoods trained by the end of the week."

His henchman nodded deeply and bowed low in fear. "Yes, Lord Axegrind, as you command it."

Axegrind dismissed him with a flick of his wrist and a screwed up sour face that looked as if he had tasted dirty socks.

* * *

"So, what's the guild status now?" Conrad asked one of the Obsidian Owls on patrol in the sewers of Oakthorn.

The veteran answered, "Our hall is destroyed, and our numbers are cut by two-thirds. Worse, nobody left in the barony can afford our services but Alex the Wise and the abbey. Our days could well be over."

Conrad smiled. "Not quite yet. Here," he said as he took a handful of coins out of his pouch and gave it to the veteran. "I am calling a gathering together to discuss the future of the guild, and a quest that I have been given."

The veteran bowed. "Yes, right away. I know a place we can safely discuss these matters."

The veteran led him southward for half a mile before Conrad asked, "Where are the others, and why are we taking the south tunnel?"

The veteran spun without speaking and attacked with his daggers drawn. Conrad blocked one with his chain-mailed sleeve, and the other cut his cheek as he ducked. Then, on instinct, Conrad's leg thrust out and made a sickening crunch under his assailant's kneecap. The veteran buckled and fell. Conrad followed up by stomping on his wrists in succession.

"I could *expel* you from the guild for this, as Tyton left me in charge, but I'm tired of being nice. You will explain yourself, or that kneecap will be the least of your worries," Conrad growled.

The veteran hissed, "You don't deserve the leadership or the gold. I've served him for years, and you take over for beating a few Blackwolves? It should have been ME instead, you spoiled rotten blue-blood! Everything was handed to you on a platter since birth!"

Conrad kicked him in the face and shouted, "YOU DARE pass judgement on my life, you blind, delusional, rabid dog! I have been framed for murder, I have fought zombies, skeletons and vampires in the bowels of Shadval trying to save this barony and all of you, and sent the ghoul of my father back to his grave for your ungrateful hides! I have had all I can stand of fingers wagging at me. I should leave you tied to the grate by the waterfall and let you starve, you coward!"

As Conrad weighed his options, the veteran tried to bite him in the ankle, but chipped his teeth on the hardened boot leather. Conrad reached down and snapped his neck. "You just cheated yourself out of being second in command, you stupid gutter rat." Conrad spat at the corpse. Conrad fished out his gate key and dragged the body south to toss him out through the waterfall. After the body hit the rocks on the west edge of the river, Conrad sat down on the ledge with his legs hanging over, wondering why he still bothered defending these townspeople. He did not return to his barony proper for many hours.

* * *

Tyrianna went alone toward the dungeons, confident her invisibility was enough as she floated through the corridors and stairwells. She, therefore, did not see the wire in time, and she set off the powder charges in the adjacent chandeliers and torch braziers, some covered her in white dust, revealing her position, and the others were deafening within close range and enclosed spaces. She was stunned and unable to conjure a spell as she lost concentration, falling twelve feet to the hard floor and breaking a couple fingernails. An elderly Dwarfish man with dark goggles and white hair stepped out from behind a wall tapestry and removed his earplugs. Tyrianna's ears were still ringing, but she saw him approach. He raised a hollow tube at her with a trigger on the bottom, and then her world vanished in a blinding white flare, and the acrid stink of magnesium. But before he could grab her, Tyrianna vanished in a beam of pale silvery light that faded away in a split second. Behind the Dwarf appeared a very angry, tall goddess; it was none other than Syrene. Her shadow fell across him, and he gulped as he turned around, and Syrene's right foot hit him so hard he flew all the way to the staircase thirty feet away. The Dwarf groaned once, and passed out before Syrene vanished.

Tyrianna felt her way blindly within a cave that she knew very well. But it had been changed. There were shards of broken pottery near the altar and signs of a struggle here. She called out in fear, "Mother?"

Syrene appeared in moments, answering, "I am here, my child. I did not see your danger until it was too late. I am still in mourning for your father. I am so very sorry."

Tyrianna turned at the displacement of air to one side, but heard nothing. She was both deaf and blind now and horribly alone. Tyrianna screamed and sobbed in terror, as helpless as the day her father died so many years ago. A hand touched her cheek, and Tyrianna clasped it in desperation, and then followed the arm to her mother's torso, hugging for dear life as she continued to sob, "Mama, I'm blind!"

Syrene stroked her daughter's hair and held her close, kissing her forehead. Then a faint voice in Tyrianna's head spoke, "He has made you deaf, also. I am so sorry, sweetheart. I should have never let you go alone into the world of men. I can teach you to see in other ways, and will keep you safe until then. This, I promise."

Tyrianna kept weeping in her mother's arms, rocking like a small child.

* * *

Back in the land of Korath, Tyrus heard a loud noise somewhere nearby. It had come from under the ground. Then he realized, "The dungeons! Curse me for a fool!"

He quickly donned the monk's robe and hid the trident under it, while striding hurriedly in the direction of the blast. Some knights barred his way at ground level. "It's after hours for visits to the prisoners, Father. We cannot allow you in."

Tyrus bowed slightly. "Of course, my apologies, kind sir. Praise to the Lawgiver."

As they recited the praise in turn, he punched them both in the throat to silence them, and followed with simultaneous hammerfist blows to the backs of their helmets. They fell, and Tyrus propped them against the wall at their post. Then, he descended the stairs behind them. Down three flights of steps he went before he discovered an unconscious Dwarf with dark goggles at the foot of the stairs. Then, a familiar voice spoke in his head, "My daughter is safe now, but will be unable to help you. Your quest is now in your hands alone. You must leave before you are cornered. But first take cover behind the tapestry. There! Luck be with you."

Then the voice was gone. Tyrus hid as instructed in the alcove behind the tapestry, and stayed there until the knights swept past, with one shouting "She has to be here! Look, the outline of the white dust where she hit the floor, search the cells, the confession chambers, and the washbasins! Hurry! Find the Elf witch!"

As they spread in a search pattern, the way clear emptied out, and Tyrus made his exit.

"Whatever has happened to Tyrianna, you will all pay, this I swear on my father's throne!" he whispered to himself.

Tyrus turned north toward the lake, passing the Falcon's Perch on the way. Tyrus scowled in recognition. "A pox on this house, and the vermin who drown their wits in it, to cheerfully swallow a caravan of lies!" he growled as he turned his back on it.

* * *

"Sandhaven is going to kill you, demon," claimed Frederic as he sighted the outlines of Kozos in the distance. Wayne kicked his rump, causing him to fall in the snow again. "Call me that one more time, moron, and I'll feed you to the wolves like your friend on the mountain.

You have no idea what kind of evil you blindly serve. You were nothing but a sacrificial lamb to him, or he would not have sent you into harm's way so young and naive. Don't be a fool!" Wayne admonished the boy.

Frederic clambered to his feet and brushed off the snow; he was still stiff and sore and now hungry. But the mention of his dead friend made him queasy.

Curse this demon, Father, and deliver your servant from his clutches, I pray, he thought to himself. Wayne saw the hands in the prayer position, and the lips moving and said, "Forget it, kid. If some power in the sky answered them all, your cult would have exterminated everyone by now. Stop wasting your breath."

Frederic snapped, "You cannot win; you are outnumbered. Every year, we grow stronger, and you will have nowhere to hide."

Wayne answered, "That is exactly why the people need to learn the truth about Malsain and the cult. So the rest of us can live in peace."

Frederic just stared in confusion, "You expect me to believe that?"

Wayne smacked him on the head. "No, of course not. You are young and stupid. That's why I don't tell you what my plan is, aside from not trusting you half as far as the axe flies." Wayne did not actually have a plan; he was making it up on the spur of the moment, but he had no need or desire to divulge that.

* * *

"Sire, the body of Sir Gregor was discovered in the woods, and Prince Adam is gone.

Gregor had many wounds matching the width of a big sword. What is your wish?" reported Sir Skavund the Unremarkable.

Nathan grumbled, "This means Marcy knows. Adam could not so much as kill a mouse. Best not to antagonize her further. Her foreign devils are a dangerous lot. And I still need her family's resources. Therefore, what I want you to do is put a stop to the rumors about Corbin. Give them some other juicy gossip to occupy them. Make something up, the peasants will believe anything. Thank you, Skavund."

The knight saluted and bowed, then spun on his heels and left on his errands.

Next was Sir Bothun the Brave to report, "There are five marriage proposals for the hand of young Minerva, sire. From one Raimondo Napoli of Agama, another from Prince Mark Goldlion of Stonehaven, one from Prince Andrei Kristos Aristodemos of Agama, one from Prince Katsuro YamaNeko of Ama, and a name I cannot decipher from the land of Zagtu."

Nathan clenched his fingers. "Confound it! Already? Her courting birthday is still two months away …"

He paced back and forth like a caged panther, biting his nails. "Gaaaaa, send our apologies to Zagtu and this … Raimondo. Minerva will not be married down. Learn what you may of these three princes. Be as quick as you can. Thank you."

Bothun saluted and bowed, and as he passed Sir Vornadin the Serpent, he whispered, "His temper is stoked; I'd be delicate if I were you."

Vornadin smiled in acknowledgement and continued his approach to the king's platform.

"Sire, the alchemist has sustained a concussion and reports a tall, powerful, red-haired woman appeared from nowhere as the young girl vanished. We saw the outline of where the girl fell, and the scatter pattern of oxidized magnesium. All three devices were on the mark. There was some blood from the ears. Unfortunately, Sir Fergus overheard. Marcy knows. She will ask questions," Vornadin concluded.

"Damn that woman!" Nathan snarled, as he took to pacing again.

"Damn, damn, damn, DAMN …"

Sir Vornadin interrupted, "If I may, sire …"

Nathan stopped and gestured with his palm up to continue.

"Make an alliance with Father Sandhaven and with the academy headmaster. The Cloverhills and Mollenbecks will turn on you when Marcy does. You need support whether you get along or not. Forgive my bluntness."

Nathan frowned, "I see. Do you think Bradagar the Irreverent will agree to this?"

Vornadin hesitated, "That is difficult to predict, sire. But I think it safe to say he highly dislikes Marcy and Adam. He may or may not take your side."

Nathan clenched his teeth and put his hand over his face in exasperation and resignation.

"Very well. Do it. Make him an offer. Go."

Vornadin saluted and bowed and took his leave.

* * *

"Baron, it pains me to say that I cannot go with you after all. The pervasive corruption in the council will destroy all I hold dear if I do not pull it up by the roots myself. Sandraz is overwhelmed. The queen ..." Ravenna tried to explain.

Bravane the Younger held his palm out vertically. "Say no more. I understand. What little has reached my ears has convinced me that you are correct, and you are the only one who is both capable and willing. I shall pray that others exist who may assist me in my quest. I cannot hold that against you. Again, I am sorry about your brother. I hope his spirit finds peace and justice."

Ravenna gave a slight nod. "Thank you. May your journey be fruitful and victorious."

The exiled baron bowed. "Thank you, good lady. Victory to you as well."

With that, Bravane left the chamber.

Lady Ravenna then paid a visit to her sister-in-law, the queen regent in name only, as poor Lissa Firebird, born of Xantir though she was, lacked the strength of their convictions. Lissa was drained of all courage and will since her husband's death and was losing weight from her diminished appetite. Her two children, Lorraine and Mark, were given a nanny by Sandraz. Lissa stayed in her bedchambers with a seat by the window, staring out over the garden courtyard, pining for her dead husband, King William Goldlion. Lorraine ran to the door as Ravenna entered and hugged her aunt hello.

"And how old is my niece this year? I've been away a long time ..." Ravenna admitted.

Lorraine declared, "Seven summers old, Auntie. And Mark is five."

Mark stood up from his studies. "I'm going to marry Princess Minerva, then ride into battle and avenge my father on the biggest horse ever born, and after the enemy is defeated, we will eat all their food. The end!"

Ravenna chuckled. "My, but you are brave, young nephew! May you also grow strong and wise!"

The nanny admonished, "Dreadful fantasies for such a young lad. I've told him too many children's stories, and he won't sit still to listen to anything else."

Ravenna patted the nanny's shoulder. "I wouldn't worry. His auntie has tales of her own. Might I have a word alone with my sister?"

The nanny curtsied. "Of course, milady. Come along, children."

The royals protested, but grudgingly did as requested.

Ravenna hugged Mark good-bye and kissed Lorraine on the forehead on their way out.

After the door had closed, Lady Ravenna spoke, "Lissa, I did not want to trouble you earlier, but this matter cannot wait any longer. The council is taking over and making our people suffer. I must ask you for the Rule of the Right Hand. It is the only way I can mend our troubles. Will you approve it, sister?"

Lissa slowly turned from the window and weakly nodded yes. The queen's eyes were heavy with sadness still, and Ravenna walked over to offer comfort. "Your loss is also mine. I am sorry he is gone so soon."

Lissa held out her hands and broke into sobs as Ravenna first held them, then lifted her touch to stroke Lissa's hair as the seated queen hugged Ravenna for dear life.

"I'm sorry I failed our people, but I miss him so ..." Lissa wailed.

Ravenna continued petting. "I know, sister. I know."

* * *

As the thunderstorm got to within a few miles of shore, the opening roar of the sandstorm began, lifting off the ground behind Adrian, Garzon, and company. All but Adrian were helping the women get to the foothills. They were still too far away to take shelter. Garzon yelled, "Brace yourselves! Here it comes! Stay together!"

Bernice, Moira, and Mandy all screamed in fear, as did Adrian. Kazius neither screamed nor flinched; the land of Razadur had known many sandstorms in his time. Sal just pressed on in silence. The fury of the storm was upon them, gusting at fifty knots. Their makeshift head veils and hoods stayed on, but the women stumbled, and Adrian ran in blind panic. Garzon swept his hand in a dismissive gesture. "Waste of good swordfish he is! The fool!"

The remaining party walked steadily east, guided by Garzon's sense of direction. Ahead, Garzon saw a small keep, manned by men in familiar red hoods. Garzon warned the others, "Enemies ahead. Follow me and stick to the wall!"

Mandy stopped cold when she saw the uniforms. She shook her head no and refused to approach.

Garzon chastised, "You will die out here! Don't be a fool! I will handle them."

Mandy dug in. "No, no! I'm not going in there with those evil hyenas!"

Garzon motioned for Sal to pick her up and toss her over a shoulder, as Mandy wailed, "No! Stop!"

It was too late. They were now close enough that the enemy could hear, even in the storm. A small team of them issued from the front archway of the keep, and Garzon sprang into action. More sounds of metal and bone splintering under the impact of his battle axe followed, and many bloodstains dotted the sand. Two men dropped their weapons and ran in the same direction as Adrian had gone. One hid deeper inside the keep. The structure was now otherwise empty. The party took cover inside the walls and sighed in relief. Kazius, in particular, knew this place well. It was the Red Keep, Razadur's western port on the desert trade lane and an outpost of the Crimson Hoods, who collected the tributes and taxes.

* * *

In the tiny fisherman's market, Belinda noticed two male strangers, dark-skinned like desert people were, and their accents were that of Vaja. Thoughts of another man from long ago filled her with disgust. A man who never returned from the fire of '33.

"Backstabbers," she whispered, as she turned her face away and carefully avoided the newcomers. Belinda pretended to look over the crabs and oysters of a vendor she did not know yet and nudged Layla discreetly, whispering, "Don't look, but there's two men behind us at the mackerel cart. Do not speak to them, and never trust them. They move like assassins."

Layla just shrugged. Clearly she did not know Belinda's history or trust her judgement in such matters. This left Belinda thinking she had to expose them before her friends became their victims. But how? Belinda needed to get Layla safely away and then come up with a plan.

"Layla, could you find some more seashells for us? I'd like to have a supply for when the weather is too cold; it's already rather chilly. It would be most appreciated."

Layla frowned. “Oh, all right. But I want some smoked salmon for dinner with carrots and onion!”

Belinda nodded yes.

Nearby, Sanjay whispered to Raj, “That blonde heading toward the pier has been staring at us. I think she is on to us.”

Raj replied, “Tail her. If she bolts, take her hostage or get rid of her. And do be quiet about it.”

Sanjay nodded once and left.

Each corner Layla turned, she looked over a shoulder, and each time Sanjay had his back turned or had ducked out of her line of sight. Layla could not shake the feeling she was being watched, and hurried her pace. The pier was busy with the loading and unloading of fishing boats, and a select few small merchant vessels looking to score some bargains and resell the goods elsewhere at markup.

There was also one canoe from the nearby tribal island of Ye-Ho, with another armload of star charts for navigators in leather scroll cases, plus their surplus paddles, and bottles of exotic purple ink. What did not sell here was taken to a Dabani trading post south of Korath. At the pier, Sanjay had no more hiding places and stuck out like a sore thumb. Layla spotted him and bolted. The woman’s gasp of terror and her quick footsteps got the attention of Jai and Vasanti. The temple sister signaled Jai to go topside. Jai nodded once and wasted no time. As Sanjay wove his way around the fishermen and merchants on the pier, Jai cut off his retreat.

Layla turned to look again and stumbled backward over an uneven board. Sanjay closed in, certain of his prize, when a dagger sprung up between the boards into his foot from below. He fell, clutching his foot, and grunted in pain.

Vasanti withdrew her dagger and changed position under the pier while Jai readied his chakram for a clear shot. Layla spotted Jai and believed he was with the other man. Her look of fear alerted Sanjay, who turned to see his enemy. He cursed himself for getting cocky and hobbled away to buy time, what little he could get. He was almost upon the blonde, gaining her feet, when Vasanti made her appearance at the east side of the pier behind the blonde.

Vasanti's chakram was also at the ready. Sanjay dove off the west edge of the pier, and Vasanti had the only clear shot. She nailed him in the ribs and the right lung. Sanjay hit the water hard, and it was all he could do to tread water with his right side in such agony. Vasanti dove after him, and Jai stood watch. Only then did Layla understand what was happening. She was an innocent, caught between two sides of a conflict, and the side that would have wished her harm, just lost. Layla sighed in relief.

Vasanti swam under the target and surfaced behind him with a dagger drawn, and Sanjay reacted too late. The dagger came down on his left side, taking his other lung. He gasped for his last breath and slowly sank while Vasanti removed her weapons from his doomed flesh. With the chakram in one hand and the dagger between her teeth,

Vasanti swam for the shore under the pier. Layla turned to the dark stranger standing nearby to say thank you.

Jai bowed with his open left hand extended sideways, and his right hand over his heart, holding his chakram. Jai informed the blonde, "There's one more of them in the village, with more on the way. You had best get to safety."

Layla gasped, "Belinda was right! Oh, shit! I have to warn my friends!"

Layla started to run before Jai grabbed her arm. "Wait! Running will tip him off if the gossip has not already done so. Be careful!"

Layla gave him a puzzled look, then nodded to humor him. She walked very briskly, not wanting to leave anything to chance.

Vasanti nodded to the blonde as she passed by, then motioned for Jai to follow. They split up, walking southward on solid ground with Vasanti flanking to the east, and Jai flanking west. Out of sight, around the narrow street corners and packed huts, Raj was met in the tiny market by the other survivors, his own men Samir and Udai, plus the last of the Whispering Tigers, Chapal and Kumar.

Udai reported, "There's at least one enemy on our trail; several were wounded or killed in the ruins. We may need hostages."

Raj mulled it over for a minute. "Not until we know their numbers."

Udai simply nodded once and kept his thoughts to himself.

An elder appeared in their midst, blind in one eye, and frail, requiring a cane both for walking and compensating for his poor vision. He addressed them all, "Please, no weapons here, we are a peaceful village and ..."

Kumar cut the man's speech short with a crossbow bolt in his chest. Raj slapped Kumar,

"Now you've done it! Paint a target on your head next time and have the words embroidered on your shirt that says 'cocky bandit for sale to lowest bidder.' You just blew what little cover we had, you stupid brat!"

Kumar whined, "Worked fine in Vaja."

Raj got in his face. "We are not in Vaja anymore, and your tigers have grown lazy and stupid in the one year that Nikita took power in the temple, and called off the manhunt on your sorry band. Preying on easy targets has made you all into lambs."

Raj spit on Kumar's shirt to accent his point.

Chapal intervened, "I am the leader of the tigers, not him. Leave him alone.

Raj sneered, "The two of you are all that's left of the tigers. And you are nothing compared to my father when he was in charge!"

Udai nudged Raj, and pointed toward the pier, along the alley where Vasanti stood.

Raj ordered, "Get her!"

Kumar refused, leaving Samir and Udai to chase after their enemy. Samir was the first to raise his weapon, firing a crossbow bolt, which Vasanti deflected with a sweep of the chakram. She then ducked behind a hut and lost them in seconds.

The Creepers took to overturning barrels and smashing crates in their vain search, and as they split up, she seized her opportunity. Jumping from a rooftop, she delivered a flying sidekick to the back of Samir's neck, driving him hard into an adobe brick wall, knocking him out instantly. She ran before Udai could aim.

Jai appeared fifteen yards behind Chapal and Kumar, and before Kumar could react, Jai's chakram cleaved into Kumar's left shoulder, making it impossible for Kumar to reload his crossbow. Chapal and Raj put aside their differences and gave chase. Jai weaved west and south, zigzagging between huts and then leaving the village for the sparse cover of the plains.

Raj hissed, "He's heading for Lake Maha. There's no cover there on the north banks!"

He was so certain of victory, that he did not notice Vidur and Prasad approaching from the southeast and splitting up. Vidur sped toward the village, while Prasad shadowed Raj and Chapal. Udai grew tired of the chase, exited the east side of the village and waited for a target to present itself for his longbow. Udai saw Vidur on open ground, and was taking aim when Vasanti's chakram cut his bowstring, which left huge red welts on his left arm and the right side of his face. The chakram embedded into an upside down small canoe under repair. Udai drew his sword, cursing, "Come and die, bitch!"

Vasanti drew her long daggers, and stalked the outer perimeter of Udai's reach. Vidur was forty yards away now, and took aim with his longbow, waiting for a clear shot. Udai noticed and charged Vasanti to spoil that clear shot. Vasanti rolled under the charge, slashing his ankle as she did. It was a shallow cut, but Udai felt the sting, gasping. Udai dove to one side, tucked and rolled onto his feet, and charged again. As Vasanti dodged to the side, he threw sand in her face.

Vidur took his shot, merely grazing the back of Udai's right leg. Vasanti tucked her face into her left elbow and took a blind-fighting stance with both hands holding daggers in the reverse grip. The air displacement to her rear triggered her reflexes, summersaulting backward over his swing, and raking his back with both blades before springing backward away from his return stroke. Vidur slung his bow across his torso and readied his own sword for melee as he went to aid Vasanti. Udai feinted to one side, Vasanti blocked, and opened her right side to the real attack, taking a slash to the lower ribs. Vasanti dropped one of her daggers and fell clutching her bleeding wound. Vidur saw the blow, and yelled to distract Udai as Vidur charged to her aid. Swords rang as they met, throwing sparks. Vidur began to tire again, as the minutes dragged on, his parries growing weaker, and his attacks slower … Udai pressed his advantage with a desperate flurry that cut across Vidur's pectorals, his right forearm and left shoulder, before knocking the sword out of Vidur's hand with the force of the last blow. Then, as Udai raised the sword for the killing stroke; Vasanti's chakram took his left arm off at the elbow. Udai screamed, dropping his sword and running to the emptied market for rags to stop his bleeding. Vidur and Vasanti both passed out from pain and exhaustion.

Near the lake, Jai turned to face his pursuers with his sword drawn in the high guard position, and Chapal loosed a crossbow bolt, which sailed high over Jai's head from the recoil. Raj took more careful aim with his longbow and shot low under Jai's defense, striking his calf. Jai fell to his knees and felt the awful burning of the scorpion venom. Prasad came in ninety yards behind the enemy and swung south to angle his line of fire away from Jai. Chapal was reloading as Raj shot again, Jai deflected the arrow this time, but knew he would eventually lose, due to his injury and their numbers on open ground. Prasad took his shot just as Chapal fired the second bolt. The bolt grazed Jai's cheek, and Chapal took an arrow through the kidney, and his shock registered in slow motion. Chapal looked down at the point protruding under his rib, his mouth open as if to speak, before turning about to see who had shot him. Raj was already firing in return at the greater threat. Prasad had dodged left and flattened onto his belly with his bow horizontal and his next arrow nocked. Chapal sank to his knees, gasping, "Not … fair …" while Raj crouched into a kneeling position, shrinking his profile. Prasad and Raj kept aiming, firing, and dodging until they were out of arrows.

Raj turned to Chapal, "Give me that!" and he grabbed his crossbow.

As Raj was loading the bolt, Prasad plucked an arrow from the ground nearby and nocked on the run. Raj shot high from the recoil, and Prasad's arrow hit Raj in the left shoulder. His own scorpion venom began to burn inside the wound. Raj threw the crossbow down and ran north. Chapal crawled weakly toward the crossbow, determined to go out in glory. He passed out just as his fingers brushed the body of the weapon. Prasad arrived, inspected Jai's wound, and helped him up. When they got to the village, their path was blocked by the injured Kumar, with the chakram still in his shoulder. "You will pay for this indignity, you filthy rats ..." he declared, with only a stolen paddle to defend himself.

Prasad eased Jai against a barrel and set his bow aside. As Kumar shambled toward them, Prasad took a defensive open handed stance. Kumar swung with only his right arm; Prasad caught the paddle with both hands and yanked it downwards at an angle, before lifting it over Kumar's head whose momentum tumbled him into a backspin, landing well past Jai and impacting the wall of a storage shed. Kumar clambered clumsily back onto his feet, dazed and angry. His vision had blurred, and his feet were unsteady. Such that, as Kumar advanced to attack Prasad with only his fists, Jai easily tripped him. Kumar did not get up.

Jai retrieved his chakram and gave Prasad his bow back. Villagers were just now re- emerging from their huts, which Prasad took as a good sign until he saw Vasanti and Vidur. Vasanti had lost a lot of blood, and Vidur was not looking well either. The material evidence of a dismembered arm and a dropped sword told Prasad that another body was unaccounted for. But right now, caring for their own wounded was a priority. Vasanti needed help. Layla saw from a distance, that the people who saved her life were in bad shape, and begged Belinda to help them. Belinda shook her head no. "But I owe them my life! They may die! How can you ignore that?" Layla demanded. "If Krisa or Kendra or Bernice were hurt, you'd help them, wouldn't you?"

Belinda scowled, as nobody had EVER talked to her that way! Belinda was old enough to be Layla's grandmother! Her fingers clenched as if to strangle the young blonde and gritted her teeth, snarling and cursing. "You were not there when the Blackwolves were nearly exterminated by Arius before switching sides. They sold me into slavery to the Bloodhammers ten years before you were born! And the people you want me to help look the same as a man who joined the Blackwolves after they turned to evil!"

Layla repeated, "Belinda, they saved my life ... is there nothing good left in this land? In you?"

Belinda cursed again, in incomprehensible languages. Then shoved Layla out of the way to go have a look at the wounded. "Fetch me a needle, some rat gut, a small fire, and some strong drink," she ordered some locals.

Once the needle was sterilized, she dabbed the alcohol on the wound, which caused Vasanti to wake, screaming and thrashing.

"Hold her still," Belinda barked.

Prasad finger jabbed several pressure points, and Vasanti was out again.

Belinda flinched, looking at Prasad as if he were a ghost. But no, this was not the same man. Prasad motioned to continue. Belinda paused a split second, and then started to sew up the wound. Vidur's cuts were shallow by comparison, but he too, lost a fair amount of blood. Once they were sewn up, Prasad asked if they could stay here for two nights. The village began their debates, but Layla's testimony swayed the decision to a yes.

Kumar reappeared one more time, still stumbling in a daze, with his right fist up, and his left still useless. Prasad accepted his challenge. Kumar stumbled forward to attack, and Prasad was content to keep dodging and leaning for a minute, before Kumar starting wrecking crates and baskets when he missed. On the next swing, Prasad caught Kumar's right fist in his left palm, and twisted counterclockwise until Kumar was on his knees facing away from Prasad, with his arm bent over his head. With his own right hand, Prasad delivered a chop to Kumar's trachea, and that was the end of him.

Chapter Forty-Eight
Friends and Enemies

As the sandstorm subsided, Garzon made the decision to stay another night and live off the supplies in the keep. Nobody argued until hours later when the sole remaining hood locked the door to one of the supply rooms. Mandy and Moira notified Garzon, and he strode to the door and announced, "Open the door and I will let you live. If you refuse, you will meet the same end as this door! You have one minute to decide, you scurvy dog!"

The Crimson Hood answered back, "You and whose army? There's not a sword made yet that can break this door, and the turn is too sharp for a battering ram!"

Garzon cracked his knuckles and let an evil grin steal over him. "I'm not using a sword, and if you persist in this folly, you will learn why the Syndicate pirates run in terror at the sight of me or quake at the sound of my name!"

The hood challenged, "Bold words from a nobody out of the desert!"

Garzon turned his back to the door, brought one knee up, and mule kicked the door clean off its hinges, and the hood was trapped under the door as Garzon walked over it, all 6 foot 9 inches and 416 pounds of muscle and bone, plus his ultra dense, huge battle axe. In a squeaky wheezing voice struggling for air under the weight, the Hood pleaded, "Mercy! Please ... get ... off ..."

"You ignored my warning and will not get another chance, impudent one. This is the price of your folly as I already told you. Good-bye!"

As the weight on the door shifted, one last plea was heard, "No! Wait!" And then the axe cleaved both door and human. The look on Sal's face while witnessing the scene was catatonic. Mandy, Moira and Bernice had all covered their eyes when Garzon kicked the door. Adrian was somewhere out in the desert, probably lost, and Kazius silently vowed never to cross this behemoth of a man.

* * *

Lord Alex the Wise heard a knock at his door and wondered who could be visiting at this hour of the day; it was well past dinner. He opened the door to see Henry the Lorekeeper of the abbey. "Dreadfully sorry to bother you, but Conrad insisted. He has gone west on a long errand, and he reports that he must decline the leadership of the Owls. He trusts that you could relay the message to the right ears upon their return to the barony."

Alex scratched his beard, which was growing back and covering some of his burns, "If Bethany or the others appear before his return, I will pass it on. Anything else?"

Henry mused, "Yes, as a matter of fact, we are starting another rotation of winter crops in the Abbey's botanical window garden, do you have any special requests?"

Alex thought for a moment, and Myra spoke, "Tomatoes would be nice."

Alex added, "Kale, too, and squash, snow peas, carrot, potato and onion."

Henry smiled. "Consider it done. We are also adding garlic, cilantro, cabbage and rhubarb. Do enjoy your evening, sir and madam."

With that, Henry shook Alex's hand, hugged Myra, bowed and left.

* * *

"So, which is the northernmost tavern in these parts, kid?" Wayne inquired of his reluctant companion.

"The Lawgiver does not approve of such places, where men turn to sin and lechery," Frederic replied with a sour face.

Wayne challenged with a sarcastic tone,

"But he has no problem gaining more followers who were born or conceived in such places, seems rather incongruous to me, but naturally, you did not ask, and a devout standard bearer of the faith such as yourself, would never entertain such logic ..."

Frederic hissed, "Demon!"

Wayne coldcocked him hard for that. "I warned you about that, one more time and you'll be crow food like your friend ..." The mention of the crows and the missing Stuart made Frederic vomit again.

Wayne saw a fruit vendor nearby, with the last fresh pears of the season, and a cart full of jams and jellies.

"Pardon me, where's the nearest tavern?" Wayne requested.

The vendor just pointed to the sign of the Falcon's Perch and then gasped in shock as he saw who he was giving directions to. Wayne's likeness was drawn on a wanted poster not ten feet away.

"Fifteen gold crowns, eh? Why in..." Wayne began, as Frederic ran in panic, attempting to alert the knights. "There goes that plan ... well, no use going to the dungeons on an empty stomach."

As Wayne entered, the hoots and hollers of the crowd inside were almost deafening, all faces were on this ugly old woman, Karina Cooper, ranting away about the many enemies of Father Malsain. How the Elves attacked a Dwarven alchemist, seduced the townsfolk who marched to war, bribed a hunter and farmer, and tricked a woman in the mountains, all to enslave or destroy Korath and its people. Wayne shook his head as he sat down to order his food. Nearby, a drunken lecher was being teased by a young, curly haired blonde lady.

"I don't understand all this fuss. I'm a simple girl who wants to raise a family and mind her own business. What about you?" the girl whispered so Karina would not hear.

The drunk replied, "Only too happy to help with that situation, Miss ..."

The girl added, "Call me Morgessa, handsome."

The drunk was about to speak, when Morgessa put a finger to his lips, mouthing silently, "Let's talk somewhere less crowded."

Something about the girl's mannerisms reminded Wayne of Belinda and some other women from Black Falls. She was deceitful, but Wayne said nothing. The drunken fellow was no friend of his, and Wayne was a wanted man. A low profile was best for enjoying a meal before trouble caught up with him. Alas, before a serving wench could even take his order, Karina pointed at him. "I seen your face on the posters! What's Nathan want you for?"

Wayne shrugged, "Me? I have not the faintest idea why he wants me. I was just helping out at the orphanage and got tired of it. So I left. The hell with the prince's pretentious declarations ..."

The entire tavern went wild with cheers and laughter, and Karina grabbed his hand, raising it high in clasped fists. "Here's our fellow, balls of brass and talks plainly! What's your name, Sonny?"

Wayne fidgeted. "Uh, call me Danny."

Karina bellowed, "A drink for our Danny boy! Bring the wench over here!"

Wayne was still ordering his food when four knights arrived with swords drawn. The locals protested but gave way grudgingly to the pointed ends of rude steel.

Karina called out, "Kurt, get over here! Where the blazes is that nephew, tan his hide!"

Kurt was nowhere inside the tavern. The knights soon surrounded Wayne, and called out, "Bring the boy in!"

A fifth knight forcefully dragged Frederic inside and demanded, "Is this the one?"

Frederic vigorously nodded in fear, "Y-yes, he's the one," and turned to vomit before he could even form the first syllable of the name Stuart.

Sir Bothun the Brave announced, "You are under arrest for espionage and now murder. Take him away!"

Karina wagged her finger at the boy. "You! I knew it! You abandoned Malsain and took up with Father Sandhaven, didn't you?"

Frederic gulped and scrambled to get away from Karina the Whale. Sir Ulmadast the Round nudged and shoved Karina away. "Leave the boy alone, you ugly old hag ..."

Karina hissed, "If Barton or Malsain ever return, you'll be sorry, Sonny!"

Ulmadast retorted, "Shut your gums, or you'll spend a night in the dungeons, too!"

Wayne's stomach grumbled as they left; nothing had gone right today. And it was going to get worse.

* * *

Tyrus was sorting papers in the document room, cleaning up the mess that Alex the Meek was forced to leave behind, when one caught his attention.

> *DEED TRANSFER: Twelve Marble Lane property, to Kitra Cooper, effective August third, 1539, for services to the Lawgivers.*

It was instinct and the word *Lawgivers* that told Tyrus this was important information; now he had to find out why. The title history showed the previous owners to be John and Sarah Mill, most likely the parents of Alex! Further rummaging showed that both parents died in 1539, of some "accident." Tyrus did not believe in such coincidences. The last scrap of information of any relevance to his quest was about Alex Mill himself. Kitra was the nanny for Alex when Mill's parents died, and Alex was thereafter raised in the orphanage, instead of at home.

Further clues would be in the king's castle, or in the church of the Lawgivers. And there was not much time, for once he was on the trail, these cult people would hunt him also. Tyrus headed north toward the lake. Once there, he gazed into the water, and spoke: "Syrene, if you can hear me, show me what I must do." Tyrus waited long minutes before her image appeared on the surface. Her voice spoke to him, "The evidence you seek is within the church. Beware, the town is turning against you, and Daniel is now captive. Your greatest trials are near, and this path takes you there. Trust carefully, few are deserving of it."

* * *

All eyes at the table turned when Lady Ravenna marched right up to her brother's old chair at council and sat down with a ferocious look on her face. Bravane the Elder showed relief, Sandraz was absent, Clark was clearly displeased, and Darla smiled like the cat that caught a juicy canary. Lady Ravenna Freebird turned directly to Clark Russell Whitetree, and hissed, "So sorry to tell you that the rumors of my demise were exaggerated, and that you are now the first member to be expelled from the council, by the power vested in the right hand of the crown, and by the many provisions of ancient law. You have harassed our people, exercised undue influence over the council for your hidden agendas, and I will soon have evidence that not only was the late councilman Vamanastral an Alpha clan infiltrator of this council, but SO ARE YOU, Clark!"

Clark turned red with rage, yelling as he stood, "This is an outrage! I won't honor these blatant lies! You will regret this, Ravenna!"

Moments later, as Ravenna clapped her palms together twice, the doors opened, and the Goldcrest Knights who served only the Goldlion family line, entered to escort Clark out. As Clark begrudgingly left the room with snarls and shoves, Darla Mae Copperhill cheered, as did Vaude Krantz, and Adam Walter Coppergrass. Franz Leon Croix scowled in disgust. Lady Ravenna pointed, "Franz, you are next! Get out!"

Franz gaped in shock, "What did I do?"

Ravenna hissed, "You knew about the poison that killed my brother, and you did nothing! Which makes you an accessory to a capital crime! Your sentence begins immediately!"

Franz bolted for the second story window, but as he opened it, a freak gust of wind blew straight up and carried him ten feet before dropping him to his death, impaled on the iron fence-works surrounding the building.

Emil Jacques Fleur stared in horrified disbelief. "What in heaven's name was *that*? Mon Dieu!"

Ravenna grinned evilly, she knew but was not telling. She merely declared, "I am reversing all council actions for the past thirty days, and we shall reconvene on the morrow. Thank you."

Nobody dared challenge her, especially now. They all left in silence.

* * *

"A word of caution, young ones, Korath is not known as a hospitable region for strangers in recent years. Stay close to me and try not to speak to unhappy people. Especially if they wear shiny armor. Do you understand?" Thomas said, bowing to see eye to eye with the two children.

Molly said yes and nodded. Carol merely blinked her eyes. Thomas hefted his silver studded walking staff in one hand, and slung a bag over the other shoulder, with their travel provisions inside. "We will get a horse when we are south of the river, and hope for fair weather along the way."

* * *

"So, Prince Mark is the youngest suitor, you say?" asked Nathan.

Sir Vornadin the Serpent nodded. "Indeed, sire, a mere five summers. I take it you think this is somehow to your advantage."

King Nathan grinned, "Precisely, he will be the easiest to control if his father is out of the picture, and he can't sire any children for, at least, another seven years... perfect for my plans. Send our acceptance letter this evening."

Vornadin cautioned, "Young Minerva may have ideas of her own, Your Majesty."

Nathan scowled and then smirked, "You let me worry about her."

A knock at the doors announced the return of Sir Bothun the brave and the other knights with their captive.

"Perfect! This is a splendid day, just splendid! Bring him here, Bothun!"

Wayne was led in chains and forced onto his knees.

"Now, SPY, your friend admitted passing through Valantir, but he is too cowardly and meek to be the true asset of your mission. Who are you working for? Speak!" Nathan barked.

Wayne stared in silence, allowing his defiant anger to show in his eyes. Nathan backhanded him, "I will brook no self-righteous upstarts fomenting rebellion and disloyalty! Who are you working for?"

Wayne spat blood as he sat up again. "You would not believe me anyway, which means we are just wasting our time here."

Nathan kicked him in the ribs and yelled, "Take him away! Insolent dog!"

Another knight arrived with bad news, "Your lordship, the Headmaster Bradagar the irreverent declines your offer, he will not take sides. He advised you to rethink your strategy, owing to Marcy's keen observations, her family connections, her obstinate will and political clout, and her Knights. He also ..."

Nathan interrupted, "Bah! The coward! I don't need him anyway! Leave me!" The Knight bowed dejectedly, "Yes, sire."

Lastly, a Herald returned with news. "Sandhaven accepts an alliance with you and Corbin. Lawgivers loyal to him are already working to undermine our opposition. In fact, the boy Frederic is one of Sandhaven's people."

Nathan smiled, "We shall have a feast then, a private one, away at the Academy so Marcy cannot eavesdrop… I want Sandhaven and the boy to know I am grateful. Leave the Headmaster out of it. Thank you, you may go."

The herald, too, bowed dejectedly, "Yes, milord."

* * *

In the guest house on twelve Marble Lane, Kurt Blackhammer sighed with contentment and rolled onto his side with his face still buried in Morgessa's cleavage. She cooed, "Oh, baby, such passion and stamina! (giggle) Have any more of that?"

Kurt sighed, "No, baby, three times in one night did me in. But Mama will kill me if she finds out, her and Auntie both, keep telling me I need a righteous woman who will raise their grandchildren to obey the Lawgiver and all that…"

Morgessa pretended at innocence, "You didn't know? Baby, I'm a devout listener to the ways of the Lawgiver, truly and honestly, I swear!"

Kurt groaned, "I don't care half as much as Ma does. I just want you, in your naked glory, with kids or no, until I die, no lie!"

Morgessa kissed his arm, "So you love me then? And want to marry me and raise strong sons and cute little girls?"

Kurt nodded, "Yeah, if Ma approves …"

Morgessa slapped him, "What do you mean 'IF'? You either love me or not!"

Kurt protested, "What the bloody hell! Ya want me to be disowned and ostracized? You even know who my Ma is?"

Morgessa lied, "I don't care who she is! If you love me, you'll marry me!"

Kurt rubbed his cheek, "Damn! If you don't hit like she does, too! Malsain made her the burgess of this estate and the headmistress of the orphanage, more than twenty years ago! Her and me auntie got their positions from him!"

Morgessa probed further, "I hear a beast attacked the orphanage, and neither Malsain nor Kitra suffered so much as a scratch!"

Kurt bristled, "My ma is too old to make the trip every morning, she took on help to run things in her absence, and Malsain, I don't poke my nose in his business, I hear he's got a right nasty temper!"

Morgessa knew she hit a nerve, and intended to exploit it. "I also heard one of his apprentices was mauled by a beast, just like the orphans, and a farmer."

Kurt suspected something amiss, "What are you on about? You said you was a simple girl, just wanted kids and what not, ye gots a mighty keen interest in Ma and Malsain for some simple girl ..."

Morgessa lied again, "I meant humble, I'm a humble girl, just like the Lawgiver says we ought to be, humble and sweet ... and ..." Kurt was not convinced, "My ma ain't humble. You hit just like her, and ye not so sweet anymore! Yer just like all the rest! You just use me and leave me! Bitch!"

Morgessa crossed her arms, pretending to pout and sulk, turning her back to him. As Kurt got up to get himself a drink, she reached for a vase and cracked it over his head. Kurt fell unconscious. Morgessa then broke a couple more to give the illusion of a big struggle and overturned a chair, then she got dressed and exited the guest house, then broke a window with a rock. For all her efforts at stealth when leaving the property, she failed to notice a lone figure by starlight, returning from the lake, dressed in brown monk's robes. Morgessa whispered to herself, "Should have told Sandhaven I'd sooner die than seduce that clumsy oaf!"

Tyrus let his hood down, and announced his presence, "So who is Sandhaven, I might ask?"

Morgessa practically leaped out of her skin, eyes wide as saucers, spun around and fell backwards in fright.

"You stay away from me! You hear? Sandhaven is very powerful, and you'll be sorry if you touch me!" she declared as she drew forth a dagger from her bodice.

Tyrus took one step back, and produced the trident from under his robe, Morgessa gaped at it in horror. Tyrus feinted a thrust, making the girl jump, and before she could recover, struck the tines on the ground, causing her ears to ring painfully. Morgessa dropped the dagger, and clutched her ears in agony. Tyrus quickly kicked the dagger into the tall grass near the forest to the east of the road, and placed his steel grip on both of her wrists. Morgessa struggled to get free, but this stranger was stronger than anyone she knew.

Tyrus warned her, "You will tell me what I wish to know, or we shall find out exactly how well you can swim!"

His tone left no doubt that Tyrus could swim with total confidence, and that Morgessa would not enjoy the experience. She relented, "Sandhaven is the new Alpha Minor, in charge of the Lawgiver church. He plans to install Corbin Birchgrass as prince in place of Adam Silverlane. That's all I know, I swear!"

Tyrus corrected, "Really? I think not. To the lake, then!"

Morgessa pleaded, "No, wait! What else do you want to know?"

Tyrus probed, "Why has Kitra inherited the Mill Residence, when it was not Malsain's to give? Was she involved with their deaths?"

Morgessa sighed with relief. "I can help you, if you oppose Malsain. I don't know why Kitra got the estate, I swear. Kurt was going to tell me, but he doesn't trust me anymore. I'm telling the truth!"

Tyrus pressed on, "Who is Kurt?"

Morgessa got a suspicious look on her face. "Wait a minute! You know Malsain and Kitra but not Kurt? Who are you?"

Tyrus gave a guarded explanation, "I am from a faraway land, and Malsain has caused trouble for someone I am sworn to protect. Now tell me who Kurt is!"

The girl replied, "You really are from another land. Kitra is Kurt's mother! And he's right there, in that guest house, where I left him, the ass! I was just starting to like him, too."

Tyrus glanced at the entryway between the hedges, and a sign upon the small gate read: Twelve Marble Lane. Again, instinct told him there were vital clues here, and he had no idea what they were, or where they were hidden. But this was indeed the Mill property, adjacent to a couple vineyards.

Tyrus bowed, "Thank you. Perhaps you could introduce me to this Sandhaven fellow, and instruct me on the local customs."

Morgessa mused, "Maybe I could, and maybe I will."

Tyrus raised an eyebrow. "I knew a young lady even more stubborn than you are!"

Morgessa asked, "Where is she then? What happened?"

Tyrus regretted his remark, answering, "She bit off more trouble than any mortal can handle, is what happened. She is safe with her mother, which is all you need to know."

Morgessa suspected something, exactly what he could not tell. But she let it drop, and began walking toward town, and Tyrus had to play along for the moment. Until he could formulate a better plan.

* * *

When Jailor Esmund the Plain took his lunch break, Wayne called across the hall to Alex the Meek, "Fancy meeting you here. They say we are spies, but I have not spied anything worth talking about!"

Alex gave a weary reply, "Ha... Ha..."

Astrid in her adjacent cell said nothing; she was too weak from her ordeals down here. Alex did not ask about her bruises and tattered clothing, but instinctively he knew, from her downcast and melancholy expressions, that she was abused for someone's ego. Awkward silence fell over them for long minutes, and then Ognar the terrible came to sit at his post. Wayne thought to himself, he was spending a lot of time in captivity since being caught by the Elves and that the only place worse than here in the dungeons of Kozos he had seen up close was the blood arena of Black Falls. He sighed and attempted to sleep.

* * *

Tyton finally had some use of his arm, and led his team hobbling away from the ruins. Bodhan, Bhadran and Shankar were in worse shape, Vedanga was now buried near the pine trees, and Amala had to be carried on a litter. Off in the distance, away to the northwest, a tiny village became visible. They would rest there awhile, and decide later what to do. Tyton counted fifteen enemy bodies dead at the ruins yesterday, and there were a few who were known to have fled the scene. He could only hope that Axegrind would not be this difficult when the time was at hand.

* * *

"By your leave, milady, I wish to discover the fate of my grandson, and therefore resign my seat at council," declared Bravane the Elder.

"Permission granted, and thank you for your efforts here during your long exile, may your quest be to your satisfaction," Lady Ravenna answered. "Might I suggest you enlist help on this journey? Zara-Mogai is an unforgiving place, and Nug-Za is far to the Northern reaches of it. The crown will grant you a small sum for your years of service. Godspeed to both of you," she concluded.

Bravane the Elder bowed, "Thank you, milady, may your reign as right hand be satisfactory as well."

Ravenna gave a nod of thanks.

Darla Mae Copperhill appeared, kneeling in petition, "Begging your permission to lead the search of Franz Leon's quarters, milady. I have long suspected he was involved in the death of my own brother."

Ravenna nodded again. "You may. I hope your brother will find peace."

A herald stood near, awaiting his turn.

Darla bowed, "Thank you, Milady."

The herald spoke, "Your excellence, Jonah and the wizard have returned. Lebiced wishes audience with the crown, both of you."

Ravenna replied, "And he shall have it on the morrow! Thank you."

The herald bowed and saluted.

Now a middle-aged male peasant appeared, "On behalf of my family, madam, thank you for restoring justice to our town. Thank you from the bottom of our hearts."

Ravenna smiled, "I am glad to hear it. Here, a penny for your troubles." She gave him six pence and a leftover crust of bread.

The man wept with joy and kissed her feet. "We are honored, Lady Ravenna, by your gesture and ever so grateful."

Ravenna nodded once more before the close of court for the day.

Upon retiring toward the royal chambers to update her sister-in-law, three knights drew their swords to attack at the base of the grand staircase. Ravenna morphed into her bird form, and fled to the rafters, where she took human form again and summoned a gust of wind to blow out the lanterns, plunging the room into darkness. Then, honing in on the clanking of their armor, Ravenna fried them where they stood in a bolt of lightning. Ravenna morphed twice more to land at the top of the stairs.

"Well, Clark, wasting no time I see. You are a dead man next time we meet."

* * *

"Here, we will load some supplies into the wheelbarrow for our journey to Black Falls.

Kazius, you will lead the way. But I warn you, one false move will be your last," Garzon announced.

Kazius wanted to say he expected as much, but held his tongue, out of more respect than fear. For all his savagery, Garzon was a fair and honorable man. Kazius would have never believed the two could co-exist in one and the same person before this bizarre turn of events.

He dared not admit he actually admired that, for it was antithetical to who he once was.

The thought of what he used to be began to disgust him. The people hated him, his father used him, and only

Bernice had ever loved him. The woman who now carried his child and gave him hope. She had grown on him, and he actually loved her in turn after all they had been through together. Her love was everything now. But it was Garzon's code of honor that completed the template for his future, whatever lay ahead. He would meet his destiny as a man, and for once, he felt pride in his decision. He would take them to the narrow pass on the western face of the Iron Ridge Mountains. It was perilous to be sure, but unexpected for that reason. Axegrind was unlikely to have anything but token security there, which Garzon would make short work of. Onward they went, with Kazius holding his head high leading the way.

* * *

"YOU! How dare you show your face here, you bootlicking slime! You carried out the marching orders of Arius and helped enslave or bankrupt entire nations! I don't care what your real name is, and I don't care what your story is!" Belinda screamed at Tyton as he neared the outskirts of the village.

Tyton tested her, "Really? You were a Blackwolf yourself, before they switched sides. I know what they did to you, they boasted of it often. How they sold you out to Arius and the Bloodhammers, and I heard much later of your son. He is in charge there now, is he not?"

He had stepped onto thin ice by bringing that up, but it was true. Axegrind was her son, and the shame of it ran deeper than her hatred of the Blackwolves. "What does it matter now, you backstabber?" Belinda asked with a tone of resignation and despair. She had failed as a mother, her son stolen at a young age and raised by bullies. There could be no deeper wound for her, not even her slavery.

"Do you ever wonder what happened after the Raid of 1533 and the great fire in Oakthorn? I can tell you. Much has changed since then," Tyton added.

"Why should I care, and why should I trust you?" Belinda snarled.

Tyton began anyway, "Because you are haunted by your past, just as I am. The memory of your son gnaws at you. You have nightmares, I see it in your eyes. I have my own. I paid dearly for infiltrating the enemy and attempting to destroy them from within. I lost the love of my life long before Black Falls became my new home. Many times a year, I dream of her still. And every month, I see people in the flames begging for help. Some were beyond saving, and these people I dispatched to end their suffering. Until I was struck unconscious from behind and fell among the bodies of the slain. Everyone, even Arius himself believed me dead. I started over, SO CAN YOU."

At those last three words, Belinda broke down in sobs, "It's too much to bear ..."

Layla hugged her. "I had no idea how bad it was, you never told us this. My god..."

Belinda sniffed, "It was long before your capture, you were not even born yet."

Layla admonished her, "You are like a big sister to us, how could you think to keep this from us?"

Belinda had no answer but to look up with sad eyes.

Bhadran interrupted, "Sorry to intrude, but Amala needs tending, she has barely survived."

Tyton nodded, "Yes, of course, may we bring our wounded here? I can compensate you for the trouble."

Belinda weakly nodded yes.

Tyton bowed, "Thank you."

The villagers quickly helped with the litter, and Tyton's other brethren limped behind them. Belinda took a breath and followed. She was bewildered and exhausted, but also felt a great weight had been lifted from her. She was not quite so alone as she had believed.

* * *

D'aarzane shambled weakly into the cavern where his master Arius sat meditating with a frosted black globe of polished opal. The rogue's mask had fallen off and his uniform hung loose on a now withered frame, his skin looking ancient in years. "I found Barton, destroyed in Valantir … I could not undo it. The backlash is … destroying … me …" he declared as he slumped to his hands and knees. Arius probed the magical aura surrounding his senior assassin, and it was true; some godlike power had accelerated his metabolism beyond all hope. The very elixirs in his blood that gave the man such deadly speed were now augmented such that his body ate itself faster than he could acquire food to replenish it. A spell custom made for D'aarzane alone, which no mortal could have designed. "Barton... was... a... demon..." were his final words before the assassin died.

Arius roared in horrible fury, with such vehemence that the cavern shook and all his chaos fanatics fled for their lives. Fireballs sped down the tunnels and claimed three of them. Dozens escaped with smoldering robes.

"What... *godling* has done this to me!" Arius queried to the empty air.

Arius felt anew the crushing abandonment of his youth. His mother Helga Mollenbeck died giving birth in 1513, his father fled to lands unknown, leaving him with his uncle Elbert Mollenbeck and Grandfather Roland. Elbert died in the battle of Shadval in 1540, as did Elbert's son Edgar, and Arius's wife Lorenna. While Roland died earlier in 1529 of a hunting accident.

Arius overturned several tables, bookcases, bookstands, threw his opal globe in rage and cracked it against the cavern walls, and roared again. Then he incinerated the body of D'aarzane. Arius raged for hours until utterly spent. Hundreds of books and scrolls lay burnt, dozens of tablecloths and tapestries, and Arius himself crumpled into a kneeling position, rocking back and forth, mumbling incoherently. Were he still mortal, he would have drunk himself to death. The only escape left to him was meditation. He probed and stirred the ashes of his servant, and bent his will to deciphering who cast the spell, and the same energies that created the dome around Oakthorn exploded in his face, propelling him backwards into the stalagmites with such force they shattered. One fact and one fact only, he gleaned from this event. The originator of the two spells was one and the same enemy, and this enemy was powerful beyond even Arius's dreams. And for once in many decades, Arius again knew the icy chill of fear. And fear was a dangerous thing in a stone cold, psychotic narcissist such as he.

* * *

Thomas and his two charges had secured a pony, and were traveling into the eastern border of Korath when two bandits appeared, drunk and thinking this man with two girls was an easy mark. How wrong they were. Thomas gave a twist in the middle of his walking staff, and the twelve silver studs raised out of their sockets. As Thomas struck the man on his left in the leg, an arc of electricity played on the man's trousers, making him fall and jerk like a fish out of water. A high blow to the man on the right in the shoulder did the same. Thomas twisted the staff again in the other direction, and the studs clicked back into their housing. "Designed for the wolf, that was, but effective on ordinary enemies as well. Just hope it has enough charge to get the job done," he told the girls. Carol and Molly both nodded.

Chapter Forty-Nine
Dirty Laundry

"Well, well, well, if it's not our old pal Adrian! Must be out of your bloomin' mind, crossing the desert by yourself!" declared a scruffy pirate near the treeline of Pirate's Marsh, situated about midway between the fishing village of dirt, and the fortress of Black Falls. Adrian could not speak with his parched throat, and motioned for a canteen.

"Oh, the poor lad wants water, do he? Whaddaya say, boys? Yea or nay?" the leader asked. The men all guffawed, and one said, "Charge him full price for a sip! What's that, 300 hunnerd percent markup? HAHAHA!"

Adrian gave a sarcastic half smile and the one finger salute.

"He gots hard feelings now, tsk tsk, the poor lad must have pissed off the locals or gambled all his winnings again," the leader taunted.

Adrian marched up to him and grabbed for the canteen, which the leader held away out of reach. Adrian was the shorter man, and near to collapsing from dehydration.

One pirate took pity as he tossed a waterskin, "Fine, ya beggar! Can't stand this pathetic look no more! Here!"

Adrian snatched it out of the air like a dying man, chugged his first three gulps; and then drank slowly until he was sated. After a couple of minutes, he spoke, "There's a party … of men … marching toward Black Falls … their leader … wants to find the children … been attacking the Syndicate …"

The band started arguing about AxeGrind and centaurs and this monster named Garzon, at which point Adrian boasted, "I met him and lived to tell about it! I just escaped from him!"

The leader clapped him on the back, "Aye, that's wot yer best at, RUNNING!"

The men nearly died laughing. Adrian scowled. Then a few took turns punching Adrian in the shoulder. "Wussy landlubber! C'mon, we gots rum and wenches that will knock you on yer arse!"

Adrian decided to play along in case they meant it.

* * *

"You summoned me, milady?" Amanda Redoak inquired with her head bowed.

Lady Ravenna nodded, "I have indeed. Did your cousin or uncle say anything about their quest?"

Amanda shook her head. "Very little, milady. My cousin Bravane has a pained and embarrassed expression whenever I am near. I do not understand what has happened."

Ravenna mused, "Whatever it is will wait. But with so many empty council seats, it is time to fill them. Some of the knights have complained of your protests concerning the refugees. This is precisely the kind of voice we need in council to end the stalemates that prevailed in the past, you could also speak for Oakthorn. Do you accept?"

Lady Amanda stammered, "Me? I don't have much experience in councils, and have only been deputy Mayor a very short time ..."

Ravenna corrected, "No matter, you have a skilled wit, a stout heart and you care about the people. Too long has the council been corrupted by ambitions and greed. We need you."

Amanda bowed on both knees, prostrated, "I am humbled and honored, Milady, I shall pray I am worthy of the task."

Ravenna smiled warmly. "Good. We shall dine tonight to celebrate. And have you fitted for a wardrobe."

Amanda bowed again, "Thank you, milady."

Ravenna snapped her fingers twice, and one of the Goldcrest Knights answered. "Amanda is now to be escorted, under your protection."

The knight nodded and saluted, "Yes, Your Highness."

Ravenna gave a single nod. "Thank you both."

* * *

"Well, we must part ways for a while, I am no closer to finding my wife than when you hired us, sir. But I am honored to know thee." Skorvald admitted, with his hands on Jonah's shoulders.

Jonah gave a sad half smile.

"Good fortune to you, I am glad to know you also. Where will you go?"

Skorvald grinned. "We will try the northern regions again, and accompany your Baron. The Syndicate is very active in Zara-Mogai. Whether we find loose tongues is another matter."

Jonah nodded and bowed.

Skorvald saluted in turn, to Jonah, Lebiced, Lady Bethany and little Devi.

Lebiced then spoke, "I too, will have business elsewhere. After meeting with Ravenna, I must return home to confer with my peers. Our work is never done."

Jonah took his hand. "Thank you for all your help."

Bethany was starting to show in the midsection and holding her belly with one hand while cradling Jacob with the other. Nell was there, too. Not long afterwards, as Bravane the Elder and Bravane the Younger, plus Skorvald and his men, left the front gate, Conrad arrived to see them off, startled to see the Baron and Bravane the Elder in close proximity and in outwardly peaceful relations.

"Do my eyes deceive me? Or is this ..." he began.

Bravane the Younger interceded, "No, my friend, your eyes are fine. It is a long story. I have learned that I have a son, and we are making a journey to find him. I am embarrassed to say, the mother is Winter Auguron. I did not know the name until Lady Ravenna told me. And no, this is not something I would have done sober."

Conrad was stunned almost speechless. "But, how..."

Bravane waved his hand, "Time is short, we must be off. But congratulations! You are going to be an uncle again!"

Now Conrad sat in the saddle, his mouth unable to form coherent speech. And he remained thus, watching his friend and cousin fade into the West, making for Xantir and then Iglar, to traverse the Narrow Pass from Bal Dar into Zara-Mogai. Then, with a heart full of doubts and bad memories, Conrad turned to enter the city of West Bend as the sun began to set. At least here, a few men still recognized him as the great grandson of James Redmane, who fought alongside King Reginald Goldlion and Prince Andrew Goldlion almost a century ago, against the invading forces of Izimal. While most commonfolk here paid him no mind at all. In his heart, there was no returning to Oakthorn. His parents were both gone, half the barony was ruined, and the other half filled with gossipy rumormongers, betrayers and bitterness. And yet, his journey was not over yet. He had come here to say his goodbyes, and his melancholy was consuming him.

* * *

Amala, Vidur and Vasanti were still in poor condition, and unable to fight effectively.

Tyton did not want to leave them behind, but their enemies were still out there, either waiting in ambush, or taking refuge. On the reports of his people, Tyton concluded refuge was the more likely, due to the enemies' injuries. Tyton would need to rely on just Prasad and Bhadran to complete the mission. He confided to Belinda, "More assassins are still at large, and I have to stop them. Injured arm or no."

Belinda said nothing. Outwardly, she was stoic, but inside, her thoughts were at war. She just shrugged and walked away.

Layla whispered, "I've never seen her like this. She has always been the strong one."

Tyton nodded once with a palm up, suggesting to leave the topic be. He went to gather Prasad and Bhadran. "We need to go, we will return for the others when we can. Raj must not roam free to prey on more innocent people."

Prasad and Bhadran nodded in agreement. Within the hour, they were supplied with provisions for a more careful journey. Tyton would not run them to exhaustion a second time.

* * *

"Father, I have met a foreigner who opposes Malsain, he is waiting outside. He is stronger than even Ogun, I would not have believed it possible for one of his size," Morgessa reported.

Sandhaven stroked his whiskers. "Be careful, my dear, foreigners can be treacherous."

Morgessa chimed, "He seems honorable enough."

The Father scowled, "Even more reason, if his faith differs from ours in even the slightest. What do you know of him?"

Morgessa began to doubt if she should tell him, "Well, he wears the cloth, and is well-mannered ..."

Sandhaven prodded, "Is your faith wavering, young one?"

Morgessa composed herself, "And what if it is? Frederic and Otto are not so different ..."

Sandhaven bit the hook. "Frederic can still be molded, and is loyal like Stuart was. You, however, had best be careful ... do not let this foreigner put ideas in your head."

Morgessa frowned and bowed, then left the hall. Sandhaven instructed Walter the sullen to keep an eye on Morgessa. "And report only to me." Walter shrugged and bowed.

Outside, Morgessa found Tyrus pacing the gardens. "The Father says to not trust foreigners. But I've never been appreciated here for all I do. The only women to be rewarded for their loyalty are hard and cruel like Kitra and

Karina. Do you think women are born sinful?" Morgessa asked.

Tyrus raised an eyebrow. "Why do you ask me this?"

Morgessa whispered, "I felt loved by Kurt, before he deferred to his mother's authority, and I feel bad for betraying him to Sandhaven. How can love be sinful, and betrayal for a cold and hard man be good? Men who love and hate women in the same breath ..."

Tyrus deflected, "These things I cannot answer. I am a man of action, you need a sage."

Morgessa gave a sad dejected look.

Tyrus added, "The things you seek are not found in this Kingdom, I fear."

* * *

"What do you mean, they are dead? How?" Clark demanded of his servant.

"Their armor was discolored, and their flesh burnt to a crisp, sir," the man replied.

Clark shoved at him, "Get out of my sight! Go!"

Clark paced his carpet furiously. "First the Lawgivers tell me she died in a cabin fire, and now this! They are all unreliable, doddering fools! Like all the deluded commoners, blind, begging, stupid and pathetic sheep!"

Clark kicked over several chairs. "Confounded witch! I had the council right where I wanted! Bickering and stalemated while their rightful masters gathered power and influence! I'll show her! I'll show all of you!"

A blackbird descended from the rafters, and took human form. "I expected as much from an Alpha, you leech!" Ravenna announced, just before she fried Clark with a lightning bolt. "You were indeed the most slippery and dangerous. Now you will serve as a message," she hissed before taking wing again.

The servant opened the door to the dining hall after hearing a noise, and stood aghast at the sight of Clark's smoking corpse. He soon ran to fetch others and clean up, pretending nothing happened, as few would hire them as servants now. No, they would keep a charade going until the money was exhausted.

* * *

Conrad strode into a tavern named the Cider Barrel and ordered a pitcher of their strongest mead. Talk in the town about his distinctive armor had already reached the market section, where Lady Bethany asked familiar faces for more details. Conrad was on his third tankard when she finally found him. "Brother! Why did you not let us know you had arrived?" she pleaded.

"I came to say goodbye. I have had all I can ever stand of Oakthorn and spiteful commoners dragging my name through their pig filth. And I have no happiness here either, I've been given a quest to go to Xantir. Mother talks to me now. And other people you would never believe. My life is cursed, Bethany. Is it wrong for me to want to abandon a quest for a chance at a happy day before Arius destroys us all?"

Bethany's eyes went wide in shock; this was so unlike her brother. "Wait, you say Mother talks to you? What did she say? What quest? What happened to you?" She babbled.

"Mother warned me about the ghouls. Do you remember when the fevers began?" Conrad tested.

Bethany nodded. "Yes, of course I remember; that was just before the thunderstorm in September. What does that have to do with ghouls?"

Conrad explained, "When I was in Shadval, I fought ghouls down there, they gave the same foul odor as that fever. And the people who died of the fever, came back as ghouls; ALL of them."

Lady Bethany fell backwards into an empty chair, "Oh, dear Gods..."

Conrad poured himself another drink. "Oh, yes," he continued, "And the commonfolk of our scorched Barony have no idea of the horrors I fought on THEIR behalf, they just look at me the same way Eledar did... well, piss on them all, I'm done!"

Bethany took his hand, "I'm so sorry. I remember the funeral. You deserved better."

Conrad took a gulp, wiped his beard, and exclaimed "Damned right I did!"

Bethany tugged at his hand, "There's someone here who would be overjoyed to see you."

Conrad began to slur, "An' who might that be?"

Bethany jabbed him in the shoulder. "You big oaf! It's Rebecca! She loves you, I've seen it in her eyes."

Conrad had a bewildered look. "Wait, the barmaid? You sure?" His memory was fuzzy at the moment.

"Yes, I'm sure, go see her before you leave on this quest of yours," his sister suggested.

Conrad mumbled, "I did not say what my decision was …"

Bethany rolled her eyes, "Brother, I know you better than you know yourself. Even if Oakthorn has done you wrong, and even if West Bend got corrupted by these Lawgiver zealots, Stonehaven still needs you, and you have long prided yourself on Redmane honor. It's like your great grandfather James would say: 'Honor must prevail' and so it shall!"

Conrad rubbed his eyes, and shook his head. "So much for drinking in peace," he groaned with a touch of sarcasm.

Bethany answered with disdain, "Have it your way then, brother, you shall have your peace!" as she turned to leave in anger.

Conrad regretted his remark at once, but had not the presence of mind to undo it. He got up to pay his bill, leaving the rest of his mead untouched, and walked somewhat unsteadily toward the door. "A fine kettle of fish this is …" He sighed in sad resignation.

* * *

"Now, what does your nose tell you?" a voice asked in Tyrianna's head.

"I smell oil on a blade, and I smell animal fur, and mothballs," the teenage girl replied out loud.

"Yes, and what do you feel?" the voice continued.

"I feel a breeze from over the water, and sunlight, and a tremor in the earth… what is it?" Tyrianna inquired.

"A storm rages south of here. We are out of its path, but we have just identified your strengths. You are not as blind as you thought, and in time, you may even recover a small portion of what you lost. The Gods have regenerative powers beyond that of mortals, and you are half mortal, never forget that," her mother answered.

"Will I see again?" Tyrianna begged.

"You may, but not as before. You will still require your other senses to compensate. This is the way of all wisdom, paid for by experience and by the will. Our decisions bear fruit, and not all of it is sweet. There is no other way to it," Syrene advised.

The daughter wept. "I am sorry I did not listen before, I…"

Syrene took her daughter's face in her palms, and kissed her forehead, "I know, my child. I know. Many centuries ago, I was young, too, and twice as stubborn."

Tyrianna hugged her mother and smiled. Love and hope had returned at last.

* * *

"The season of greatest snowfall is almost upon us, you only have but a few days before the secret path to Gamble Pass will be blocked off. Since the Syndicate has put a price on all of you, every mercenary in Kozo-Makan will be after you. The honored brethren of the silver lotus cannot hide you long, there is no safe place in this land, you must go very soon," the woodcarver told Rachel and the centaurs. "We value our friendship with yourself and the Icefang Alliance of Nordranaya, but we cannot promise protection against two companies of mercenaries. I beg your forgiveness," he added with a nod, a bow and supplicating hands.

Rachel asked, "What about the tunnels into the mountain?"

Chen Li Pao shook his head no. "Tunnels made for short people, not for tall centaurs, I am most sorry."

Rachel nodded, "We appreciate your providing shelter and food until our wounded could recover. Thank you, we shall not forget."

Chen Li Pao bowed again. "Remember, turn west at the pass, and we hope you arrive safely in the land of Karn. Do not trust the people of Korath, we hear the Syndicate does much business down there, many children and slaves pass its borders in all directions. Bad place for you."

Rachel inquired, "Do you know of the poachers?"

Chen Li Pao shrugged. "Many, many, poachers, give tributes to Syndicate in return for protection. Money goes west to Zara-Mogai and to Syndicate controlled towns in Agama. This all I know."

Rachel took his hand, "Thank you. We owe you."

Chen scoffed, "Owe nothing, we are even."

The Woman Rachel Longarrow bowed and mounted on the back of Brenathea, the bridemare of Xandannus as she announced, "Northwind Nomads, let's ride!"

* * *

After council, Lady Amanda spoke with Ravenna in private, "I am grateful for the confidence and the stipend provided, but I wonder how my people will last until spring..."

Lady Ravenna smiled. "I have a solution for that, they can all stay in Vamanastral's old mansion, and once a week, they shall dine here as guests and I will call it the good will feast. More than that shall have to wait."

Amanda bowed. "Thank you, on their behalf and my own. We are grateful."

Ravenna nodded, "It is my duty to our people. And as Lebiced would say, 'Our duty to lead by example. Xantir will not remain free if Tyranny exists everywhere else, therefore we must preserve our history and knowledge so others may free themselves.' Many people wonder how all of Xantir is sovereign, and yet exist in peace. It was not always so. It began as a breakaway from the Empire of Itana which is now fragmented."

Amanda bowed again. "Yes, as my family well remembers."

Ravenna blushed. "Of course, pardon my error ..."

* * *

"Father, I have followed the girl as you commanded, and I heard them speak in cryptic riddles. She defers to this outlander you warned about. What is to be done?" asked Walter the Sullen.

Sandhaven answered, "Then we must isolate her from the church, no Lawgiver is to speak with her ever again. <u>Not even</u> her relatives, under penalty of disgrace."

Walter bowed and nodded. "Yes, Father. It shall be done as you instruct. How else may I serve?"

Sandhaven mused a moment. "Learn all there is to know about this foreigner. Where he sleeps, what he eats, how he moves, everything!"

Walter bowed again. "I will."

* * *

"I sent for two dozen southland assassins and you bring only the THREE of you?

"Explain yourself, Raj! I do not accept failures nor excuses!" barked Axegrind.

Raj prostrated on his knees. "The temple assassins of Kali chased us down, somehow they knew about us, some old blind man ratted us out, and..."

Axegrind interrupted, "Your enemies are YOUR problem, as for MY problem what to do with you, I will give you one more chance to prove yourselves, IN THE ARENA! Away with them!"

Raj begged, "Wait! Some of the Temple has survived! Their leader is still after us! You need us!"

Axegrind scoffed, "We will see about that! I think you have it backwards..."

Several Bloodhammers grabbed the three assassins and dragged them away.

Axegrind called after them, "The one armed man goes first!"

Raj protested, "Udai will make you eat those words!"

Axegrind countered, "Perhaps, but I look forward to his attempt, I've not had decent entertainment since the last minstrel choked on his dinner!"

His henchmen cackled with drunken stupor.

* * *

A farmer heard the squeal of pigs in distress, and raced to their pen with his pitchfork, only to stop dead in his tracks when he was close enough in the dim light of sunset to see what the matter was. A bipedal monster with the head of a wolf knelt over a fresh kill gorging itself on pig flesh.

"G-g-go away, w-we d-don't need trouble around these parts, n-now back off and leave us alone, you hell-spawn, I command you in the name of..." the farmer began.

One leap, and the beast was upon him, swatting the pitchfork out of his hands and landing with all fours on his adversary. The farmer raised his arms to protect his head and neck, but his belly was vulnerable. The were-beast thrust his claws deep and ripped the ribcage apart, and removed the doomed farmer's heart, still beating. The monster then ate it before returning to the pig, dragging it away from the town of Kozos toward the mountains.

An hour later, the wife called out, "Wally, get in here an' put the kids to bed, it's ... AHHHH! NO-oooo-oooooo! The beast is back! He took my Wally!"

And within minutes, the entire town was on high alert again. Tyrus showed up to inspect the body, and the savagery of the attack stunned even him. He called out, "All of you, stay in your homes, the beast that did this is more than any of you can stand against! GO! Now!"

They knew not who Tyrus was, but they obeyed. The truth of his words and his tone of authority were enough. But the knights who appeared to inspect the ruckus took exception to his tone.

"Who do you think you are? This is OUR Job! A man of the cloth should have fetched Sandhaven and then left well enough alone matters that are not in his circle of influence!" the obese Knight barked.

Tyrus retorted, "There's no time for this! Out of my way!" as he punched them square in the chest and knocked them twenty feet backwards to the complete astonishment of all still present. Tyrus sped after the tracks of the monster in the failing light of the evening, until he was deep in the shadows of the foothills, following the scent of blood and the traces of heat rising from the footprints.

The knights struggled to get up, but had to take their armor off first, the dents were interfering with their breathing. Upon inspection of the chest-plates, they remarked, "Who the devil was that? Never seen a bare fist do that EVER!"

* * *

Kazius still led the way up the winding narrow mountain path, but as the wind got colder, and the sky dimmer, he called behind him, "There's a cavern not far from here, around the next couple bends on the trail, we'd best make camp there."

Garzon warned, "No tricks, or it will be your last."

Kazius sighed. "I know you don't trust me, but it's no trick. Just watch for the animals up here. There will not be any sentries for another day or two."

Garzon laughed. "You have it wrong. The animals need to watch out for ME."

Kazius rolled his eyes. "Of course, how silly of me."

Sal made no comment, and the women made stifled nervous giggles. It was another hour before they found the cave, by which time everyone but Garzon was shivering.

They had been forced to leave the wheelbarrow behind long ago, as the path was too narrow and twisted to steer it effectively. Garzon had broken it down for the wood, and everyone was glad he did. On his third attempt, he struck some sparks on some dry bits of straw and oatmeal, and began to smolder. He nursed the fire enough to throw the wood on, but it was only enough for a single night. Their situation could not be helped. Deeper in the cave, they could smell they were not alone, either. Everyone but Garzon huddled for both warmth and safety. Something lived here, and it knew they were here.

* * *

A cloaked and hooded female ambled toward the crowded bar at the Sleepy Mermaid Inn, whispered to the innkeeper, who pointed upstairs after accepting two silver coins. The woman bowed, and retired right away to the upper stories. She counted the doors on the right, until the seventh, and then knocked three times.

A grumbling voice asked, "Who is it?"

The lady replied, "A woman who loves you."

She then heard footsteps, and the clicking of the latch.

The door opened, and Conrad squinted through the gap.

Rebecca let down her hood, "See? It is I, as I said."

Conrad took her hand and allowed her in. No sooner had he closed and locked the door, then they met in a searing kiss with their arms entwined. They moved, inch by inch, closer to the bed, her hands woven into his hair, and Conrad's hands feeling her waist under her dress. They tumbled onto the bed, with Rebecca on top. Conrad hooked his fingers under her lacy briefs, and worked them down as Rebecca unclasped her cloak and let it fall. She worked her legs out of the briefs, and then settled her skirts over Conrad as he yanked his nightclothes off. Conrad felt her wetness sliding against him, and his passion grew. Rebecca snuck a hand under and guided him in. Conrad unlaced her top to free her breasts, and suckled them as Rebecca took his phallus all the way inside her. She moaned happily, "Ahh, yes, my love, how I have wanted you there for many moons."

As he sunk to the hilt inside her wet folds, Conrad sighed with both relief and hunger, and buried his face in her cleavage. Rebecca bucked on top of him, and giggled. They kissed some more, and Conrad rolled on top. He took an easy pace at first, but in minutes, he was consumed with desire, and bucked harder. Rebecca hummed in surrender to him, wrapping her legs around his waist, embracing his hunger with her own. "Yes, love, take me now, claim me, and promise to return soon. Do it, finish inside me, I want to feel your glory, and look in your eyes when you spill your seed. Want us together always, with fine children on our knees, and a warm hearth to call home..." she whispered to him in her most sultry voice.

He lifted her legs over his shoulders and dove in harder, his breaths fast and shallow as he moaned, "Oh gods, so close..."

Rebecca cooed, "Yes, so big and full ..." as she began to convulse and quiver under him, sending him over the edge.

He thrust all the way in and emptied his essence deep inside with many grunts of bliss. Conrad crumpled on top of his new love, and sighed, "Ohhh, such a wonderful catch you are, I am most grateful, milady."

Rebecca teased, "Shut up and kiss me."

He did.

* * *

"Who are those dark-skinned bandits cutting across the marsh? They move like phantoms and carry more weapons than I've ever seen!" hissed Adrian to the pirates nearby.

Club-leg Fred whispered back: "Looks like more Southland assassins, on their way to Black Falls, I reckon. No concern of ours. We don't pry in Axegrind's business so long as we get paid for the cargo. Speakin' o' which, ye oughts be earnin' yer keep about now, ya scurvy pup!"

Adrian rolled his eyes, "Gods, forget I asked ..."

Fred lost his temper, "Well excuse us ugly pirates for expecting work outta some worthless, two-faced, greedy merchant who left a bastard behind in West Bend after ordering a hit on the whelps' grandfather Ugval! Even for the syndicate, that's pretty low, you slimy wet dog!"

Adrian lunged at him to strangle the old codger, and they fell into the shallows of the Marsh, venting their pent up resentments and misgivings. Away to the Northwest, the sounds of their conflict had alerted Tyton, Prasad and Bhadran to their presence. Tyton gave the signal to fan out and assess the value or threat level of the combatants. Fred was at a disadvantage with his club leg, and Adrian was not a lightweight.

The other six pirates were taking bets on the fight, and did not see the assassins returning. Adrian was slugging away with both fists, and Fred was pinned. In desperation, he threw mud in Adrian's face. As Adrian brought his hands up to wipe it off, Fred tugged at his shirt and yanked Adrian to his right and rolled on top to return the same treatment. Adrian grabbed him and did a badly executed headbutt that left them both dazed.

Three of the pirates suddenly found knives at their throats, and the other three still standing hesitated to do anything. Tyton spoke, "Drop your weapons, and keep your hands up. Slowly, or your friends are dead."

Adrian mumbled, "This is your fault, Fred!"

Fred kicked him in the jimmies for that.

Tyton ordered, "You two will cease, and shut up!"

Adrian wheezed, "What do I care? They don't matter to me..."

Fred spat, "We just fed your worthless hide and gave you water and wenches..."

Tyton finger jabbed one pirate's neck and threw his dagger hilt first at Adrian, knocking him out cold.

Fred winced, "Well now, thanks for that..."

Tyton commanded, "Your names, NOW."

Fred pouted and complied, "That there is Adrian, no-good greedy ass merchant from hell's rectum..."

Tyton K.O.ed another pirate to make his point.

Fred chuckled nervously, "Right. These guys call me Club-leg Fred, this is Rat-fink, Salty Jack, Dog Hump, Pork rind, Whiskey Jim, and Sourpuss."

Tyton pressed, "What manner of pirates are you?"

Fred answered, "We ship cargo for the Syndicate, fresh fruits to Razadur from the Dabani plains and the Bazu pines, and rubies from Razadur to the Dabani post where it travels overland to Maza, then through Talos to Kozo Makan. We don't ship any slaves in the Dabani gulf or the Vaja Strait. That's all done on the West end of Razadur or else up north of Korath."

"If that was all you transport, you would not be pirates," Tyton stated matter of factly.

"Okay, so we handle Opium sometimes... the poppies grow in Izimal, and ship from the port city of Zamul to the Red Keep where they go overland to either the fishing village or here. Can we go now?" Tyton glanced at Prasad and gave a slight nod. They jabbed two more pirates who fell unconscious, and Fred limped away as fast as he could. Jim and Jack fell to their knees, "We don't want any trouble..."

Tyton then told the others, "Tie them up. Take all their blades and any powder they carry."

Minutes later, when the three of them were beyond earshot, Tyton whispered, "Bhadran, I need you to return to the village and safeguard the others if the Syndicate makes an appearance."

Bhadran nodded. "May your mission go well."

Tyton bowed. They rearranged their equipment to account for change in circumstances, and then went their separate ways again. Tyton was not pleased with the past few days at all, and was saving up all of his rage for Raj. The man who killed Sidhuri.

* * *

"Bad news, Father. Walter the Sullen is dead. Some horrible beast got him and ate his heart, and one of your new people I never saw before, dented our armor so bad with his bare hands, the smith said it took five hammer strokes to bend 'em back, bruised us pretty bad, too. He gave chase to this creature, but nobody seen or heard either one since," said one of Nathan's knights.

"This must be the one Morgessa spoke about, for I have not recruited such a man.

Thank you for bringing this to my attention," Sandhaven said with a nod of his head.

After the Knight left, Sandhaven waited a minute before following. He found Nathan himself once again within the academy, and called to him, "Your Kingship, I wish an audience with you."

Nathan grumbled, "What now?"

Sandhaven stated his case, "I believe we have a solution to the Malsain problem. A very strong and resourceful outlander with a sense of honor. He has no fear of him, and I know someone he seems to care about. We can use this to our advantage, you and I."

Nathan gave a gruff reply: "Why would I care about Malsain? He's old news."

Sandhaven ignored Nathan's tone, "Because Malsain is the Were-beast responsible for both the Cloverhill murders of 1509, and the deaths of the Mill family who were about to expose him. He is the one who damaged your orphanage, and cost you many children. Did you really think your connection to the Syndicate was a well-kept secret? You are a patron after all..."

Nathan clenched his fists, "How DARE you take that attitude in front of... of... HIM!"

Corbin was in shock.

Sandhaven chided, "Come now, if he is to wield power one day, he must come to terms with unpleasant realities. Malsain was up to his neck in the slave trade, and you are in it to the *hip*."

Nathan bristled at the double meaning meant for his ears alone.

Corbin begged, "What does he mean, Father? Are we..."

Nathan nudged him out of the room, "Not another word, go practice your archery."

Corbin pleaded, "But..."

Nathan hissed, "NOW."

Corbin shuffled away dejectedly.

Nathan slammed the door. "Are you blackmailing me?"

Sandhaven demurred, "I've been known to use such strategies, but no. Let us be plain."

Nathan begrudgingly agreed, "Yes, LETS."

Sandhaven continued, "We need each other. The Mollenbecks wield considerable influence within the

Alpha Clan, much more than you ever will. Marcy will not hesitate to use that in her favor. Malsain only wants Adam, the boy is pliable to his will. He wants power the same as we do. The Cloverhills hate Malsain more than anyone, they know, and have kept it secret. The truth would hurt all of the Lawgivers and expose the Alphas. And trust me on this, if the Alphas did not need you, then you would never know we existed. Need I explain further?"

Nathan hissed, "Yes."

"If we encouraged a conflict between Malsain and an ignorant outlander, the Lawgivers and Alphas could emerge blameless. You may even win some support from the Cloverhills, however unlikely. I have use of Corbin, Marcy will not. We are on the same side here," Sandhaven suggested.

Nathan grumbled, "So you say and wish me to believe..."

Sandhaven relented, "Fair enough. But think on this: how much time do you have? Rebellion is brewing among the people, you need allies. Mark my word, Marcy is resourceful and determined, she will not wait. If I know about the woman you keep in the dungeon for your appetites, there is a fair chance that the Mollenbecks, and Marcy, also know. Time is not with you, my King. You must decide, and soon. Corbin's future may depend on it. As well as your own."

On those words, Sandhaven bowed and left.

* * *

Tyrus returned to the town exhausted, and morose. He was greeted by Morgessa, "What happened? Did you get him?"

Tyrus shook his head no. "There was nothing for me to follow once he reached the riverbed; no scent, no thermal traces, he got away."

Morgessa tried to comfort him, "I'm sorry." But her words could not get past his hurt pride. She took his hand, and he pulled away, "Please stop. You are a beautiful woman, but I will not be satisfied until Malsain is put out of his misery."

Morgessa ran away in tears. Tyrus complained aloud bitterly: "Is there no reward for honor left? Must I be tormented so? Failing my duty thus, not once, not twice, but many times?"

His melancholy voice echoed far away in a cavern, his face fading within a crystal ball between four hands, mother and daughter. "I did not know before, that he carries such weight on his shoulders... I treated him so badly... I..." The mother interrupted, "Focus, little one, reach the stillness below the churning waves, and listen."

Tyrianna did as she asked, reaching down into her core, her breathing slower and slower, searching out she knew not what. Long minutes drifted by, and then, she heard a pulse.

Tyrianna strained to identify its source.

"Gently, don't force it," Syrene advised. The girl repeated the process, reaching into her core, and soon heard another pulse; strong, ancient, pervading all around and within. It was the planet itself.

"Now, marry your thoughts to it... and reach out to him on that wave." Tyrus fell to his knees in wide-eyed shock. "Tyri?"

She willed the words, "Yes, it's me. I don't blame you for what happened. You've done so much for me all these years, and I treated you badly for it, I'm sorry. I ... wait, something is wrong..."

Tyrus panicked, "Tyri? TYRI!"

The connection was broken. Tyrus ran to the woods in his rage, cursing loudly, and kept going until his second wind was utterly spent. And he fell into a dreamless slumber.

Chapter Fifty
Landfall

Two voices thundered at the watery entrance to the cavern: "WHERE is Father? What have you done with him, witch!"

Syrene put a finger over her daughter's lips and whispered in her head, "Your enraged half-brothers have come knocking, we are leaving now. Come."

In a flash they were gone. In retaliation, the two sons leveled the entire island, by fire and flood and angry quakes that sent thirty foot waves in all directions across the winding sea, toward Agama first and foremost, then Stonehaven, Izimal, Mojara, Razadur and Valantir. Many ships and ports were damaged or destroyed. And still, the twins went seeking revenge, combing the oceans and conjuring great storms in their fruitless search for Syrene and Tyrianna.

* * *

Conrad kissed Rebecca goodbye one more time, "I shall return, Love, this I swear."

Rebecca taunted with a sly grin, "I will hold you to that, and more, Captain."

Conrad held her hand tenderly and winked at her as he turned to mount his new horse.

"Send letters!" she called after him as he cantered toward the gates.

He called back, "I will! Often!"

Then they blew kisses from afar, and he faded from sight.

"Well, I'm glad you improved his mood," said Lady Bethany.

"He's had a sad life, I'm sorry you two had words. I don't think he really meant them," Rebecca replied.

Bethany huffed, "The brother I know is very honest when drunk. I'm rather certain he did mean them, but enough of that, I couldn't bring myself to punish you for my brother's moods."

"Thank you for telling me, it would have crushed me to hear he left without saying goodbye," said Rebecca.

Bethany simply nodded and weakly smiled, not wanting to dwell on the subject any longer. They both returned to Vamanastral's Mansion as more snow began to fall.

* * *

"What purpose you summon me for?" asked the cantankerous Gizrog, goblin war chief of the gutripper clan.

Arius glared at him, "You will assemble the other war chiefs for a renewed campaign against Valantir, they are weakened from their losses, and must be laid low while the opportunity exists."

Gizrog protested, "You promised us victory last time, we burned like moss on hot coals; TWICE we did. Gizrog not like burning."

Arius let loose a fireball that consumed Gizrog's 2nd in command, and twelve other goblins. "I can arrange the same fate or worse for the rest of you knuckle dragging, worthless vermin! You will march or die horribly!"

Gizrog gulped, "Why we die for you? You no care about goblins, ever. You hates us, we hates you. No land for goblins but here, forever hunted elsewhere. We do this for you, we want land of our own..."

Arius levitated Gizrog over a stalagmite, "The only land you will get is your GRAVE, you sniveling upstart!!!! You will obey or I will destroy each and every last one of you!!!"

Gizrog relented, "We obey. But not forget."

Arius hurled the Goblin into the wall, "See that you do, or I will have the Dragons hunt you to extinction, *pawn*!"

Gizrog scurried away without further comment. Arius paced alone in circles amidst broken furniture and burned tapestries, charred books, and piles of bones. The chaos cult had finally abandoned him after his last purge. Decades of work had been lost, all his plans gone sour, to be reduced to commanding scrawny savages the size of children ... it wasn't fair. It had to be the godling's fault. He or she had undone all his plans. Why would Stonehaven or Valantir matter so much to such a God? It had to be the daggers. Five enchanted bits of metal whose origins were long forgotten, their purpose as well, hidden for centuries from the eyes of men … and Arius hated any power that was not his to command.

* * *

"I see movement at the eastern mouth of the pass, the mercenaries know we are here, we have no time to lose!" Rachel opined.

Xandannus countered, "Let them follow, make for the southern wall of the pass, I have a surprise for them."

The Nomads followed Xandannus' lead, and he led them as if trying to escape pursuit in the mountains again. He called to his friend Blodias, "When I give the signal, set a torch and light it."

They rode hard for the South, then wheeled westward at the wall of the valley. The mercenaries gave chase as expected, confidant they could overtake the centaurs before they reached Karn. The minutes dragged on, and both parties saw a faraway mist forming at the western mouth of the pass. The mercs knew the legend of Gamble Pass. Some who attempt the passage never return from the mists. Few return at all, thus the gamble. The leader of the Dragon Tail Pirate company drove his horse harder, to catch his prize before the mists closed in. His men followed suit, all but a few in back, whose horses collapsed in exhaustion and cold. Taking the long way around had cost them, and now big ominous clouds rolled in from the South, dark and flat at the bottoms, heralding heavy snow. Tang Min wanted that reward money.

He was a quarter mile away from his quarry when he saw what looked like a flare being launched at high arc toward the wall. Too late he realized, it was not a flare at all. It was something much worse! Tang wheeled his horse around to go east again, just as the arrow reached apex and fell toward the mountain face.

"Go back! It's a trap! Go back!" he called in vain.

Seconds later, the arrow exploded in mid-flight, two hundred feet off the ground. The shock wave rippled across the mountain face, and the thunderous roar of the avalanche began. That was the end of the Dragon Tail Pirate company. While the Centaurs raced to the far side of the mountain, Blodias was not so lucky. His ankle turned, and his bridemare Tegemis helped him hobble under an outcropping. There was nothing Xandannus could do for his friend once they vanished from sight under a blanket of white fury.

* * *

"What do you want now, Kenneth?" Queen Marcy inquired with a sullen, exasperated tone.

"Is that any way to greet your brother? It's good to see you too," Ken replied with a touch of sarcasm.

"Well, out with it, why are you here?" Marcy insisted.

Her brother bowed, "I actually have useful information for you. The Lawgivers are infighting again, and rumors have surfaced of a kept woman somewhere in the dungeons, I think Nathan has *pressing* business with her in the confession chambers by the sound of it..."

Marcy slapped him hard. "You had BETTER be right about this! If your information is wrong, we will be the laughing stock of all Korath!"

Ken added, "Well, we might bribe that old Dwarf geezer a bit, wasn't he found in the dungeon where that Elf girl was injured?"

Marcy scoffed, "He'd betray us to Nathan for the same sum or maybe less, absolutely not!"

Her brother mused, "Well, that leaves the much less reliable kitchen maids..." Marcy shoved at him, "Get out! Not another word about this, to anyone! You leave it to me and me alone."

Ken brushed himself off and left in a dark mood. After he was gone, Marcy summoned her Knights to convene in secret. "Lugnai, I need you to capture Bothun alive. Lochar and Cernach, you will inspect the newest prisoners... make sure they don't have the plague. Fergus, you will accompany me on another errand," Marcy commanded.

The knights all bowed and saluted.

"Go forth and make me proud," she said with a sweep of her outstretched vertical palm.

They went to perform her tasks. Fergus thumbed his axe to test its edge, and smiled most evilly. Marcy then paid a visit to the Academy. The sentries tried to deny her, but her cruel eyes, and the threat of Fergus the Cleaver unmade their resolve. Once inside, Marcy sought out the headmaster, Bradagar the Immodest. He reacted stoically, "To what agenda of yours do I owe this visit?"

Marcy smiled coldly, "To the point as always. I like that about you."

Bradagar brushed her off, "Flattery will avail you nothing, Madame. You should know that by now."

Marcy relented, "True. I've come to inquire about my husband; he's been here more often than usual. He must be up to something."

The headmaster chuckled. "Is he ever not, madame?"

"See? There's no dancing around with you. I think Nathan is hiding a great deal from me, and even dared to confine Adam against his will. I want to get to the bottom of this, my patience is at an end," Marcy confided.

Bradagar smiled briefly. "Imagine that. Adam is loved only by you. But yes, you are correct. Nathan wanted my allegiance earlier, and I refused him. Exactly what for I can only guess. But I daresay it revolves around Sandhaven and a boy named Corbin. Do you know of him?"

Marcy snarled, "Why should I?"

Bradagar baited the hook, "Benson, Clay and Otto say that Corbin is Nathan's bastard. And of course, the mother is paid to keep quiet, but fifteen years is a long time to keep a secret like this. Word gets out one way or another. I may not like Adam, but I think you should take him to safety."

Marcy clenched her teeth and hissed, "The truth at last. Nathan will regret this indiscretion. Thank you, Headmaster. I'd lay low if I were you."

Bradagar replied, "Your concern is appreciated of course, but I take my own advice. The wisest course will present itself when we don't expect it to."

Marcy scoffed, "Spare me your tea leaves and old crone's babble."

Bradagar nodded, "As you wish, madame."

Marcy left in a seething fury, slamming the door. After Marcy was gone, Bradagar tapped a chessboard, commanding, "Bishop to Queen's rook six." He smiled and began to pack one of his knapsacks.

* * *

"I almost don't care anymore what happens to Oakthorn. Arius can do what he likes there... I'm quite done defending people who hate me," Conrad complained aloud to Lebiced as they rode past Agama's borders.

The wizard answered: "Not even to Henry who is in charge of the Abbey now, or Alex the wise?"

Conrad grumbled, "Okay, maybe I do care about those two, plus Savadi, but I cannot go back. There's nothing but torment and misery for me there. Not for all the gold and silver would I go back to that dung pit ! I have enough to settle down somewhere else. And send for the lady who loves me. Start over. I deserve that, right?"

Lebiced nodded. "Certainly. But all choices have consequences. Arius will not leave any of us alone, what he plans for Stonehaven he will do to other lands, you and your lady would not be safe forever. You must surely know this in your heart. I ask you to defend your loved ones as you already have. You have the courage and will, but these alone are not enough."

Conrad stopped his horse, snarling, "LISTEN, old man, I have done more than ten of my peers put together to protect this land, faced certain death more than once, and earned myself nothing but scorn, ridicule and hatred in the process! Spare me your fucking hollow lectures!"

Lebiced raised his eyebrows in startled apprehension, and try as he might, whatever words he could conjure at that moment, seemed inadequate. So, the remainder of their journey to Xantir was dominated by awkward silence, and punctuated by more snowfall. Conrad's thoughts turned darker, etching a deep frown on his face and made his eyes cold and hard.

Lebiced hoped it was a passing mood. The prophecies suggested that one of the three champions was Conrad. Xantir and Stonehaven needed him.

* * *

Thanks to Garzon, the others now had fur to reduce the effect of the elements, but still the cold winds battered them almost senseless. Their fingers cramped and ached, their ears burned, and traversing the narrow ledge was increasingly difficult. The very reason this approach was so undermanned. Kazius faltered several times before finding the will to make his limbs obey. The women were also not sure-footed up here. Moira sneezed and lost her balance.

Reflexively, Sal grabbed for her without thinking. He held on but could not look in her eyes. He shut them as he pulled her up. Many minutes passed before her feet were steady again. Sal said nothing and Moira tried not to think about it. She knew what he had done in Mojara. It was still unforgivable. Onward they crept in single file, Kazius leading the way, with Mandy close behind, then Garzon, then Bernice, then Sal, then Moira. Garzon moved as if he was born in the mountains, and Bernice thought it impossible that a man his size could navigate this ledge. But as he kept her from falling, she was glad for it. Moira was less lucky, she fell a second time, and Sal was pulled down as well, but managed to hook his left arm onto the ledge for support. He did not have long, the snow was melting and refreezing underneath, causing his grip to fail, and his arm to go numb. He struggled with all he could muster to pull Moira up, until she could climb on his back. Sal knew he was done for.

His voice pleaded to her, "I'm sorry about the girl. I hope you find her..."

Just as Moira crawled onto the ledge to his right, helped up by Bernice, Sal felt his fingers seize up. He lost his grip and fell without another word, as his body was swallowed by the flurries below. The eeriness of it would haunt Moira for many weeks. It seemed like agonizing hours, crawling along a treacherous ledge before the path widened again. They passed under a frozen waterfall with great trepidation, and soon came to bare rock under an overhang. Kazius's teeth chattered as he stuttered, "T-there's a-another c-c-cave ahead, j-just another m-mile or t-t-t-two..."

Even Garzon hoped he was right. He needed Kazius's knowledge of this place, and if anything happened to Bernice, Kazius might be capable of suicide. It took another hour to reach it, but the cavern was there as promised. Full of icicles and crevices, but the wind lessened in here.

Again, they huddled for warmth, but got no sleep at all. Everything was too cramped, and the broken shale did not make for comfort. Nonetheless, they stayed put for a day.

* * *

A rowdy crowd pervaded the atmosphere of the Drunken Dungeon Tavern, full of howls of laughter and of pain, arm wrestling, drinking games, isolated brawls, darts, billiards, greasy food and Dwarven serving wenches, with the clanging of industry in the background as smiths pounded hot irons over their anvils across the alley in the city under the mountain. This was the border town of Bal Dar that secured the western mouth of the narrow pass to Zara-Mogai against intruders. Bravane, Skorvald and company had stopped here for food and rest.

Skorvald sensed a particular human nearby, a seedy character even for this place. The fellow had a huge scar on the right side of his face, framing both sides of a glass eye. He also had red runes tattooed on his arms and chest, big fat sigils with wide serifs, and long curving leftward downstrokes that narrowed to a tip. The man was also bald on top with gray whiskers, a nose ring and many missing teeth. He was flashing a gold coin asking in whispers if Jonah Saint Noir had passed through here. Skorvald smelled a rat. Skorvald discreetly joined in the dart games nearby to the seedy stranger, after giving a quick nod to his cousins from Frost Pillars.

Skorvald arranged an accident when the strangers back was turned, with a dart in the ass. The stranger howled in rage as he spun around, "Who the bloody hell? You have worse aim than a pissing bull!"

Skorvald bowed in pretended remorse, "My deepest apologies, sir. Here, allow me ..."

Whereupon he knocked him flat with a headbutt and then grabbed his collar. "What is your business with Jonah?"

Skorvald was instantly surrounded by three more humans sporting similar red tattoos. Skorvald's men surprised them from behind before they could unsheathe their daggers, and held their arms fast. "I'll ask you one more time, what is your business with Jonah?" Skorvald repeated.

The man lied, "His mother sent us; he is needed at home."

Skorvald tested, "Where is his birthmark?"

The stranger was sweating now, "Uhh, everybody knows that. It's ... it's ..."

Skorvald slammed his head on the floor, "Wrong answer! Who paid you to seek him out? Speak!"

The stranger lied again, "His mother..."

Skorvald headbutted him a second time, breaking the man's nose. Dwarven royal security showed up to restore the peace and threw the two parties behind bars.

Bravane the Younger whined sarcastically, "That plan went well."

Skorvald teased, "It gets better."

Bravane retorted, "Oh, I can hardly wait..."

His father, Bravane the Elder added: "Oh, yes, loads of fun, this is the best stage production I've seen in twenty years ..."

After several hours, a Dwarven general appeared with a decree: "We have identified your adversaries as 'Blood Fangs' from Thalu, a sorry lot of mercenaries, and thus you are pardoned for your behavior. HOWEVER, you are henceforth forbidden to return here. We want no part of human conflicts. You will be released tomorrow. They will be let go two days after. You have until then to vanish from sight. That is all."

Bravane the Younger protested, "What? My great-grandfather ..."

The general interrupted, "I know who you are, Redoak. The decision is final. Good-bye!"

Bravane pounded his fists against the bars and grunted in exasperated fury. "Ungrateful bureaucrats!"

* * *

Tyton recognized at once the main road up to Black Falls, a winding ledge zigzagging up the eastern face of the Iron Ridge. "There," he pointed, to a tower halfway up the nearest mountain, "The first outpost, vulnerable at sunrise if we attack from the cliff to the north. They will be blind to the shadows there at first light. We will move at sunset to begin the climb."

Prasad nodded in acknowledgement. The plan was good. By day, they gathered herbs in what scarce quantity could be had in the bleakest and foulest part of Razadur. By sunset, they made their approach at the base of Mount Sandhorn. Barren at its base, it quickly changed to sparse and withered scrub, and then bare rock again. Prasad donned his climbing spikes, as did Tyton. They did not need the grapnel, yet. As the land descended into darkness, the risks of their climb quadrupled. But onward they went, methodically and cautiously, true to their craft.

* * *

"Have you ever been to Xantir before?" Lebiced asked to break the tension.

Conrad said: "No I have not, but my Grandfather Seamus left accounts of it to my father." Conrad's face went dark at the thought of it … what he had to do to his father's ghoul because of the Augurons.

Lebiced quickly changed the subject, "Yes, well, Xantir is older than I am; it broke off from the Itana Empire by 1311, and was already home to roving herds of centaurs. Clan Freeborn stayed here, and the Sunset Sovereigns sometimes pass through. They disagree with the notion of Kings and Kingdoms, and with our practice of marriage alliances with Royal families, but we do have similar goals in mind."

Conrad grumbled, "And what would that be?"

Lebiced continued, "We and the centaurs both cherish freedom; they accept no masters, while we seek to free people's minds in other lands. Truth and knowledge are necessary for freedom. Tyranny anywhere is a threat to our own freedom. So we have made it a sacred duty to preserve and promote knowledge. It's why Amber Silverwing married your great Grandfather James."

Conrad moaned and rolled his eyes, "So you are going to tell me I inherited this duty…"

Lebiced tried a softer approach. "Is that such a bad legacy? We hold freedom to be a fundamental right. The Greenwood Order of Xantir is dedicated to defeating tyranny, and your own Emerald Order had similar ideas. Before Eledar and his ilk poisoned it…"

Conrad hissed, "Do not speak his name again in my presence, the very mention makes me ill." Lebiced let it go. They rode in silence for the many miles inbetween Twin Hill and Dromon Hill, the center of Xantir. The snow fell here also, Xantir was the South terminus of the Terran Sea frost current.

Conrad did not want to be here, he wanted to be far away on some sandy coast or near a tropical forest with only Rebecca for company, the hell with duty. He stopped his horse and turned around to go back to West Bend.

Lebiced called after him, "Conrad, please reconsider! Your great Aunt Susan was very skilled at magic, and died in Shadval defending and avenging the people she loved. Arius is stronger now than Lorenna was then. I am getting too old, my time is near. You are Stonehaven's best hope against Arius. I implore you to search your heart, who will protect Rebecca and Bethany and Devi but you? Jonah is not made for the ways of magic. Nor can he fight the chaos cults, he is bound by the blood curse."

Conrad stopped cold. "WHAT? Explain yourself, old man! What business does my brother in law have with some blood curse?"

Lebiced sighed, "Jonah is the nephew of Lorenna. I thought he told you..."

Conrad growled, "The blazes with all of you! I've had enough of secrets and skulking bandits, traitors, backstabbers and wagging tongues! You can deal with Arius yourself, old man!"

Lebiced sighed again, "The stakes are too high for this nonsense..."

The wizard weaved his hands in spherical motions, and then thrust a bright blue ball of light outward in front of Conrad, which became a swirling wind that lifted a veil of snow from below, and then hardened into heavy walls of solid ice, enclosing the patriarch of the Redmanes.

Conrad yelled, "Is this how you promote freedom, old man?"

Lebiced countered, "You of all people should understand, Conrad Redmane, that freedom is protected by brave souls who did their sworn duty! There can be no freedom without responsibility! I will do mine, and ask you to do YOURS! Did you or did you not swear an oath to the land?"

Conrad snarled, "Damn your hide, you crusty old bastard..."

Lebiced challenged, "Is that a yes?"

Conrad answered, "FINE! Now undo this wall!"

Lebiced closed his eyes and raised his staff ... he hummed in a low tone, and then struck the wall with the staff, creating cracks and fissures in the ice. He hummed again and then struck the ground, the tremors expanded the cracks and finally the wall crumbled. Lebiced then advised, "Remember this, and remember it well, Arius commands fire and air and dark chaos magic. You need to use Earth and Water to defeat him. The ways of Light and Harmony will take longer for you to learn. The anger festering inside you makes our task more difficult.

Unless we brought Rebecca here..."

Conrad shook his head, "So be it, you crazy old man."

* * *

Kazius led the party deeper into the caves, explaining, "One of these tunnels is directly under the arena of blood, there will be a grate blocking the way, it's locked from above by gears and levers, and it will be many many feet up from the floor. This won't be easy."

Garzon scoffed, "It matters not. We are going."

Kazius replied sarcastically, "The council has spoken."

Garzon growled, "Got any better ideas for damaging the Syndicate network and finding the children?"

Kazius backed away, "No, not really..."

Garzon barked, "Well, here's how the plan goes then, YOU lead the way after I break the grate, and Bernice comes up last when the way is clear. Any tricks..."

Kazius groaned, "Yes, I know."

Garzon punched Kazius in his left shoulder, causing the arm to go numb, "Good, do not forget it."

* * *

"Now remember, there will be no talk of wolves, we are to listen in the marketplace for news of your father if he is still alive. Follow my lead, please," Thomas instructed the girls.

"Okay," said Molly.

Carol nodded yes.

Molly tugged at Thomas's sleeves. "Can we get muffins and tarts? Please?"

Thomas smiled, "Very well, yes ... but not too many. I think it's going to snow again, and I don't want you two catching cold."

The girls frowned and gave a sad resignation.

"Okay..."

The muffin cart was not hard to find, and Thomas paid in silver coin for seven muffins, four he divided among the girls, and three he ate himself. Most of the gossip in the market was about the Elves stealing children or killing Barton or about the "new lover" of Prince Adam, all conjecture and hearsay as Thomas could tell, not a shred of verifiable proof was given by anyone. Thomas hid his disgust under a very stoic face, and nudged the girls away from such malicious rumors. Then a middle aged man with a round midsection whispered, "Hey! Over here!"

Thomas and the girls turned their heads, and wondered if the man could be trusted. He walked past and beckoned them to follow, not pausing but a moment to see if they understood. Thomas decided to see if this man knew anything.

As they rounded a corner, the man did an about face and pretended he forgot something at the market. Some priest was approaching with several of his followers. Thomas sensed something wrong, but was too late to act on it. A young lad among the followers pointed, "That's them! The girls who stole the food and hid in the stables!"

Thomas turned the girls around and began a brisk walk back through the market, attempting to buy time. As they passed a side alley, the man from earlier whispered again, "In here! Quick!"

They followed.

The man led them through a blacksmith shop and out the other side, then down the opposite alley, through another vendor's tent full of hanging linens and silks. They continued dodging and weaving through shops and alleys, until they were well clear of pursuers.

"Pardon my asking, kind sir, but who are you?" asked Thomas.

"Call me Peter. I recognized the two girls from the orphanage, and I'm blessed with many cousins in that market, whose shops we wandered through … I'm the foreman in charge of repairs after the beast tore up the place," said the fellow.

"And I know where your Dad is," he told Molly.

The girl jumped for joy. "Where is he? Can we see him?"

Peter frowned, "Sorry, Lass, Alex is in the dungeon. King Nathan thinks he's a spy, and nobody dares tell him no."

Molly shrieked, "That's not fair!"

Peter knelt in front of her. "I know it's not fair. I do. That's the way of this kingdom, lass. The royals are born with silver spoons, and the rest of us got fitted for saddles and wagon hitches. We don't like it either."

Carol finally spoke also: "He has my mommy, too, down in the dungeon. We came by boat a year ago to the dead place, and then by wagon here. My brother Avnand is dead. Pirates did it."

Peter cautioned, "Careful where you say that Lass, the Syndicate has ears here, a right evil lot they are, all the big fish answer to them. Yer not safe in these parts, ye best git gone from here."

Molly protested, "Not without Daddy!"

Carol was also adamant: "I want my mommy! And I want to go home!"

Peter warned with annoyance: "You have no idea what kind of monsters run this kingdom. It's a hopeless task I tell you. I've done all I can already."

A voice behind him announced, "It is not hopeless."

Peter jumped out of his skin when he saw the Monk's robes, mistaking him for someone else: "By the gods, you scared the corn out of me, lad! What are you doing in those robes?"

Tyrus pulled the hood down. "I required what no other garment could afford me. And I must find the records for the Mill property."

Peter griped, "You keep this up, Nathan will chop my head off! You and your stubborn honor..."

Molly chimed in, "Does that mean my Daddy lived here? Will you help us?"

Tyrus nodded, "Yes, little one, I will help."

Peter waved his palms dismissively, "No more, the less I hear, the better, I'm in enough trouble, I'll be off now..."

Molly grumbled, "Then you're a coward like my daddy..."

Peter raised his voice: "Look here, Lass, ye have no idea what your daddy survived, and if you had half a brain, you'd be scared too! And don't expect my help again! I'll have to report the robe as stolen, and I can't be seen with any of you henceforth. There, I've said my fare thee well." And with those words, he left.

"Well, pleased to make your acquaintance at least, mister..." inquired Thomas.

"Call me Tyrus," said he.

* * *

The first outpost was cleaned out before anyone knew what happened. The topmost sentries died without a sound, with arrows in their throats, and the two temple assassins worked downward from the top with complete element of surprise, despite the forewarning of Raj and company. The cliff of Sandhorn was considered to be a suicidal climb, and thus they never looked. Even if they had, the sunrise would have blinded them. The next outpost would be trickier, but Tyton had a plan for that as well, drawing on his memories of many years ago, Tyton would fake his way in with borrowed uniforms from the dead. It was a necessary risk. To add to the deception, Tyton carried Prasad as if bringing a wounded and unconscious man back to the fortress. He would be visible at the next switchback in the trail, and watched from then on. It took another half hour to traverse the distance to the next tower. At the doorway, the senior Bloodhammer demanded, "What happened? Are we under attack?"

Tyton responded, "I think he got food poisoning, he became violently ill… and then collapsed. You need to double check your rations."

The sentries instantly wrinkled their noses and put their hands up to ward themselves against contagion, "Take him away from here at once! We'll hold down the fort here, get going before we all get the heaves…"

Tyton turned away grinning like a well-fed cat. Once they reached the next switchback, and were out of sight, he let Prasad down. It was time for the grapnels again. "I'll take the North side here; you take the last post from the South. Meet you on top of the wall," Tyton announced.

Prasad nodded and began jogging southward along the wide ledge.

"Soon, Sidhuri, I will avenge you or join you," Tyton promised to thin air.

* * *

Given their sudden notoriety and the abrupt timetable, Bravane the younger and Skorvald were unable to locate a willing guide for their journey into Zara-Mogai. And only Kendrus Cedar Keg would explain why, "There's bad blood between here and Zara-Mogai, that land is full of Trolls, goblins, Syndicate scum, chaos fanatics, and exiled Dwarf clans. The rebellion of 1431 was started by Tarza Igneous and Judas Redeye, who both died in the effort, but not before they killed King Gravnar Anvilhammer's wife Krisi Stonelantern, and several other women. Gravnar remembers like it was yesterday. They made war on us again in 1513, we drove them back until the great Quake sent both sides running. Gravnar's son Seamus died there, and his grandson Dendrius as well. We love our King, and my ancestors died defending him, three generations of them. That's not counting the plague of 1517 that almost cut us in half. Nothing against you folks, but there's not a soul in Iglar that will help you, sorry."

Bravane the Younger nodded and bowed, "Thank you for telling us, and my sympathies to your people."

Kendrus scoffed, "Words. Less than air in the bellows. I'll give you some advice. If you meet a Redeye, an Igneous, Blackstove, Redcoal, or Oakstout, you have three options: keep walking, slit their throat, or cutoff their jewels. Those names are forever cursed. Now, if I was you, I'd go home and forget this errand of yours. Lacking that, keep to the mountains and don't cross any dragons."

Skorvald nodded, "Oh, we'll be certain to tickle them and then run for our lives."

Kendrus grinned sarcastically, "Oh, you're funny... under different circumstances, I might even like you. My call would have been send the Blood Fangs back home in chains and let 'em face justice there for whatever is on their records. Queen Margo up North has had enough of these mercenaries and cultists. But, as it is, they will be hot on your tail come morning. Now get going!"

Bravane the Elder waved. "Thanks."

* * *

"Is that the only way up?" Garzon asked.

Kazius groaned, "It's the best way, and the other drainage chutes are no wider. Unless... there is a shorter one..."

Garzon protested, "My shoulders will never fit in here. where is the shorter hole?"

Kazius grumbled, "The shorter one is directly under the slave pens, and it's guarded both day and night."

Garzon prodded, "What's the other catch?"

Kazius replied wearily, "It's guarded by a Wyvern. An underfed, chained, cranky and mean Wyvern."

Garzon harrumphed, "It bleeds, doesn't it?"

Kazius conceded, "Well, yes, but it's poisonous ..."

Mandy exclaimed sarcastically, "Oh, is that all? Throw my husband in and wait for it to take a nap..."

Garzon laughed. "Woman, how bad is he to merit such a fate?"

Moira interrupted, "Adrian kidnapped my daughter to sell her to pirates..."

Garzon stopped laughing. "I see. Then we shall keep the Wyvern alive for the day we find him again."

Mandy sighed, "I was joking. If we have to kill it, we kill it. Plenty of other fitting punishments for my husband."

Garzon added, "Woman, he has sided heart and soul with the Syndicate pirates, which makes him a threat to women and children everywhere. Men like him took small babes from their parents in the lands of the Bazadani, my adopted people. And they will pay dearly for the affront. Do not speak again of mercy for such as he."

This left Kazius wondering uneasily what was in store for him or Bernice and his child.

Chapter Fifty-One
Breaking Point

"Lugnai, if you would..." Marcy commanded.

Sir Lugnai the savage raised his war hammer for another blow, and Sir Bothun the Brave closed his eyes tight. He screamed as his other hand was smashed. Then hissed in agony, "G-go... to... hell..."

Marcy sighed. "Enough, Lugnai. Obviously he requires a different form of persuasion. Leave us."

Lugnai scowled, but he bowed before leaving the enclosure. Marcy whispered to Bothun, his arms bound by ropes to a stone bench in a secluded garden. "Tell me what Nathan is up to, or I shall have your niece and your sister dragged here for the same treatment. You don't think I will? I know about the boy Corbin. And I know about a woman in the dungeon. If you don't tell me, someone else will, and I'll find a way to pin the blame on you for it. Your honor would be forever tarnished."

Bothun snarled, "What ... would YOU ... know of honor, bitch?"

Marcy donned her thick canvas and leather gloves and plucked a purple flower, before waving it in Bothun's face. Marcy purred with a sinister grin, "Do you know what this will do to a child, Bothun?"

The knight whimpered, "No … leave her alone … she's innocent…"

Marcy giggled. "My, yes, but that can be corrected, as well …"

Bothun strained at his bindings, only to collapse in agony again from the pain in both of his ruined hands. He whimpered with tears in his eyes, "No, anything but that …"

Marcy jabbed his right hand with a gloved finger and smiled as Bothun winced. "Tell me what I wish to know, and the niece will remain unspoiled. But cross me and they both die in agony," Marcy hissed.

"Why … would I trust … your word," Bothun wheezed with pain and fatigue.

"Oh, you poor dear, have me all figured out, don't you?" she whispered mockingly in his right ear before licking him.

Bothun cringed.

When Marcy nibbled on his ear, Bothun cried in turmoil, his mind torn between many impulses. Disgust warring with hungers, one for freedom, and others for unspeakable passions, such as to kill her, or to be mounted by her. Marcy saw the effect in his eyes, how his sanity was crumbling. She straddled him fully clothed on the bench, and gyrated her hips before caressing his left cheek with the flower. He felt the side of his face starting to tingle and go numb. Bothun moaned, "No more ... stop ..."

Marcy purred again, "Tell me and I will give you a clean death."

Bothun moaned again. "He plans to marry Minerva off to the prince of Stonehaven, and to have Corbin inherit the crown here ... Sandhaven backs Corbin as well ..."

Marcy glared in fury and jammed the flower in his mouth. His eyes went wide as his face muscles went rigid, and the poison continued to spread. "THIS ... IS WAR, Nathan! You cheating dog!" Marcy snarled with clenched teeth, furrowed brows, and curled lips. She kicked the bench over with Bothun still tied to it and screamed incoherently in animalistic grunts and growls. Her servants all ducked for cover as she passed by.

* * *

"You remind me a bit of another student from years ago. He was even more reckless than you, and just as wild than the centaurs who roam here. His name doesn't matter, only that he is eleven years older than you, full of ideas to change the world, but chafed at the notions of duty and responsibility. He was brash, rude, spiteful and full of rage ... tell me Conrad, do you know what a disciple is?" asked Lebiced.

"A student or apprentice ..." mumbled a melancholy Conrad.

"Quite so, and that is the root of discipline. Without self-restraint, we are slaves to whatever impulse may arise, and honor loses all meaning or relevance, such men do not wield power, the power wields THEM. Arius had no honor, and this other fellow had little. It's why he had no support here, he caused his own alienation and isolation ..."

Conrad interrupted, "Are you saying the masses have the moral upper hand?"

Lebiced corrected, "No, NO, not at all. Tyranny by one madman or by many is still tyranny. Numerical superiority has nothing to do with honor."

Conrad mumbled again, "Yeah, I've seen the stupidity of mobs..."

Lebiced stood up from the grassy incline, "Why don't we take a walk and introduce you ..."

Conrad groaned, "Why?"

The wizard added, "You have ancestors from these hills. Do not forget..."

Conrad sighed, "Okay, fine."

Lebiced added, "Just not any surviving direct ancestors in these parts, I'm afraid... just cousins in West Bend and in Agama... and as it turns out, you are actually a distant cousin of Jonah."

Conrad growled, "Right now. I don't care! I want nothing to do with the Augurons until the day I mangle their sorry bags of bones ... is that clear?"

Lebiced had a word on his tongue, but then thought better of it and remained silent. Something was bothering

Conrad terribly, and Lebiced knew only the barest details. He regretted sending for Rebecca, but saw no alternative if Conrad were to master the challenges ahead in time. The poor girl was going to find herself with a very prickly cactus.

* * *

"Have you gone completely mad? Shelter YOU from my Father? Are you so eager to see my head on the chopping block, goblin?" snarled Winter in her throne room.

Chieftain Egraz of the blackspike clan prostrated himself at her feet, "No, Queen Auguron, never wish such a thing as that... your beautiful but cruel face must not suffer such an end. We will ever be your servants."

Winter softened her voice a shade, "There is but one ruse that would work... that I have caught you attempting desertion to Vostiok and have thus held the lot of you for questioning. You must pick someone to be the scapegoat. If Father is not convinced of our tale, we are all dead, do you understand?"

Egraz begged, "A scapegoat, Madame, why?"

Winter hissed, "To be beaten, you fool! It must appear that I have interrogated one of you, MOST thoroughly!"

Egraz whimpered, "Have you no other way?"

Winter shook her head no. "They will not like this..."

Egraz said mournfully.

Winter scowled, "It will be done this way, or you can take your chances up North in even colder climates. You have but an hour to decide. Now get going!"

Egraz shuffled away with his head bent low. Winter strode forward to her long table and knocked some of the goblets clattering to the floor for effect. There could be no mistakes with her once mortal father if what she suspected was true.

* * *

Garzon entered the last chamber where the Wyvern was chained, and the beast screeched in anger, sensing this was not a helpless meal like the others whose bones littered the floor.

Garzon advanced warily with his axe held in front of him, warding against the barbed tail. Far above, over the grate that the Wyvern was set to defend, Raj and Udai heard the beast.

"That's not his gloating tone, there's trouble down there," whispered Udai.

Their third man had become Wyvern food after losing a match in the arena only a few days past. The clanking and scraping of the chains heralded enraged movements of the beast, in response to some threat below they could not see or hear, and anyone bold enough to face a Wyvern of his own will, was not someone they wanted to meet on the business end of his weapon. The sounds changed from clattering chains to gnashing teeth and the whipping of the barbed tail, but no cries of pain followed. Again the teeth closed on empty air, and the tail missed. It seemed to be circling its prey, but they still could not see who else was down there, only the motion of the chain and part of the Wyvern's body. Then they heard the sound of metal breaking stone, and the wailing of the beast as it danced in pain and fury so loudly it echoed in their cell and assaulted their ears.

The monster thrashed in agony and screeched madly until a great thud and clanking of chains interrupted. Now the sounds became howls of panic. It passed under the grate, and there was a large man fastened to its neck as it tried to shake him off. The tail was bloodied and missing the barbed end. As the head jerked to and from, attempting to dislodge Garzon, he struck at every pass near the chute in the ceiling leading up.

Udai hissed, "The bloody bastards' trying to break in! I can't see what he's holding …"

Bits of gravel flew on the next strike, and the side of the chute showed hairline cracks.

Raj panicked, "We have to get out of here! Guards! Help! Enemy at the grate!"

Udai snarled, "You may have signed our death warrants you fool!"

Raj did not listen and kept shouting.

As the minutes passed, the strikes were less frequent, not because Garzon grew tired, but the starving beast did, given the powerful legs that were locked around its neck.

Finally, several Bloodhammers entered the cell to verify Raj's claims.

"Tell Axegrind we have an intruder below," ordered the biggest Guard.

Raj pleaded, "Let us out of here!"

The Guard answered by head-butting Raj and then punching him in the gut. Raj doubled over, wheezing. "Take them to the forward cells," the next largest declared.

Gongs sounded in the distance as the alarm was raised.

* * *

Dear Rebecca:
Please forgive my strange request, there are urgent matters in Xantir, Which only you can remedy.
Something festers in the heart and mind of your beloved Conrad,
and all my probing only angers him.
It is imperative you join him here before he can make any progress in his training.
You may or may not know me, The Wizard Lebiced.

"What is this?" Rebecca asked of Lady Bethany.

"My Brother has had all he can stand of Oakthorn and the people therein, except for you, and I can hardly blame him. But the wizard is right, something is eating at him, and only a woman he loves has any chance of reaching him," answered Bethany.

"But why Xantir? Conrad training under wizards? Since when?" begged the Barmaid.

Bethany nudged Rebecca to take a walk with her away from the prying ears in the Manor. "Conrad has changed since his battle in Shadval, so my husband says. He has begun to speak with the dead, and having visions. He is also one of the few survivors of the fever, his level of exposure would have killed anyone else. He and I are both descended from Xantir bloodlines among others. Certain abilities often skip generations. Savadi and Andar once told me that Conrad has a hard road to travel, and I suspect he truly needs your help now. He has been alone too long. He is proud and stubborn, and turns away his own sister rather than accept help. You may have better luck. You will have to heed your own instincts," advised Bethany.

"I will do my best," Rebecca replied.

They hugged, and Rebecca went to arrange for a horse.

* * *

Dear Lebiced:
Blood Fangs are seeking Jonah.
I have dealt with Douglas for his crime,
but was too late to stop the mercenaries.
My youngest son is in danger.
Please look after him.
Much love, your great niece Margo.

"Oh, dear, this is not good. Not at all," Lebiced moaned in a melancholy tone. He immediately folded the letter, and went to search out any of the three centaur herds that roamed through Xantir. Conrad would have to fend for himself.

* * *

"Your Majesty, more disturbing news..." announced Sir Cernach, "While combing the mountains for clues to the activities of this Danny fellow who was arrested weeks ago, we found, THIS." Cernach held out an Elven crafted bow with claw marks on it. "The skeletons were picked clean, the corpses look to be months old. There were only two of them, I discovered a message tucked away in one of their quivers. It's a plea for help, from Valantir to Talos, claiming Arius has made war on them. The claw marks on the bow match several murders here in Kozos."

Marcy pondered the import of all this. "Take the evidence to the attic at the Cloverhill Estate, treat it well, be discreet and do not delay."

Cernach bowed. "As you wish, My Queen."

Marcy then summoned Sir Lochar, "Who is on jailor duty today?"

Lochar answered, "Tergomir the Brash, and Gerundin the Glutton."

Marcy smiled cruelly, "I have something for Gerundin's appetites. Fetch one of my flowers, and a bottle of wine. We move in when he takes his shift."

Lochar grinned, "Yes, My Queen, it will be done."

* * *

Tyton cleared the wall crenellations just as some sentinels were pulled away by cries of "Intruder under the arena! He's wounded the Wyvern!" Tyton stayed in the shadow of the tower, listening. He thought to himself, Who could have found the tunnel in these mountains? Only a handful of men, including himself, knew that secret. Now Axegrind had to make double certain to shorten that list. No wonder the wall was a lower priority. He saw Prasad gain the other tower a hundred meters south of him, and they nodded to each other. It was now child's play for them to knock out the few remaining men on the wall, and prowl the many rooftops of the closely packed granite buildings inside. This was now more of a waiting game, as Tyton knew from their reputations alone, that the younger Axegrind would not make the same mistakes as Kazius, nor would he emulate all of the flaws of Arius. Tyton and Prasad would wait, listen, watch, and pounce when the best opportunity presented itself. The real question was, who is the visitor down below?

* * *

A piteous whine emanated from the mass of ropes and rags tied about a post in the cell, "Please, I beg you… I need the pipe… please…"

The burly middle-aged deputy just raised one eyebrow and grunted.

Darmid pleaded again: "Please, I'll do anything, I'll give you names, locations, passwords, anything!"

The deputy snarled, "Should have made the offer long before you killed my Uncle, you two pence backstabbing drifter!"

Darmid sobbed and cried, "The pain … please … I'm sorry about your uncle … I … must … unnngh … m-must …"

His eyes were wide in shock and agony, as his bony chest went rigid with crushing pain. Darmid gasped for air, but his body would not take any in, as his face reddened with the effort and beads of sweat covered his skin. His mouth no longer worked, and he died with a squeak. Darmid was no more, his heart had seized up for lack of his drug.

The deputy snorted with contempt, "Took you long enough!"

He sauntered to the forward room, noted the day and hour in the log book, and scrawled, "Scribe Darmid dead of heart failure."

Then he waited for his shift to end before making his report to Magistrate Blackhull.

* * *

Since the beast was near the end of his strength, and thus no further use to Garzon, he slid off the creature to sever the chain that bound it in place, setting it free. The Wyvern only needed a few seconds to understand what happened, and it gave no more contest. The beast folded its wings and slithered wearily down the tunnel, past Kazius and the others. While above, the sound of many boots above heralded pending company. Kazius whispered, "Find us some rocks, we may need them soon."

Bernice nodded without really understanding why.

Mandy went straight to the task, while Moira stood helpless.

Kazius explained: "We are about to have armed and hostile visitors, and I will not have my… partner and child defenseless against them."

Bernice and Moira finally understood, and both joined Mandy.

Garzon heard the stretching of bowstrings, and hoisted his axe up as a shield just in time to deflect the first volley from above. He backed away from the hole in the ceiling, forcing the archers to shoot at his feet, and still they missed. A voice from the cell commanded, "Bring the oil!"

Garzon wasted no time waiting for it, and broke into a run, warning the others as he did, "Clear the way! Get clear!"

Kazius grabbed Bernice and was about to speak when the first barrel struck the floor and burst open. Mandy and Moira were too late to react when the torch fell, and their clothing caught fire. Garzon grabbed one burning dress with one hand, and used the axe with his right to cut it off. He quickly nudged Moira farther westward down the tunnel as the second barrel fell. Garzon only had time to shield Mandy by leaping in front of her. He caught the second rush of flames full on his back and fell to the ground in agony. Kazius and the others dragged him down the tunnel until they were under dripping water.

Kazius whispered: "Get him to the Southern fork in the tunnels and then hide there, on your left... I will draw their attention, go!"

For once, they all obeyed, and did their best to drag Garzon quickly and quietly, with straining neck muscles and gritted teeth, Mandy whispering in turn, "By the gods, he is heavy!"

Kazius then spotted the glinting of metal below, and picked up a severed link of chain. He poked through his handful of rocks for the right size and shape, and then searched for a proper flat surface somewhere far west of the Wyvern's chamber. Men in armor were still descending single file from the metal rungs in the access shaft, and sliding down the rope held by ten of their comrades above. They heard the pounding of a rock in the distance, and with a nod to each other, they marched in haste after the sound. Inbetween the crude hammer-strokes of improvised tools, Kazius heard the clanking of their plate armor a hundred yards away, and he knew the archers would be trailing behind in chain mail and leather. He yelled in a taunting voice, desperately stalling for time, "Tell that cowardly two face weasel Axegrind to face me himself!"

A whistling of arrows was his answer, and Kazius dove to the south wall, taking two nicks to the left leg and a crack to the head as he did so. Dazed, he rose unsteadily onto his knees and elbows, as the bowstrings were being nocked again. He shook his head and stumbled farther west toward the south fork. The next volley was vicious, and left a shaft buried in the right leg, with two gashes to his midsection and shoulder. Kazius did not pause; he pushed on, limping and crawling until he turned the corner.

He lifted one finger to his lips to silence the women, who gasped anyway in spite of his warning. Bernice began to cry, "No, don't leave me!"

Mandy and Moira had to cover her mouth, whispering, "They are going to kill us all, be quiet."

Kazius continued crawling and whispered, "Can anyone lift his axe?"

They tried, to no avail, until all three tugged in unison. It was all they could do just to hold it off the ground. Kazius decided to himself he was not going to beg for mercy. He was going to meet his end the same as Garzon. He counted silently as the cadence of boots drew closer. Fifty paces, forty, thirty, twenty ...

"NOW!!!" Kazius exclaimed in his nearly forgotten commanding voice.

The axe thrust out like a battering ram and felled several men in a pile with the wind knocked out of them. Kazius raised up on both knees and his right arm, lashing out with the crudely sharpened chain link in his left, and slammed it into the neck of the nearest soldier trying to get up, who dropped like a severed tree limb, his blood spraying everywhere. Kazius rolled away on his back, groaning as the arrow in his leg snapped in two. Garzon whispered in a pained hiss, "MY ... TURN ..." and grabbed two heads while kneeling, slamming them together so hard the helmets crumpled, and red rivulets ran from their noses as their eyes went still as glass. The women handed Garzon the axe. He leaned on it like a walking stick as he raised up slowly onto both feet. The archers had just formed ranks twenty feet away and could not help their terror at his size. Axegrind was not among them to give orders, and the captains did not have visual contact yet, two arrows loosed in panic, as the others turned tail and ran. Garzon twisted to one side and in a single arc, snatched one arrow to swat the other. Bernice fainted.

Garzon knew an advantage when he had one, and bellowed with all the anger and pain still raging in his burns, "RUN, weaklings! FLEE for your pathetic lives or kneel and beg for mercy!"

The enemy morale completely collapsed, and confused ranks ran in both directions, west toward the mouth of the cave, and east back to the arena. When all enemy eyes and ears were far away, Garzon finally sank moaning and hissing to all fours again, and whispered directly to Mandy, "Next time I tell you to move, MOVE ..."

* * *

Conrad had settled into yet another inn, known as the Lord and Princess, situated on the north face of Dromon Hill, but after three meals alone, he began to get bored. Lebiced was nowhere to be seen, and Conrad was a complete stranger here, a stranger in armor wearing the sword of his ancestors, the last thing he had any pride in. All other reminders of home he had forsaken. He also knew the money would not last forever. Eventually he would need a permanent home, and work; the hell with nonsensical prophecies and wizard training.

"Excuse me," he said to the innkeeper, a round-bellied, middle-aged man. "I'm a bit lost. Do you know any Redmanes out this way?"

The older gent raised an eyebrow and mused, "Nope, not a one, but if you don't mind paying a tribute, that will get you a few hours in the archives of the Greenwood Order, maybe you can find some other relatives in the records there."

Conrad had no better ideas, so he tipped the man ten pence, and thanked him as he wandered in search of the Order. Streets in Dromon Hill (and many other parts of Xantir) were not the same as Stonehaven ... some were tunnels, many were wooded paths, and some were elevated walkways weaving between trees and hillsides, It was more like Valantir, and yet not. Directions from one location to another were like: "Take the North- South tunnel to the third stairway, go east a hundred yards, turn right at the tallest cluster of cedar pines, and take the creek to the second bend ..."

It was no wonder most visitors who grew up in towns or cities got lost here. It was half-forest, half-scattered village and countryside.

It was many hours later, past sunset under a misty rain mixed with sleet, that a cold, exhausted Conrad found the Order. The main door led underground into a network of more tunnels framed by oak timbers and cedar panels. He was soon met by a red-bearded bald man in a white linen tunic, a brown leather belt and a green wool vest, who presented three objects on a tray. A silver chalice, an acorn, and a scribe's quill. This had to be some kind of test, Conrad surmised. Was there a wrong choice, or was this a method of deciding where one belonged? The man's eyes were warm, but mysteriously aloof. If the latter condition were true, then what did each object symbolize? Or, yet another possibility was that this was simply to gauge his reactions. Conrad could not make up his mind, and before he could speak, the man jerked the tray, sending all three objects into the air. Conrad caught the acorn and the chalice, but dropped the acorn when he grabbed for the quill. He made an animalistic grunt of consternation, feeling as if he had just failed the test. The bald man just smiled and stood observing what Conrad might do next. He was still being tested.

Finally he had enough. "What do you want from me?" Conrad challenged.

The man spoke reverently, "I merely presented a mirror to show you your own nature. When you understand why, then you will be ready."

Conrad barked, "But I came here to find my relatives, not to play silly games!"

The other man simply nodded and bowed before adding, "Many Redmanes reacted as you have, it is written. But I also see a man who is not at peace. You fight against your own nature, because you believe it should be other than what it is. When you begin to ask why, you will find the answers."

The next instant, Conrad was outside in the cold night next to an empty log cabin at the crest of a low hill near a pond and a grove of cedar pines. "What! How did you do that? Where are you? GAAAA!"

Conrad fumed for several minutes cursing the stars and the wind before taking refuge in the cabin and attempting to get a fire going. The blankets and furs on the bed reeked of must and mildew, Conrad grunted in disgust as he tried to keep his nose away from it and still get warm. He felt a draft behind him, and discovered several holes in the blanket. Rats had taken parts of the blanket to line their nests. And other animals had left marks as well.

"Think this is funny, old man? Do you? I should have stayed in West Bend… with a woman to warm my bed, and … never mind…"

Conrad did not want to say the words. He missed his sister Bethany's cooking, and yet had grown to hate her husband Jonah for keeping dark secrets, just as he now hated the abbey for what the Arbiters had made of it, despised the gossipy peasants, and hated Arius and all the other Augurons. Not one happy memory remained.

His dark thoughts made sinister shapes out of the dying fire and the shadows, and images formed in his tired mind, of his father's ghoul, and the Veteran Owl sick with envy, and even Jonah. "Eledar punished us because of you, 'Captain.' Darmid poisoned me because of you! Even Mandy is too good for you! It's your own fault for losing that hunting knife where the Bandits could find and use it! You may as well have killed Ramus yourself! And did you know Amanda was kidnapped while looking for you?" the voice of Jonah castigated.

Another voice broke in, Bethany's: "Mandy never loved you, only your armor and rank got you into her bed! Devi loves you because she's too young to know how wretched your heart is! Nobody else will ever love you! You will die alone, childless and forgotten!" Finally Conrad could take no more and ran from the cabin screaming in the freezing cold.

* * *

Gerundin the Glutton greedily accepted the wine bottle and took three gulps before he knew something was wrong. By then it was too late. Even one of his bulk was affected in seconds. His muscles seized up almost on contact, just like Bothun. His face reddened for lack of ability to breathe, and his twitching hands attempted to grab Lochar or Marcy, but his arms and legs now froze also. Gerundin flopped onto the floor, squeaked like an old man after climbing a hundred stairs, and died pissing himself.

Alex Mill cried, "No! Don't kill us! Whatever I did, I'm sorry!"

Marcy just coldly stared him down with her eyes squinted in icy fury until Alex was cowering in the farthest corner of his cell. Then Marcy turned to Astrid, "Are you the foreign redhead that my husband Nathan takes to the confession chambers and then plants his seed in?"

Astrid glared back, "I hope my husband kills him. That is my only answer, bitch!"

Marcy gave an evil grin, "That could be useful someday. You may live. Right now, I only have need of your testimony. I want Nathan to suffer. I want to destroy his power base, and you are going to help me."

Astrid scowled, "And why should I do that?"

Marcy clicked her tongue, "Because I will do whatever I must, even if it means scarring your features beyond recognition, drowning you or making you watch as this cowardly weakling (points to Alex) is tortured beyond endurance."

Astrid stalled for time, "You know nothing of northern women then. Our gods are stronger than your pathetic Lawgiver!"

Marcy gritted her teeth and growled, "Lochar, it's time to teach this mongrel a lesson, take her to the stables and send my other knights to me while I decide what to do with the men."

Lochar flashed a knowing, evil, and eager grin, and lifted the keys off of Gerundin's dead body to open Astrid's cell.

Alex screamed, "No! We are innocent! Please let us go!"

Wayne admonished, "Shut up, Alex! She never cared about innocence and never will."

Marcy purred to Wayne, "Well, aren't you the smart one? I like reasonable men."

Lochar dragged Astrid upstairs after handing Marcy the key ring.

Wayne smirked, "And what, exactly, is your definition of reasonable?"

Marcy taunted, "You sound like a mediator. Oh, I can see why my husband locked you away down here … he hates anyone who can see through his facades."

Wayne answered, "That could well be true, but that's no reason to like you any better. I can't see that the poor jailor here did anything to you …"

Marcy smiled. "Of course not. But he kept you here, which serves my husband's purposes. My offer is quite simple, you help me, I help you. Don't tell me you actually like the sleeping arrangements and the food down here …"

Wayne countered, "Razadur has worse."

Marcy raised an eyebrow. "Is that simply rumor or a bluff?"

Wayne smirked again. "Am I to believe that a queen such as you has never heard of the arena of blood? I've seen it with my own eyes, it was carved out of banded red sandstone by the Dwarves who first lived there. It is neither rumor nor bluff."

Marcy curled her lip in a half-frown, "Hmmmph, much as I find this entertaining, time is a luxury at present, and I must have your decision. Help me, or rot here indefinitely."

Wayne replied, "On the following conditions, one, you allow Alex to go free today. Two, after thirty days, I leave unharmed to go where I choose."

Marcy scoffed, "*Really*? What madness leads you to think you are in any position to make demands?"

"Because I know a chess player when I see one, and you love a challenge," Wayne declared with satisfaction.

Marcy stood silent, weighing his words for a minute before answering, "Done. The game begins."

Alex Mill stammered, "H-how did…"

Wayne interrupted, "Alex … it is both bad manners and bad luck to pry the stonework of a gift house before you even sleep in it."

Alex did not quite understand, but nonetheless kept quiet. Marcy unlocked their cells and giggled as she cupped Wayne with her left hand. He thought to himself after a moment of shock, this is a new twist.

* * *

Above, a lone man with a trident stood in Lochar's way.

"Stay out of the queen's business, you! Or else …" the knight threatened, before being brought to his knees by the tuning fork effect.

Astrid also fell, and Tyrus pulled her up by the arm, whispering, "Run! I know a cabin up north of here. Your daughter is safe there for the moment …"

Sir Lochar pulled his broadsword free as he stood up, calling below, "He has the woman!"

Queen Marcy Elaine Cloverhill panicked on the stairs, "Who? Who has her?"

Her knight answered, "Some dead man with a trident!"

Wayne paused at that last word, and the hissing words of Tyrianna echoed in his head, "I'm never speaking to you again!"

Wayne whispered, "I think I should stay here until the excitement is over ..."

Marcy taunted with glee: "Afraid of someone, are you?"

Wayne answered, "Yes. There are *some* things, and *people* that ordinary folks in their *right* mind *should* fear!"

Queen Marcy gleamed with anticipation, "I will find out who, and I will never let you forget..."

Wayne sighed in exasperation and dread; he was out of the skillet and in the fire yet again.

Tyrus heard the clanking of plate armor as Sir Lochar attempted pursuit and, with one deft motion, lifted Astrid up and put her over his shoulders, and then ran as fast as he could manage. The sound of pursuit grew dimmer and more distant, and by the time Tyrus reached the forest, it had stopped altogether. Lochar stood with hands braced on his knees, gasping for breath just beyond the park. Queen Marcy was going to be very displeased.

* * *

Morgessa was now a beggar in the village of Pine Slopes since her family had cast her out on the orders of

Sandhaven and all of Kozos had turned her away. Her face and clothing were dirty and ragged from sleeping in the only places she could find to stay warm, often in barns or storage sheds and stables. Once a week, the tiny Church of the Dove gave her food and a bath. The Lawgivers usually left this place alone because the population was small, remote, and had limited resources. They were not a threat here. The only threat was Morgessa herself and the truth she carried.

That Sandhaven was cruel, heartless, and full of political ambitions. And that something was very wrong with the concepts of the Lawgivers. Morgessa fell often into despair, asking herself what kind of God created both animals and humans with the same desires, and yet reserved the harshest punishments for humans when those desires are acted upon?

When she voiced her doubt and despair at the weekly bath, Sister Serena answered, "That is a God who appeals to the desire for power and control, which is in opposition to our true needs for love and harmony. There are two sets of law, the laws of men, and the laws of nature. And only when the two are in agreement, do they lead to happiness. Nature is the more powerful; it is everywhere. Some laws of men hold that women are born sinful; this is a contradiction if we hold that life is sacred. Who nurses the babies? Who carries that life for nine months and loves them the most selflessly?"

Morgessa despaired again. "But why are we told such confusing things? Why have we been made to suffer thus?"

Sister Serena offered in sympathy, "You are young and innocent, child. You know not the ways of men and politics. But know that you are welcome here and loved. We do not judge you. We wish you harmony and happiness. That is the way of our faith." Morgessa broke into tears and held on tight when Serena hugged her.

Chapter Fifty-Two
Reversals

At the Falcon's Perch Inn, Karina the Whale went into a raving lunacy when the word got around that "Danny Boy" was now in the company of Marcy.

"Sold out to save his own skin, he did! The coward! When I catch him, I'll smother him until he's deader than a smoked fish! I'll make his ears bleed and pluck his eyes out, that two-faced, heathen gutter rat! I'll kick him in the jewels and break his fingers! I'll ..."

From twenty feet away, Kurt interrupted, "Why is this 'Danny boy' such a bloody big deal? I ain't never heard of him before ..."

Karina turned on him, "YOU! Where the heck was you when the knights came to arrest him? Me sister tells me you took some sinful woman to bed that night and this heathen wrecked half of the guest house thanks to your pickled brain and wagging cock! Ye ain't my nephew no more, and I'd a thrown you out on the street after knocking yer thick skull with the iron pot! Your wickedness brought this fate upon ye! Ye keeps scoffing at the Lawgiver, and now ye gots to pay the price! Me sister been too merciful this time! It's on her account I didn't beat ye bloody half to death you daft twit!"

"Have it your way then, you old nag! I'm packing my things and leaving the sorry lot of you to these confounded, finger wagging know-it-alls! Know what? Yes, I do have a thick skull. I would have followed my younger sister Vanessa away from here when she took the two orphans with her out west twenty-four years ago if I had half of her sense!" Kurt bellowed in rage as he slammed his tankard down, left to pay his bill, and slammed the door on his way out.

Karina was shocked into silence for half a minute before she began muttering incoherently.

* * *

A faceless black wraith hissed and groaned in the gray mist that covered the world, and Conrad was held to a gravestone by thorny vines as many figures emerged to torment him. A headless Eledar cradled a ghoulish white face under its left arm, and in the right hand, it held a noose with Bethany in it. She begged Conrad to free her. A rotting hand clawed through the ground below Conrad and raised the middle finger in Conrad's face. An empty suit of armor held out a burned contract as the ghoul of Obsek clung to the right leg like a puppy. The armor spoke, "Look what your bravery has gotten you, worm … your people hate you, and many have died for nothing. You cannot win…"

Conrad bolted out of bed, tangled in the sheets and flailing against things that were not there anymore, "NO-ooooo! Get away from me!"

Conrad had another startle when a charcoal gray housecat growled and hissed at him and jumped off the foot of the bed.

"Where the blazes am I?" Conrad whispered to the darkness.

A male child's voice around the corner said, "Mom! He's awake!"

Conrad thought he was going to die of embarrassment. Conrad heard the rush of air as a lantern was lit in the other room, and then the flickering rectangle of light against a far wall that moved with someone's footsteps.

"By the heraldry of your armor, you must be a Redmane, descended from James and Amber, am I right?" queried the brown-haired woman.

Conrad moaned, "And you are?"

The woman dodged, "I'll tell you when you are better rested. What sent you to the north coast of Xantir in the middle of a freezing night yesterday?"

Conrad probed, "So where am I exactly?"

The woman replied, "You are in Birch Hill, next to the Terran Sea and the frost current. You would have frozen to death, if not for us wandering after the cat who got stuck in the well. We found you minutes before the storm came in."

Conrad rubbed his temples and closed his eyes as he sank back into bed, "I could not even begin to tell you the horrors I have endured this year alone … and cannot even say I am glad to be alive."

His host mused, "My father was like that before he died of cirrhosis when I was eleven. I ran away from my mother six years later. Had all I could stand of my family and the Lawgivers. So tell me, what do you Redmanes believe in?"

Conrad grumbled, "Lately, I believe in only three things: food, shelter, mead, four actually, the last being a good sword."

The brunette scoffed in defensive tones, "If you are just another version of my father, do not expect to be welcome here. I, for one, am quite glad he is dead, and I would put you in the ground myself if you touch my children, mister!"

Conrad hissed, "If this is what the world is like now, I shall be glad to be rid of it; everywhere I go, nothing I do is good enough! What have I done to deserve such scorn?"

The woman called to the other room in subdued anger, "Thomas, will you take the children to their lessons? I need to use the barn."

A tall, dark-haired man emerged from that other room, and nodded. The host left without another word, and Conrad waited five minutes before curiosity got the better of him.

He found the barn fifty yards from the house, and the sound of a wooden pole beating on bales of hay was accompanied by screams of "I hate you, Father! I hate you! DIE you stinking drunken fucking coward!"

Conrad quietly went back to the house and collected his things to find some other shelter.

* * *

The sound of boots echoed once more in the tunnel, coming from the west, the men had discovered the bone-chilling winds from the sea out there. Kazius and the others were now trapped. Garzon whispered from his sitting position, "Where is the narrowest part of this south passage?"

Kazius whispered back as he lifted weapons and shields from the three bodies of the dead: "Just under the inside sloping wall of the Arena, about forty-five feet from the drain. But the archers will have a straight shot there. The bend between here and there is more advantageous to us."

Garzon nodded. Kazius gave the shields to the women. Then they dragged off one of the bodies to the bend in the tunnel, and made their plans.

* * *

"Father, we lost track of the blonde girl. She has been gone for two weeks. What is your wish in this matter?" asked the boy Frederic.

Sandhaven mulled it over for a moment before responding. "We start a rumor, that she has succeeded in prying secrets of Malsain from Kurt. And thereafter fled Kozos. This will send him hunting if he is still in the region. Then, we wait."

Frederic bowed. "Yes, Father. As you command it."

As Frederic left, Sandhaven muttered to himself, "Now is the time to deal with Marcy, Danny, and Prince Adam."

* * *

As the biting cold wind picked up, the motley party slowed to a crawl.

"This Dwarven map leaves much to be desired, begging your pardon," Skorvald complained aloud after their second near encounter with the great Wyrms in the Dragon Ridge Mountains north of the Pass.

Bravane the Younger answered back, "My pardon takes much begging of late..."

The Elder Bravane chimed in sarcastically, "These god-forsaken mountains have not improved my moods either, and, oh, yes, we ran out of food sometime yesterday..."

Sigurd Izmond (son of Dagnar, and the husband of Roxanna Saint Noir) interjected dryly, "Let us hope the Blood Fangs prove to be palatable to dragons."

Jonak (father of Astrid and Vithgar) taunted, "That bunch needs marinating in pepper sauce to mask their stench ..."

Gormund (nephew of Jonak) admonished, "Have you actually smelled a dragon's nest?"

Jonak laughed and clapped him on the back.

Dagnar gave the signal to duck, and they all watched as many leathery wings moved nearby, no more than half a mile away, going east by northeast toward the center of Zara-Mogai.

"What the devil are they hunting now?" spoke cousin Grimhorn.

Cousin Balnir added, "Gods have mercy on whoever the prey is ..."

* * *

A bent-over man with dark skin and many blackish-purple warts hobbled to the sentinel's post, with a tremor in both hands, as he carried a basket of food toward the eastern lift of Black Falls.

"For the prisoners below," the man said in a raspy voice.

The guards let him by, afraid to catch disease from this peasant.

Many minutes later, as the lift finally arrived at the sublevels, he hobbled off and stumbled. Nobody dared touch him to help up. So the one load of passengers left him behind. When a sentinel glanced back, he had vanished. A thorough search of the area turned up dyed fragments of mushrooms and the urine stained cloak he had borrowed. By that time, Tyton was prowling in the rafters of the Blood Arena under-structures, where these men had no hope of spotting him. Prasad was still descending the narrow chimney that joined the arena to a vent in the side of a high vertical cliff. The sentinels had long looks on their faces as they decided not to report the stranger until they caught him. They did not like bearing bad news. Especially not during high alert. Axegrind was known for his bad temper.

* * *

Conrad found an abandoned country cottage on a sharp slope facing the Terran Sea, and upon cursory investigation, decided he would stay for a week. But everywhere he went, the nightmares followed. He could not find peace. When he returned at last to Dromon Hill, Rebecca was waiting for him. "You broke your promises! My first letter was from a stranger, not you, and you left no messages where you were going, making me crazy with worry that you got trapped under the ice or broke your leg or, Gods forbid, were dead! Where is the Conrad I fell in love with? Tell me!"

Conrad hung his head. "I'm sorry. I don't where he is, or who I am anymore."

Rebecca implored, "Tell me what happened, let me in, don't shut me out. I want to help. I want us to be happy. Please…"

Conrad sank to his knees on the verge of collapse. "Everything is wrong. The world I thought I knew was all lies…"

Rebecca kneeled with him and hugged him close, "Darling, look at me. Do you not see how I care about you? I'm real. I came here for <u>you</u>. Look at me. Look in my eyes. Feel…" She put his hand over her heart.

Conrad tried, but the fear was strong and he shut his eyes, crying. "The nightmares will not stop. They are driving me mad, ever since returning home from the Quest in Shadval..."

Rebecca soothed: "Then we will find a warm bed together and I will hold you until they go away. Whatever is in me to do, I will. I will listen, I will love you, I will *simply be here*, with *you*, the man I adore. Let the rest of the world wait. There is only us."

Conrad kept his eyes closed and hugged tighter for dear life, sobbing.

* * *

Dragonfire ravaged every last goblin clan, leaving only the few scattered members who escaped into narrow winding tunnels or into the sewers, even the ones in Nug-Za, with an occasional Dwarf or human victim thrown in. Winter Auguron knew exactly who was responsible for this attack, and she was not at all pleased. "You... Are NOT my father anymore, you deluded, blind, reckless *monster* ... I will never forgive this last affront and yet one more broken promise to my servants and to me, *never again* will I serve you ..." hissed an ashen faced, singed, and irate minor chaos witch from the shelter of the caves of the dead.

* * *

Under a starry sky with scattered stringy clouds, in the low hills of the border region between Xantir and Iglar, Clan Freeborn greeted the wizard in his own custom: "Live free, die well, o Lebiced of the Stormcloud lineage. What errand brings you in such bitter cold wind as this?"

The old wizard answered, "An urgent situation, in which a relative to myself is endangered and unaware. His jealous, corrupt, and spiteful brother has put a bounty on his head. And the mercenaries known as the Blood Fangs aim to collect on it. I aim to stop them, with your help."

Agathon scoffed, "How does this concern the Freeborn Centaurs?"

Lebiced snarled, "Because evil will spread further if this plot is carried out … the Alphas and the Syndicate already have enormous reach, and the target could one day be a king. One who could stand up to these bandits and scoundrels … do you care nothing for the Elves, humans and allies who would be affected by adding yet another nation to Syndicate dominion?"

Agathon countered, "Not a tangible concern, Wizard. Speculation and hearsay near as we can tell. Who is the target? What is the evidence?"

Lebiced began shouting, "Damn it, Agathon, if you ever trusted my word, trust it now, my grand-niece Queen Margo has compelling reason to think her son is in danger! Do as you will, but Jonah is a loyal and honorable man, one who deserves better than this nonsense …"

Agathon frowned. "Perhaps. We will consider your problem."

And then the clan turned to leave. Much later, the wind carried to Lebiced the words he was not supposed to hear: "A token effort then, nothing more. We will make one sweep to the east and then turn south for the winter."

Lebiced scowled, griping aloud: "I am far past the age of such juvenile dodgery being the *least* bit amusing … remind me not to overestimate the honor of Freeborns … the *ass*."

* * *

Kazius pulled out the remainder of the arrow from his leg, and Moira bound it up while Garzon scavenged any and all usable items from the dead bodies, and was tying belts and bowstrings together. The sound of company was fast approaching, not more than a hundred yards away. Garzon laid down the shirts and chain mail on the floor in front of them and then waited.

At this spot, the women with three shields edge to edge, backed with spare leather, spanned the whole width of the tunnel leaving only small gaps at the floor. This bend in the tunnel put the enemy archers at major disadvantage, no straight shot was possible beyond melee range.

As the first wave of attackers rounded the turn, Garzon pulled the belts taut, and the trap snared a dozen pairs of feet, impaling the men on the weapons behind them and giving Garzon an opening to swing his axe with complete surprise at the second wave. Their morale shattered yet again, and confused ranks collided before they retreated in unison. Between the trampled, the impaled and the beheaded, three dozen enemies had fallen in mere seconds.

Garzon was pleased. He could rest a few minutes again, and the plan had worked perfectly.

* * *

At the bottom of the chimney, Prasad had a dilemma. There was nothing to grip between the chute and the arena floor hundreds of feet below, and even if he had, that required more rope than they had left after descending the cliff of Sandhorn. He had to pray that the last two pitons could find purchase in the chute itself. His heart stopped when the hammer slipped from his fingers, falling toward the drain grate and impacting with a loud clank in just under five seconds. "Great Mother, preserve me!" he whispered.

The sound of metal on metal carried, and cries rang out from the stadium exits, "Intruder! Intruder in the chimney!"

Prasad had to quickly improvise before they decided to pour boiling oil from above … he squirmed his way back up about three feet before he found a crack in the chimney. It would have to do. With the pommel of a dagger, Prasad banged and wedged the piton into the crack, praying it would hold long enough for him to reach safety.

* * *

"Carol! Honey! It's so good you are safe! I prayed for you every day…" Astrid sobbed as she hugged her daughter.

Tyrus was glad to see it, that finally one of his efforts was not wasted. Molly pouted, her only friend seemed to have forgotten her, and her daddy was not here. But Thomas had not forgotten and had produced a spyglass to see what could be seen from this vantage point on the mountainside. Not knowing what he was looking for, or who was who, it proved to be of little to no value. Until Molly noticed his odd behavior.

"What's that pipe thing?" she asked.

Thomas explained, "This is a device that magnifies faraway images. I was hoping to find clues to your father's whereabouts, but you would have to tell me what he looks like, or see for yourself."

Molly inquired, "Can it see the other side of the world?"

Thomas laughed. "No, never that far. Now, see the lights of the village there?"

Molly nodded yes.

Thomas offered the spyglass and instructed where to point it. "Look again through the eyepiece here…"

Molly lit up. "I can see tiny people in the snow!"

Thomas added, "Yes, and your father is farther away to the south in the other town we just left. I won't lie. Our situation is difficult. King Nathan is a cruel man, and so is Malsain. They can do bad things to us and to your daddy. I will do my best to give this story a happy ending, but I get hurt just like you do. I might not survive. If anything happens to me, I want you to stay near Tyrus, okay?"

Molly cried. "Please don't leave me!"

Thomas cradled her hands as he promised he would do his best to stay alive.

* * *

Garzon heard the noises above and laughed. "The new leader of Razadur has his hands full today. This should be most amusing!"

Moira quipped, "We could still die in here, and you think this is amusing?"

Garzon wasted no time, "Woman, all men die one day, whether they have a sense of humor or not. You may waste your short life however you see fit. But I pray that the gods have a sense of humor … and mercy as well. A humorless or merciless immortal is a truly fearsome prospect."

Mandy cackled, "I like you!"

While Bernice whispered to Kazius alone,"Thank you for protecting us. I have never been prouder of you, or happier to be with you, as your woman. I have seen a change in you since the sandstorm. You have become more wise and courageous." Kazius looked into her eyes, and therein he saw truth. He *had* grown. Where he had once felt paranoia, jealousy, rage, and resentment, he now felt peace. And this was worth more than the throne he was ousted from. There were no regrets anymore or rather, very few. He reflected for a moment why this was so, and it came down to this: he finally belonged somewhere. He had a clear purpose, protecting his new family first and foremost. He was loved ... he never got that from his parents, NEVER. He never got that from military power either. There was no comparison.

Finally he said to her, "Thank you. This is going to sound very odd, but I only know your first name..."

She told him, "I was named Bernice Marie Jean Baptiste, in the year 1543, after my mother and grandmother, my lord."

Mandy teased, "Get a room!"

Kazius ignored that remark, and leaned in close, bowing until his forehead touched Bernice, and whispered in his most reverent tone, "Will you marry me?"

Bernice wept with joy, her voice failed and she simply nodded yes and hugged him tighter than ever. Moira, however, scowled and sulked; her life, for all she knew, was destroyed. The image of Sal vanishing into a white void still haunted her, and her last words to her husband Alex Mill were spoken in great anger. She wanted to be able to tell him she missed him so, half as much as she wanted their daughter Molly safe in her arms again. She had no room to forgive anyone.

* * *

Alex Mill had fled to the village of Pine Slopes because King Nathan's Knights would be after him for false charges of espionage and throw him right back in the dungeon or kill him. There was no work for him here, so he, too, was a beggar. Naturally, in a place this small, he met the other three beggars, one of which was Morgessa, who led him to the tiny Church of the Dove. Alex liked it here, but never felt truly at peace. Nightmares of Malsain plagued him, joined by a roster of other tormentors such as Kitra the rail, who chastised every hair that strayed out of line, every hint of rebellion, every spark of skepticism, and every speck of curiosity into things that the Lawgivers deemed heresy, sin or blasphemy.

For a feeble old woman, she terrorized even the strongest and bravest orphans, and Alex had long ago stopped being brave. As Alex bolted awake from one of his nightmares, Morgessa heard from the other corner of the barn and tried to calm him. "What is it? We are safe here..." she whispered.

Alex shivered badly and stuttered, "M-m-malsain ... I-i told my parents what he did, and that s-same year, th-they died. I-it's all m-my fault ... and K-Kitra whipped me with w-willow branches ... I'll n-n-never be free ... never ..."

Morgessa crept over to his side to cradle his head and rock him back to sleep. "Sister Serena can help you... rest now."

* * *

Prasad had only seventy-five feet of rope, and with each swing, he could feel vibrations in the line. He dared not look up at the piton. It could wreck his nerve and determination. After a dozen swings, he began to hyperfocus on the pillar's edge fifteen feet beyond his reach and forced his breathing to be steady.

"Now or never," he whispered to the spirits, and at the apex of the next swing, somersaulted off the rope toward the lip of the pillar, and reached his hands out on the second rotation ... and he touched the lip but could not keep his grip on it. He slid down the pillar at sufficient speed to burn through his gloves and he was forced to let go. He somersaulted again off the pillar in a much slower rotation, timing the spin to put his feet under him, and he felt something give when he landed. He had twisted his ankle. Above him in the seating area, sentinels began sliding down the 20° sloping inner wall to surround him. Until grunts of pain betrayed the presence of another enemy picking off targets from behind.

Another dark-skinned man had stolen some weapons from their comrades in the corridors, and was now shooting them like they were just canvas targets on hay bales. Prasad smiled; Tyton was here to even the odds. After a dozen sentinels fell, Tyton was out of arrows. There were now ten men standing on the benches, and eleven on the arena floor. The ten closed in, highly overconfident in their chances. Two daggers flew and reduced that number to eight.

Now Tyton drew his Adya Katti Sword. Prasad had a chakram and a dagger, taking his time to study the men he was facing as they slowly advanced, testing his reactions. Two men on the benches charged, Tyton ducked low and slashed their femoral arteries; they fell screaming.

Three more lunged, and Tyton leaped over their heads, and as he landed, slashed an enemy in the Achilles tendons. In minutes, only one Bloodhammer was left standing on the benches, who panicked and fled while Tyton slid to the arena floor.

One opponent had ducked under Prasad's thrown chakram and was closing in with two bullwhips, keeping Prasad off balance on his injured ankle. Until Tyton's sword sailed point first into the attacker's kidneys. Six men advanced on Tyton, who retreated to grab Prasad's chakram, and threw it such that as two men sidestepped out of its path. It struck another in the back who was closest to Prasad. Prasad repeated the maneuver against Tyton's opponents and picked up the Adya Katti blade. Nine enemies remained, who lasted but two more minutes.

Prasad sat down to rest his foot when the last enemy fell. Tyton collected the enemy's weapons, and then dropped them through the grate in the floor, before leaving on his real errand to hunt down Raj and Udai.

* * *

Sir Vornadin the Serpent had left his empty plate armor where Nathan nearly tripped over it.

"What is the meaning of this?" Nathan demanded of his remaining knights.

Sir Ogun the Massive remarked, "He will return after his task is finished, sire."

King Nathan barked,"Task? There is no task, but what I give you. This is not acceptable!"

Ogun merely added, "Neither is the loss of Jailor Gerundin, Sir Bothun, and Sir Gregor … sire."

King Nathan snidely commented, "Oh, he thinks he will take retribution, does he? And who is Marcy going to blame? ME! This is all that the Cloverhills and Mollenbecks need to mount a rebellion or a blockade … there will be no more defiance of my orders!"

Seconds later, an exhausted herald raced in to the audience chamber, "Sire, I bring bad news …" and dropped to one knee.

King Nathan clenched his jaw and fingers before hissing, "What transpires in my kingdom now?"

The herald finished, "Vornadin and Lochar are both dead, by each other's sword … sire."

Nathan grumbled, "Assemble all the men … at the academy where Marcy has less access. Lock the gates when all are inside."

* * *

A crying, blubbering Karina Cooper was startled by Father Malsain near the woods, and she did not notice the tatters of his robe. She rushed to take his hands and blurted out: "Me nephew. Lawgiver save me. The Fallen One has me nephew … full of defiance he was, Father. He has abandoned us and taken me sister's best heirlooms, the chalice, the candelabra …"

Samuel Malsain interrupted, "Where did he go? Have you told anyone else?"

Karina sobbed, "No, Father, nobody else knows how loyal I am ... they would curse me and abandon us both if they found out ... he went north, Your Holiness..."

Father Malsain snarled, barely able to contain his rage, "Those accursed Doves again ... and foreign interlopers ... I will ... I mean, the Lawgiver will, punish these blasphemers... you must deal with Sandhaven. He continues to usurp my work, my authority, you must rally the people against him."

He dared not say more, how he needed a royal puppet such as Prince Adam, and he knew Karina hated Adam. No, his servants must be ignorant of his secrets. Because all who knew his secrets would have to die.

* * *

After the screams died out and the last weapon was dumped, Garzon called up to the grate sixty feet above, "Hello up there! Who do I have to thank for these gifts of arms?"

Prasad was taken aback. He had forgotten that someone was in the tunnels below. "You may thank the nation of Vaja and the temple brothers" was his cryptic reply.

Garzon chuckled, "I only hear one of you."

Prasad added, "Our temple leader has an ancient score to settle. He is not available for comment."

Garzon responded, "Rumor was that the leader was a woman..."

Prasad corrected: "Was. Things have changed."

Garzon laughed again, "So they have."

Now Kazius called up: "You sound exhausted. Axegrind will not be merciful. The lever for this grate is at the eastern end of the bench area, in the third row. You can join us if you wish. Our friend here is too big to fit in the hole. We might have company again soon."

Prasad taunted: "You think so? How do I know I can trust you?"

Kazius replied: "We only know that the luxury of time is slipping away. And we could die either way... it's your choice."

Prasad stood up on his one good foot, and declared, "True enough. Who will catch me? I am out of rope ..."

Garzon answered, "We will not have all day, unless Axegrind invites us in for tea..."

Prasad laughed. Then he dragged the eleven dead bodies toward the wall and piled them up until he had a crude scaffold, and on his fifth attempt, finally got a handhold on the top of the wall and hauled himself up and over into the bench area, crawled to the lever and tugged. The creak and groan of metal machinery told him it worked.

* * *

At long last, Conrad related all the events that haunted his nightmares, as Rebecca simply snuggled his head against her shoulder while they kept warm under the covers in the medium sized room of the Lord and Princess Inn of Dromon Hill.

"I had no idea, darling ... how awful that you bore all these horrible burdens alone for this long... I'm so sorry..." she half-whispered in a sympathetic tone. "You deserved so much better than this, baby..." she opined before kissing his forehead and stroking his hair.

Conrad continued weeping, holding tight to her shoulder and bosom. Rebecca rolled on her back and let him snuggle in closer. Minutes later there was a familiar stirring down below. She cooed in his ear and gently guided him in with both hands; he sank deep and slow, as they both savored the renewed contact and passion. She looked in his eyes, and there she saw gratitude, love and tenderness. They kissed, and gradually their strokes increased in tempo, until his ragged breathing and grunts of primal hunger announced his pending climax, and with a last thrust, he sent them both over the edge into delirious bliss, and fell asleep in each other's arms.

* * *

In an unheard of rare act of charity, Queen Marcy Elaine Cloverhill told Danny to run for the hills, because war was about to begin in earnest. "My knight Sir Lochar was found in the embrace of death, his throat slashed by the sword of Nathan's man Sir Vornadin in his dying act of vengeance. It's been fun meeting you, dear boy, but I can tell you are ill-suited for prolonged battle. I will give you thirty minutes before I launch the assault. Go quickly and quietly, or I may kill you myself. Leave before I change my mind…"

He did. Turns out she lied; she really meant ten minutes.

* * *

Moira brooded in the farthest corner of the chamber under the grate where Prasad had dropped in, while the others made cursory introductions.

Kazius spoke last, "Men once spoke my name in fear or disgust, and many still do. I no longer wish for the power I once had. It is a very long story."

Moira snorted in derision. It had to be a ploy to win over his new allies. She indulged images in her mind, of the wyvern out there somewhere, gorging itself on Adrian and the remains of Sal … when the image of Sal took a mind of its own: "I saved your life! Ungrateful bitch!"

Moira put the image out of her mind, and walked out of the chamber into the tunnel.

Garzon called to her, "Where in blazes are you going, damn fool woman? You are going to get yourself and possibly US, killed!"

Moira ignored him, and tried to block out the memory of Sal falling backwards into the white void, but she could not. Worse, she could not remember the face of Molly, only that of her husband Alex the Meek. Alex as an innocent choir boy, then later as a gangly timid orphan, and lastly, as the bumbling, cowardly overgrown child.

She asked aloud to herself, "Why did I marry such an immature, asinine weakling?"

Another voice answered: "Because you never met ME, darling!"

Moira stood in shock, not realizing how far she had gone, or that she was talking out loud until now. She was facing an armed host of two dozen men with knives and swords, led by a scruffy short man with several scars and tattoos, and Moira was completely defenseless. She bluffed, "My brother is here with me, and he will make you pay for this!"

The leader laughed, "Funny, if he was anything to fear, I reckon I'd know his name, now wouldn't I?"

Before she could stop herself, she lied: "His name is Sal, and he's twice your size!"

The short man snorted, "And when I cut off his knees, he can suck me off! Somebody gag this wench; she's starting to irritate me ..."

Moira ran back in the other direction and screamed.

Chapter Fifty-Three
Day and Knight

Kazius openly complained that Garzon's prediction just might come true as the echoes of Moira's screams reached them.

Mandy commented: "I don't know what has come over her lately ... she is acting very strange."

Prasad said nothing; he considered it best that he see for himself what everyone was like.

Bernice asked Garzon, "Can you save her?"

He responded, "Can? Yes. Will I? We are about to find out..."

Garzon plucked a body from the pile at the bend in the tunnel and used it as a crude shield, measuring his steps as he crept closer to the sound of the screams.

As Moira rounded the fork in the tunnel, he hurled the body such that it looked like someone attacking the mob, and in the two-seconds of frenzied thrashing and hacking it took them to realize it was one of their own, Garzon took a wide stance and indulged an evil bloodthirsty grin with his axe raised high, poised to drive fear into the first pair of eyes to notice him. The short leader was stunned speechless and his trembling fingers dropped his weapon. Garzon yelled and cleaved him in two down the middle to the pelvic bone. Half of the men ran and half dropped to their knees and surrendered, throwing their weapons aside.

Garzon called out, "Exile! Bring the belts and bowstrings! We have a dozen prisoners."

Kazius complied and remarked, "Axegrind is running out of men. He has lost. He will not press a hopeless cause."

Garzon gave an incredulous look. "We shall see soon enough."

Back in the chamber, Moira was still shaking and huddled against the wall. Mandy did her best to calm her friend, but nothing was working. So Prasad finger jabbed a nerve cluster to put Moira under. Mandy looked at him with fear and backed away.

* * *

The two sentinels at the cells were very nervous when the patrol did not show up. As one peeked around a corner to investigate, the second one felt a body land on top of him before his world went black and silent. A thrown dagger ended the other one before he could even speak. Raj and Udai backed away from the door, certain of what was next. Tyton lifted the keys off the dead sentinel, and unsheathed the Adya Katti blade before unlocking the door.

Raj protested, "So this is it, then? The same fair fight you gave my father?"

Tyton whispered, "You call killing a family of nine including a blind man fair? You call murdering a fourteen-year-old girl fair? If that is your idea of fair, then YES."

Tyton took his high-guard position and stalked the middle of the cell, wasting no more words. Udai feinted a lunge, Tyton swung in a wide, low arc. Raj leaped high and Tyton ducked under him, mule kicking as Raj landed, sending Raj face first into the bars, and onto his back, dazed. Udai kicked Tyton in the shin, and Tyton fell. Udai tried to stomp on him, but Tyton rolled on his side and with his good leg, swept Udai's feet off the floor. Udai fell on top of Raj, and rolled off just before Tyton rolled into an axe kick to Raj.

Udai tried again, and missed. Raj weakly rolled away, Tyton moved to block the exit and borrowed a club off a dead body. Udai got tired of waiting, and charged with his one arm extended to claw, strangle or suffocate. Tyton sidestepped and hit Udai on his unprotected side with the club, before slashing hard at his kidneys. Udai knew he was dying, and weakly lunged one last time, straight into a fatal thrust to the gut. Raj began hyperventilating, and called desperately for a sentinel. Silence followed his echoes.

Tyton limped toward Raj, taunting, "There's nobody left to save you, Raj. Now you die."

Raj tried to run and circle behind Tyton, but he just spun and slashed. Raj ducked under the sword sweep, but the club hit him in the ribs. The return stroke of the sword slashed his throat, and Raj gurgled in shock as he fell.

"Now at last, Sidhuri is avenged ..." Tyton said as the last members of the southern creepers bled and hissed away their last few minutes. He then crawled away to a safe distance before applying a salve to his throbbing shin. Then he looked for a safe place to conduct a ritual.

* * *

"Milady, the peasants are staging a rebellion. What is your wish?" reported Sir Cernach on bowed knee.

Queen Marcy asked: "Who are they targeting?"

Cernach replied: "They are unfocused. Spies says they are split between hatreds of Sandhaven, Nathan, yourself and Adam."

Marcy concluded, "That sounds like Malsain's rabble. We wait awhile behind the fence of the Cloverhill Family Estate, he dares not enter the grounds, he knows what is in the garden. When my husband Nathan or Malsain become vulnerable, then we will move in. One further task, if you would, Nathan took something from the choir boy he accused of espionage, and left it in the castle. Bring the item here."

Cernach bowed, "What item, my Queen?"

Marcy added, "A silver dagger. Now rise, and do me proud."

Cernach rose, bowed again, answering, "Yes, Your Majesty."

* * *

"I want to see the village up close," said Molly.

Thomas asked, "Why the village? I thought you wanted to find your dad."

Molly nodded. "I do. I think he's in the village. I can feel it, I just know!"

Thomas sighed. "All right then, but remember what I said. If anything goes wrong, stay near Tyrus, okay?"

Molly gave a sad frown. "Okay. But remember your promise."

Thomas took her hand again. "I will, young one. I will."

* * *

A disembodied voice spoke in a gravelly whispered hiss to the mercenaries still prowling for their newest enemies in the mountains: "Speak your business, mortals. Why have you entered my domain?"

The senior-most Blood Fang answered: "There's a bounty on some Jonah Saint Noir, and some Northlanders got in our way… we have a score to settle with the lot."

The voice roared in utter disgusted wrath: "Do not speak his name again … but make him suffer or kill him and I may also reward you. You may live. Tell me, how did these Northlanders enter without my notice?"

The gang leader replied, “Got no idea. But we seen their tracks a ways back, they came through a couple days ago. We don’t know magic...”

The voice of Arius declared, “I will accept your word. Now go prove yourselves useful and do something about them...”

The leader inquired, “What kinda rewards we talking about?”

The voice of Arius snarled, “You have ceased to amuse me, puny mortal. Now GO!”

The gang then muttered under their breath about the bad omens in this place, including the occasional piles of dragon shit.

* * *

In some secluded chamber, Tyton lit the incense in a seashell, placed in front of Sidhuri’s likeness cast in a small silver statuette, and prayed.

“Forgive me. I never loved anyone as I loved you. I’m sorry I could not save you, sorry I drove you away ... I miss you so much ... I wanted to return someday ... to have our own family. I wish you were here ... Nothing was ever the same without you. I cried many times on your ribbons, long after your fragrance had faded. Nothing was ever enough after you died. Not even avenging your death. That became my only purpose ... I was so foolish then ... and so empty now... someday, Sidhuri, some day...”

* * *

The fourteen remaining Bloodhammers fled to the inner keep within the mountainside, and the few witnesses gave a feverish, panicked account to Axegrind: "There's a giant down below, in league with Kazius and three witches ..."

A second man added, "There were two demons in the arena, they were unstoppable..." Axegrind clubbed both of them unconscious. Then he withdrew to the west-facing window of the sanctum. None of his men dared speak, until Axegrind finally reached a decision.

"Open the doors, and signal our surrender," he ordered in a melancholy tone. "But let us drink first. Our last comfort ..."

* * *

"Father, why do they hate us so much?" asked Corbin.

Nathan barked, "WHY? It's because we make the rules, we have the gold, the land, the firewood, and yet, despite our protection of them against lawless and godless bandits, sinister Elves and starvation, they resent all that we have ..."

Corbin pleaded, "And what about my mother?"

Nathan scoffed, "She is just another peasant who wants things she cannot ever have..." Corbin cried, "She loved you, and you treat her like ... like..."

Nathan interjected, "A mongrel at the dinner table? A fish that lay in the sun too long? A worm in the garden?

She was a good lay, but there's nothing she has that I could not get somewhere else..."

Corbin was horrified at what he heard, and did not want to be here anymore. Suddenly the Academy was too small and confining, and his father was a selfish jackass. Corbin made a show of going to the archery range again, and then looked for the secret tunnel that Sandhaven had used between the academy and the castle. King Nathan was too self-absorbed to even notice.

* * *

Winter surveyed the damages everywhere, she had lost three-quarters of her servants, a tenth of her supplies, a third of the rooftops and wagons, half of her livestock and gardens of tubers, wheat, squash and grapes, and still no sign of her son. She smirked as she calculated that despite the damages, she was not so bad off. With less mouths to feed, she had plenty to go around. Her mood turned darker than coal when she saw the burnt corpse of a carrier pigeon, with the scroll it had carried turned to ashes. It could have been an update on the Centaurs, or some other news of great importance... lost. She kicked at broken pottery and animal bones, snarling, "You were <u>never</u> a good father, NEVER! I <u>*hate you!*</u>"

Below in the sewers, Rod wondered, did she mean her own father, or his? She never told him who his father was. All his life, that word conveyed a great emptiness to him. Was he some wandering minstrel like the notorious Jordano of Agama, or a philandering pirate for the Syndicate? Rod hoped it was someone he could be proud of, like a cartographer, a diplomat or an alchemist. Someone who could explain the great mysteries to him. But most especially, someone kinder than his mother. He imagined she drove his father away, or worse, executed him for some slight to her ego.

His melancholy sank so deep that even his rat Wilbur did not cheer him for long. The aching for his other roots was heavy like soaking wet canvas. He longed for the story of how they met, some adventure long forgotten, something that would give his existence more meaning. Rather than the caged bird he was, who starved for a kind word, and who was punished for singing off key. His birthday on November twenty-seventh ceased to matter long ago, it was no happier than any other day in this unforgiving place, with only Winter for his family, and his only companions were the rats. Without them, he would have died of loneliness. But today, they could not save him from despair.

* * *

"Tell me, and be honest," said Rebecca after another session of lovemaking with Conrad. "If you are not returning to Oakthorn, *wait, I am not blaming* you… they have treated you horribly, I know, but how are we going to provide for children in our future?"

Conrad sighed. "I don't know yet. I was hoping to find relatives here who could give me work. But all I got was more riddles ..."

Rebecca was glad that he made an effort so soon and kissed him. "We have time; we have been lucky. But I need you to understand, when Arius destroyed homes and crops, my income vanished. Most of our people had to rebuild, and I sacrificed many bottles to stop the advance of the Undead across the bridge. I came to you here in Xantir with nothing but my clothes. WE have to rebuild. This is not your fault, this is the hand we are dealt, Love."

She kissed him again on the forehead and cheek as she waited for his answer.

Conrad sighed again. "I do not know yet what we will do. I have enough, that we may survive until spring. I will think of something, I promise."

Rebecca snuggled against him, stroking his beard, "That's all I needed to know, my darling."

* * *

Father Samuel Malsain arrived in the village of Pine Slopes during a light snowfall after sunset looking for Kurt Blackhammer, which was as simple as seeking out the one and only Tavern that existed there. Kurt felt the hairs rising on his neck when a hooded stranger walked in, and pretended he did not notice the man.

Malsain whispered, "Hello, Kurt..." just before Kurt threw half of his drink in his face and bolted for the door.

Malsain lost his control, and reverted to his wereform, shredding another set of clothes which he would have to replace soon. The tavern emptied in thirty-seconds as half the patrons left through any window or door available, and the other half were ejected in pieces. Kurt heard the death screams and the bestial snarls behind him and kept running in blind panic, and around a corner came more strangers that Kurt noticed too late to dodge, and they tumbled together in an awkward heap to the ground.

"Watch where yer goin'!" yelled Kurt as he fought to regain his feet.

A young girl snapped back, "YOU watch it, mister! You..."

Another bestial snarl silenced all of them, and Kurt bolted away again. Thomas whispered to Molly, "Stay behind me, Tyrus and I will handle this monster."

Kurt was in hysterics as he ran further north to he knew not where, "Oh, my god! Oh, my god! Oh, my god! He's a fucking werewolf ..."

As Malsain exited the tavern, he saw Kurt running away, and then the young girl.

"One of the brats that got away! I will have to eliminate ALL of you!" said the were-beast.

Tyrus advanced inbetween them with his trident drawn and struck it on a lamp post while pointing at Malsain, and the monster howled in agony before crawling away and then loping on all fours like a jackrabbit toward the forest to the northwest for cover. Tyrus gave chase again. Then Molly saw the dead, mangled bodies by the tavern and screamed, it was just like the carnage at the orphanage. Thomas tried to pull her away and keep her quiet, but she ran south right into the Church of the Dove.

* * *

From a nearby barn, a panicked and paralyzed Alex Mill heard the death screams, then the familiar voice of Kitra Cooper's son, Kurt, and lastly, the screams of a young girl, and pure instinct propelled him into action; he ran with all his strength, augmented by a burst of adrenaline, following the scream of what his heart knew to be his daughter. Indoors, Sister Serena appeared in her night robes, with a candle in front of her, checking what all the uproar was about, and a young girl almost knocked her over, spinning as she collided with the grown up.

"The bad wolf is back! Don't let him get me!" said Molly, almost out of breath.

Serena was about to speak when Alex rushed in. "Molly! You're alive!" he said as he got to his knees after colliding with the doorframe; his vision had not fully adjusted yet to the dim evening light of the streets.

Molly ran again, bowling Alex over, "Daddy! Take me home! Don't let the wolf get me!"

With his first real courage, he said, "He won't, honey, I won't let him. Not while I live!"

Serena whispered, "This way! Hurry!" She believed there might be something useful nearby, but no longer had the words to say what.

Alex and Molly obeyed and followed the sister to a storage room. Thomas and Morgessa both arrived just in time to do the same. Serena rummaged through the shelves and barrels, crates, jars and baskets, and finally gave up.

"The silver is gone, it must have been sold to support our charities… I am sorry," Serena said sadly.

Alex Mill stood up to his full height and declared, "Then I must return to the capitol, a silver dagger was taken from me there."

Molly tugged at Thomas's robes, and Thomas spoke, "Here, Molly knows how this works," as he gave Alex the staff. Thomas instructed: "Twist this way here, to raise the studs, and strike with it to stun him, but I think you will still need the dagger to do more permanent damage…"

Alex shook hands with Thomas. "Thank you."

Morgessa stood silent, both in admiration of Alex's newfound courage, and in envy of Molly's mother, whoever she was. Serena noticed her conflicted expression, but held her tongue.

* * *

Danny heard the sounds of pursuit behind him, and ducked behind a tree just in time to see Malsain bounding past him. He froze in abject terror, hoping the were-beast did not notice him, which was astronomically unlikely. A minute later, one enraged Myrmidon named Tyrus appeared farther east among the tree cover and the pale light of the moon. Danny wondered how this man could track a werewolf at night, but his thoughts were interrupted as Tyrus came in his direction, waving him southwards, whispering, "Go! Protect the women in the cabin..."

Danny complied instinctively, only later questioning how Tyrus knew about the cabin or Astrid. By which time Tyrus was too far away to answer. He was about to thank his lucky stars when a cloaked and hooded blind girl appeared in front of him. Her eyes were glowing a pale white, and she called out in an eerie high baritone: "Daniel Darkmoon, I have a message for you. Tell the women that Skorvald is alive. His quest is not over yet. As for *you*, I have not forgiven you. If not for the visions, and your desire to redeem yourself, I would be your worst nightmare. Now go."

Danny gulped and ran. She was already his worst nightmare.

* * *

As Garzon walked Axegrind into his cell to await a people's tribunal, Kazius led the eldest and least threatening citizens to the inner sanctum with the clean spring, and let them fill their waterskins before making a short speech: "Many of you don't trust me or like me, and I can't blame you. In fact, I'll be leaving soon. But before I go, I will appoint a council to run things in my absence... and it will be from among you. First..."

A hysterical cry interrupted him, "You LIAR! I don't believe you!" as Moira lunged with a sharp rock at Bernice beside him, but never reached her target. Prasad tripped her, and Moira fell backwards, instinct made her spin to catch her fall with her hands, but she fell upon her own rock, and lay there impaled.

Mandy wailed and pounded her fists in anguish on Prasad's arms and shoulders. "You killed my *only friend*! You monster!"

Kazius had shielded Bernice with his own body, but now stood aghast. He only wanted to make peace, and in mere seconds, it went horribly wrong. There was no help for this. He sank to his knees, crying, "This is not what I wanted … not at all. I am so sorry …"

Tyton was still nowhere to be seen and was believed to be dead. Prasad pushed away from Mandy, and left without a word to anyone. He stopped only when he reached the southmost tower at the gate wall, and had climbed to the top to gain solitude. There were three primary roads and several variations on those for one of his kind, who dealt both life and death. There was madness, which dominated Nikita and led to her death, and there was melancholy which haunted Prasad. The third road was to stop caring at all, becoming a nihilist or cynical and self-destructive scavenger and that way was true horror, such as his younger brother Korvandu had become before Prasad was forced to destroy him.

* * *

Malsain bounded up into the trees, twice he was knocked down by a sonic burst, and twice he bounded away again, until he was too far away and too deep in the cover of trees. Tyrus had to give up the chase yet again. He cursed Malsain before leaving, "By Neptune's beard, I will bring you down, murderer! You will answer for all the children you have stolen from their parents! You will not escape forever!"

* * *

Corbin brooded in one of the towers of the academy, thinking to himself. His father was a callous, arrogant, selfish jackass, and because of his father, Corbin had no real friends to speak of, except maybe Torveld the senior trainer. Corbin had neither pity nor love for his half- siblings. They were both spoiled rotten. Corbin just felt an odd mix of jealousy and apathy. In fact, the only people Corbin admired were his mother, plus Torveld and Bradagar the headmaster. Whatever love Nathan may have felt toward him was both weak and muddied. He knew Marcy hated him, and Sandhaven was just using him for political agendas. Finally, Corbin tired of his own thoughts, and sought out Bradagar the irreverent. Problem was Bradagar was nowhere within the academy.

* * *

Word had gotten around concerning the destruction of Oakthorn, the sacking of Valandrassil, and the death of King Goldlion, even here in Razadur. Tyton had nothing to return to up north, and lacked all desire to return home to Vaja to be reminded of Nikita, Sidhuri and other sorrows. Tyton despaired of crushing loneliness, and he looked at the figurine of Sidhuri one last time. He tied her ribbon around it, and kissed it reverently before letting it slip from his fingers into the river just above Black Falls. Then he collapsed on all fours in tears. He had neither bathed, eaten, nor shaved for days. Everything he lived for was gone. He later walked aimlessly in delirium, toward the Dabani plains.

* * *

The bodies piled up on both sides of the academy gates, many of the peasants outside riddled with crossbow bolts, and some knights within cooked alive by burning grease. Karina the whale escaped the carnage with a bolt in her shoulder. But not before she spotted Corbin combing the grounds in search of someone.

"Coward! You and Sandhaven are to blame for all this!" the old nag spat in his direction as she fled for safety.

As Karina staggered into the Mill property occupied by her sister, the feeble Kitra Cooper held the door open.

"Why is Malsain not leading this attack?" Kitra asked.

Karina wheezed, "He said the Lawgiver had business with Kurt."

Kitra sighed in despair. "You don't know Malsain as I do, sister. Malsain himself will hunt him and kill him, if he is not dead already. I cannot keep his secret anymore."

Karina stammered, "What secret? What are you babbling about, sis?"

Kitra looked Karina squarely in the eyes. "Listen well, sister. Our leaders belong to an inner circle called the Alpha Clan. And worse, Malsain is the werewolf."

Karina blurted, "Heresy! The Fallen One got to you, too! How dare you turn on our teacher!"

Kitra chided, "You are the bigger fool, sister, so was I once, when I agreed to lure the Mills into the open, using young Alex as bait. They knew what Malsain was. I saw him kill both parents with his bare hands. He killed two of the Cloverhills as well. It is you who have sealed our fates, sister, by sending him after Kurt."

Karina grunted as she pulled the bolt out of her shoulder, and stabbed her sister to death with it.

* * *

Cernach reported on bent knee, "Our spies say Nathan's men have sustained casualties, my Queen. What is your wish?"

Marcy gave an evil grin and purred, "We wait a day or two for their morale to crumble. No, wait. I have another idea ... has anyone seen Sandhaven or Malsain?"

Cernach shook his head no.

"Keep our men at the ready to move in on my order. They will tip their hand soon. They can ill afford not to. Prep my horse while I go suit up."

Cernach bowed, "Yes, my Queen. As you command."

* * *

In the cabin once occupied by Ravenna, and later repaired by Danny:

"Where is my daddy?" Carol pleaded.

Danny answered with sympathy, "The oracle did not say, little one. I am sorry."

Astrid chimed in, "He will find us, sweetheart. He loves you very much."

Carol cried. "But I miss him *now*..."

Astrid hugged her tiny daughter close, "I know, baby, I know... Mommy misses him, too." Danny went back outside to chop firewood.

* * *

With a sour look on his face, Kendrus Cedar Keg called in a disgusted tone: "What foul business do you have *this time*, Wizard? Every time I see you, it's a tale of woe or portents of dire calamity for a people entirely too familiar with both..."

Lebiced replied: "I ask only if you have heard or seen anything regarding a gang known as the Blood Fangs, nothing more, good sir."

Kendrus relented, "Oh, THAT nasty lot. They were released two days after we let the other humans go into Zara-Mogai on some crazy quest of theirs. Bad blood, pardon the pun, between those groups. Why the interest, old man?"

Lebiced measured his words: "As you say, bad blood. A nephew of Lorenna has put a bounty on his brother. The mercenaries are after him, and I am related to them all, in ways I won't bore you with."

The Dwarf taunted, "That's the kindest gesture we have had from you yet, old man."

Lebiced scoffed, "I had this silly notion you had better breeding than the Freeborns."

Kendrus grinned, "But <u>we are</u>, bred quite lustily with the best vintage of spirits, in nice cozy beds locked away from nasty horseflies!"

Lebiced scowled as he wheeled his horse south toward home, muttering, "I'm far too old for these foolish errands ..."

* * *

After a dinner in the former mansion of Vamanastral, one of the refugees lingered a moment near Lady Bethany, who was now starting to show in the belly that her third child was underway. The fellow was middle-aged, with a few gray whiskers among the brown, and his frame was scrawny except for his midsection. He spoke timidly, "I'm sorry we misjudged you and your brother..."

Bethany was in a mood today, and let him have it, "My brother is never coming back because of your kind! Your fickle wagging tongues drove away one of the most noble and courageous men I have ever known! It's rather late for your tepid apologies..."

The fellow shrank away from her angry glare, and turned to shuffle into whatever corner of the mansion he slept in. Jonah stood up to comfort his wife, "Is something else wrong, dear?"

Bethany broke into tears, "*Everything is wrong*! Your family, the Saint Noirs and Augurons, their horrid plots, my father is dead, my brother has chosen exile, my bakery and the Co-Op were both destroyed, our home wrecked, our name slandered and sullied, we are beggars like all the rest now, I'm going mad… if one more thing goes wrong I don't think I can take it!"

Jonah hugged her close. "I … I'm sorry honey. Really."

Bethany pounded weakly on his chest, "I can't take any more pity, or empty words … I want a home of our own again, a safe place for our children, away from these gossipy backstabbers and Eledar's fawning sheep!"

Jonah whispered, "We'll find a way, I promise."

Bethany scowled, "You better."

* * *

Alex Mill prowled the grounds of the castle, trying to think of a way in, when Queen Marcy rode up behind him, followed by her knights. Alex had never seen Marcy in full armor, and the look on her face was scary to any man who knew her history. He froze where he stood, expecting to die any minute.

"Looking for this, little orphan?" Marcy inquired as she held up the silver dagger.

Alex nodded his head, still looking scared out of his wits.

Marcy tossed it over to him and advised him, "Don't touch the purple flowers, but if Malsain should get near any by some accident, drive him into the thick of them."

Alex stuttered, "W-why are you helping me?"

Marcy replied icily, "An old family debt you might say. My great-grandfather and his father were both murdered by Malsain. They were obstacles in his bid to become Alpha Minor. And because Malsain has made such a mess of things, the other Alphas would not complain if you were to somehow destroy him. I don't expect you to live anyway. But if you do, remember the trouble I saved you of finding this item."

Alex disliked the sound of that, but saw no choice but to accept. "Y-yes, o-of course…"

Marcy grinned evilly, and signaled her horse to resume cantering toward the academy. Lugnai, Cernach, and Fergus followed her. When they were farther than a stone's throw away, Alex returned to the grove where he left Molly and Morgessa.

He whispered, "Now we need shelter and food, and I have no money…"

Morgessa told him, "I cannot go to my family or anyone, I have been ostracized by the Lawgivers. I have no money either…" It was also late evening, and various fires had broken out during the rebellion. So they ventured toward the forest that bordered dagger lake.

As they passed the Falcon's Perch Inn, Alex froze in midstride, "Wait, I remember this road… Marble Lane, this... *this is where I was born*, where my parents died ... oh, god ..."

Molly interjected, "It safe to go in?"

Alex shrugged with trepidation and confusion, "I don't know, sweetie, I don't know ..."

Morgessa cautioned, "Kitra and Kurt might be inside ..."

Alex gulped, "I'm not worried about Kurt, but Kitra scares me..."

Molly tugged at his sleeves. "But it's cold out here, Daddy."

Alex summoned his nerve again, "Yes, it is. Let's go have a look then."

Morgessa found herself wishing yet again that Molly was her own daughter and that Alex was her partner.

* * *

Garzon lingered after breakfast, thinking aloud, "I still require your services in locating the children, o King for a day..."

Kazius complained, "It will be more difficult, having lost Adrian in the sandstorm ... but yes, we will do what we can."

Garzon corrected, "Nay, it *will* be done, as surely as I fed you in the desert, secured shelter from the storm, danced with a Wyvern and made many widows and orphans, exile."

Mandy was nowhere to be seen. Kazius was in a pensive mood, wondering where he might retire that

Bernice would be safe. He knew Korath and Stonehaven were out of the question. And he wanted to be farther away from his father anyway, far, FAR away from all his bad memories.

* * *

Now that the beast Malsain knew the foreigner's scent, he made certain to stay far downwind and under cover at all times, also avoiding farms where he was expected to strike. He lived off of wild birds in the meantime, including ... the most tempting wild turkey he had ever seen. It sensed him and ran for all the good it did. The wereform of Malsain caught up in three great leaps and landed on it, wrapped both paws on its neck and with one twist, it was over. Malsain gorged himself while he had the luxury. Then, he hid the remains and took refuge in the largest tree he could find. Revenge would wait one more day.

* * *

Ravenna, the right hand of Queen Regent Lissa Firebird, protested, "I advise against this, the Prince is too young! And Father Malsain has influence in Korath, I don't trust them! This marriage is a disastrous idea!"

Queen Lissa sobbed, "I don't have the heart to say no to him, the children are all I have left besides you. Please don't ruin his hopes..."

Ravenna stood firm. "Malsain, Nathan and Marcy would do far worse than dash the hopes of a young boy who is *our* duty to protect!"

Lissa pleaded, "I beg you. Let him dream a little longer..."

Ravenna snarled, "As you wish, but mark my warning, we will both regret this. The younger Minerva is a prissy spoiled brat, and her parents are scheming pigs..."

The melancholy Lissa withdrew to her window again and crumpled into a ball, she lacked Ravenna's spirit and determination, and any quarrel of any kind took all of Lissa's energy.

* * *

Astrid woke up to a bout of nausea and crawled out of bed to hurl in the pail.

Then she cried: "*No*... not by *him*, please... no..." Danny pretended he did not hear and went back to sleep, dreaming of Marcy exacting revenge on Nathan Silverlane.

* * *

Karina's lack of medicinal knowledge and her stubborn pride, combined with her small circle of friends, made certain her shoulder became infected, and a fever was making her delirious. She stumbled outdoors in the cold, seeking relief and heedless of the dangers all around the town proper to the South. Alex recognized her from a hundred yards away, and shooed his two companions into cover of the trees on the East side of the road. Karina heard something, and babbled, "I'm not afraid of you, demons! The Lawgiver protects me! You and all the heretics will suffer! The judgement is coming!" Molly ran shrieking deeper into the forest, Karina's insanity was too much like the big wolf that ravaged the orphanage in a fit of rage.

Alex called after her and gave chase, "Molly! Come back!"

Karina yelled into the darkness, "You! The insipid little orphan boy, ye ran off with my rebellious niece Vanessa and that little bitch Moira! I'll fix you when I find yer heathen bones, boy!"

Morgessa waited in silence for Karina to get closer, and when she did, punched her in the temple.

Karina stumbled and fell. Morgessa began kicking the old nag, and Karina put her arms up in defense, taking many blows to her flabby hands until she yanked a shoe off and made Morgessa lose her balance. Karina crawled in her direction, taking more kicks to the face as she did, but finally got within reach of Morgessa's neck, and put all her weight into strangling her.

Morgessa clawed and kicked, but it was a losing battle. Until a blind girl with glowing eyes approached, and waved her hand. Karina was propelled backwards with great force into a large oak tree.

"Your menace ends here, you stupid tub of lard!" said Tyrianna in her high baritone voice, and she gestured again, forming her extended hand into a clenching fist, whereupon Karina's head cracked and caved in. Morgessa was out cold, almost dead. Tyrianna levitated the girl off the ground and moved her toward the empty guest house of Twelve Marble Lane. Then left the girl at the doorstep before vanishing.

* * *

Malsain detected two scents moving toward his tree, one was the small girl who escaped the orphanage, and the other was Alex the choir boy. An evil grin stole over his face, as he imagined the satisfaction of taunting and tormenting them. He waited for a few seconds before dropping directly into Molly's path. Molly shrieked at the top of her lungs, and ran East toward the lake.

Alex heard the scream, and redoubled his pace, "Oh god no, please let her be safe, please…"

Ahead of Molly, the woman in the mist reappeared, and gestured for Molly to follow. The little girl did, and vanished within the mist, suddenly lost even to Malsain's bestial senses.

He snarled, "What foul sorcery is this? Show yourself, witch!"

His answer was a wide bolt of blue light that knocked him backwards two hundred yards in two-seconds, careening at oblique angles off several pine trees as he did. Then the mist also vanished.

Alex arrived where he last heard any sounds, and stood scanning the area for any signs of Molly or menace, calling out to her, "MOLLY!"

The voice of Syrene whispered in his head, "Follow the path that I show you, do not stray, and marshal your strength for tomorrow. You must find it within you to prevail. Only thus will you prove yourself. I have helped all that I may."

Alex did not question, and followed the weaving images in his mind to safety.

* * *

Tyrus heard the sounds of struggle and came running too late to do anything. He kneeled over the body of Morgessa, and placed his ear to her chest to verify she was still alive. Her pulse was weak, and her skin was cold. He carried her inside to the rug near the fireplace, and attempted to get a fire going.

"I won't leave you again, I'll not have your death on my heart..." he murmured to the girl. He went to the bedroom and yanked a blanket off the bed, returning to wrap her up in it before seeking out the tea kettle and other possible items of use. He was still boiling water when a mist appeared at the door and then vanished, leaving Molly in its place. She blinked a couple times before recognizing who Tyrus was.

"Tyrus! The wolf is out there again!" she cried.

Tyrus replied, "Yes, little one, but you are safe here, where is Alex?"

Molly was horribly confused, "I ran from this crazy old lady and I don't know where Daddy is anymore... I just want to go home!"

Tyrus spoke soothingly, "This *is* home, little one, your father lived here as a child. Before Kitra... ummm, stole the house from his parents..."

Molly was perplexed, "How do you steal a house?"

Tyrus sighed, "I'll explain another time. I need to find your father."

Molly cried, "I'm sorry I lost him! I didn't mean it! The wolf gives me nightmares! Please bring Daddy back!"

Tyrus took her by the shoulders. "I will search a few minutes. I cannot leave the two of you here defenseless long. You are now my responsibility..."

Molly just looked at him blankly, she did not know what the word responsibility meant. But the possessive word in front suggested burden or duty. She did not want to be a burden.

Reflexively, Molly asked "What happened to Miss Morgessa?"

Tyrus told her: "I do not know, little one, I arrived too late to tell."

Then Molly inquired, "Why Thomas not here?"

Tyrus considered the question for a few seconds before responding: "I think he is a man of peace, ill-suited for such as Malsain, and I sensed he has visited that village before."

Molly probed again, "Does he know sister Serena?"

Tyrus shrugged, "It is possible. I cannot really say. Enough questions, I must find Alex."

Molly nodded and went to check on Morgessa, who was moaning faintly and not yet awake. Tyrus stepped outside into darkness, and stood for a minute to let his eyes adjust. Several hundred yards away, he saw the thermal speck of a figure walking and weaving its way south toward the house. Tyrus readied his trident in case it was Malsain. It turned out to be Alex.

Benson found Corbin brooding in the Academy tower again, and taunted, "The town hates you, and your father too."

Corbin glared in anger. "You know nothing. They don't care one bit about me or you, they hate Adam, and my father is a pig."

Benson tried again. "Sandhaven is just using you…"

Corbin responded flatly, "Let him try. Why would you care?"

Benson was taken aback, "I don't, really… I… thought you were full of yourself, maybe I was wrong."

Corbin just sat there, then answered, "You were. Apology accepted."

Benson asked, "So what do you plan to do?"

Corbin groaned. "I'm not made for politics. I just want to leave this madhouse, but I can't abandon my mom. This place is hopeless."

Benson sympathized, "I know what you mean…"

* * *

Poor Sir Jorna the Dull had been left behind in the castle all by himself, and now he was surrounded by angry peasants.

"I've done nothing to you, please let me be!" he implored.

But he was too easy a target for their vengeance, and they swarmed him with clubs and rocks, denting his armor and knocking him senseless, thereafter beating him to death before binding his legs and dragging him behind a mule outside. They marched to the academy once more, where the gate had been beaten down, and the body of Cernach lay there, riddled with crossbow bolts in the front of his chestpiece. Other knights lay dead, felled by the great war-hammer of Lugnai the savage, and the battleaxe of Fergus the Cleaver, and they were hacking and bashing at the doors of the main hall while Marcy sat on her horse watching. She heard the clamor at the gates, and turned to glean the meaning of it.

"So, you witless beggars have managed to slake your bloodlust on the least threatening of all the Knights, thinking he will be an example to my husband, who obviously abandoned the poor wretch. Your stupidity astounds even me, you craven mongrels!" said Marcy with venomous disgust.

"Take them!" she ordered her knights. Hundreds of peasants fled in terror, and dozens fell. Lugnai and Fergus were the most feared of knights in all of Korath for good reason.

* * *

When Morgessa finally awoke, her throat was swollen and she could barely talk. Alex was taking in the sights of the guest house, which he barely remembered. It was built only two years before his parents died. He remembers his father sweating away at constructing it, which often deprived him of his father's presence. And one day, his father, John Mill, took him aside and showed him the cornerstone that he had just begun engraving.

"One day, son, this will be yours. All yours."

Alex did not understand then. The cornerstone meant nothing to him. But now, he had a burning desire to go outside and find the stone, it was his last link to his father.

He made a full circuit of the guest house and did not see anything. He tried one more time, and then… the morning sun caught just right on the northeast corner, revealing what looked like a blemish in the stone. He looked closer. There was painted wax covering parts of the stone, and the mortar around it did not match the rest of the masonry. Alex raced back inside to fetch a wooden spoon, and Molly followed him back out. He scraped out the wax, to see:

"For Alex Mill, b. July 18, 1534, our beloved son. Love, John and Sarah Mill, 1537"

Alex broke down in sobs. Molly hugged him. "What wrong, Daddy?"

Alex just mutely shook his head and hugged her back, rocking on his knees, still sobbing. It was too much to explain to a young child. Tyrus found them there, and presented the few documents he liberated from the orphanage. It was a slap in the face to see Kitra's name in them.

DEED TRANSFER: Twelve Marble Lane property, to Kitra Cooper, effective August third, 1539, for services to the Lawgivers.

Kitra was the nanny just before then, but his torment at the orphanage had erased that knowledge. Kitra ran the orphanage for Father Malsain for many years. Where Alex had grown up until Kitra's daughter, Vanessa Blackhammer, helped him and Moira escape to the west.

Alex was now seething mad, as the enormity of his loss was laid bare before him, made possible by Kitra Cooper, Father Malsain, Adrian, and so many others. Alex went back inside, grabbed the staff and dagger, and strode toward the main house with his teeth clenched in a murderous rage, snarling and growling the entire time. Molly hid inside the guest house with Morgessa; she had never, not once, seen her father angry like this. Alex opened the door, and then turned back, vomiting. Flies were swarming over the corpse on the floor. And across the road, crows were picking at another corpse in the tall grass.

* * *

A party of three made their way northward from the barren plains of Razadur dressed in a single layer of light fur against the late autumn chill. The winter solstice was almost here.

Bernice inquired, "Why are we not helping Mandy seek after Adrian?"

Garzon grunted, "Enough food and bother has been wasted on his account…"

Kazius said nothing. He did not want to go north at all. But he grudgingly agreed to go, because his past still made him an unwelcome guest in many lands, and he needed Garzon's help.

* * *

Marcy made a temporary retreat to allow her knights to recover their strength, and while consumed with boredom, she went rummaging in the attic of the Cloverhill Mansion. She found something interesting in an old journal kept by her great grandfather John Cloverhill:

A merchant friend confirmed the timing of events since 1501 through his own sources, that there was a Dabani She-Wolf since the late 1400s, and she was slain by an Elf before spring equinox in 1501. This set the stage for the Dabani-Talos alliance from that time forward, and it is precisely that summer of 1501 that Samuel Malsain began trying to influence an organized campaign here in Korath against all Elves, whether from Talos or not. The Alphas have been content to leave the Elves alone, as they tend to isolate from humans, and in this, my father agrees with me. Malsain's personal vendetta suggests a direct link with the Dabani She-Wolf and her parent who is still at large. The Alphas would not care if Malsain was a werewolf himself or not, but the fact of his instability is of great concern. He may one day expose our society, and undermine the hard work of many generations, this we cannot allow. Father and I have yet to find a suitable solution to the problem. — December 11, 1508

Marcy also knew, that Samuel Malsain was one of the few survivors from the battle of Shadval, autumn of 1540, while Jack Saint Noir still occupied the position of Alpha Leader. But unlike John Cloverhill and many others, Queen Marcy Elaine bided her time until carefully planted seeds and "beneficial weeds" bore fruit. She was the most cunning and ruthless of all the Cloverhills put together.

* * *

"Where is Corbin? It's time for him to take an active role and prove himself worthy ..." muttered King Nathan as he paced nervously in the Great Hall behind the battered doors that still stood, with narrow cracks in them where Fergus had landed a telling blow. Sandhaven sneered in contempt, thinking to himself that Nathan was far less subtle than the King believed himself to be. But, being the political figure he was, Sandhaven saw an opportunity as well.

"Pardon my bluntness, sire, but the boy needs inspiration. He needs a heroic figure to show him how history is made, he hides because he is young and inexperienced. And because he doubts your faith in him. You are the Elder, sire, he does not have faith in himself yet. You must be his guiding star. You are his example, he will rise up when you do," the new Alpha leader suggested.

Nathan's vanity got the better of him. "Yes, you are right. I will retake the castle, and grant conditional pardons to those who will pledge peace..."

Torveld the senior trainer held his tongue, but his eyes were cold and disgusted. While Sir Skavund the unremarkable sank his head in dismay and melancholy. Retaking the castle was suicide for their reduced numbers. Sir Gregor, Sir Bothun, Sir Jorna and Sir Vornadin were all dead. Ogun the massive was the best man they had left, and even he was no match for the ferocity of Fergus and Lugnai.

Only Sir Ulmadast the Round dared to challenge the idea. "Begging pardon, my king, but this plan is madness. Our best knights are dead, and hers remain. Our allies are few, and our enemies are plenty. Is there no way to make peace without sending us to die in vain?"

King Nathan bristled, "You COWARD! Are you taking Marcy's side?"

Ulmadast replied, "No, sire, I was merely..."

Nathan backhanded him in the face and yelled, "Get out! Beg her mercy if you wish, but I'll not be made a fool by a vassal!"

Ulmadast gave a sullen look and then turned without a word to leave. Sir Skavund followed directly after him, and now even Ogun showed doubt in his eyes, weighing his options.

After a few moments, Ogun drew his sword and ran Sandhaven through with it, stunning everyone who witnessed it. Then Ogun left to join Marcy's faction. The cadets of the Iron Hand Academy were now all Nathan had left, he looked in their eyes, saw their doubt and fear writ large, none of these grown children were a match for the knights. Nathan finally saw the error of his arrogance, and retreated in morbid silence to the bell tower, where he hung himself.

Marcy heard the bronze bells ringing wildly in D-Minor from afar in her estate, and wondered if this was a war summons or a desperate trick. While Corbin, who had taken the tunnel back to the castle proper, intuited the meaning of the bells right away. His father was dead, and so was Sandhaven. It was time to take his mother away and run, their lives were in danger now. The body of Jorna at the Academy gates was proof of the peasants' blind rage.

Even Benson would understand, and Corbin did not have time to say goodbye.

* * *

Word spread quickly from the Academy, "The King is dead! The King is dead!"

Many peasants cried or cheered, which occluded the news of Sandhaven sharing a similar fate.

Without Kitra, Karina and Sandhaven, the Lawgivers (and even the Alphas) were in disarray, demoralized, leaderless and disorganized, many attempting to fill the vacancies, but none with the force of personality and the alliances needed to gain a clear advantage, except ONE: Queen Marcy Elaine Cloverhill. But Marcy had other plans at the moment. She insisted on seeing the bodies herself, and had no difficulty getting there unchallenged.

"So, the Knights abandoned him, you say?" Marcy inquired.

Torveld nodded. "Yes, Your Majesty, and Ogun himself slew Sandhaven before deserting the king. Nathan's ears were poisoned in a moment of weakness by Sandhaven, and would have stormed the castle just to prove himself to a boy who also abandoned him. His pride cost him everything... I can't say I miss him. But it is a tragedy nonetheless."

Marcy smiled. "A fair assessment. Tell me, where did the boy go?"

Torveld kneeled. "I have not seen him since yesterday, my Queen. He has preferred solitude much more than usual of late. I suspect he and Nathan had differences which could not be reconciled..."

Marcy gave a suspicious look. "Stand up and look at me," she ordered.

Torveld did so, and after a moment, Marcy relented, "I believe you. For the sake of peace, I will leave the boy be. But this academy is now mine, as is the rest of the kingdom. I expect to make some changes, and there will be no debates. Has anyone seen Malsain?"

As she spoke, he was prowling within earshot in the shadows of the watchtowers above them, and he was sniffing the air, something was not right. Marcy was missing two knights, and all of Sandhaven's lackeys had gone to ground. Then he realized in panic: Prince Adam was vulnerable, and some of the Lawgivers were likely to kill the Prince as misguided retribution for the death of their leader. Speed was of the essence now, as Adam was Malsain's last puppet left, and desperation made him throw caution to the wind. He leaped off the North Wall, away from the south gate and the courtyard, and sped on all fours toward the Cloverhill Estate in full daylight. Peasants ran in all directions away from him, shrieking: "The beast is back! The beast is back!"

He ignored them all. He ran right to the edge of the Iron fence that surrounded the Mansion grounds, and took cover within the nearby trees. The odor of the hated wolfsbane was strong even here, until the wind shifted. A storm was blowing in from the Westlands, and even now showed on the horizon as a mass of dark clouds. Inside the mansion, sounds of struggle confirmed Malsain's worst fear: he was too late.

Prince Adam's nasal voice whined, "I order you to disperse at once and leave this house!

I am the rightful heir to the throne, and you are trespassing on family property! Now go away!"

Three men and a boy just laughed at him. Heinrich the wretched took a fistful of Adam's hair and yanked his head back while William the spiteful took a lit candle from off a small table, and proceeded to drip hot wax on Adam's face. Adam screamed in agony and fear, which brought Malsain running to the fence again, stopped short by the scent of the poison flowers. He grabbed at the bars and rattled the fence in frustration, snarling and cursing whoever was inside. Dennis the acrimonious punched Adam in the gut, knocking the wind out of him, thereby putting an end to the noises. It was the boy Frederic who approached with a

short sword in his hand, and slashed at Adam's throat. The first cut was too shallow and merely oozed angry red trickles. Dennis prodded, "Finish it, boy! Do it like a man!"

Frederic yelled and lunged and gave it all his strength, taking Adam's head off. Blood spattered all over Frederic and the nearby window. Malsain saw from below, helpless to do anything from outside. He hid once more in the trees, waiting for Adam's murderers to emerge. They chose the eastern gate to make their escape, and Malsain circled south to catch them. He was upon them in a great leap from a nearby rooftop, Dennis and William were dead in seconds, and Frederic was next. Heinrich picked up a nearby pitchfork from a Farmer's wagon, and hurled it at Malsain. The points struck but did not penetrate. Malsain picked it up and threw it back.

Heinrich gasped in shock and fell, wheezing. Frederic could not run fast enough, and in two leaps, Malsain landed on him and bit his arm off before he could land a blow with his sword. Frederic screamed in horror, and Malsain tortured him for long minutes until the boy was dead.

The storm was closing in, and Malsain caught the familiar scent too late. The second he stood up to run, he was knocked down by the sonics of Tyrus's trident.

"Now, Monster, it is time to end your miserable existence..." snarled the avenging Myrmidon. Malsain threw a dead body at Tyrus, who ducked, and before Malsain could get away, he was struck from behind by a silver studded staff and the electric charge made his body convulse as he fell. There stood Alex Mill, his own anger was a close copy of the look on Tyrus. Malsain got hit by another sonic burst, and in desperation, Malsain threw dirt at both of them before dashing to the South again. Malsain's mind was reeling. How could that possibly be Alex? How did he not notice their approach? How did they know where he was? And where did this staff come from, that could stun him so? Malsain was still preoccupied with his questions when he collided with Sir Ogun the massive in full armor. Again, Malsain did not smell him in time. Everything was suddenly wrong. He must have gotten too close to the flowers.

Malsain ran off to the West, his enemies seemed to be swarming him from all sides, he had to get away or go out in a blaze of glory. The sky grew dark, the clouds were rolling in fast, and far to the North, lightning flashed. The momentary distraction allowed yet one more enemy to surprise Malsain. It came in the form of an uppercut from Lugnai's war-hammer that made Malsain spin backwards for five and a half rotations as his momentum took him forward. Even for a steel weapon, that hurt. Dazed, Malsain had lost all sense of which direction was which. He ran in fear again, he needed high ground away from these ambush tactics. The next opponent caught him completely unawares, he never expected a young female to attack him.

But she did, with a forcebolt a fraction as hard as what hit him in the forest. Malsain was now hopelessly confused. How did this Elf-witch become this powerful? Who was the woman in the mist? Were they related? Why did some human child matter so much to their kind? Malsain stumbled north, straight into another sonic burst.

Malsain dodged the next one, and bounded onto the rooftops to get away. On the third leap between houses, he was struck by another forcebolt. They were everywhere, and his senses were dulled by the horrid things that he had long suspected were Marcy's doing.

It was her style to keep silent until she had a clear advantage. She had to know for many years that Malsain was behind the Cloverhill murders. It was just dumb luck that Sandhaven's minions led to his peril this way. Malsain wound up somehow at the grounds of the Orphanage where it all began. The repairs were almost finished, it looked just as it did many years ago, when Kitra was a mere child instead of a withered old crone. The Orphanage was a perfect cover for the slave trade, and the Lawgivers were the perfect pawns. It kept the hands of the Syndicate "clean" of direct involvement, and cemented their alliance with the Alphas. But now, it seemed too fragile. Twice the lady in the mist had intervened, and now suddenly, Malsain's enemies were legion. Had they all put aside their differences to eliminate him? How was it possible for them to unite and organize so quickly?

His thoughts were cut short by a peal of thunder and lightning from less than a mile away. The misty rain came down, and visibility kept getting worse. The rain also cut the effective range of his already dulled sense of smell. Malsain ducked inside with great haste, and made directly for the stairs going up. His pursuers straggled behind, Lugnai was closest, but his armor slowed him down considerably. As Tyrus rounded a corner trying to ascertain which way Malsain ran, Tyrianna stood in his path, blind and yet not blind. She could never again see flowers or printed words, except in her visions. But her ability to detect heat signatures now dwarfed that of Tyrus. "He has fled into the Orphanage. He knows his last pawn is dead, but has not yet realized the entire town has turned on him, they know the truth at last. I think Marcy has known all along. You will find him in the upper floors..." Tyrus nodded, "Good to see you." Tyrus then dashed on his way, while Tyrianna stood waiting for Alex to catch up.

Tyrus quickly caught up to Lugnai, not knowing who he was, only that he too, pursued the beast. Tyrus was the first to the door, just as the misty rain turned to hail and sleet. He bounded in long strides to the stairway, and took zigzagging leaps all the way up to the dorms.

Down below, Lugnai shook his head, "Crazy foreigner must be eager to die..."

Above, Malsain frenetically bounded from one spot to another in the upper storage rooms among the emptied nests of birds and rodents to attempt a hurried and panicked decision on the best angle of setting ambush. He finally settled crouching behind a pile of leaning, stacked paintings and mirrors, and forced himself to slow down his breathing, and feared his rapid pulse would still give him away. His thoughts raced out of control, cursing the Wolfsbane at the Cloverhill Manor, cursing the Elf-witch, and the nation of Talos that sent their assassin after his brood, and the meddling foreigner with the trident, and that Queensknight, Lugnai as well, he could still feel the impact of the warhammer, and that of being hurled through the tree trunks by a Godling. And what of Lord Barton? If he could change into the form of Friar Toby, he could become anyone... Malsain's enemies were suddenly legion in a single day. Kurt had gotten away, and there was no telling what he confessed to that wench Morgessa. Word had also gone around about a hunter who suspected his identity. Everything Malsain had worked for all these years was coming apart.

Alex Mill arrived out of breath, at the spot where Tyrianna stood. The sleet was turning to snow, the sun was down, and the street lanterns could not quell the shadows of terror and doubt rising within his mind. The Oracle planted one hand on his shoulders, and spoke, "To you, I appear blind, but I still see possible futures. Only by killing the beast can you claim yours. All other choices lead you to ruin and sorrow. I hear your thoughts, and must tell you this. Do not concern yourself with anything but Molly. Her future is up to you. Now go! Hurry! You cannot prevail alone, and Tyrus needs you."

Alex nodded and sped once more in pursuit.

As Sir Lugnai the savage turned the first corner of the stairs, he removed his helmet to open up his peripheral vision, and rested it on a post. His queen had sent him to join Malsain's enemies and put an end to the monster at long last. The time was right, with Malsain's support base completely eroded. Lugnai could almost smell the blood. He grinned with battle lust.

Power and glory would fall to Marcy and himself. Songs would be sung of this night for many years. Wine and mead would fill his cups and wash down the taste of roasted meats and vegetables, and wenches would hang on his every word as he filled in what the songs left out. Lugnai ascended once more toward the 2nd story dorms of the Orphanage as Alex entered the doorway below. Lugnai scoffed when he saw the staff in Alex's hands, but reckoned that fodder might be useful. Alex passed Lugnai at the 2nd level, following the faint signs of claw marks on the bannisters and steps in the dim torchlight.

Outside, Tyrianna sought out the women hiding indoors to the east ... they needed to know what she could not tell Alex. The truth that would have destroyed him, and sealed the doom of so many more innocents including Molly.

Queen Marcy Elaine Cloverhill and her other remaining knight, Fergus, stood in a window facing the orphanage, watching events unfold. Malsain had no more support, and was outnumbered by armed opponents on all sides. Even if Malsain survived, he would be forced to flee and start anew. Malsain was obsessed and unstable, but not stupid. Marcy calculated the odds as she indulged a taste of the finest red wine of 1466, the last vintage ever made by Simona Ganza, and acquired at great expense from Simona's grandson Leon seven years ago, including the swap of an extremely rare Orchid from the Cloverhill courtyard. Yes, Marcy grinned to herself with another sip, Malsain's time here was nearing an end.

Tyrus followed the heatprints right to Malsain's hiding spot, and looked for a way to the rafters above without Malsain hearing him. The Myrmidon was in bare feet, unlike Alex in his leather boots, and the Knight in full plate armor. Tyrus meant to seize that advantage to the utmost. He tested the crates and barrels along the South edge, and satisfied that they would hold, ascended toward the ridge beams and supports. None too soon, Alex was getting near, and might have given away Tyrus' position. Alex hesitated at the top of the stairs, his terror was returning. He could smell Malsain close by. His hands trembled and he gripped the staff so tightly his knuckles were white. The chatter of his teeth told Malsain exactly where Alex was. An evil grin curled his lips, as he prepared to pounce. Alex nervously whispered, "T-Tyrus, are you here?"

Now Malsain knew the name of the foreigner; they WERE all conspiring against him. He would show them their folly, before finding a new home. He would give them a plague of werewolves to remember him by.

Paintings and mirrors crashed to the floor as Malsain made his move. Alex heard the sound and raised the staff by instinct alone, his eyes were not adjusted to the dim starlight in the windows yet. Malsain was nearly upon him when Tyrus threw all his weight into the pommel of his Trident right in Malsain's back. The impact broke the floor under them and they landed in the dorm just below. Lugnai turned to assist and caught Malsain full in the face with the warhammer just as the beast stumbled to his feet. Malsain collided with a bedpost and spat blood. There had to be some silver in that steel to do this to him. Malsain retaliated with a lunge for the throat, which Lugnai barely dodged, the claws struck his cheek and his brow, but he barely noticed with the lust upon him. He spun to hit Malsain again, but the beast had sailed past his reach. Malsain reached another bed and threw it at Tyrus, who one handedly tossed it aside as he used the other to smack the trident's tongs against the wall, assailing Malsain's ears yet again. Before Malsain could run, Lugnai clocked him over the head, knocking him flat to the main carpet. Malsain lashed out blindly and leaped through a stained glass window, clambering up the outer wall back toward the attic.

Alex was still trembling at the top landing.

Malsain roared, "You! Why have you returned after all these years?"

Alex stammered: "To save my daughter from YOU!"

Samuel Malsain scoffed, "I should have known her scent was oddly reminiscent… this is all your fault, little boy! You and your accursed whelp! You will be the last to die after I ravage her right in front of you and grind her bones to splinters!"

Alex did not remember what he did next, his mind overtaken by fear and rage, eyes shrunken to pinpricks. He screamed incoherently as he beat Malsain bloody with the silver studded staff even after the last electrical charge had been spent, and only when his breath had been spent, did he collapse against a wall. Malsain staggered away as Tyrus caught up to them. Again, the

Trident's sonic attack rang in the werewill's ears. Malsain threw a mirror at him, Tyrus shoved Alex out of the way and raised both arms and Trident over his head. The shards bit through the Monk's robe into his arms and the lower part of his back. Malsain climbed outside to the roof before Lugnai could rejoin the battle. Malsain was sore all over, and the bitter cold just made it worse. He needed his claws dug into the roof through the thin ice and snow just to stay upright, and his muscles did not want to obey. The Myrmidon had no such claws, he knew, which was Malsain's only advantage out here now. Below, he could hear the sound of his enemy pounding the planks loose to gain access to the roof. Shingles tore away as two planks creaked and groaned. Tyrus then stood on the ridge support beams. Malsain snarled to himself, this foreigner was not stupid. Malsain lunged before Tyrus could attack his ears again. Tyrus deflected the attack, and Malsain lost his footing, falling four stories to the street as Marcy watched above. Despite the blanket of snow, Malsain hit hard. Gradually, his sense of smell was returning. He realized that's why his wounds are not healing as fast as they normally do. That accursed poison was still vexing him. Malsain weakly raised up on all fours and limped away toward the Academy. If he was lucky, he could take hostages there.

Tyrianna finally found the women in the tavern. They answered the private door only after hearing her say, "I come as an ally of Alex the Meek. I am the daughter of the woman in the mist."

Molly remembered how the voice in the mist saved her life.

"Listen closely," Tyrianna continued more discreetly. "You must be strong for your father. His wife, your mother, Moira, there is no gentle way to say this. She is dead. I am sorry."

Molly wailed, "No! Not my mommy!"

Sister Serena gasped in shock and hugged Molly close.

Morgessa hesitated to reach out, not knowing if Molly would accept her. She wanted to be with Alex, but dared not say so. And now was the worst time to bring it up. Envy of Moira and sorrow for Molly tugged her in two directions. Tyrianna cast a knowing yet blind look at Morgessa, but said only, "Alex will need all three of you if and when his task is done."

* * *

Marcy saw where Malsain was headed, and ordered Fergus to accompany her in pursuit.

The queen donned her leather gloves and pulled another purple blossom out of a pouch hanging on her belt, and then they went to mount the horses below on the ground floor. Marcy dabbed the blossom on her sword first, and then on Fergus's axe. She was leaving nothing to chance. Regardless what happened to the academy, Marcy would not let it go without a fight. She also needed popular support, which she could gain by saving the cadets and the first years. Marcy always had her reasons.

Tyrus stripped off the monk's robe to leap onto a shorter building, skidding down the roof and somersaulting off the edge to the street in hot pursuit of Malsain. While Sir Lugnai the savage stripped off more armor plates that were slowing him down, before leaving the dorm.

The voice of Tyrianna sounded in Alex's head, "The monster still lives, now GET UP!! Every minute that he is free to seek vengeance, the more lives will be lost, INCLUDING Molly! He is headed for the Academy! GO!!!"

Alex rose as if half dead, stumbling down the stairs.

Lugnai shoved him aside, "Leave this to the fighters, choir boy!"

Alex felt his anger returning and shook off his fatigue. Tyrianna's words echoed in his head, "I hear your thoughts, and must tell you this. Do not concern yourself with anything but Molly. Her future is up to you. Now go!" Alex did not waste words with the knight, and followed on his heels until they were in the snow-covered street. Alex gained the lead, and far ahead at the limits of his visual range in the flurry, a distant Tyrus turned north into the broken gates of the academy. Malsain's prints still held faint thermal traces, leading the outlander straight to the monster's point of entry. The beast had climbed the walls to the second level and ducked for cover in the same bell tower where Nathan hung himself. The cord was still severed where a vassal had cut the carcass loose. Tyrus saw the thermal silhouettes of bats dispersing from the belfry, leaving Malsain alone and exposed. The monster had made a grievous error in picking this spot to hide, and Tyrus planned to exploit it to the fullest. The wind was still blowing from the west; thus he ascended the outside of the east face.

Malsain lost the scent of Tyrus, and picked up the spoors of Alex, Lugnai, Queen Marcy, Sir Ogun the Massive and Fergus the Cleaver. And another scent was hidden among them, a sickly resin mixed with the tang of metal. His eyes went wide when he finally realized what it was. More wolfsbane! That accursed witch intended to finish him once and for all! He was tensed for the leap to escape when Tyrus got the drop on him, his trident ringing right in Malsain's face, the echoes resonating in the bells.

At this close range, and in this location, the attack made his ears bleed. Malsain howled in agony and collapsed to his knees. In desperation, he grabbed the lip of the main bell, and shoved it into Tyrus, knocking him off the tower, but at great cost to Malsain. The ringing of the bell just added to the noise still in his ears, the beast fell backwards into the belfry and bounced off a landing before hitting face first at the bottom. His enemies were closing in, he needed an advantage fast. Right now, Marcy was the biggest threat. She had the hated poison.

Malsain stumbled up only to fall again. His balance was off, and his body was wracked with pain. He struggled again and again to get up, and finally crawled away toward the water tunnels. There was only one way he could go, as the main tunnel had locked grates on both sides preventing entry from its tributary junctions. The tunnel curved north toward Dagger Lake, and if his luck was good, he could escape before they caught up. There was nothing he could do about the noise of the water displacement. They would know where he was every time he moved. The horrible indignity he was reduced to, him, once second only to Barton, until the appearance of the damn Elf-witch. Malsain snarled as he limped away, he knew he was in bad shape. Only the godling had ever hurt him this badly, and Barton was a close second.

Tyrus groaned as he rose onto his hands and knees outside the tower. The rest of Malsain's pursuers were rushing through the broken gates now and fanning out in search of the monster. Their heat patterns now masked the trail of Malsain. Tyrus wearily entered the tower again, searching for signs. Alex followed him. In the dim starlight, they could not see the hairs, but Malsain's scent was here. And it triggered Alex's revulsion. He fought the sensation, and forced himself to focus on Molly as Tyrianna told him. Tyrus had a suspicion, but said nothing.

They followed the faint trail to the water tunnels, and then it was clear there was only one direction to go. Tyrus and Alex were both exhausted, but Malsain was too dangerous to go free. They pressed on. Above them, The knights and Marcy continued searching with torches in hand, combing the entire academy.

Sir Ogun the massive spoke up, "Permission to speak freely, my Queen?"

Marcy nodded.

"Malsain must know we are here. He is outnumbered. If he had hostages, he would have announced himself by now. He is either waiting in ambush or he has fled. What is your command?"

Marcy weighed the options with a furrowed brow, and finally decided, "Lugnai, with me into the water tunnel, Fergus, I want you to keep watch in case he reappears, the rest of you take the high ground where you can see him coming." They all bowed and nodded their compliance.

Meanwhile, the snow flurry continued to blanket the land, filling in the footprints of anyone who was still outside on the surface. Tyrianna announced to the women and Molly, "My role here is finished, I am needed elsewhere."

To Morgessa, she added, "You will not need to wait much longer."

Morgessa gave a weak smile. Her hopes were dim, but it was all she had.

She was still an outcast because of Sandhaven. While Molly was lost in sorrow, her Mom was gone, her best friend vanished, and Alex might be next. Serena tried to be strong for them, but even her composure was thin. Nonetheless, Tyrianna stepped out into the snow, and then in a flash, was gone. The emptiness left behind was tangible.

Malsain thought he heard echoes behind him, and began loping faster on all fours toward the exit many miles away. Still, the winter chill and his bruises hindered him. He wondered if this is how his spawn felt before the end.

Alone, afraid, exhausted and trapped... it was all up to his three survivors if Malsain perished. The world was always against him... the Dabanis, the Taloshim, the Cloverhills, the Mills, the Doves, the Elves of Valantir and their Bitter Rose, even that arrogant Kazius in the end, there were no allies left. His best hope was to take as many enemies with him as he could, or miraculously flee to freedom. The echoes behind him were unmistakable now. Someone was hot on his trail. But he couldn't tell the distance. It was only a matter of minutes until they caught up. So many miles left to go, and he might not have the strength left to make it. That Elf-witch was still alive somewhere, he hated her the most. It was the cancellation of her bounty that began his downfall. Revenge was a hopeless dream now. His strength was waning, and he just wanted to reach safety and rest.

Alex could hear the splashing several hundred yards ahead in the curving tunnel. So did Tyrus, of course. The intensity of the sound was diminishing, their quarry was succumbing to the same fatigue that they were. Tyrus knew this would be a battle of will, and worried Alex would falter. But he also knew Alex would never vanquish his inner demons unless he saw this through. And Molly hung in the balance too. Tyrus therefore said nothing. There was little energy to waste on words anyway. The minutes dragged on, in the cold, damp, almost pitch black tunnel, punctuated by occasional beams of starlight from above. Alex collapsed long before Tyrus did. He would have to rise up on his own strength;

Tyrus had little to spare. And the sounds ahead had stopped. Malsain was waiting. For all the good that did, as Tyrus could see his heat trail. The outlander braced his Trident in front with both hands in case there was a trap down here. Tyrus slowly advanced.

Malsain heard the change. Only one pursuer was moving, and taking a cautious stride. He estimated this was the foreigner. The sound was getting closer, and would soon be in line of sight. The Were-beast studied his options. There was nothing he do against the sonic attacks, and the shape of the tunnel itself would concentrate the effect right at his head. The prospect of repeating his experience in the bell tower dissuaded him from attempting to stand and fight.

Malsain summoned the last of his strength to spring into a crude gallop.

Tyrus heard and gave warning, "He's getting away, HURRY!"

The Myrmidon's cry redoubled Malsain's fear into panic, and he picked up his pace.

Alex dragged himself upright and stumbled against the wall. His second wind was spent. Farther away, Marcy and Lugnai heard the notice.

Lugnai's torchlit grin was one of battle lust. The quarry was here, and running in fear. Marcy could hear the change in his breathing, and let him take point.

Tyrus was saving his strength for the battle. Malsain had no hope of outswimming him, and his tracks in the open would be evident to anyone. It was only a matter of time.

As Alex appeared in view of Lugnai, he spat, "Useless choir boy ..."

Alex felt the anger rising again, and gritted his teeth as he stood up after Marcy had passed him by. He imagined beating the Knight over the head with the staff, and then realized the tunnel was too confining and let the staff drop, discharging the last feeble spark it had left. Alex drew the silver dagger out, and followed at a distance.

On the western bank of the lake, two huddled adults and a child moved southward toward Kozos.

Wayne grumbled, "This couldn't wait until morning?"

Astrid apologized, "Carol wanted to say goodbye to Molly. I'd like to be out of Korath soon as possible, and get to a friendly port city. I'm sorry for your trouble."

Wayne relented, "Well, I can't fault you for not liking this place..."

Their voices carried in the wind, to the exit of the tunnel, where Malsain had just arrived. He could smell one of the girls who eluded him earlier. What luck, for perfect hostages to show up, he might yet live and escape! Except that the snowdrifts covered half of the grate, and icicles had formed at the top, freezing it shut!

Malsain cursed, "Nooooo! Not fair!"

He howled and snarled, struggling to budge the bars. Carol heard the howls and broke into a blind run, screaming. Malsain threw all his weight and strength into the effort, and exhausted himself to no avail. He whimpered as the sound of pursuit got closer, and turned around just as Tyrus struck the Trident against the tunnel wall. Two things happened: first, the tunnel amplified and focused the effect even more than Malsain had imagined, shattering his eardrums beyond repair, and the buzzing in his skull felt like it would shake all of his teeth loose and knock him unconscious. Second, the ice shattered and sprayed Malsain with icewater. This was ten times worse than the bell. It hurt so much at first he couldn't speak or even breathe. For a moment, Tyrus even believed he killed him. He got too close, and Malsain yanked him off his feet, slamming him back and forth into the walls, whereupon Tyrus dropped his weapon.

Malsain threw him back into the tunnel, picked up the Trident and struck the pommel against the grate, breaking the lock and the hinges in turn. Then he tossed the weapon into the lake and limped and stumbled clumsily away into the starlit snow. Malsain attempted a leap only to fall on his face because he had no balance left.

A walk on the ice in this condition would be the end of him. He took cover among the trees, but kept tripping over tree roots under the snow. He kept going because he knew begging for mercy was not an option. They would kill him, fast or slow did not matter. Marcy alone could finish him, if she was near. He felt the sound of a very heavy hammer knocking the busted grate aside, it was definitely Lugnai again. Malsain winced and whimpered again. Just the vibration from the warhammer reminded him how badly that uppercut hurt. Malsain tried a new tactic and tunneled under the snow. Lugnai followed his trail until he got to the burrow.

"This won't save you, Malsain! We will find you and destroy you yet!" he yelled.

Lugnai hit upon a plan. He dug around for fallen twigs, and lit them with the torch, and let the smoke fill the burrow. Malsain stifled his coughs and held his breath. The smoke was stinging his eyes, and he steered around to the far side of a tree blocking line of sight from the entrance. He poked his nose up through the snow and took a deep breath, then dove down again and burrowed away from the tree. Lugnai grumbled, this was taking too long. Marcy swung around to the left of Lugnai, and spotted a hole with specks of soot. She unsheathed her sword, and took blind swipes in the snow near the hole, making the burrow collapse. Then she stepped into the sunken spots and kicked her way through. Malsain could feel the air displacement and could smell both Queen Marcy and the resin on her sword. His worst fear was getting closer. Malsain broke cover into a loping gallop, misjudging his stride often and clumsily colliding with several trees in his desperation. Marcy gave a hand signal to Lugnai to flank the monster from the south while she covered the lakeshore.

Ahead of them, Tyrianna appeared. "Looking for me, sinful one?" she taunted.

Malsain could read her lips. "HOW DARE YOU speak to me that way!!!!!" Malsain roared as he charged at her position.

Tyrianna teleported out of the way, and Malsain collided head first with a large boulder. Tyrianna just smiled wickedly and vanished again. Malsain was flat on his back, stunned.

He grumbled, "Witch! I hate you!"

Marcy answered sarcastically, "Oh, you wound me, Samuel. But that's nothing to what awaits YOU. But you already know that."

He could feel her voice if not her words, and Malsain blurted, "Fuck…"

He rolled away from her swing, but took a shallow cut to the shoulder, and the effect was immediate. His left arm could no longer hold up his weight, forcing him to lope on three limbs while his arm dragged nearly useless. He fled right into Lugnai's path, taking another uppercut by the warhammer, knocking him backwards into a tree trunk. Malsain lost his bearings, circling Lugnai back toward the water tunnel. He realized his error too late when he saw the familiar shoreline. And behind him, Alex stood with hate in his eyes. Malsain smelled him just as the dagger hit his back and sank to the hilt.

Malsain gasped, "No…"

Alex twisted the blade and then kicked him to the ground. Malsain feebly tried to reach the handle with his right hand, but it was under his left shoulder blade. The gurgling noise was a sign that his lung was filling with blood. Malsain tried to beg, but his voice did not work anymore. The eyes of the beast rolled back and went forever still. He was finally dead. Alex fell from exhaustion again. Marcy and Lugnai found him there.

"Maybe not so useless after all," Lugnai admitted.

A weary and battered Tyrus arrived to carry Alex to shelter before he froze.

The following day, Alex awoke on the bed inside his house at Marble Lane once more. On the table was a royal pardon, and two bodies slept on either side of him. One was Morgessa, the other was Molly. Next to the pardon was a pine cone that Carol gave to Molly. Tyrus had vanished without a word of goodbye or any mention of where he was going to anyone. Wayne left a note by the front door that he was leaving with Astrid, and that he would not return here where the Lawgivers held sway. Later in the afternoon, Tyrianna appeared, to tell Alex that Moira was in fact, dead. (She knew the other ladies did not have the heart to tell him.) Alex was deeply conflicted, his chief concern was how did Molly take it.

"As any child who loves their mother would, in sorrow. But she bore it well, all things considered," the Oracle said before vanishing again.

Alex remained conflicted and confused for a few days, and on the fifth day he finally lit a candle for Moira and tearfully apologized for all the things that happened since moving to Mojara. Two more weeks passed before Morgessa finally confessed her feelings for Alex, and another month went by before they were comfortable enough to act on it.

The townspeople were still disillusioned by the loss of Malsain and Sandhaven, a few blamed Alex, but the fact of Marcy's reign and Alex's pardon discouraged them from expressing too openly their misgivings. Molly did not make any friends in Kozos, but during travels to Pine slopes, made some there, and came to accept Morgessa's presence in her Dad's life. Alex was still known as Alex the Meek, but little by little, also became known as Alex the humble hero. As such, was usually left alone and nobody questioned the addition of a small white dove on his door.

Alex settled into his quiet, boring life, and for the most part, was happy at last. He tended the grapevines that his father planted long ago, and taught himself the arts of winemaking and gardening, while Morgessa took up herblore and knitting. What happened in Korath and the other kingdoms after that, is another tale.

Made in the USA
Charleston, SC
10 February 2017